The Sc

Bliss and Chandler Series Book 2

By Tony J Forder

First published in 2018 by Bloodhound Books

www.bloodhoundbooks.com

Print ISBN: 978-1-912175-97-0

Praise for Bad To The Bone

"It's an excellent beginning to a new series, I could even see a prequel at some point as Bliss' history was fascinating." **Amy Sullivan - Novelgossip**

"A good solid crime thriller that will keep you guessing till the very end." **Joanne Robertson - My Chestnut Reading Tree**

"A pacey, invigorating read that offers plenty of thrills and a solid entry into the genre." **Mark Wilson - Author**

"Forder is a talented author, who lent authenticity to every word that was written." **Jane E. James - Author**

"Forder has created well-rounded main characters - I warmed to Bliss immediately with his non-nonsense approach and also his rapport with his partner, DC Chandler." **Clair Boor - Have Books Will Read**

"This is a well told tale that has been thought out, several threads coming together with excellent descriptions." **Misfits Farm - Goodreads Reviewer**

Praise for Degrees of Darkness

"I found this to be a compelling yet gruesome read. Great praise to this author." **Philomena Callan - Cheekypee Reads And Reviews**

"An absolutely brilliant page turner that will give the reader much to think about." **Jill Burkinshaw - Books n All**

"Degrees of Darkness is an engrossing and haunting thriller!" **Caroline Vincent - Bits About Books**

"This is an awesome read that for me that put it on a scare factor alongside Stephen King and Thomas Harris." **Susan Hampson - Books From Dusk Till Dawn**

"Beginning with such a petrifying opening chapter, Tony J Forder sets the tone quickly for a chilling and claustrophobic thriller." **Kate Noble - The Quiet Knitter**

"Had me hooked from the outset. Strong characters and no-nonsense descriptions kept the story rolling. Chilling and wonderfully suspenseful" **AB Morgan - Author**

Praise for Scream Blue Murder

"Forder didn't spare the horses when writing Scream Blue Murder. This book rockets along, a breathless action-packed ride. Perfect reading for fans of Simon Kernick and Jeff Abbott." **Matt Hilton, author of the Joe Hunter thrillers.**

"An action-packed, twisty thriller. Great stuff." **Mason Cross, author of the Carter Blake thriller series**

"This was a heart in mouth, adrenaline-fueled thriller that set off at a relentless pace and just kept going!!" **Steve Robb - BookieWookie**

"Wow!! What can I say I was totally addicted from the prologue." **Jill Burkinshaw - Books n All**

"This is an extremely well written, action-packed book. With great opening scenes to set up the plots." **Alexina Golding - Bookstormer**

"Holy Moly you are in for the ride of your life with Scream Blue Murder. It begins with a bang and just doesn't relent." **Alison Daughtrey-Drew - Ali - The Dragon Slayer**

For Sean - uncle, brother, second father, and friend. Thank you for believing in me. I miss you, 'Mickrick'.

ONE

Despite the late hour and the early start due the following morning, Bliss was not woken by the sound of his mobile ringing close by on the bedside cabinet. He had been reading for an hour, his back pressed into a pillow, another supporting his neck. In recent years, sleep had often been elusive, and he was beginning to feel the incremental nature of fatigue deep in his bones. A call at this time of night meant something important, however, so he set his paperback aside and snatched up the phone.

"DI Bliss," he said, with more of a growl in his tone than he had intended.

He ran a thumb and forefinger over eyes that felt swollen and scratchy. He listened for a moment, then swivelled so that his legs hung off the side of the bed. Bliss reached for a block of pale blue Post-It notes and a pen, then hurriedly scrawled a few words and tore off the top sheet.

Glancing over at the alarm clock, he said, "You know I'm not on call, right? I mean, I don't officially start until seven in the morning."

Bliss did not recognise the name of the officer who had called. He wasn't about to give her a hard time for carrying out an instruction, but neither did he wish to fall foul of regulations before his first day back in the post had officially begun.

Without pause, as if expecting this response, the constable informed him that the Detective Superintendent with oversight for all major crimes in the city had insisted on Bliss attending the murder scene.

"In that case, I'll be there in about twenty minutes," he said, surprised to be summoned ahead of other detectives of equal or higher rank.

After ending the call it took several seconds longer to gather himself. Anxiety swiftly replaced the initial surprise, and Bliss found himself taking a couple of deep breaths before moving. He dressed quickly, splashed cold water over his face, smoothed down unruly tufts of short hair on the crown of his head, then stopped in the kitchen to make a flask of strong black coffee. It was a chilly night, and he had no idea how long he might be outside.

Ten minutes later, Bliss's black Insignia rolled up on the throng of official vehicles in a parking area by the man-made lake at the leisure spot known as Ferry Meadows, located on the western edge of Peterborough. As he killed the engine, a figure wearing a luminous yellow waterproof jacket appeared from out of the gloom. As the police officer approached the vehicle, Bliss grinned, both startled and pleased to see a familiar face beneath the peaked cap.

He retained the warm grin as he climbed out of the car and retrieved his heavy woollen overcoat from the back seat. Shrugging into it, Bliss reached out a hand. "How the hell are you doing, Lennie?"

Inspector Leonard Kaplan pumped the hand a couple of times and slapped Bliss on the upper arm. "Not so bad, Jimmy. Yourself?"

"Oh, can't complain. Well, I can, but who would listen?"

He regarded the other man more closely. He and Kaplan had worked cases together a few times before, when they were stationed in Dagenham, Essex. Both were sergeants in those days, and had struck up an immediate friendship.

"What are you doing up here in Peterborough?" Bliss asked.

"Transfer option came my way and I accepted it. Fancied a change of pace. Started last month. I'm surprised I haven't seen you around before this. How long have you been up here now?"

"Seems like forever, Lennie. And yet hardly at all. A long story."

Kaplan nodded, glanced at his feet then back up again. "I was very sorry to hear what happened to Hazel. And to you, of course."

Bliss forced a half-hearted smile. "I know, mate. I got your card and wreath at the time. They were appreciated, believe me."

"You're more than welcome. So, things working out okay for you up here?"

"I think they will. This time."

"This time?"

"I just came back from another posting. Listen, how about coming over for a beer and a ruby sometime. It'd be good to catch up properly."

"I'll hold you to that," Kaplan said, then frowned. "Why are you looking at me so suspiciously?"

"It's just that you've changed so much, but I can't pinpoint how. Have you grown a moustache, Lennie?" Bliss's eyes narrowed as he tried to work out the difference in the man's appearance.

Kaplan laughed out loud. "No, you prick. I've shaved off my beard."

Bliss rolled his eyes and laughed at his own foolishness, though it had been almost twenty years since he and Kaplan had worked together. He yanked up his coat collar and breathed warm air over his hands.

"This mist is a bit nippy. Damp, too."

"You've gone soft, mate."

"Yeah, especially around the middle."

Behind Kaplan, floodlights stood grouped in a circle – emitting a low hum and a strange glow in this two-dimensional light. There were bodies milling everywhere around the scene, carrying themselves with a respectful air of solemnity. Bliss nodded his head in that direction.

"So, what have you got for me, mate?" Bliss asked.

Kaplan shook his head, thin lips pursed beneath the wild, greying moustache. "Not a nice one, old son. Not a nice one at all, which is why I put a call in for your lot in Major Crimes."

He turned and headed towards the bustling area of activity, where men and women in white protective coveralls hovered like inquisitive spectres.

"The forensic videography team have finished with the body," Kaplan went on. "Pathologist is on her way. The rest of the CSI people are waiting for you to give the go-ahead before they do their stuff. Basic searches going on around the crime scene, as you can see, and a fingertip search crew have been ordered for first light."

The two men paused before a white tent, now erected over the body to protect it from the elements and to preserve as much trace evidence as possible. Bliss glanced across at the lake, dim fragments of reflected light now barely visible through the gradually thinning mist.

"We'll need a diving team in there."

"You think we'll find the murder weapon in the lake?" Kaplan asked.

"You never know. Murder weapon, Nessie, Lord Lucan and Shergar, I shouldn't wonder."

Kaplan gave Bliss a tight smile and said, "I've seen all I want to see tonight. I'm sure you're more familiar with what's waiting for you in there."

Bliss nodded. He would like to have told his old friend otherwise, but, unfortunately, he thought it likely to be true.

A uniformed officer approached with a clipboard and had Bliss note his attendance. The uniform also handed him a white bundle wrapped in cellophane. Bliss reluctantly took off his overcoat and handed it to Kaplan. He unwrapped the package, climbed into the protective garment, zipped it to the neck, then pulled up a snug hood around his head.

One more ghost to add to the congress.

Finally, Bliss pulled on some plastic booties and snapped on a pair of latex gloves. Without another word he stepped inside the tent.

The elderly woman lay on her back, arms and legs spread out as if she were forming a large X. The hood of her beige parka was like a saucer for her spilled blood. In the unnatural light it gleamed like a halo of slick crude oil. Other than a couple of minor abrasions, her face was untouched. Across the rest of her body there were too many puncture wounds and lacerations to count, but it looked to Bliss as if there must be several dozen. He squatted down beside the body to take a closer look. The victim's green tartan skirt had been yanked up to her waist, tights shredded and her vulva brutalised, most likely with the same weapon that had punctured the flesh so cruelly. The remainder of the wounds appeared to be randomly distributed, though her breasts had been left completely unscathed. The final, sickening debasement, was that all ten nails had been ripped from her fingers.

They were nowhere to be seen.

Bliss drew saliva into his mouth. It tasted like dirt. He leaned forward, inspecting the lacerations and deep puncture wounds more closely still. A large blade, he thought. At least six inches. A carving knife, possibly a cleaver. He cast his eyes around the immediate area, but saw little more of interest other than what appeared to be a trail of scuff marks leading away beneath the tent. Still squatting, Bliss shuffled awkwardly lower down the body and checked the heels of the woman's shoes before standing upright once more. He was done, but he took one more look and lingered over the woman's face. He shook his head, wondering what tale this victim's body would tell.

They might be mute, they might have had all signs of life drained from their still bodies, but they each had their final story to tell him. He just had to find a way to extract it.

Back outside of the tent, Bliss appraised the entire scene of crime as he stripped off the protective garments. The mist continued to thin, the glow from the city and a pale moonlight affording him something approaching a view. A bank of hills on the far side of the lake ran up to a handful of scattered buildings. To his left the car park and the angular features of the Nene Outdoors Watersports and Activity centre, to his right a gathering of trees just yards away. Murdered in there and then dragged out here where she would be easily found, was his guess.

Kaplan came alongside him, smoke coiling from a cigarette held loosely between his fingers. He handed Bliss his overcoat.

"It's times like this I wish I'd taken that up," Bliss said, staring at the glow as his colleague took a long drag.

"I know what you mean." Kaplan nodded, then inclined his head towards the crime scene. "There's been two similar cases recently. This the same MO?"

"Pretty much. As far as I can recall from the notes I read, anyway. The DCI who had the case has had to take some leave, so this is my first taste. I wasn't expecting to land this, but I have. For now. From what I know, this would appear to be the same killer. He's not touched the vulva before, though."

Kaplan winced, whipping his head to one side as if having received a blow. "I haven't seen anything like that in quite a while."

"Which of us has? He's escalating. And it was bad enough before. Who found her?"

"The husband. Poor bastard. She took their dog for a walk around nine-fifteen. They live close by and every night it's once around the lake, a little short cut back home, followed by a hot toddy on evenings like this. He didn't get bothered about her absence right away. His wife often stopped to chat with neighbours, so walks could last from anywhere between thirty and sixty minutes."

"What's the victim's name?"

"Annie. Annie Lakeham. Her husband is Joe."

"So what time did he start to think something was wrong?"

"Ten-fifteen, ten-twenty. They're not the sort of people who like to bother others, so he came out looking for her on his own. He travelled their usual route, but in reverse, thinking he'd meet her on the way back. If he'd come the other way he might have missed her altogether. As it was, he all but stumbled right over her body."

"And the dog?"

Kaplan dipped his head. "In amongst the trees. Skull caved in, throat cut, left to die. Looks as though the killer made an attempt to bury it, but stopped for whatever reason."

"Bury the dog?"

That made little sense to Bliss, but there was always something about a murder scene that didn't seem to fit, one thing out of kilter with the rest. Still. He didn't like *odd*. Didn't appreciate *unusual*. When those two characters were attached to a crime scene, they usually spelled trouble.

"I used to bring Bonnie and Clyde over here pretty much every day," Bliss said. "I stopped coming once they were gone, and I've missed the place. Not sure I will anymore."

"Who and who?"

Bliss tapped his own head. "Of course, after your time. They were my two Labradors. Bonnie and Clyde."

Kaplan chuckled. "So typical of you, Jimmy."

"What is?"

"Using the names of villains. Couldn't be, say, Holmes and Watson."

Bliss screwed up his face. "Ugh. Those would be absurd names for dogs."

"Of course. What was I thinking?" Kaplan's forehead creased. "You said you missed the place. That they *were* your two Labradors?"

"Yeah. Both of them are dead now. Clyde hung in the longest."

"Sorry to hear it."

"Cheers. They were a good age." Bliss made light of it, but their deaths had hurt. He had thought more of his dogs than he did most people. Their absence in his life remained a raw wound that he did not think would ever heal.

He stared out across the park at an area where the lights of many vehicles gathered, and a series of small flames flickered in hastily prepared braziers. The local TV, newspaper and radio media were being held back until forensic and search teams were through.

"They'll eat this up," Bliss said, with no small measure of disgust. "Granny-butcher, and all that crap."

"It's the nature of the beast, Jimmy. They wouldn't write it if people didn't want to read it. It'll be all over social media before you even get back to your office."

"I know." Bliss was appalled by human nature's capacity to dwell on all that was evil and base. He turned his head to look back at the tent once more, still seeing Annie Lakeham's body though it was hidden from view by the zippered flap. "I often think that's what bothers me most of all."

Bliss shook off the morbidity. It had no place here. Not when there was a fresh crime to solve.

"Where's Joe Lakeham now?" he asked.

"Paramedics took him to the hospital. Shock. I sent an officer over with them if you need some questions asking."

Bliss shook his head. "They can wait a while. Though I am interested as to whether it was him who closed her eyes."

One of the floating spectres loomed up out of the darkness, pausing by the tent. "Are you finished in here, sir?" A woman's voice, her question directed at either of the two men.

Bliss nodded and Kaplan gave the head of the forensic science department the okay to move in on the immediate scene of crime; they knew what could and could not be disturbed prior to the pathologist's attendance. He took hold of Bliss's arm and steered them away, brushing through the narrow line of trees and back out onto a large expanse of open land. He indicated a landscape of bulky structures, metal glinting vaguely in the meagre light.

"A kids' playground," Kaplan said. "Plus a barbecue and picnic area. Just a nice, picturesque recreation area. I dread to think who might have discovered the body if the old man hadn't."

Preoccupied, Bliss said nothing for a moment, his mind processing too many disparate thoughts. Kaplan was right: such atrocities were not meant to happen in places of natural beauty. They often did, but that would never make it right. When eventually he spoke, his voice was low and even.

"Fucker's got a taste for it now, Lennie. This is one sick puppy we're dealing with here."

"Agreed. In a way I'm happy to be handing it over to you and your squad." Kaplan thrust his hands deep into the pockets of his voluminous jacket, the damp air apparently settling into his flesh. "Will you be taking it from here?"

Bliss nodded. "I'll head over to the station and start rounding up my own team. I'll get someone down here to take over from you within the next hour or so."

Kaplan held out his hand. "No problem. You'll be back yourself, will you?"

"Later in the morning, I suppose. Unless anything new turns up here before then. The pathologist will know where to find me."

They walked back over to his car, where Bliss took off his overcoat once more before sliding into his seat. He reached across to the passenger side, uncapped the flask and poured himself a coffee.

"Fancy a cup?"

"No thanks. The catering truck will be here soon, and I have a date with a sausage bap and a big mug of tea."

Bliss nodded. Held out his hand. "Fair enough. Good to see you again, mate."

Kaplan gave a faint smile. "Just a shame about the circumstances." He closed the car door and moved back a pace, but as the engine was gunned he stepped forward and tapped on the window. Bliss powered it open, eyebrows arched.

"Don't forget that beer and curry you promised me," Kaplan said.

"I won't. Give me a chance to settle in and get this investigation up to speed."

"She won't be the last, will she? Annie Lakeham." It was not really a question.

"No." Bliss shook his head and met his friend's eyes. "He'll carry on doing it if we don't stop him."

"What a twisted, sadistic freak he must be. You be careful, Jimmy. This one's a monster."

His voice weary with fatigue and experience, Bliss sighed and said, "No, you're wrong there, Lennie. He's a man. Just a man, I'm afraid." He shook his head and added: "Bloody terrifying thought, isn't it?"

TWO

It was nine-thirty in the morning, and lights still blazed inside the plain two-storey Thorpe Wood building that was the north Cambridgeshire area police HQ. Rain had started falling around dawn and hadn't let up since, the leaden sky sitting oppressively low over the city. Bliss stood by his office window staring out at the business park opposite and shivered, feeling the chill of the day emanating from the beaded panes.

Having driven directly to the station from the murder scene shortly before midnight, Bliss immediately checked his staff personnel notes and telephoned four colleagues to order them in. Detective Sergeant Oliver Bishop had seniority, even though he was essentially on loan to the unit for an unspecified amount of time. He and DC John Hunt were currently partnered up. Bliss had met neither man before commandeering them for his team, basing his selection purely on reputation. After a brief chat in his office, during which Bliss brought them up to speed, he dispatched the two detectives to the scene of crime to formally take over from Lennie Kaplan. That left DS Mia Short and DC Ian Carmichael, both of whom he had worked with during his first posting at the station. Bliss had a high opinion of them and knew they worked well as a pairing. They were sent to the hospital, first to talk to the murdered woman's husband, and then to obtain any early information from the pathologist when she arrived with the body.

At 3.00am, Bliss ordered all four detectives back home to grab a few hours' sleep prior to the morning briefing. Whilst he pushed those under his supervision hard, he also recognised the benefits of down time and the need for fresh, alert minds. Shortly afterwards he took his own advice and crashed out in his office; slumped back in his own plush leather chair, feet up on the desk, until an office cleaner with a particularly whiny vacuum cleaner woke him at six-thirty.

Thorpe Wood provided decent facilities for its staff – if you discounted the lack of parking spaces – and after a quick shower and brush of his teeth, plus a squirt of deodorant and a change of shirt, Bliss kicked off the morning briefing feeling about as refreshed as he was likely to for a few days to come.

Experience had taught Bliss that major cases like this had a habit of draining investigating officers both mentally and physically. It was hard to remain sharp and focussed throughout, but it was his responsibility to drive the inquiry forward. He hoped for a swift arrest, but at the same time he would take care of his squad for the duration. Attrition rates were high at the best of times within the service, but a murder could devastate a team if its investigation dragged on too long.

When Bliss entered the Major Incident Room to handle the briefing, everyone was there waiting for him: ten detectives, ten uniformed officers, five civilians. The third victim had elevated the operation considerably; this was now officially a "serial", and once word spread it would thrust the investigation onto the front pages of most daily newspapers. Bliss had been allocated the numbers he had requested in an e-mail to his Chief Super; a sure sign that the higher echelons were worried about this one. *As much about me and my reputation as the murders themselves*, Bliss guessed, finding an uneasy smile for his team.

"Good morning everybody," he said, striding across the room to the group of whiteboards he had updated earlier. There was an interactive whiteboard on the wall, but he'd been warned it could be unreliable. Bliss had decided to go old school.

"Thank you for being punctual, especially those of you who were either on duty or dragged in by myself late last night."

The incident room itself had been updated and refurbished since his previous posting, and was now a smart and sophisticated working environment, complete with a central meeting area surrounded by work pods and computer facilities. Bliss looked up to survey the squad. Several faces were familiar to him, while most others had been suggested as excellent officers or detectives who would not let him down. At first sight he wasn't exactly bowled over. The suits looked a scruffy bunch, and the uniforms uninterested. But the wheels were in motion now, and it was up to him to make sure none fell off. The case demanded a well-oiled machine, not a clown's car.

"For those of you who don't know me," Bliss continued, "I am Detective Inspector James Bliss. That's boss to you whilst on duty, Jimmy at any other time. I returned to Thorpe Wood last week after a break of twelve years. Since leaving here I have been posted to the NCA, and SOCA before that. Primarily I was based with the Eastern Region Special Operations Unit.

"Recently I began looking for a return to murder inquiries, and the predicted long-term absence of DCI Harrison provided me with the opportunity to return to my old stomping ground here in Peterborough.

"Now, I didn't know your old boss, but I hear he's just as decent a man as he is a bloody good copper, so clearly I couldn't have larger shoes to fill here if I was taking over from Koko the clown. If my own reputation precedes me, all I can say is don't believe everything you read written in crayon on the toilet walls."

This brought some tension-breaking laughter as Bliss hoped it would.

"I'm sure DCI Harrison and I have different methods," Bliss said, examining the eyes looking back at him. "I'm equally certain that our goals are precisely the same: to do the best job we can. I'm not a political animal. What you see is what you get. Give me a chance, I'll do the same with you. Now, introductions are over, and I'm going to run through what we have so far."

Bliss cleared his throat and took a sip of water. He saw doubt written on some faces, but he also saw determination. That was just fine by him.

"Those of you who have been working on operation Moonstone, which covered the first two victims, should be keen for a refresher and, of course, to learn what's known about victim number three. If you've worked with me before you'll know that I prefer to take questions after my update rather than be interrupted in full flow, so please make notes as we move along."

Bliss took a step back and jabbed the thumb of his left hand against the first whiteboard.

"Victim number one: Maureen Jackson, aged sixty, murdered on Friday, August 23rd in Stanground. Maureen was walking home after a night out at bingo. Between the social club which ran the game and her front door she was grabbed, pulled into the garden of an empty house, where she was assaulted and killed.

"Maureen was a widow who lived alone, and so her body was only discovered the following day when some local kids accidentally came across her. The garden where she was found was a favourite haunt for some kids because the house had been abandoned for about a year. We have to ask ourselves whether the killer knew this and waited there deliberately, or took a chance on where he carried out the attack. There is no evidence either way, but the gut feeling so far is that he knew. Did he choose Maureen Jackson, therefore, or did she just happen to be in the wrong place at the wrong time? Trace evidence is weak, so we can't answer that question other than with another best guess, which is that she was simply unfortunate.

"First MO has our killer stabbing Maureen in a frenzied attack, but taking care not to harm either her face or breasts. The significant signature, however, is the removal of all ten fingernails."

Pausing for breath and a swift sip of coffee this time, already feeling in need of the caffeine boost, Bliss ran his eye over the crime scene photographs. Ugly and depraved, they portrayed the very worst that mankind is capable of.

"Let me remind you of something at this point," he said to the team. "The shots on these boards are deemed fit for your consumption. Others, far more graphic, are available in the crime scene logs database."

He inched forward to the second board.

"This is Joan Mitchell. At fifty-eight she is the youngest of our victims. Joan lived with her husband in a housing project for the elderly over at Paston. She had been attending a function at their community centre and was walking home when she was attacked. This happened on September 15th. Same MO alerted the team to the fact that Maureen Jackson wasn't a one-off as previously suspected."

Running a hand down cheeks he'd not yet shaved, Bliss moved on. The third board held the least amount of information.

"And now we have Annie Lakeham. Killed whilst out walking her dog last night. Unfortunately, the MO has stepped up a gear, as this time the victim's vulva was also brutalised. This now confirms we have a serial killer on our hands, and sadly I think we all know what that means: every move, every decision will be in the full glare of publicity. What I would ask you all to do is ignore that fact. I don't want you second-guessing yourself because you fear making a mistake. Let me make myself clear on this point: the only blunder is keeping something to yourself. If you think it, I want to hear it. No theory will be shot down in flames. Now, questions?"

A uniformed hand shot up. "Boss, is there any connection between the victims?"

Bliss nodded and waggled an extended finger in the direction of the officer who had spoken up. "Good question to begin with. Like me, you must be new to this team. The answer, bearing in mind that we're still piecing together last night's murder, is that no evidentiary link has been discovered so far. But it is one avenue we will continue to explore."

Another hand. A detective this time. Another face Bliss did not recognise. A male face that had not seen a razor in a couple of days. "How well planned were these murders, boss?"

"I wish I could answer that with some degree of confidence. The thinking on the first murder is that Maureen Jackson was probably a victim of circumstance. As the second took place in a residential area for the elderly, it seems likely that the murder, if not the victim herself, was pre-conceived. It is believed that whoever did this went there deliberately to kill, and the chance with Joan Mitchell presented itself. I have not yet discussed last night's incident with the senior squad members who worked the first two, so you'll have to wait for a more complete answer on that one."

A few muted conversations broke out as the assembled team digested this information. Bliss cleared his throat and said, "Let me get DS Bishop and DS Short to fill you in on events that took place earlier this morning, both at the SOC and hospital."

Bliss stepped across to a desk and planted himself on its corner. He wedged two fingers between his shirt collar and neck, trying to create some more space between the two. The tie he wore had begun to feel more like a noose. Standing up in front of a large squad had never come easy to him, and with the first part over, Bliss now felt the tension start to ebb away.

Detective Sergeant Bishop, a giant of a man at well over six foot and weighing in at more than eighteen stone, lumbered up to the front, closely followed by DS Short who, by comparison, looked like a child. Bishop positioned himself to the side of the third board and crossed his arms beneath a massive chest.

"Myself and DC Hunt were at the scene for a couple of hours. Essentially, we have a similar SOC, though in addition to the escalation of violence, there are two unusual aspects this time around. The fact that our killer chose to attack someone who had a dog with them is slightly unusual. Obviously there are two major risks in doing that: first, that the dog might attack them, and second that its barking might alert other people. While we can assume he took the dog out of the equation first, and swiftly, it remains a strange decision. The second curious feature is that it looks as though he made an attempt to bury the animal. I can't think of a single good reason why he should hang around to do that."

"Maybe he's a pet lover who got upset when he realised what he'd done," someone suggested.

There were a few outbreaks of laughter at this, but Bishop held up a hand to silence them. "You may mock, but I've heard stranger things. It's worth considering, though I'm not sure how it will take us any further. Anyhow, CSI were still hard at it when we left, but I've had no word of any smoking gun turning up since."

"DC Carmichael and I interviewed Mrs Lakeham's husband, and were also able to have a quick word with the pathologist when the body arrived at the hospital mortuary," Short said. A few of her fellow officers called her "Barbie", because of her pretty face, long blonde hair and full figure. When she spoke, however, the DS commanded respect. Her thick Merseyside burr had a natural edge to it, and legend had it that many a male colleague had regretted using that nickname to her face.

"Mr Lakeham was unable to provide any worthwhile information other than a timescale. He saw no one and heard nothing unusual immediately prior to discovering his wife's body. The pathologist wasn't prepared to offer any indications or guesses, so we'll have to wait for the post-mortem results to find out if the body gave up any clues."

"Thanks for that," Bliss said, standing and walking centre stage once more. He formed and then unclenched a fist on several occasions. "It's obviously early days with Annie Lakeham, but we do have some forensics from the previous two victims. Only one link so far, and that was matching hair found at both scenes. Our killer wears his hair quite long and is going prematurely grey. Unfortunately we were unable to obtain any DNA, but we do have a blood type – he's a common 'O' and we're waiting for DNA results on that. Footprints found at or near both scenes, but no matching patterns. Size is the same, and from the depth of tread the forensic lab reckon the weight of the wearer is around twelve stone in both cases."

"You haven't mentioned witnesses, boss," one of the uniforms said. "Does that mean there aren't any?"

"That's exactly what it means. Door-to-door canvas came up with nothing at all. Last night's murder was far away from any dwellings, of course, but locals will be questioned as a matter of routine."

Bliss shook his head and took a deep breath. "Fact is, people, we have some evidence that will help us build a case for the CPS once we have a decent suspect, but absolutely nothing to lead us to him at this point."

"We are still working on victims one and two," Bishop pointed out. "But of course, a fresh case means fresh impetus and fresh evidence."

"Exactly." Bliss nodded his agreement. "Now then, DS Bishop will be going over to the scene with me after I have met with senior detectives. DC Carmichael will be handling the actions in my absence, and you are to work through him if anything crops up. DS Short will be managing the office, so if you have any queries then please approach her first. Overtime will be allowed if necessary, but only if first approved by me."

Bliss paused. Looked at the team before him. He set his jaw. "In case it hadn't already occurred to you, we are up against the clock. This man will kill again. We may have a month, we may have less. But if we don't catch him, then another elderly women is going to be murdered. Please keep that in mind. Now, for the remainder of this week we will have briefings at eight and five-thirty, and if you don't attend, you'd better have a bloody good reason. That's all."

He moved away from the boards without a backward glance. There was nothing there that wasn't now firmly fixed in his head. Sometimes he wondered how all the hideous things he had seen during more than thirty years of police work failed to coalesce into one single image that would send him over the edge of sanity. And at other times he wondered if he had already moved beyond that grey area and fallen into the abyss.

THREE

The Superintendent's office was familiar to Bliss. Throughout his previous posting at Thorpe Wood he had spent more time in it than he cared to dwell upon. Having been summoned to attend a meeting there immediately after his catch-up with senior detectives working on operation Moonstone, he was edgy despite knowing the previous occupant was long gone from the job. It seemed to Bliss that Superintendent was now the only rung on the ladder where pressure could be brought to bear from below as well as above, and as such whoever took on that role had to be a political beast first and foremost. It was virtually an impossible task pleasing everyone, but the worst type of character to accept the responsibility of that rank was one whose gaze only ever fell upward. A prime example had been a former post-holder, an arsehole of a man by the name of Sykes, with whom Bliss had butted heads on just about everything to do with case management.

This time he found two women waiting for him, one either side of the glass and chrome desk in the far corner of the room beyond an L-shaped seating area. Both rose to greet him as he entered.

"DI Bliss," Detective Superintendent Marion Fletcher said, her smile matching the warmth of her hand. "Good to see you again. Let me introduce you to Alicia Edwards, our most senior DCI during Stephen Harrison's unfortunate absence."

After the formalities, Bliss took a seat next to Edwards. He had met briefly with the Super two weeks earlier, in what amounted to an interview for the post he had subsequently accepted. Bliss had taken to her immediately. Short and slight, with a mane of light-brown curls and a firm set to her chin, Fletcher exuded a natural charm that allowed others to relax in her company. Bliss imagined that led to many a person being lulled into a false sense of security when attending meetings.

"How was your first briefing, Inspector?" she asked him.

"It went well, I think, ma'am."

"Any relevant updates for us?" Edwards chipped in.

"Nothing so far, no."

"This was Alicia's first DCI posting seven years ago," the Superintendent explained. "Ordinarily, Inspector, with DCI Harrison having arranged time off to care for his poorly wife, I would have let the DCI take over the reins of the case you're now heading. However, with so much on her plate already and the pressure building for results, I felt it needed someone with little or no caseload to get in the way of this one major operation. As I explained in an e-mail to you last week, DCI Edwards and I did discuss the matter beforehand. It was a close call. Had it not been for the most recent attack, she would have got the nod. In my view, however, a third victim raises the stakes exponentially, and you can devote your entire time to it, whereas DCI Edwards cannot."

"Yes, and I'm more than happy for you to be running with this, DI Bliss," Edwards said, shifting sideways to face him. "I don't believe I could have given it the attention it now clearly warrants."

Edwards was slim and lithe, looked as if she worked out, and despite a severe cut, her jet black hair was stylish and feminine. She wore little make-up, and didn't even need that to Bliss's mind. If she knew she was beautiful, she did not appear at pains to bask in that knowledge.

Bliss smiled and nodded. "Thank you, Chief Inspector. As you will undoubtedly be aware, I'm not new to the place, so at least I don't have to bed in completely. I still know many team members as well, which is also a big help. I trust I can come to you for advice as and when I need to."

"Of course. I was thinking we should, in the first few days at least, meet once a day so's you can update me. Please don't feel obliged to report to me every five minutes. This is your investigation, and whilst as the SIO I need to be kept informed, you make your own decisions in order to progress the case."

"Thanks. It's a tough one to start back with, especially given the third murder last night, but I have a good team on it with me."

"They are," Edwards agreed, nodding vociferously. "Some may need a few rough edges shaving off, having become a bit too comfortable and a little lax. But you'll get them into shape in no time. And I'd just like to say that it's good to meet you at last. I've heard a lot about you."

Stiffening, Bliss wondered if there might be more to come. But the DCI was still smiling at him and nodding cheerfully. He responded in kind.

"I'm sure opinions are divided. As I discussed with the Detective Super here when we met a fortnight ago, I don't believe any of that old baggage is relevant anymore. It's all history now, if not exactly ancient."

"Oh, I've heard only good things from the likes of DS Short and other detectives who were here during your time, Jimmy."

"That's nice to know. I think I have a good take on the investigation so far," he said, nodding appreciatively but looking to steer the conversation back towards safer ground. "And whilst there has been an obvious escalation with the third victim, I would hope to get some traction within the next twenty-four hours."

"Excellent. And how's your health these days, Inspector?" Edwards asked.

Bliss tried to read the DCI's face but came up short. He shrugged. "I manage, thank you. The decline has slowed. I'm never going to be entirely well, as it's a chronic condition, but I'm on top of it."

"Your absence record is not bad at all, considering."

"I find I need time off in clusters. I reach a point of saturation where the cumulative effects become too much, and rest is the only thing that helps. But I watch my diet, and I have acquired techniques that help me manage my symptoms. I'm good to go. Otherwise the Superintendent here wouldn't have taken me back, I'm guessing."

Fletcher smiled at him. "No, I would not. Actually, I have a friend who has Ménière's and I know how terribly it impacts her life. I meant to ask during your interview, but how's the hearing?"

"Not good." Bliss shifted uncomfortably in his seat. "But not bad, either."

"Good to know. If there are any reasonable adjustments we can make, you only have to ask."

"Thank you. I'll bear that in mind."

For the next twenty minutes they discussed the parameters of the case and the required communication beyond informal meetings. Pretty standard stuff from what Bliss could tell. His time spent working on cases involving organised crime had provided greater insight into twisted minds than he would have thought possible, given his wealth of prior homicide experience. It was his impression that darkness catered for every possible debasement, with murder being only one.

When the meeting broke up, the Detective Superintendent asked Bliss to wait behind. When they were on their own, Fletcher turned to him and said, "The events of last night could not have been foreseen, Inspector. I apologise for the late-night call out, but I was keen that everyone should recognise you as the senior officer on this case from the very beginning. DCI Edwards is SIO for the sake of protocol, but operation Moonstone is your case. You appear to have hit the ground running, and I thank you for that, Inspector."

"No problem, ma'am. There's nothing like being thrown in at the deep end to test whether you will sink or swim."

"I have every confidence in you. From what I hear through the grapevine you've achieved a lot in just a few hours. As tragic as it was, this latest murder may offer up some leads the previous two have not afforded us."

"That's my thinking, too."

"Good. Inspector, despite everything that was discussed for the record in our meeting just now, informally the DCI is not entirely happy that someone other than her has been given this case. She agrees that her caseload has her stretched, especially with court appearances, but she did fight to have other investigations released to you so that she could take this one on. I understand why – it's high-profile, and will become more so from today. Of course, when this was discussed last week, we had no way of knowing there would already be a third victim on your first official day back."

Bliss nodded. "I understand. If not for last night's murder, DCI Edwards would be running Moonstone."

"Whilst that's true, I meant it when I said it was a close call, Inspector. It's not as if you lack experience. Truth be told, you're a DCI in all but name. Edwards has been here throughout and has, of course, kept herself up to speed with each of the previous two incidents, so it's important that you work together well."

"Ma'am, any time you want me to step down and have DCI Edwards take over, then please go ahead. The last thing I want to do now that I'm back is to rock any boats."

Fletcher smiled back at him. "Thank you, Inspector. I do appreciate your understanding. There may come a time when I have to do just that. For the time being, however, I would rather keep things as they are. Edwards has momentum with her caseload, and it doesn't hurt to have a fresh eye on one which has clearly defeated us thus far. That said, I do want you to come to me if you feel unsupported by your DCI. This is not about personalities or career boosts – it's about solving what is now a serial case."

"I agree. I'll get on with it as best I can, and I will make sure I include DCI Edwards all the way. I sympathise with how she might feel, and have no wish to antagonise her."

"Good to hear." Fletcher stood and held out her hand again. "It's great to have you on board, Inspector. Now, go break a leg."

"Thank you. I intend to."

Bliss took one more glance around at the office, whose walls seemed to echo with the loud and often volatile disagreements between himself and Sykes, whose puce face was so often creased with rage that Bliss felt the man might have a heart attack at any moment. He allowed himself a slight, thin smile. Then he turned and walked away with the noxious odour of bullshit in his nostrils. As with the office itself, the stench was familiar to him.

FOUR

Detective Chief Inspector Edwards was waiting for Bliss in the corridor when he walked out of the Detective Super's office. She nodded mutely towards the stairway close by, and Bliss followed her out onto the landing. He noted that she walked like an old western gunslinger preparing to draw down on someone, her fingers even twitching in anticipation.

"I trust you didn't fall for all that old bollocks," she said, rounding on Bliss, nose wrinkling as if she had accidentally wandered downwind of a foul odour. "Fletcher's heart is in the right place, and she does like to see the best in people. But she is also naïve, and make no mistake, Bliss, I am fucking outraged that you got handed this case."

Bliss had expected something like this; her face might have remained impassive back in the office, but Edwards's eyes had given her away. A burning ire had remained in them throughout. He didn't much care either way about retaining the investigation, but neither was he about to take a step backwards on day one of his fresh posting. There was a time and place to do so, and this was not either.

"I don't see why," Bliss said, more casually than he felt. "It's a bit of a loser, isn't it? Two previous murders and not one decent lead. Nothing to go on with this one so far, either. You really want to own it?"

The DCI dismissed his comments with a shake of her head. "I'm not concerned about the result, Inspector. It's how it looks from afar. When my time comes to step up, questions will be asked as to why I was overlooked in favour of someone ranked beneath me."

"You could argue that it reflects well on you – that you were considered far too crucial to be wasted on an investigation going nowhere fast."

Edwards narrowed her flinty gaze. "Don't be obtuse, Bliss. It's a triple murder investigation. The only one we have on the books currently. That's a DCI role at the very least."

He had tried playing nice, now Bliss felt it was time to hit back. "In that case, perhaps you ought to be looking at yourself more closely. You said questions would be asked of you. Perhaps you're the one who ought to be asking them."

The last time he was based at Thorpe Wood his manner and attitude to senior officers had been poor. At the time he hadn't believed that to be the case, but hindsight was a wonderful thing. He'd had little self-control in those days, and could admit to it now. In the past few years, however, he had sought help with relaxation techniques, approaching life in a more zen-like way.

Most of the time.

"Are we going to have problems?" Edwards asked, looking him up and down will ill-concealed distaste.

"Not if you let me get on with my job we won't. Look… boss, I didn't ask for this case. I couldn't care less about keeping it, or office politics for that matter. Believe it or not, I just offered to hand it across to you. The Superintendent is adamant that I run it, reporting to you. You're still the SIO, after all. In truth, my reading of that is that if I'm successful, you get the credit, and if I fail, I get the black mark against my name. You never know, maybe Fletcher really is protecting you."

Bliss felt the woman's eyes drilling into his. She was trying to read him, but he kept his own gaze neutral.

"You have a reputation for speaking your mind, Bliss. That you can often border on the flippant. In my view, flippant can easily cross the border into impudence, which in turn borders on impertinence."

Bliss somehow kept his face impassive, when all he wanted to do was laugh. "That is a lot of borders."

"None of which I expect you to cross."

"That would not be my first choice, either."

Edwards continued her scrutiny of him. Eventually she looked away, then nodded. "I'll give you the benefit of the doubt for now, Bliss," she said. "But you can bet I will be riding you hard. One false step is all I need."

"I understand. I want to work with you, not against you. I'm not your enemy."

For the first time, Edwards softened her countenance. "You're not at all what I'd been led to expect," she said. "I thought you would be a lot more belligerent."

He shrugged. "People change."

"We'll see. Either way, ignore what I said back in that office. I do want regular updates, and you are not to make your own major decisions about tactics. You run everything by me. "

"And what if it's time sensitive? You wouldn't want to be seen to be slowing the investigation down, would you?"

"Of course not. Do what's necessary in those circumstances."

Edwards nodded once and left him to it. Bliss smiled as she walked away. He turned to stare out of the closest window, which overlooked the ground floor car park, dense scrubland beyond stretching far into the distance. The sky had not brightened, but at least the rain had stopped. Bliss considered the two meetings he had just endured. He had done well. He had earned himself a way out, by simply being able to claim time sensitivity. He just hoped Edwards would not keep pushing. He had changed. But not that much.

*

Bliss was sitting at his desk updating the case file when he heard someone cough close by. He looked up from the computer screen, and smiled broadly when he saw who was standing in the doorway. He rolled his chair back and spread his hands.

"Detective *Sergeant* Chandler," Bliss said. "As I live and breathe. How's life in the sex crimes division, Penny? You learn some new lewd words to call me behind my back?"

Penny Chandler had been Bliss's closest ally after his move into the area from London. Throughout their time together at Thorpe Wood they had been unofficial partners. Six years ago, Chandler had taken and passed her sergeants' exam. The first person she told was him. More recently, Bliss had recommended Chandler for the Sapphire unit, a specialist division whose responsibility it was to investigate rape and serious assault. As part of the Specialist Crime and Operations Directorate, Sapphire was based in New Scotland Yard. London had been Chandler's temporary home for going on nine months now.

For a moment, Bliss thought Chandler would flip him the finger in response to his remark, but instead she stepped inside the office and perched on the edge of his desk. Her navy skirt rose up on her thighs, and it sparked a memory of their time together that made him feel a little melancholic.

As for Chandler, the smile she had greeted him with never left her face. "Whatever I have to say to you I will say to your face, old man. Actually, boss, everything I am learning down there is entirely your doing. As I told you when we last spoke, I'll be eternally grateful."

Bliss got to his feet. Stepped around the desk and gave his friend a warm embrace. Chandler's hair was soft against his cheek, and she smelled of oranges. As was her habit, she wore a silk blouse, and Bliss felt his hands slide on the smooth material. Slight of build and barely a couple of inches over the five foot mark, Chandler felt like a child in his arms. Bliss held off squeezing too tight, as he felt he might snap his friend in two.

"You've earned every single thing that has come your way, Pen. You're a bloody good cop. People miss you when you're not around. So I hear, anyway. Me? I could not care less."

Chandler winked as he released her and they stood back to regard one another. "Yeah, you miss me, don't deny it."

It was true; he did miss her. Bliss told her so. "And I certainly wasn't expecting to see you here, that's for sure. What a pleasant surprise. Is this a flying visit to the area or are you here on a job?"

"The latter. A couple of victim interviews and a bit of grunt work. My guvnor thought my local knowledge would save time for the team. Plus, I volunteered."

"A dangerous precedent," Bliss told her. "But it is so nice to see you again. It'll be like the old days around here."

Chandler glanced around. "Seems like only yesterday," she said, her gaze falling back on him. "It really struck a chord when you told me you were coming back to Thorpe Wood. I had some of my best times here with you."

"And worst," Bliss reminded her.

"True. But they made me stronger. And better."

"You've spread your wings, Penny. Out from beneath my shadow you've blossomed over the years. I didn't recommend you for Sapphire just because we're mates. I spoke to every DI and DCI you've worked with since I left here. One or two DCs and even uniforms as well. How you handle those below you on the ladder is just as important as how you deal with those on the rungs above. No one had a bad word to say about you. Despite my so-called leadership."

Shaking her head, Chandler punched him on the upper arm. Just a tap, but he made a meal of it.

"Not in spite of you," Chandler insisted. "*Because* of you. The grounding you gave me was invaluable. I owe you, boss. Big time."

Bliss dismissed her observation with a flick of the hand. "Well, it's great to see you back here, even if it's only temporary."

"Thank you, Jimmy." Chandler indicated his desk with a nod of her head. "I see it hasn't taken you long to settle into a familiar routine. Five minutes is all it takes for you to make a complete and utter mess. You should be ashamed at the stack of documents you've got piled up already."

He nodded. "I have a system. I just forgot what it was."

Chandler laughed, and when she peered beyond him she laughed harder still. "You brought the Bliss Pissed-o-Meter back with you I see."

Chuckling along with Chandler, Bliss turned to look at the wall behind his desk. A week or so after arriving in Peterborough the first time around, some wag had stuck a cardboard thermometer on the wall behind his office chair, with an arrow pinned to the centre. It supposedly depicted his mood at any given time. The dispositions had a narrow range, none of them placid. In just shy of four years prior to moving on, he had never managed to catch the individual responsible for swinging the arrow.

"Been stuck on grumpy for a while now, Pen," Bliss told her. Looked back into her eyes. "My money is still on you being the mood-shifter."

"First of all, as I've told you a million times, don't call me 'Pen'. Second of all, has the arrow moved since you left?"

"I never took it out of the box at any of my other offices."

"How come?"

"It didn't feel right. Time and place, you know?"

Chandler nodded. She would sympathise more than most, he thought.

Bliss checked his watch. "You had breakfast, Pen?"

"Not yet. I was hoping to catch some with you."

"I could eat. Bloody hell, I can't believe you're standing here with me again. Even in just a few hours or so this place hasn't felt the same without you."

In his friend's presence, Bliss liked to pretend that he had no need of Chandler in his professional life, that she was little more than an average detective, and pretty much a pain in his rear. The truth was, she had completed him at work. No one had come close since. They were more than colleagues, less than lovers. His work wife, someone had once commented. Bliss hated the term, but he could not disagree with the sentiment.

*

Whilst the rain had relented, the sky remained a seamless cover of dense, grey cloud that looked set for the day and ready to unleash its cargo again at any moment. The crime scene appeared very different in even this meagre natural light, and Bliss was feeling a little disorientated as he switched his gaze between the boating lake and the vast stretch of land leading off towards the closest crop of buildings several hundred yards away.

The media were gathered in the recreational area's largest car park, the whole of Ferry Meadows having been closed to the public for the day. The congregation had grown substantially now that national newspaper and TV crews had arrived. It never took long for news to leak out. Particularly bad news.

"Wait until they realise we're now hunting a serial killer," Bliss said to his colleagues. "They'll wet themselves in excitement."

"Cue photos of Sutcliffe and Fred West," Chandler said, shaking her head and hunching deeper into her heavy padded jacket. With her first interview not due for a couple of hours, Bliss had suggested she join him at the scene after breakfast. The DS had seemed elated to be included.

"And Hannibal Lecter," Bishop muttered. "Anything to scare the public shitless."

"If it even does anymore," Bliss said. It was a sour observation, he realised, but valid nonetheless. It was hard to shock people these days.

"I'm not sure we have so many murders of this nature that people aren't affected, boss."

"I just think that the many hundreds of books and films available about crime and criminals, not to mention explicit video games and the graphic content you can find even on YouTube these days, has made the public fascinated by it rather than frightened."

"I think you're right, boss," Chandler said. Her nose and cheeks were flushed with the cold, and she stomped her feet to keep them warm. "The most popular TV shows are all crime related. And the stuff they have on the internet is sick."

Bliss thought of something he had noticed as they drove through the first stage of the park and onto the winding, narrow road that led to the boating area. "That barrier by the mini roundabout is locked down at night," he said. "During the summer it's up until quite late, but, if I remember right, it's padlocked fairly early at this time of year."

Bishop nodded. "I'll check, but I think that's the case."

"So if our killer came here by car, he would have had to park down that end."

"Sounds about right."

"Okay. Then let's include that in any public appeal. You never know what people may have seen without recognising its significance. And let's get a forensic team down there, too. Have them look for fresh oil stains in particular, or traces of dirt that looks out of place."

They were restricted as to where they could walk; forensic technicians and crime scene investigators still hard at work searching for trace evidence. Pathways were clearly marked by fluttering tape and flagged metal spikes, the trail following areas already searched and cleared by the scene manager. The grid, they called it. Bliss walked across to the knot of trees beneath which the small hole had been dug, Chandler and Bishop close at his heels.

"What do you two make of this?" Bliss asked, staring down into what may have been intended as a shallow grave. "Does it make any sense at all for our killer to hang around to bury a bloody dog? Not only that, but to dig the hole and then not use it?"

"He could have been frightened off," Chandler suggested. "Maybe he heard someone coming. Perhaps even the husband."

"It's possible. I just don't get why he would dig the hole in the first place."

"Some killers cover up the bodies of people they're close to. Maybe this bloke loves animals."

Bliss chuckled. "Someone suggested that during the briefing earlier. It may not be quite as absurd as it sounds, I suppose."

"It's odd, I grant you," Bishop said, stooping to peer into the hole. Tall and wide, his every mannerism appeared ungainly. "Perhaps the victim's husband saw something of note."

Bliss frowned and snapped his fingers. "Do you know who actually reported the murder last night, Bishop? I know

Mr Lakeham found his wife out here, but what happened after that? Did he go for help at all?"

"He used his mobile," Bishop replied. "Inspector Kaplan told me that the couple had been given a phone by their daughter. Annie Lakeham forgot to take it out with her, but her husband found it on the kitchen table and brought it with him when he went searching for her."

"Okay, that solves that little riddle. Now, answer this one: with what did our killer dig this hole?"

Both Chandler and Bishop scoured the leaf-strewn soil around the immediate area. Chandler looked up and said, "He could have used his hands. The ground is probably soft enough after all the rain you've had up here."

"He could've used a stick and then tossed it," Bishop suggested.

Shaking his head, Bliss pointed at the hole. "Look at the edges. Three of the four are squared off, and the soil is smooth in places. Looks to me like he used a spade."

Now it was Bishop's turn to frown. "But that would mean he came prepared. Which suggests he had already selected his victim, and knew the dog would be with her."

"Or that he wasn't here to kill anyone or anything at all."

Chandler got it first. "You mean his entire purpose here at all was to dig the hole? To bury something?"

"Makes more sense than digging it to bury the dog and then not."

"So you're thinking he was digging the hole, and Annie Lakeham stumbled upon him. He couldn't allow her to tell anyone what he was doing here, so he killed her."

"More likely it was the dog that found him. Probably ran through where the trees stand, at which point our killer caved its skull in with the spade. Annie came through after the dog and saw what had happened, our man did the only thing he could when faced with that situation."

"So why not just leave it at that?" Bishop asked. "Why carry on with his usual MO?"

"This sick fuck has a thing for women in this age range, Sergeant. Having killed her, it was probably instinctive for him to continue with the rest of the ritual. Despite the initial murder being unplanned."

Bishop was shaking his head. "So he comes here to bury something, but in addition to the spade he also brings a knife and some pliers or whatever the hell he used to rip out her nails? I'm not saying you're wrong, boss, but it doesn't completely add up."

Bliss pursed his lips. Thought about it for a few seconds. "It's just a theory at the moment. I don't have all the answers by any means. Maybe he always goes out tooled up, ready for any eventuality. I'm simply speaking out loud at the moment, voicing thoughts based on what I see and think. It's worth approaching it from that angle for a while. Might help us see things in a different light. Get us to ask different questions this time around."

"Such as?"

"Such as what was he intending to bury," Chandler interjected. "And why?"

FIVE

As he sat alone in his squalid and sparse bedroom, hunched up on the floor wedged between a leaning wardrobe and a broken chest of drawers, his body shuddered and his flesh quivered. He had done little but spasm and convulse since arriving home and dashing straight into his room to escape the stinking world that had no rightful place for him.

The old woman had come out of nowhere, following the bloody stupid dog.

The hole was barely dug. All was still in the chill night air until he'd heard a snuffling, a hurried scurrying sound that grew louder with every passing second. At first he thought it might be an inquisitive deer, but then the dog appeared from between the sprawling roots of the trees.

And a dog almost certainly meant an owner following close behind.

He had waited, spade poised in the air, as the dog scampered up to him. Friendly little thing it had been, too. Tail wagging furiously. Pink tongue lolling as it huffed at him. It took only two well-aimed blows to wipe that dopey look off the animal's face.

He then heard similar sounds, only louder and more forceful this time, from a much larger presence coming his way.

Then the woman had appeared.

They exchanged looks.

It only took that single initial eye contact for him to know he was screwed. Reflecting on it now, he liked to think she had thought exactly the same thing. Especially after she caught sight of what remained of her pet and the spade in his hands now dripping blood onto the frigid soil.

I had to kill her, he told himself, still hiding away in his room when he ought to have been out at work. *Kill them both.*

I had no choice.

At first his instincts screamed at him to make a run for it, the woman already dying in a pool of blood at his feet. But then he realised that the night had grown quiet again and that, for the time being at least, he was alone once more. His other tools were in the car, which wasn't so far away. Not if he really wanted them. If he jogged it would not take long at all to fetch them.

It hadn't.

The pliers and the knife did their job well. But then a frenzy had overwhelmed him, his mind wandering more than it usually did at this stage of the act. For some reason he grew angry with the woman. He enjoyed being methodical, working to a timetable and routine of his own choosing. This woman's death was out of place, out of time. It did not fit. It did not feel right at all. So he used the blade more than he would otherwise have done. The point of attack was clear to him, and when it was over he could not say it hadn't felt good.

In fact, in the hours that followed he'd had to confess to himself that it actually felt wonderful. Perhaps even overdue.

And yet he had left behind the hole.

After dealing with the old woman and dragging her out where she would be displayed for anyone to see, he had not been thinking straight. His head was muddled, a filter of blood-red hues placed over his eyes. Still, he accepted these were excuses. Leaving the hole exposed had been a terrible error.

What would the police make of the hole? Would they guess what it had been for? Could they possibly know? No. No, that was unthinkable.

Yes, he had slipped up by leaving the hole, but everything else was as it should be. There was not even the slightest chance of them even considering the truth. No, the hole would be a mystery for them to puzzle over but never solve.

*

Bliss bought them all a late lunch at a nearby diner on the edge of the A1. In reality it was little more than a glorified greasy spoon, but people seemed to enjoy it. There was a lot of garish Formica, the tables were sticky, and the staff were probably as underpaid as they were undertrained. As the three detectives sat and cupped their drinks, Bishop asked Bliss about his experience of working with Chandler.

"To quote Charles Dickens, 'It was the best of times, it was the worst of times, it was the age of wisdom, it was the age of foolishness…'."

Chandler set her mug down and raised the middle finger of her left hand. Bliss laughed before continuing.

"Pen and I worked two extremely high-profile and difficult cases together. In the first, a missing boy had turned up dead, while a racist killer stalked local prey. I was fortunate enough to tie the cases together, but in resolving the investigations I also unwittingly engineered a separate murder."

Chandler shook her head, before shifting stray hair behind her ears. "None of that was your fault, boss. I've told you that often enough."

"Well, that was certainly how the brass saw it. They needed someone to blame, and it was my operation. But then after a six-week suspension, I was cleared on all counts. Even so, I guess it left me feeling a little vulnerable and uncertain of my future. It was extremely unfortunate that my first major case afterwards led to a bygone murder conspiracy and corruption amongst several fellow officers. Some lost their jobs, others their lives. I think I gained the respect of some colleagues, but lost it from just as many others."

"Sounds like a nightmare," Bishop said. "How on earth did you handle it?"

"I didn't. Not really. Had to undergo the usual therapy sessions. Not sure they helped. I think my mind was set on quitting."

"I convinced him he would be lost without the job," Chandler said, smiling gently at the memory. "And that the job would be worse off without him."

"Penny was my rock," Bliss admitted. "She stuck by me, constantly finding herself having to fight my corner. When I first moved up to Peterborough I deliberately distanced myself from my colleagues. In retrospect I know that was the wrong thing to do, but the scars from my personal and professional life back in London were too raw to even consider having them exposed. Penny accepted me for who and what I was. Who and what I had been. And then she accepted me for what I became."

"Sounds like a match made in heaven," Bishop said. He sipped some coffee and nodded as their food arrived. "Just the kind of partnership you hope for in this line of work."

"You're spot on there," Chandler said. "Sometimes the mix is just right. When it works, things become second nature. When it doesn't, it just feels awkward."

"Hopefully I can step up and fill your shoes on this op."

"I have tiny feet, so you'll do fine."

Chewing his way through a cheese omelette, Bliss became fascinated by the way Bishop ate. The man shoved it away and swallowed almost without chewing. His tie carried the stains of breakfast past by the look of it, and Bishop's white shirt did not look fresh out of a wardrobe. One of the rough edges to shave, perhaps. Bliss steered clear of the investigation for a few minutes, other customers sitting too close for comfort. Instead he broached the subject of Christmas, now only two months away and looming larger with every passing day.

"I was on duty last year," Bishop complained, stabbing a sausage with some venom. "The station was like a morgue. I can understand uniforms being needed for all the minor stuff, but who the hell commits serious crimes on Christmas day?"

Chandler laughed. "A lot of suicides at Christmas. The odd family murder, too."

"Spending the day with yours then are you, Pen?" Bliss asked her.

"I suppose so. Unless a knight in shining armour comes along to whisk me away to the Bahamas."

"There's only tarnished armour around here," Bishop said, laughing at his own feeble and decrepit joke. It didn't seem to bother him that he put a mouthful of undigested food on display. "How about you, boss? I take it you'll have a day or two off."

Bliss nodded. "I booked a few days. My mother would like me to pop over to see her, but I'm not sure if I want to."

Chandler looked up sharply from her food. "What about your dad? You haven't fallen out with him again, have you?"

Bliss hung his head a little, switching away from Chandler's earnest gaze. "He passed away. Sorry, Pen, I should have told you. I meant to."

"Oh, no. How long ago?"

"A couple of years now. Died just before Christmas day."

"A couple of… Bloody hell!"

Bliss felt a twinge of guilt. If ever there was something to share with a good friend, it was the passing of someone close. That he had not picked up the phone to let Chandler know was something he now regretted. They had spoken on many occasions since, but either it had never felt right to slot it into a conversation, or he had simply forgotten to mention it. Bliss wondered what that said about their friendship.

"I'm so sorry to hear that, Jimmy. I'm sure it must have been a difficult time for you and your mum."

He rubbed a small scar on his forehead. "It was. I spent some time over there to help her through it."

"Where were they again? Spain, wasn't it?" Bishop screwed up his face, trying to recall what he'd been told.

"Just inland of Marbella. Up in the mountains."

"I'd be off there for Christmas like a shot given half a chance," Chandler said. "Don't get me wrong, I love my family, but get-togethers can be wearing. They all seem to blur into one after a while. You know exactly what's coming next."

"'Tis the season to be jolly," Bliss remarked, laughing. "I wish I'd not mentioned it now."

"So what's your early take on this case, boss?" Chandler asked him. "I mean, unless your man has left you something tasty this time, you're another victim down and no closer to him from what you've said."

Bliss glanced around to make sure he could not be overheard. "I wish I could make an argument, Pen. Sadly, we all know I can't just yet. Yes, it's early days, but nothing is shifting forwards at the moment. There's no momentum to latch onto. All we can do is pull the strands together and see what forensics we have, see what the door-knocking brings us."

"Yeah." Bishop gave a grunt. "And rack our brains figuring out what the freak was trying to bury."

"Or if he was there to bury anything at all," Chandler said, seemingly disconsolate now.

"Hey," Bliss rapped his knuckles on the table. He met their eyes. "It's called police work. We're supposed to be good at it."

"Well, some of us are."

Bliss narrowed his gaze. "Just because your current guvnor is down south doesn't mean my powers are weakened. Carry on like that and your next posting will be to traffic control."

Chandler smiled. Then allowed it to fall away as she wagged a finger at him. "You win. But you should have told me about your dad. I'm not done with you yet about that."

Bliss put a card down to pay for their meals. As they left the diner, he was wishing that Chandler would stick around for a while, wondering if there was a way he could make that happen. Bliss had a feeling that even three murders in his case was closer to just getting started than being solved, and he needed his partner back. He wanted to feel complete again, and he did not think that was going to happen unless Chandler was riding shotgun with him once more.

SIX

Cardea had a look of unfinished business about it, Chandler thought. One of the newest townships in Peterborough, its buildings, streets and parks looked shiny, new and perfect at first glance. But a more studied appraisal took in the incomplete kerbstones, sand and cement yet to be power-washed from the pavements, a lack of finishing touches here and there. Eventually it would look the part, Chandler was sure. Right now Cardea was a bit like one of those shar pei dogs that has to grow into its skin. She had never visited the place before, but it was here, in the car park of a minor shopping centre, that Chandler had arranged to meet Carly Morris and her mother.

The drive from Thorpe Wood had been an easy one, good roads allowing for decent speeds and fast times. Cardea was an important expansion for one of the fastest growing cities in the entire country, the routes in and out just as vital.

Chandler cruised around the car park a couple of times before spotting the dark grey Focus, and was grateful to find a vacant spot right alongside. She lowered her passenger window and indicated that the mother of the young girl she had come to meet should do the same from her driver's side. The two women flashed matching nervous smiles and introduced themselves.

"You want to pop over to my place or shall I come to yours?" Chandler asked. *Keep it light*, she told herself. Let them both settle to the idea of providing information all over again, when in truth it had to be the very last thing either of them wanted to reflect upon.

They settled on Chandler joining Carly Morris in the back seat of her mother's Ford. Having exchanged a few idle pleasantries, with plenty of warm smiles and nods of encouragement, Chandler got right into it before the girl had a chance to change her mind and bail out.

"First of all, Carly, I can only apologise for asking you to rake this up all over again," Chandler said, hoping her expression conveyed the genuine sympathy she felt. Empathy, too. "Believe me, after I'd been through my own tortuous story half a dozen times, it got really old really soon."

Carly Morris gasped, a hushed sound that caught in her throat. "You were raped as well?" she said.

Chandler nodded. It felt like a lifetime ago now, but every detail of every moment remained fresh in her mind. "I was sixteen – just a year younger than you, Carly. So whilst other cops may have told you they understood how you were feeling, I actually do. I know how much it hurts, perhaps more so afterwards than during. How it cramps the stomach with a vile ache even to think about it. How the shame burns your cheeks whenever it comes to mind. That reliving it becomes second nature, despite it being the last thing you ever want to have in your thoughts again. That was me, Carly. Every emotion you have had, I had as well. So believe me when I tell you that I also felt it lessen as time went by. Especially when they caught the bastard who did it. And that's what I want to give you, Carly: that release of the weight you've been carrying ever since it happened."

The girl nodded. Swallowed. Her eyes pained. "If going over it one last time helps to catch him, stop him doing it again, then I can suck it up."

Morris was cute, with a natural pout that would have made her a rock star on social media. But her hair showed signs of neglect, and her shiny skin was awash with pimples. Time that Carly might have spent taking care of herself was now given over to an innocent victim's self-recrimination.

Chandler patted the girl's leg. "Good for you, Carly. But let me be clear that if you feel you need to stop at any time, then please do so. I mean that. Otherwise, in your own time tell me exactly what happened that night."

Morris had been walking home to Hampton Hargate from the Serpentine Green shopping centre, she explained, having met with friends at Sub Express for a pizza. On the way back home, two of her friends accompanied her until Hargate Way. From there, Morris cut through the green towards her home which was just two hundred yards from where the three said their goodbyes. By the pond stood a small gazebo, and it was here that her attacker had been waiting for her. Morris became aware of him when she reached the structure, and then only peripherally as she took the path that skirted around the pond. Her recollection was of a figure in dark clothing slumped low on the gazebo's benching, a hood pulled up around his head. She didn't hear him move, had no sense of his approach, but he must have moved quickly because within a second or two of hitting the curve she was grabbed from behind.

Here, Morris paused in her recollection. Her mother reached across to squeeze her hand. The woman was in pieces, much more so than her daughter. Silent tears streamed down her face, whereas the girl herself was dry-eyed.

This kid is strong, Chandler thought. *And she will need to be if we get this prick, because once it comes to court that's when the defence team got to spread their poison.*

"He shoved a rag into my mouth, and held a knife to my throat," Morris went on. "That stopped me from screaming. He dragged me to the floor behind the brick part of the gazebo. He never said a word, and he was always behind me. He was just so much stronger than me. Plus… the knife at my throat, of course. I was wearing leggings under my skirt. He yanked them down, and my knickers came down with them. He… felt me first. Then he did it. From behind. It didn't take much longer than a minute or so, though it felt like ages at the time."

The girl hung her head, cheeks aflame. No tears, but they would come. No way of avoiding them when the night set in, the room became dark, and Carly Morris's world existed only inside her head as she struggled to find the solace of sleep.

"Well done, Carly," Chandler said gently, nodding her encouragement. "You're doing great. Now, your statement to local police suggests your attacker used protection, that you sensed he was white, neither young nor old, but physically fit. In terms of your senses, Carly, try to think back now and tell me if you saw anything else, heard anything, if anything was odd about his body, maybe if there was some specific smell, like bad breath."

The girl nodded. Desperate to help, despite the pain it had to be causing her. Chandler felt awful at putting her through it all over again, but also knew it might be cathartic for Morris at the same time. After a few moments, the teenager's thoughtful expression changed.

"I didn't see or hear anything I haven't already told you about," Morris said. "But now that you ask, there was an odour. Not aftershave, not a nice smell at all. I think it was body odour, but he'd tried to cover it up with a spray or something."

Chandler nodded firmly then said, "The odour thing may be very helpful, Carly. Well done. We can call him Stinky now, rather than just our perp."

Carly laughed, and even her mother joined in as she thumbed tears from her cheeks. It broke the awful tension inside the vehicle.

"Seriously, you've both been a huge help. I can't thank you enough. I think we'll leave it there. I'll make sure you're kept up to date by local family liaison officers."

Chandler reached for the girl's arm and gave it a squeeze. "I know it may not seem like it right now, Carly, but you will get through this. I can't tell you how many rape victims I have spoken to in recent months, but let's just say it's enough for me to consider myself a bit of an expert in predicting how girls recover. You're a strong young lady, Carly. You will have tough times ahead, let's not kid ourselves about that. But you'll overcome them. I have every confidence in you. You and your mum both."

Chandler sat in her car long after the Morris's Focus had driven away, her mind playing over the few small additional details she had learned. Rape investigations were never less than harrowing, and in most cases the rapist is easily identified. When that is not the case, it was often those small details that proved invaluable. This had been a quick attack, but not brutal in the way so many were. Other than the act itself, there was no violence, just the threat of it. From what Chandler had picked up from the case notes, the other rape had been very similar.

She took a deep breath, then prepared to go through it all one more time.

*

Bliss entered Thorpe Wood police station via the stairway leading up from the underground car park. As he emerged into the corridor on the second floor a familiar figure was ambling towards him. For a brief moment, Bliss considered turning and walking in the opposite direction. Instead he continued on, deciding discretion was not the better part of valour in this case.

"Well, if it isn't our very own form of human cluster fuck," said the uniformed sergeant approaching him. The man stopped, folded his arms in the vale between his bulging stomach and a hefty pair of moobs. The grin he wore was crooked, just like the man himself. His flesh had a sickly sheen to it, and what hair remained on his head was slicked back.

"Grealish," Bliss said, nose crinkling. "How nice to see a familiar and friendly face."

"Once again, Bliss, that would be *Sergeant* Grealish to you. I know it's been, what, a dozen years or so, but I still won't let it slide."

Bliss paused to take a breath. Ran a count inside his head. The balls of his feet twitched, and he felt his shoulder rotating. Neither were good signs. He could have reminded the man that he was outranked, but opted for a different tack instead.

"You know why you are still a sergeant all these years on, Grealish? Because you're dumb. Dumb and fat and useless. Oh, and a bully. Let's not forget that shining example of your character."

The uniform squared himself, shifting from foot to foot. "You caught me with a sucker punch back then, Bliss," the man said, gobs of spit fleeing his lips as if thrilled to have escaped the vile swamp inside Grealish's mouth. "That won't happen again. You did yourself a favour the day you ran away from this place, because you and me would have gone a few rounds, and you would not have been able to run anywhere after that."

Bliss looked him up and down, hoping his attempt to convey contempt was working. It was hard to believe this grown man had held on to a grudge for this length of time. Grealish had given Chandler a hard time, and when Bliss gave him some back, the man had taken a swing. The attempt was ponderous, and missed by some distance. But in doing so he had left himself wide open, and Bliss had not been able to resist the gut punch. It only travelled a distance of a foot or so, but it built up enough momentum to bypass the man's doughy soft centre and bite deep. From that day on, Grealish set about causing problems for Bliss at every opportunity, even going so far as to have him arrested on a trumped-up charge. Now it seemed that had not been nearly enough.

"Grealish," Bliss said evenly. "I am in a different place both inside my head and as a person these days. If you're not, that's your problem. I'm taking the higher ground, and I will do my best to forget your very existence as time passes. But right now you do exist, and we can co-exist, provided you... Leave. Me. The. Fuck. Alone."

Bliss took two steps forward. Now they stood just inches apart. "I need to go straight ahead," he said. "You're in my way, and I am politely asking you to step aside."

He stared into Grealish's eyes for fully thirty seconds, before the uniform looked away and shifted sideways to let him pass. Bliss walked on without looking back. Grealish said nothing, but Bliss had the feeling that unless something happened to turn things around, he and the sergeant were not done yet.

*

Bliss dropped in to the Major Incident Room to get an update on the case. It didn't take long. The house-to-house canvas was still on-going, but had so far yielded nothing of use. A mobile control centre had been set up on site, and placards calling for witnesses erected alongside all major roads surrounding Ferry Meadows. The post-mortem had not yet got under way, and the crime scene team were not coming up with anything worthwhile. To add to his woe, a full media briefing had been called for 5.30pm. Bliss wondered if DCI Edwards would want him alongside her for set decoration.

Back at his desk, Bliss caught up with his messages and mail. An e-mail from the Chief Inspector demanded his presence as soon as he was available. Bliss groaned when he read it. He knew he carried baggage, and no DCI wanted to go down with the ship. But being summoned this soon after their meeting earlier in the morning was not a good sign. For a moment he considered ignoring it, but then remembered he had offered his full commitment. And this was still day one.

Edwards was in her office, and she instructed Bliss to enter and close the door behind him. With a single glance away from whatever she was reading on her laptop, the DCI pointed in the direction of the seat opposite.

"What do you have for me, Inspector?" she asked, a curt edge to her voice.

Bliss settled into the chair. On the wall behind Edwards was a series of framed photographs from her training days at Hendon, plus a certificate from just about every course an officer could attend. The woman was proud of her achievements, that was for certain. It was a fast-track, qualification-based world. He was an analogue person in a digital age, and perhaps that was his main problem when it came to fitting in.

"Early days yet with the current victim, boss," Bliss said, spreading his hands. "And no progress with the first two, I'm afraid."

Edwards blinked as if the information wasn't computing. "And that's what you expect me to announce during the media briefing, is it?"

"We may have something more by then, though I wouldn't bank on it. The PM hasn't even been done yet. CSI will be attending the scene for another day or two. It really is too early."

"And of course the press will see it that way, I'm sure. It's nigh on two months since the first victim, Inspector, as they will be only too happy to point out. Two months of continuous investigation has led… precisely nowhere."

Bliss took a breath. He felt his temper kick into gear, something pulse through his bloodstream. Another breath reeled it back in.

"To be both fair and impartial, I've only just come on board today, boss. Looking at the case files it's clear that my predecessor ran things like clockwork. His team just didn't get a break. As for me, if you can think of anything I haven't done during the very small number of hours that I've been working the case, please suggest away. I've run this op by several other officers, two at DS level, and none of them have been able to pick a hole in the investigation. However, I know you've been following the case very closely, so I'm open to all proposals."

A silence ensued that would have to have improved significantly in order for it to be merely uncomfortable. The two regarded one another across the large desk empty of anything remotely resembling workload.

"Perhaps you would like to explain yourself to the media, then, Inspector," Edwards said eventually. Her eyebrows arched quizzically. "Regale them with your tale of success so far."

"I was told you don't approve of anyone other than yourself dealing with the media, boss."

"True. But I think you're up to this one, Bliss. Let them put a face to the name, and hope they don't raise the thorny issue of your past here in the city."

Yes, like that was going to happen. Clamping his teeth together, Bliss contemplated this fresh situation. Everything was such an uphill battle these days, and Edwards would be only too happy to see him fail miserably. Anyone but herself. He began to suspect that her apparent thirst for this investigation had been fake. That she considered it to be a nail in the main investigator's coffin.

His coffin, as things stood.

"I'll take the briefing if you wish," Bliss said finally. He met Edwards's cold gaze. "As for my past, I've done nothing wrong, so I'm not ashamed. Regards the case, we need a break, and there may yet be one once all the evidence is collected regarding Annie Lakeham."

"Who?" Edwards frowned.

Bliss wasn't at all surprised by the woman's ignorance. "The latest victim."

"Of course." Edwards was adjusting her blotter pad so that it sat squarely on the high-sheen desktop. "Though it seems just as likely to provide more questions than answers. That would appear to be the pattern thus far."

Bliss couldn't argue that particular point. The DCI was correct in her evaluation; the case could go either way. He nodded and got to his feet. "I guess we're done here," he said.

Edwards waited for him to reach the door and open it before saying, "Reports on my desk at nine every morning, Inspector."

"Yes, boss." Bliss replied without looking back over his shoulder.

"And don't forget to update me before you leave each night."

"Right you are, boss."

"Oh, and Bliss."

This time he had to turn. He managed to do so without sighing. "Boss?"

"Don't screw up at the media briefing. And be sure to let them know who is in charge."

"And just who might that be?"

Edwards gave a quick, prissy laugh. "Ah. That will depend on how well the case goes, Inspector."

"I thought it might." Bliss somehow managed not to slam the door shut behind him.

*

Bishop and Chandler were waiting for him in the main open-plan office area. The entire first floor was shared by three divisions: the Major Crime unit, CID and the Regional Crime Squad. Many officers were allocated to whichever division needed reinforcement during serious cases, but each team also had a core of detectives attached to specific departments. After a considerable summer reshuffle, Bliss had found himself part of Major Crime following his reposting, and had swiftly selected other officers to accompany him with immediate effect. DS Bishop's name, having trickled down the grapevine all the way to his ear, had been first on the list.

"How did it go?" Bishop asked, as Bliss wandered in from the corridor in which Edwards's office was located.

"Frank exchange of views?" Chandler prompted, her mouth curling into a smile.

Bliss sighed as he exhaled and said, "She doesn't much care if I fail, because one more strike and I'm out of here for good. But now that we're getting national media attention, she also wants the case resolved. Puts her in a bit of a quandary."

Chandler rolled her eyes. "What does Edwards have against you? She wasn't even here when you were last at Thorpe Wood."

He had been wondering about that himself. Ignoring the fake smiles and feigned camaraderie during the meeting with Detective Superintendent Fletcher, DCI Edwards had been on his back at every opportunity so far. Bliss did not think that could be adequately explained by her having been overlooked as lead on operation Moonstone.

"I have no idea. Maybe she had friends here. It could be she just doesn't like the way I pursued that case. Taking our own people down, that sort of thing. It was a dozen years ago. People change. I did nothing wrong to her. Not that I know of."

Bliss checked his watch. He felt restless, wanting to be doing something constructive while they waited for information from the canvas team, CSI and the pathologist.

"I'm going to nose around the latest crime scene one more time. You two want to come for a ride?"

"I have some work to do on my own case," Chandler said, looking up from an open file on her side of the desk that she was sharing with Bishop. "Some paperwork, some digging around."

Bliss folded his arms and leaned against a tall shelving system, in which all manner of folders and files were stored. Having recommended Chandler for the Met's Sapphire unit, he had been wondering how well she was adapting.

"How did they go?" he asked. "Your interviews? Can't have been an enjoyable experience."

"They never are," Chandler replied. She tapped a pen against the palm of her other hand. "However, I did obtain a new piece of information. Our fuckstick rapist has a body odour problem. One he seems to be aware of, because apparently he tries to disguise it with a pungent body spray."

"That's interesting," Bliss said. "On the one hand he could be some tosspot who simply doesn't bathe, but equally there could be a cause. I understand some medications, some health conditions, like diabetes, can cause issues with odour."

Chandler stopped tapping her pen long enough to make a note. "Good thinking. I don't exactly have a smoking gun to take back down to Sapphire with me, but it's a little bit more than we had before I came up here."

"Yes, well done. We'll make a decent detective of you yet, DS Chandler."

Bliss ducked to avoid the pen Chandler lobbed at him. "You sure you don't want a trip out?" he asked again.

"Certain. I'm waiting for a call back from someone. Your own sergeant here is at a loose end, though."

Bishop nodded. "I'll go with you, boss."

Bliss clapped him on the arm. "Good man. I have to be back by four to prepare for the media briefing, but we'll take a look and see if something stirs up the little grey cells."

"Never was a fan of Poirot." Bishop got to his feet and began tugging on his jacket. "If you don't mind me asking, boss, how come DCI Edwards is putting you up to speak to the media later?"

"She's hoping they'll bury me, Bishop. Or that I'll spit-roast myself."

"You be careful, boss," Chandler said, her voice taking on an edge of concern. "You know what those maggots from the press are like ."

Bliss winked at her. "I do. And I'm ready for them this time."

Chandler laughed. "I've seen that glint in your eyes before. I don't know who I feel more sorry for. Them or you."

SEVEN

There was football on the TV, but instead Bliss opted for the director's cut of *Minority Report*. He loved the premise of crime being prevented before it happened, and though he wasn't a huge Tom Cruise fan – especially after seeing him try to play Jack Reacher – anything remotely associated with sci-fi got his vote. He lay back in his soft leather recliner, one hand clutching a bottle of Budvar, the other feeding himself from a bowl of dry Honeynut Cheerios. Halfway through the film he felt himself relax enough to start enjoying it. But long before the end his mind made the inevitable switch back to work.

His crime scene visit with Bishop earlier that afternoon had been a wash-out. He hadn't expected anything of great value to come of it, but sometimes you had to get back to basics when you felt a case needed a kick-start. Crime scenes were the starting point. The most recent was the freshest, the most likely to still retain anything worth adding to their pool of knowledge. It was hard to believe that the investigation into the murder of Annie Lakeham had been running for less than a full day. Bliss realised he was wrong to think of the case as stalling less than twenty-four hours into it, but when you stacked up the lack of leads together with such meagre findings from the previous two murders, stalled is what it felt like to him.

The forensic operation at Ferry Meadows was winding down, and within a day or two the park would be opened up to the public once more. So far, the door-to-door had thrown up one witness: a man who thought he had seen a dark, hatchback vehicle driving away from the parking area that night. The timeframe appeared to fit, but the man could not describe the car, and could not recall having seen the driver, nor did he get the plate. Bliss had spoken to the officer in charge of the canvas and asked for the witness to be driven over to Thorpe Wood the next day for further questioning.

No further evidence had been obtained from the post-mortem, either; the pathologist had only been able to confirm Annie Lakeham's cause of death and the approximate time, which they had known anyway. DCs Short and Carmichael had attended in Bliss's absence. Something neither would thank him for. His excuse for not attending had been a good one, however: the awful media briefing.

Heading into the cauldron of journalistic frenzy, Bliss had been concerned that he had nothing of interest for them. No fresh news meant digging for some, and the more unscrupulous journalists might decide to raise spectres from the distant past. Bliss decided he could handle it; he also accepted he had no choice in the matter.

The briefing room was twice as full as he had expected. Camera flashes started winking at him the moment he stepped through the door. He took a breath before sitting down at a small table, on which stood an array of microphones. Behind him a large screen displayed the Cambridgeshire County Police Service logo. Usually for briefings on this scale there would be two or three people sat at the table, including the local police press officer. On this occasion, Bliss was on his own – and felt exposed because of it. There were roughly two dozen media people in the room, and he was the sole focus of their attention. He was not a fan of this aspect of the job, but sometimes it came with the territory, so he got on with it.

Bliss gave them his rank and name, and informed the gathered journalists and photographers that he intended reading from a prepared statement. He then went on to confirm the fact that the police were formally linking the previous night's murder of Annie Lakeham with two earlier murders currently being investigated under the operation Moonstone name; also that he and his team believed all three elderly women had fallen victim to the same perpetrator, and therefore the investigating team were looking for a lone killer.

"Forensic evidence from the latest murder is still being gathered," Bliss continued. "We are confident that our efforts in this investigation will bear fruit. For reasons relating to the on-going inquiry, we are unable to release precise details of the murders at this time. What I can tell you, however, is that the attacks on these women were extremely violent, and the person responsible is a dangerous man and should not be approached directly by members of the public."

Bliss exhaled and sat back, waiting for the clamour of voices indignant at receiving so little new information. Less than a heartbeat later the room was filled with noise and raised hands. He pointed at a familiar face; one of the feature presenters from the regional BBC TV news station.

"Can you tell us what, if any, progress has been made today, Inspector?" the man asked.

"I can tell you that significant anomalies pertaining to this most recent attack are being investigated as we speak, and we are encouraged by information received from local residents."

Half-truths dressed up to make for a more interesting overall package. Bliss hated doing it, but felt he had no alternative.

"Are you able to be more specific?"

"I'm afraid not." Bliss shook his head dismissively.

"Is this now being listed as a serial killing?" someone else asked.

Going for the throat, hoping to elicit fear amongst their readers. Bliss wondered if these people even cared if what they wrote set fear into the hearts of vulnerable men and women.

"We do believe this to be the third murder committed by the same person."

"So you'll be launching a manhunt for a serial killer?"

"I personally wouldn't use those terms, no. I don't believe the use of hyperbole does any of us any good." Bliss quickly found the eyes of a female reporter and nodded in her direction.

"Inspector, this is your first major investigation back in this area for more than a decade. How do you feel about tackling something as high-profile as this after your mishandling of that inquiry?"

Good choice, Bliss, he chided himself. *You went from a piranha to a bloody shark. Just because she looks good, too. What was that old saying about not judging a book by its cover?*

"I would take exception with your description of that outcome," Bliss responded. "And the fact that I am not only back here in Peterborough, but also working as part of the Major Crime division, should suggest that I am fully able to work cases pertinent to my rank."

Initially cursing himself for having selected this particular journalist, Bliss now saw that she had opened up a door for him, and he decided to rush through it.

"Now, as you clearly have no further questions relating specifically to this particular inquiry, I'll call a halt to this briefing and will get back to my investigation team. Thank you."

Despite the torrent of protestations echoing around the room, Bliss stood and walked out of the briefing without another word. As he did, he caught the eye of DCI Edwards standing in the far corner, arms folded across her chest. Her face revealed no emotion.

Looking back on that moment now, Bliss was a little confused by his reaction to her presence: he was apprehensive about Edwards, but for some reason he found himself also eager to please the woman. Perhaps to prove her wrong about him. She would not have approved of the way he had ended the briefing. There was no doubt in his mind that Edwards would be having words with him about it in the morning.

Especially, he realised now, since he had forgotten his scheduled update meeting with her before he left for home. Bliss groaned and went in search of another Czech beer.

*

Following the briefing, Bliss had wanted to get out of the building equally fast, but then he remembered that Chandler might still be around. He took the stairs two at a time and found his friend once again on the other side of Bishop's desk.

"Hey, how'd it go?" Chandler asked, looking up from a blue file. She seemed a little peaked, he thought.

"If I said dreadful I'd be talking it up. My DCI will be after my guts, so I'm having it on my toes. You fancy a drink, some grub and a decent catch-up?"

Chandler looked down at her file, thought for a moment, then nodded. She took her jacket from the back of her chair, folded it over her arm and then picked up the file. "I'll take this with me, just in case I don't come back here in the morning."

"You staying over, Pen?"

"I am. My boss is coughing up for a night at the Marriott, so rather than drag my sorry arse back down the A1 tonight I thought I'd take advantage."

Bliss was happy that Chandler had accepted his offer. He could use the company. And she was the right sort of company. As they left squad room, Bliss literally bumped into DC Carmichael.

"Thanks for that PM today, boss," Carmichael said, recovering quickly from the collision. "Nothing I like more than the sights and smells of a mortuary in full flow."

"Someone has to do it."

"Yeah, but why me? Send some newbie next time, will you. I'll have that stench in my nostrils all night."

Bliss was about to walk away and let it go, but that did not sit right with him. As Carmichael continued on his way, Bliss summoned him back. "Constable," he said, emphasising the first syllable more than was necessary. "When I need advice on who to send where, I won't be coming to you for it. A good detective would know when to keep his big mouth shut. A good detective would know that the more he protests about a shit detail the more likely he is to continue being given them."

"Yes, boss." Carmichael nodded. "Sorry, boss."

"Are you a good detective?"

"Yes, boss."

"Then prove it to me next time."

Bliss shook his head as he rejoined Chandler, who had overheard the exchange. "You've mellowed I see," she said between smirks.

"I must have. Not a single swear word."

As they both had cars, Bliss suggested they meet at the Windmill in Orton Waterville, less than a mile from his own home, and less than two from Chandler's hotel. The air was fresh with a bite to it, so although he felt it would be good to get some into his lungs, when Bliss arrived first he headed for the bar rather than the many empty tables out front. Bliss ordered himself a pint of Guinness and a lemonade and lime for Chandler. By the time she walked in he was sat at a table for two.

"Bar meal or restaurant?" he asked, as Chandler settled in.

"I'm beat. Just a light meal for me."

Bliss nipped back across to the bar and returned with two glossy menus. He set them on the table and drained a third of his drink with a couple of gulps. Then he held his glass up.

"I forgot," he said. "A toast. To a fine sergeant, having climbed her way all the way up from lowly constable."

Chandler clinked her glass against his. "Bloody cheek. It's the constables who do all the work."

"That mean we can get rid of your rank, Pen?"

"No. Someone has to be accountable."

"Isn't that the role of us DIs?"

"As if. Yours is to sit back and take all the glory."

"Yeah, and all the bollockings."

Chandler softened her feigned glare. "Your DCI really shouldn't be giving you a hard time already. I'm surprised. Usually it takes a while for you to piss people off, Jimmy. At least two days."

Bliss chuckled. "She's being a bit of a bitch, but then I can sort of understand it. It was natural for this DCI Harrison to catch the first murder, and so of course the second as well. But then with him out of the picture, Edwards must have been rubbing her hands together at the thought of it being shifted across to her. To have someone from the outside sweep in and scoop it up must have been a kick in the bal– teeth. And then to find out the someone was me, that seems to have been the cherry on top."

Chandler took a pull from her drink. "You can't be blamed for this third murder coming along on day one, though. And then she stitches you up with the first briefing. That's not on. Not good management."

"Hark at you. Studying for the Inspector's exam are you, Pen?" The look on Chandler's face told him he was bang on. "So you are. Well, good for you. You'll make a great DCI eventually, no matter what division you end up in."

"Thanks, boss."

"Pen, I'm not your boss anymore."

"You'll always be boss to me. And boss, don't bloody well call me Pen!"

They had a second drink, ordered food from the bar, and spent a couple of hours just talking. Nothing more about either of their current jobs. Over their burgers, Bliss asked Chandler how things were going with her custody case.

A mother before her eighteenth birthday, Chandler had worked damned hard to achieve all that she now had. Until her daughter came along she had been a demanding teenager, drifting through school and emerging with little in the way of academic qualifications. Born and raised in the heart of the Fenlands, Chandler grew up in an agricultural community, where innocence lingered only long enough for her to realise it had been lost.

"What custody case?" she said, shaking her head in obvious frustration. "The whole bloody thing is a complete waste of time. You know, I entered my teens accepting my destiny: a small-town life, marriage to a local farmhand or labourer, no horizons beyond those I could see across the flat, bleak landscape. Having Hannah changed all that, and changed who and what I was forever."

Bliss nodded, understanding his friend's plight. Putting herself through college, and then joining the police, had taken a lot of guts and determination, as well as a good deal of help from parents who overcame initial scepticism. All for the sake of her child, whose father had fled during her fifth month of pregnancy.

"It changed you for the better, Pen. You can have no regrets about that."

"I don't. I wanted Hannah to be proud of her mother. I also wanted security for my child. Being a single parent was tough, but also the most enjoyable experience of my life."

From their many discussions on the subject, Bliss was aware that Chandler had matured and blossomed as both police officer and single mum, facing the world with a smile. Until the day her daughter's Turkish father appeared back on the scene. Chandler had taken his renewed interest as a positive thing. They had even all visited Mehmet's family in Izmir in the summer. Then one day, two-year-old Hannah did not come home after spending the day with her father. When Chandler drove to his flat in Market Deeping, she discovered it abandoned, cleared of furniture along with everything he owned.

The last time Bliss had discussed the situation with her, Chandler revealed that in the darkest, most unwelcome reaches of the night, her mind replayed the moment she had last seen her daughter, cradled in the arms of a man who had first taken and then broken her heart. It occurred in a sequence that ended only when Chandler rose from her sweat-soaked sheets, torment crushing her insides, bruising her very being. She saw herself waving goodbye. Mehmet waggling Hannah's hand by way of a response. Nothing suggesting the betrayal that would follow. Sometimes her subconscious allowed Chandler a horrified cry to stop Mehmet in his tracks. On other occasions she was able to sweep her child up and away from his loving arms. But when Chandler's cognisant thoughts took over, the dreadful reality of that moment ran like a movie sequence in her mind's eye.

Chandler shook her head wearily, setting aside her food. "The Turkish authorities still claim they haven't located either Mehmet or his family. All these years on and apparently, they have disappeared in a puff of smoke. I can't get the Foreign Office to move beyond what they did at the beginning, which was to compel the Turks to investigate. We're still at an impasse, Jimmy."

"That must be so hard on you."

"I won't lie, it still hurts. Every single day. But Hannah is now seventeen, and Turkey is the only life she has ever really known. She may not even be aware that I am alive. For all I know they moved elsewhere long ago. I'm still fighting, but I also now accept that I'll probably never see my daughter again."

Bliss felt awful for his friend. He had tried on Chandler's behalf to move matters on with the FO, but they were adamant that, given the political regime in Turkey, nothing could be done if the Turks refused to assist. He had even volunteered to go out there on behalf of the UK police, once again falling foul of the useless FO. He hated the fact that Chandler now had only hope in her favour, but, in accepting the realities, had also prepared herself for the worst.

Bliss moved the conversation on to safer ground, and they began to relax once again. They were on their post-dinner coffees when Chandler took him to task – as he had known she eventually would.

"So, tell me what happened to your old man," Chandler said, working her way through a tall latte.

"His heart. He'd already had one major scare, as you know. He claimed he took it easier after that, but my mum tells a different story. Anyhow, he was out for a stroll getting some exercise of all things, collapsed, died on the way to hospital."

"I'm sorry, that's such a shame. How's your mum doing now? No desire to come home to her baby boy?"

Bliss laughed. There was no one else he could talk to this way. "She is as well as could be expected. In fact, she sold up the bar and restaurant and moved to Ireland. It's where my mum's family came from. She jokes that she'll come home to die, which is a lovely thought. I told her she might not have a say in that."

"Ireland, huh? You disappointed she didn't move back to the UK, to be closer to you?"

"Not at all. Don't get me wrong, we get on great. But we're independent people, independent of each other. We don't need one another in that way. A couple of weeks a year does us just fine. Plus she's always wanted to spend more time in Ireland."

"Good for her, taking it easy I hope. If she's happy, then why not? So how about you? Any plans to move abroad in a few years' time?"

Bliss was fifty-five. He could take a part pension now and do exactly as Chandler had suggested, or wait until the pot was bigger and retire at sixty. But in the past dozen years he had yearned for a return to a Serious or Major Crime division, and nothing other than settling back in was in his thoughts right now. He explained all this to Chandler, wondering whether he was attempting to convince her or himself.

When they were done and back outside in the car park, the night air now damp and frigid, Bliss gave Chandler another hug. Again he was struck by how tiny she felt in his arms.

"Stop by in the morning if you can," he said. "One last canteen breakfast."

"I might do. Depends on what time they want me back in the office."

They said their goodbyes, and, as Bliss watched her drive away, he felt more alone than he had in many years.

*

Much later, when the night was set in, TV switched off and the house lay in darkness, Bliss padded barefoot around his home. He wore pyjama bottoms and an old Stevie Ray Vaughan T-shirt. He carried a bottle of beer, but it was warm now and he did not drink from it. As had been the case on too many nights to count, he felt haunted. Shadows moved, far away and not his own. But there were no ghosts here. Hazel, his wife, had been murdered back down in London before even his first posting to Peterborough. If the spirits of Bonnie and Clyde were close by, then they would be harmless and joyful.

It had taken years, but Bliss had reached the stage where he could not picture Hazel without first seeing her photograph. Eventually he had learned to cope with missing her. And it had been the same way with Bonnie and Clyde. They may have been just dogs, household pets, but they were also the children he and Hazel had never been able to have. He missed them so much at times that it caused him physical pain. But pain can be controlled, and now instead of sadness he felt elation at the memory of them bounding around the house, leaping upon him as if they wanted to devour him, slapping their tongues against him and nuzzling him until he buckled and joined in. Not this house, though. Only new memories would be carved out here.

So no. No ghosts.

Bliss sighed. Long and filled with pain. In order to conquer his temper and sour attitude when it came to dealing with people he considered fools – or worse – he had sought professional help. Not the kind offered by his employers, whose assurances of privacy he could never entirely trust. Together, he and his therapist had discussed many paths open to Bliss if he truly wanted to overcome what he now recognised as a problem.

A committed atheist, Bliss revealed during one session that he did admire the Buddhist approach to mass mind-control (as he had put it). This interest had deviated towards the zen philosophers, and the search to attain enlightenment. Bliss became a keen student of Confucianism, also Taoism and the works of Lao Tzu. His study had led to practice, self-imposed periods of both meditation and movement exercise. Bliss was aware that a person could follow these paths for a lifetime and never find enlightenment, but he also accepted and embraced the advances he had made in such a short period of time.

Now he was being tested: a violent and newsworthy crime, a potential adversary in the form of DCI Edwards, and a certain one in the as yet unknown figure of the man responsible for three murders. Tested and found wanting already, Bliss believed.

Hence his current state of angst. And no amount of booze could mask the awful feeling of inadequacy he felt right now.

In one of two spare bedrooms, Bliss maintained a mini gymnasium. There was also a rectangular green mat, on which he practised his old karate katas – a series of choreographed movements, forms of both attack and defence. For exercise alone, Bliss went through these katas at full pace, a legacy from his youth when he had found Shotokan karate interesting. When needing to rest his mind, he practised the same movements, but in a slow rhythm, more along the lines of t'ai chi. It was here that he went to next, seeking the repetitive movement, the discipline. Pursuing a quiet and rested mind.

After no more than a minute, Bliss felt himself sway and almost swoon. His right ear ached a little, whilst high-pitched squeals and squawks raged in both. He felt a rush of heat, neck to brow in a moment. He stood perfectly still for a few seconds, legs spread far apart, regaining his equilibrium. Bliss first closed his eyes, and then when opening them again fixed his gaze upon a single object. He stared at it until it remained steady. The moment passed, and he returned to his exercise, albeit at a more leisurely pace. Control over his condition was essential, and down the years he had learned valuable tricks.

Fifty minutes later, Bliss was done and had found a little peace. In his bedroom he pulled aside the curtains. Rested his forehead against the chilled glass. Breathed and closed his eyes.

"I know you're out there," he said. "I know that if you look up you are seeing the same sky as me. So we are close. And I will see you. I will see you appear before me, piece by piece, little by little. But at some point you will be fully formed. And then… then I will have you."

When Bliss opened his eyes, fog had formed on the window and his own street was vague and distorted. He closed the curtains, but before he did he peered out one last time.

"You're mine, arsehole," he said.

Five minutes later, Bliss went to bed, and this time he was able to sleep.

*

In his home close to the city, he awoke from a fitful sleep. The images reflected within that sleep disturbed him. Mouths open as wide as they could stretch, teeth bared, tongues bobbing as the piercing, shrieking screams both erupted and died in an instant. Eyes bulging, coated with fear. Blood: spurting, jetting, oozing, dripping, bubbling, pooling. Slicing, thick lacerations, yellow fat and white bone laid bare. Jagged nails, pink and crimson pulp left behind.

Yet it was not the horror of these images, nor even the depravity behind them, that had disrupted his night. It was the simple realisation once again that there were not enough of them. The catalogue – the inner reel that spun inside his head – repeated itself far too soon, to the point where it became stale and fruitless.

He had to add more.

Many, many more.

And soon.

That was essential. He did not merely desire them. He needed them. They would be his lifeblood, without which he would crumble and blow away like dust.

It was his secret.

His guilty, dirty little secret.

EIGHT

In a change of plan that occurred to him as he was leaving the house that morning, Bliss decided to pay a visit to Joe Lakeham. It was hard enough losing a wife of such long standing, but to have discovered her brutally disfigured body would surely put anyone over the edge. More than the possibility of Lakeham remembering something fresh at this stage, Bliss merely felt he needed to reach out to this man at what had to be the worst moment of his long life. Bliss drove the short distance from Longueville to Wistow, which took him by the golf course, along Ham Lane and into the Cherryfields estate. Less than five minutes door to door.

Bliss remained sitting in his car long after the engine block cooled. He was a little early, he figured. By six he had showered, dressed and made himself scrambled eggs on toast for breakfast. As usual he wore a suit and tie; he owned only three suits and simply rotated. When it came to ties he was a little more fussy, and there were at least two dozen hanging in his wardrobe. As for shirts, anything that didn't need ironing when it came out of the dryer got his vote. After breakfast he listened to the radio whilst reading the morning paper, glad of the distraction. He had intended driving straight to the station, but then as an image of Annie Lakeham's devastated body flashed before his eyes, he gave thought to the man she had left behind. There was no question of him being involved in his wife's death, but Bliss could not shake the image of Mr Lakeham waking to a morning which would bring with it only pain and misery.

At five past eight, the two men sat in a comfortable, snug living room that reeked of a woman's touch. Floral flourishes against plain cream walls added as much colour as the room's dimensions would take. A sofa and two armchairs in plain material, colour added by throw cushions. Bliss imagined Annie Lakeham carefully planning every inch of the décor. She would not do so again though. Not anymore. The thought angered him, but he quashed it. Outrage would do him no good here. Lakeham had made them both a mug of filtered coffee, and Bliss sipped from his as the new widower spoke.

"This beast has to be stopped, Inspector Bliss," Lakeham said. His hands, so obviously affected by arthritis, were interlocked, thumbnails constantly worrying their neighbour, his own drink set aside. "What he did to my Annie was obscene. Beyond monstrous. So much so that I felt even the medical people were disturbed by what they saw."

Lakeham spoke with little emotion. He seemed scrubbed raw. His grieving was put on hold, determination to help the police as much as possible now holding sway.

"We're going to be doing everything within our power, Mr Lakeham," Bliss insisted. He meant every word, but even so the inadequacy of them left a sour taste on his tongue. "We will have every available detective and dozens of uniformed officers working tirelessly on your wife's behalf."

"If you don't mind me saying so," Lakeham said, eyes gleaming intently, "I imagine that's pretty much what was said in regard to the previous two victims. I don't doubt the sincerity, yet none of it prevented this animal from murdering my Annie."

The older man's eyes became watery, but Bliss met his gaze and held it.

"There is nothing I can say to you, Mr Lakeham, that will take us back in time and prevent that attack from happening. I wasn't on those two investigations, yet I can tell you in all honesty that from what I have read and heard, nothing was missed. Everything that could be done was done. There is no single element of either investigation with which I can find fault. He was simply cleverer than us. He left us little or nothing. His rage is building, however, and that may well lead to mistakes. This may be hard to hear, and it's certainly difficult for me to say, but the simple fact is that we need a break and someone else may have to die in order for us to get it."

Lakeham blinked several times behind his spectacles before responding. "That's a very honest assessment, Inspector. And I thank you for it. For treating me like an adult. I am able to process such news without seeking to apportion blame."

"I'm running this investigation now. I owe you honesty, Mr Lakeham. I won't tell you we have leads if we don't. I won't rest until either this man is caught, or we have completely exhausted every line of enquiry."

"Thank you. I appreciate it."

"You're very welcome. I have one more question about when you discovered your wife out there. Tell me, did you close Annie's eyes?"

"No, Inspector. To me eternal shame I pretty much crumpled into a heap when I saw Annie lying there. I don't believe I touched her at all, and I certainly didn't close her eyes."

Bliss thought about what that meant. Unless shock was preventing Lakeham from recalling correctly, the killer had paused long enough to close his victim's eyes. The gesture suggested tenderness. Perhaps even a sense of guilt, maybe even shame.

"Is it important?" Lakeham asked.

"I doubt it. Something for us to ponder."

Bliss paused and glanced around. On every flat surface there were photographs. In each of the shots, Joe and Annie Lakeham stood as one. There were none of children, just the two of them.

"Do you have anyone who can stay with you?" Bliss asked.

Lakeham offered a faint smile. "Your liaison people have been through all that with me. But thanks for asking all the same, Inspector. No, Annie and I had no children, and the only sibling between us passed away a year back. But if you're wondering if I'm going to do anything stupid, then you can rest assured. I want to be around when you catch this beast."

Setting his mug down and rising, Bliss said, "Then I hope we don't keep you waiting too long, Mr Lakeham."

"Please call me Joe," the man said, holding out his hand. "And if I may say, Inspector, when you tell me you hope you won't keep me waiting too long, I rather suspect you mean it."

*

As Bliss had suspected, DCI Edwards was in an unforgiving mood. She collared him the moment he entered the station. In her office she tore into him about the previous evening's media briefing.

"It had already been hijacked," Bliss explained, determined to be defiant. "The questions would not have been about the case after that last one. It's not my job to sit up there like a sideshow coconut and let them take pot shots at me. Had they stayed on course, I would have seen it through. They didn't, so I put a stop to it."

Edwards looked him up and down, like a specimen she had just been asked to evaluate. "You're no spring chicken, Bliss," she said. "You've been around the block. You must be aware of how much we need to keep the media onside. Once they start ignoring the headlines and making us the story instead, they won't shift until something has been shaken loose."

"But that's just my point," Bliss said. "They *were* trying to make me the story."

"Only Evette Jordan, from the *Peterborough Telegraph*. The nationals would not have had any information to hand about your previous case here."

Bliss cursed silently. Had he known the woman was from the local rag he might not have been so quick to walk out. Still, it was done now. He had no intention of backing down.

"She was from the *PT*? I didn't know. But it changes nothing. I'm sure some of them there would have been prepared by their production team. What happened here twelve years ago was not confined to this community, boss. They would not have given up on that line of questioning."

"So you say."

"Yes. I do. And I would suggest that if you really don't want us to be the story, you don't send me out there again."

Edwards inclined her head. "Oh, don't worry, Bliss. I won't let you anywhere near the media again if I can possibly help it."

"Fine by me."

Edwards had been standing throughout, but now she settled into her chair behind the desk. Yesterday she had been wearing trousers, today it was a knee-length skirt. It irritated him that he noticed how good her legs were.

"Another thing, Inspector. I take it you have a good excuse for not attending our scheduled evening update," Edwards said.

"No. Not at all. Truth is, I forgot. I'm unused to having to do such a thing, so it's not part of my routine."

"And your daily report? Also not part of your routine?"

"Filed and logged at six this morning from home."

Bliss waited whilst Edwards tapped something out on her computer keyboard. Eventually she nodded, apparently satisfied with what she had read. "So, you're able to do at least one thing you're told to do."

"Look, I made a mistake, boss. I realise I missed the evening update, but like I say I forgot. It was not deliberate. I apologise. I'll try getting it right today."

Edwards regarded him thoughtfully. "You had better. If this situation were to continue, it might be considered insubordination."

Bliss looked at her with equal intent. "Excuse me for saying so," he said. "But you seem determined to make our working relationship as difficult as possible. And given you were not here during my last stint in the city, I can't help but wonder why that should be."

The DCI took only a beat before responding, eyes narrowing. "Because you lit a fuse under this place, Bliss, and it exploded. Not only that, but by the time the dust settled, you had fled and were nowhere to be seen. I didn't have to be around at the time for that to impact on me when I started. Do you imagine things were ever the same? Can you possibly comprehend how much scrutiny this station – this entire division – has been under ever since? And then just as things begin to settle down, you come waltzing back in as if nothing significant ever happened."

Bliss sat for a while chewing that over. It was harsh, and Edwards did not have all the facts. But for the first time he was hearing about the shadow his last investigation had cast across the station and its people. Chandler had avoided discussing it. He had only ever wanted to forget it. The cost had been too severe.

"You're right," he told Edwards eventually. "What I did here had and may still be having terrible repercussions. You can't expose murder and corruption within the job and not have any fallout. But where you are most decidedly wrong, DCI Edwards, is that I did not choose to move away. I had established clear objectives with Chief Superintendent Flynn. He and I were going to work together to steady the ship. But then the powers that be swept in, and when they were gone so was he and so was I. My move down to the new SOCA was not suggested to me as a way out, it was not offered to me as a new beginning. It was an order."

"I didn't realise that," Edwards admitted after a moment of contemplation. "I suspect many others do not, either."

"People will believe what they want to believe. You did, and you could easily have found out the truth if you'd wanted to. You pre-judged me, based on groundless supposition of the worst kind. As for my coming back, well there you may have a point. But I have worked damned hard these past dozen years whilst feeling like an outcast, and I have earned my return from the cold. And when the opportunity arose, I took it. And no, maybe I didn't care whose toes I trampled on. But then, I didn't see any queues of colleagues lining up to hear my side of the story, either."

Bliss watched the sharp angles in Edwards's face all but disappear. They may not have been replaced by soft curves, but there was a definite relaxation of hostilities.

"All right, Bliss. You want to be given a chance, you've got it. You run this investigation. You report to me, but we can set aside the evening updates. I will still be watching. I may just have a different perspective from now on."

He smiled. Nodded. "Yes, boss. I'll crack on then, shall I?"

He left believing a battle had been won. He did not feel secure, exactly. But he felt he had taken a significant step in the right direction.

*

Chandler was waiting for 'Bliss outside the incident room. "Any chance you're free, boss?" she asked him. There was both excitement and anxiety in her eyes.

Bliss was surprised to see her standing there. "What's up? I thought you were heading back down to London this morning."

"That was the plan. But one of my rape victims, seventeen-year-old by the name of Kay Devonshire, has thrown a spanner into the works. She was a little reticent when I spoke to her yesterday afternoon. Now she's here. Dropped in and asked to speak with me. I got a call just as I was packing my overnight bag."

"So… where do I fit in?"

"This is a little awkward," Chandler said. The look on her face was as if she had just bitten into a doughnut and found half a wasp in the jam. "You see, Kay's mum told me that her daughter was a real daddy's girl. Her father passed away last year. When Kay clammed up during our meeting, her mother told me she wished her husband was there, that Kay probably needed an older man to bond with again."

Bliss squinted at Chandler for a second, not quite getting it. Then it dropped. "Wait a minute. You want me to sit in on your interview and be a father figure?"

"That's what I was shooting for, boss."

"You know I have a murder investigation to run, right?"

Chandler gave one of those shrugs she had always given. The kind Bliss found impossible to ignore. Or resist. He checked his watch.

"Okay. She must be here for a reason, so let's go see what it is."

They headed downstairs to interview room three, where Kay Devonshire sat with a female PC. The room was designed to relax its occupants, painted in pastel colours and filled with neutral furnishings. Bliss remembered it as an old stock room, a dank and dusty place which even the mice avoided. and was glad to see its current function. He smiled at the uniform, who left them to it.

"Kay, this is DI Bliss. You can call him Jimmy if you want. I'm Penny, if you remember? Is there anything I can get for you before we begin? Drink? Snack?"

The young girl shook her head. Bliss was pleasantly surprised at how Chandler had got straight into it. No fumbling around searching for a way to begin the conversation. He liked that. It told him an awful lot about Chandler's progress since they had first worked together. Bliss then switched his attention back to the girl. Kay Devonshire was thin, tall, good bones. Her eyes were hollowed out. Lack of sleep he guessed. That and constant weeping. But she was in good hands with Chandler.

"Are you happy with me being here, Kay?" Bliss asked the girl, smiling as his eyes drew hers in. He sat and took care to lean back, psychologically offering no threat. "I can step outside if you would prefer."

Another shake of the head. She looked hard at him for several seconds. "No, that's fine."

"So, what can we do for you here today?" Chandler asked, opting for a soft chair directly opposite the girl.

Kay put her head down. Her hair was lank and a little unkempt. It hung in clumped strands down past her eyes. A moment later she pulled the hair behind her ears and sat upright.

"I wanted to let it out," she said, her tone devoid of inflection. "My mum says I have been bottling it up – you know, what happened to me. So I want to tell you everything that happened, and how I feel about it all."

Chandler reached a hand out, wrapped it around the girl's. "Then you do that, Kay," she said. "And we'll sit here and listen."

It had been a damp, breezy evening. Kay and her friends had been to the Showcase cinema. Afterwards they grabbed milkshakes at McDonald's. Kay lived in the opposite direction to her two friends, Sonia and Francine, so rather than force Sonia to drive out of her way, she insisted on walking home on her own. It was no more than a ten-minute trek.

On the edge of a housing estate Kay heard something which alerted her, but by the time she reacted a hand was already clamped over her mouth and a long, angry-looking blade was flashed in front of her eyes. Without a word, she was dragged off the pavement and in between some bushes onto open land. The hand that had been wrapped over her mouth fell away and roughly mauled her breasts. Then she felt her jeans being unbuttoned. After an initial struggle, the knife was shown to her again, its meaning clear.

"For the record, Kay," Chandler said, interrupting the flow of words, "what exactly did you take that meaning to be?"

"That he would stab me with it. Or worse. If I didn't let him do what he wanted." The young girl cupped both hands either side of her face and drew them slowly down, remembering things she could only ever want to forget.

"I think that's a fair assumption, Kay," Bliss said. "So in telling us what happened next, please know that at this stage you can leave out any of the more personal details you find embarrassing. This is an informal interview, not a witness statement. And if there's anything you wish to tell only Penny here, then please do so."

"He pulled down my jeans and my underwear," Kay continued, her voice lower now, as if somehow their strength might sap her own. "Then he… he put a finger inside me. A couple of seconds later, he raped me. But I don't want to just say he raped me and leave it there. Rape is just a word. His finger was enough, because I didn't invite him to touch me. It was an intrusion. The whole thing was rough, from behind me, and he just smashed in and out of me."

Kay's lips began to tremble as she switched her gaze between the two detectives. "I wish I could say that was the final humiliation. But then I had to go home and tell my family. After which I had to tell the police. Then I had to tell the doctors. I had to be inspected, combed, prodded, poked, blood taken, scraped. I had to take the morning after pill. And at the moment I still don't know if he gave me any diseases. I feel debased. I feel abused. I don't want to go out, see my friends, talk to my family. I really don't even want to get out of bed. All I do is think about what he did to me and what he might have given me. But the very worst thing is seeing how my mum looks at me now. As if when I lost my virginity she lost her little girl. And I can't get it out of my head that she must wonder why I gave it up to that bastard so easily."

That was when she broke down. Her shoulders rose as her chest expanded, and then Kay let go a long and pitiful sob that just about broke Bliss's heart. He hung his head as Chandler rushed to her side, pulling her close and allowing the girl to weep openly. It was brutal to listen to, this young girl – little more than a child – expelling emotions she ought not to have even been aware of, let alone be feeling. What pained Bliss most of all was that he thought she might be right: that her family would never look at her in the same way again, that whilst her mother would be completely devastated and protective, that ugly thought of whether her daughter could have done more to prevent it, would forever lurk around every corner. In the shadows. In the same place where Kay's attacker lived.

Eventually the girl pulled herself together. Blotched and puffy, her face nonetheless took on a renewed strength. Bliss smiled kindly at her.

"Kay, your mum will be finding this every bit as difficult to cope with as you are. No, she did not suffer your indignities and pain, but if she is anything like me then I'm certain she would gladly have endured it all on your behalf. This happened to the most important, cherished person in her life. Your mum has her own form of grief to overcome. You need time, but so does she."

Bliss hoped the girl's mother was as loving and centred as he had described. She would need to be if her daughter was going to get through this.

An hour later, in the station canteen, Bliss and Chandler sighed and fretted over a last cup of coffee together for the foreseeable future. Having witnessed the breakdown of a rape victim, having heard how the young girl felt about the emotional and physical fallout that followed the attack, Bliss asked himself if he had been right to recommend Chandler for a posting that must have had her placed in that position countless times.

Bliss voiced his concerns, but Chandler brushed them off. "Jimmy, it's been a great posting. Yes, I need wringing out at the end of every week, but if I have made even a slight difference in the lives of the Kay Devonshires and Carly Morrises of this world, then it's all been worthwhile."

"Well, good. They needed someone like you in their corner, because you're wonderful at it."

"Thanks. Of course, by the time I see them the local police have been and gone. So whilst I would not have missed the opportunity for anything, I'm not sure how much longer I want to stay in the post. Maybe I need to be at the frontline again."

Bliss was not about to talk her out of it. When they said goodbye, Bliss embraced Chandler again and wished her well. He promised to call more often, to share more with her. To be the kind of friend he wanted to be. As he watched Chandler leave, Bliss hoped he would see her again soon, but for the right reasons next time. Then he drew in a deep breath. Chandler was making progress. He had his own case to attend to.

NINE

Between the alleyway behind a row of shops whose paint peeled like sunburned skin, and an abandoned, boarded-up house showing every sign of neglect, stood a line of garages and wooden sheds. The garages were constructed from a mixture of materials, from brick to corrugated sheets of tin and even concrete-cladding. The driveway that led from the road to the odd array of structures was broken up and patchy, uneven, eruptions of weeds tearing through the raw mix of gravel, slate, cement and brick chippings. Bliss kicked out at a stone and sent it skittering across the drive towards a broken and leaning fence that looked as if it had not seen a protective coating since it had first been fitted.

Following the path of the stone, Bliss found himself standing by a section of the fence that had three vertical slats missing. It looked like the diseased open mouth of a meth-head. He turned to look back over his shoulder.

"This must be where he dragged Maureen Jackson," Bliss said.

Less than thirty minutes earlier, Bliss and Bishop had been sitting in the office, batting theories back and forth, when Bliss decided he'd had enough of inactivity. He had visited the new crime scene on several occasions, but his knowledge of the first two was sketchy and restricted to what he read on the computer screen and heard from other detectives. He decided a ride out was in order.

Bliss drove across to Stanground, home of Maureen Jackson until she became the victim of a deranged and angry killer. He parked up outside the double-width Salvation Army store, scant yards from the murder scene – not that there was any sign of it that, two months on.

The wild and overgrown garden of the empty house pressed up against the fence as if attempting to force it down by sheer bulk alone. Ivy threaded its way in and out of the wooden vertical boards and posts. Bliss took it in for a minute or two and concluded that, whilst it would have been a difficult feat to wrestle an unwilling sixty-year-old woman through the gap created by the missing planks, once inside there would have been no chance of being observed.

"Remind me where Maureen lived and where she was coming from," he said to Bishop.

"From bingo, which was held at the Powerleague social club. Just the other side of the playing fields we drove by on our way here. We know when she left, Maureen headed down Peterborough Road. A pathway from there leads onto Whittlesey Road. Then down Desborough where we are now, towards Poulter where she lived alone. Maureen was a widow. There are two other routes she could have taken, and the word from friends and neighbours is she favoured none in particular."

Bliss nodded his approval. "I like that about you, Sergeant. You take information on board very easily. Good job. I also like the fact you use the victim's name. Never lose that, no matter how high up the ranking ladder you climb. All we need now is to smarten your appearance a little and we'll be golden. So three different possible routes suggests Maureen Jackson was not targeted, but simply went the wrong way at the wrong time. On the other hand, the bingo was a regular outing, so the possibility remains that she was targeted and followed."

Bliss played it out inside his head. From all accounts, Maureen was a fit and sprightly woman for her age. The walk was not overly long, but despite that and her physical condition, she might well have been feeling it by the time she reached this point. He turned a full circle, moved back out to the road, did a 360 again. The pavement Maureen would have been walking along was opposite the garages and sheds and the empty house. Her attacker could have been skulking in the area behind the shops, or by the garages, but his approach from across the road would have been noticeable. Would have given Maureen pause, even time to cry out. But there was an alleyway between two houses closest to the pavement, the entrance to which she would have walked right past.

Bliss turned back to Bishop. "I don't recall any forensics from this alleyway," he said. "I think it was missed. I also think this is where he waited for her. For someone, at least."

The DS surveyed the area in the way Bliss had. Thought about it for a few moments. Nodded. "You could be right, boss. And no, I don't think the alley was part of the CSI scope. But it's a two-month-old crime scene now."

If Bishop was at all put out over the sly dig concerning his appearance, he did not show it. Bliss walked across to the alley, moved deeper into it, looking hard at the floor. Hoping for a collection of cigarette butts, chewing gum wrappers. Something. Anything that might suggest someone had stood in one spot for a length of time waiting for a potential victim to pass by. But there was nothing other than a ring pull from a can of drink, a wad of gum now trodden into the paved surface, and the residue of dead leaves.

"It is an old scene," Bliss admitted. "But I'm having this lot anyway."

He jogged back to his car, and popped open the boot. Came back at a canter, clutching some plastic evidence bags and a pair of long tweezers. Carefully pinching the ring pull and ripping up the gum, Bliss deposited them into separate bags and sealed each of them. With a marker pen he wrote down the day, date, time, location, and finished by adding his rank, name and signature.

"You actually think they might have been our attacker's?" Bishop asked him.

Bliss shook his head. "Not for one minute. But I'm not taking any chances. So far we've got nothing from these murders. I don't imagine I've just found the break we needed, but I won't discount the possibility until I know for sure."

"Another gem to write up in my book of learning," Bishop said. "Along with becoming a neater crime fighter."

Bliss winked. "I know we've only just met, DS Bishop, but stick with me, kid. You never know, one day you too can be a decade-long pariah."

*

Paston. The scene of Joan Mitchell's murder. The youngest of the three victims, Mitchell had been walking home from the housing association community centre to the bungalow she shared with her mother. Twice divorced, Mitchell had moved in with her mother almost exactly three years earlier after her second marriage failed. Amicably, according to both the mother and ex-husband who was interviewed two days after Mitchell's body was discovered. Bliss briefly wondered whether the fact that neither victim was married or living with a man was a factor, but it didn't feel like it.

Bliss and Bishop walked the short route. Both ways, Bliss insisted. He liked to see everything there was to see, and you could only do that if you approached it from different angles. The pathway from one end of the housing complex to the other enjoyed only meagre lighting. There were plenty of nooks and crannies, providing ample opportunity for the attacker to shelter in shadow prior to pouncing on a defenceless, overweight woman with an angina problem. To Bliss it looked and felt like an opportunist's strike rather than a carefully planned, targeted one. Joan Mitchell had been discarded in amongst some bushes squeezed between the rear gardens of two homes. Whilst the body had not begun to entirely break down when it was discovered, it was the sweet-and-sour stench of early putrefaction that first alerted the police search team the day after the woman was reported missing.

"Where would he have parked?" Bliss wondered aloud.

The residential car parks at either end of the complex were small. At night, the chances were good that they would have been full. Bliss had been forced to leave the Insignia way back on the main road. If the killer had done the same, then someone might have spotted it. It may even have been reported.

"Bishop, get on to traffic. Find out if there were any reports of a vehicle parked up on Paston Ridings on the night of the murder. I'll see you back at the car in ten minutes. I'm going for a wander."

Discussing an on-going case with colleagues was essential, but there were times when Bliss needed to contemplate everything he knew when alone. Over the years he had become adept at churning it over, like a cement mixer blending all the ingredients together to create a new and defined single product. His intention, as always, was to arrive at a fresh line of investigation, discover a path they had yet to follow. The alleyway back at Stanground and the car parking issue here were the result of physical analysis, and might yet produce good leads. Right now he needed time on his own to see it all in his mind.

A canvas of both neighbourhoods had produced no witnesses to the attacks, nobody who saw someone hanging around either on the night or at any point in the days leading up to it. No vehicles out of place, no tradespeople. No one and nothing. The more Bliss thought about it the more he became convinced that the first two victims were randomly selected after the killer concealed himself and waited for the right opportunity. The third victim was chosen by chance, having discovered the killer attempting to bury something.

Bliss stopped walking. Stuffed both hands into the pockets of his heavy jacket, head angled back as he stared up at the overcast sky. There was a potential new line of thought: it had been mentioned once before over at the Ferry Meadows crime scene, and then forgotten about, but Bliss now asked himself once again what the killer might have been burying and why? What was so important that it drew the man out on a cold, damp night? Bliss had come up with one possibility. In addition to having unique signatures, many serial killers also took trophies with them. In some cases these were body parts, at other times items of clothing, jewellery or household items were removed from the scene.

The killer would then repeatedly take out their trophies and look at them in order to relive that moment. Some hung onto the items, others disposed of them when they got bored and the items no longer had any emotional value to them. The question here, Bliss thought, was had their killer been interrupted in the act of burying a trophy?

The next logical path to follow, if so, was to explore whether he was about to bury a trophy from each of his first two victims, or from the most recent one only – Joan Mitchell. And did that mean it formed some part of the ritual for him; that he buried one trophy before he felt able to take another? Annie Lakeham may have been a victim of circumstance, but a month had passed since Joan Mitchell's murder, so the chances were good that the killer was gearing up for his next attack anyway.

Satisfied, Bliss continued on his way. This was something fresh to bring to a team he knew would already be feeling beleaguered.

*

He sat on the carpeted living room floor between her open legs, his back to her as she brushed his hair. She used only her pliable fingers, long nails trailing across the scalp, causing him to shudder at their touch. She knew how to play him; precisely and with eager manipulation. When she started at his widow's peak and ploughed a furrow all the way across his head then down onto the neck, he felt little jolts of electricity spark and flicker deep inside his muscles. The sensation caused him to gasp out loud.

It was always this way.

Always would be, he hoped.

The ticking of the old wooden clock on the mantelpiece the only sound in the room other than his low moans of pleasure.

The feel of her soft, warm hands and hard nails raking through his hair.

Her sweet warm breath wafting over him, becoming more pronounced in sync with the rise and fall of his own chest.

His toes curling and gripping the soft tufts of carpet.

The stirring in his groin that became a full erection.

When he closed his eyes it was no longer his mother sitting there behind him.

No longer his mother whose own naked groin pressed against his back, grinding into him whilst at the same time pulling him back against her.

Instead he thought of the feminine creatures he had seen earlier in the day, pulling one of them in particular to the forefront of his mind. He could almost smell the fragrant apple hair shampoo, her cherry-flavoured lip gloss, feel the slick cotton of her skirt, the warmth of her bare thighs pressed against his arms. He moaned and sighed in anticipation of what might follow.

"Mummy's little lamb thinking about the ladies again?" his mother asked, snapping him out of it as if from a hypnotic trance.

"Don't call me a lamb," he said. "You know I don't like it."

"Well, you're certainly no lion."

He let that go. There was no point in arguing with her. This was another element that always went this way. First came the soothing, followed by the scorn. She brought him so far, to a point where his weakness became apparent, his ability to resist non-existent. Then she slammed the door on it and found a way to rile him beyond mere anger. It was a dangerous game, but she played her cards well.

"You know those bitches don't even see you, don't you?"

"Please, mum."

"You pass by them day after day, week after week, and they don't even notice you exist. You might as well be a ghost for all they are aware of your presence. You're the invisible man as far as they are concerned."

He drew his legs up and hung his head until his chin rested in the groove between his knees. His erection evaporated, seed unspent.

"Here we go again," he muttered. "Why do you have to do this? Why?"

"Even if they happened to notice you, do you honestly think you would stand a chance with any of them? I don't care how fat or ugly they are, they still want a real man."

"Mum, please stop."

"A man who knows how to please a woman."

"Mum…"

"A man who is able to pleasure them, not something like you."

"Mother!"

Silence followed.

It went on longer than usual.

"I'm only telling you the truth," she said, her voice a soft whisper now. "It's not easy for you to hear, I know. Believe me, it's not easy for me to say, either. But I don't want them hurting you, my little lamb."

The fingers were back in play now.

The nails raking into him.

He heard himself groan and felt sickened by it. By himself.

And by that time she knew she had won.

Again.

Then came the inevitable olive branch. "You want mummy to do your nails, sweetie?"

Shame and humiliation burning on his cheeks, he nodded and offered up his hands.

*

"How do we find out if he took something from either of these women?" DS Short asked after Bliss had presented his new line of investigation to the team. "Mrs Jackson lived alone. If Joan Mitchell had been a teenager, her mother might have noticed what she wore when going out, but it's unlikely in this case."

Short had a point, Bliss conceded. It might be tough to establish. It most definitely would require more questions to be asked of more people. But they were stuck, inertia taking hold, so more questions of more people it would have to be. Bliss looked around at the sea of expectant faces.

"Okay, so it won't be easy," he allowed with a dip of his head. "But nothing worthwhile ever is."

"It feels like a waste of time."

"We'll only know that once this is over. Have you something better to offer by way of new ideas? If you do, please fire away."

Short shook her head. As much in frustration as in response, Bliss thought.

"I'll tell you what he does take from each of them," Hunt said. "Their nails."

Bliss nodded. "Good thinking. Yes, that's true. And they may well be enough for him. On the other hand, the nails are something we know about. Something obvious to us. Trophies are generally items whose absence isn't quite so apparent."

Carmichael held up a hand. "Boss, even if this is a line of questioning that leads us to the answer that our man does bury his trophies, where exactly does that get us? I mean, does it take us any further?"

"I understand what you're saying, Ian. It's a valid point. But it's all about intelligence gathering. Sometimes you don't know what will come of it or where it will lead until you have it. The one thing you can know for certain is that without it you will never know just where it might have led. Besides, have you got anything better to do at the moment?"

Carmichael flushed a little. "No, boss."

Bliss shrugged. "Look, granted it's thin. Nobody appreciates that more than I. But we may be able to establish two things from this line of inquiry: first, whether or not our man does take trophies. Second, if so, that he disposes of them prior to his next kill. I'm not sure where that fits in right now, but knowing those things can't hurt our investigation.

"So, I would like actions drawn up for the following: interviews with anyone who was with Maureen Jackson the night she was murdered, same goes for Joan Mitchell. Let's also ask if anyone was taking photos on their phones and have those dumped. Speak to any other friends or relatives of either woman. We need to know what jewellery they habitually wore, whether they had any particular items of clothing like scarves which are not with their bagged items.

"Let's take an inventory of items found in their bags, see if anyone can think of anything that's now missing."

Nodding to himself, Bliss was about to end the meeting when something else occurred to him. "One more thing. Have a team check out the area in which that hole was dug. If our man *was* burying a trophy on Sunday night, he may have chosen the exact same place where he buried the previous one."

Bliss thanked the team and went to seek refuge in his office. It was strange, but it now felt odd Chandler not being there. Other than one day the previous week getting his space sorted and cabinets and drawers organised, much of the time he had spent there so far had been shared with his friend. Bliss smiled at the thought. Chandler had become an excellent detective in the years they had been separated, but that came as no surprise to Bliss. His ex-DC was destined for greater things, much more so than he had ever achieved or would before he put in his papers.

As for the team around him, Bliss was largely pleased. The usual moans and groans, the odd disagreement, but that was all fine by him. Tension was a good stimulant, provided it did not boil over. He would keep it in check. They were a good bunch, and despite the whines they were no shirkers.

After updating the case logs and checking for any new additions, Bliss went to find his DCI. Her PA informed him that Edwards was attending meetings in Cambridge and that she would not return until the following day. Pleased to escape another grilling, Bliss asked the elderly, bespectacled woman to inform the DCI that he had popped his head in, and would update the progress report in time for the morning shift. An interrogation postponed rather than cancelled, was how Bliss viewed his let-off. But he would take it.

It was only as he headed home that Bliss realised he had eaten nothing during the day. Neither he nor Chandler had fancied a breakfast with their coffees that morning, the haunting words and strangled sobs of Kay Devonshire still echoing in his head, certainly. For some reason he hadn't even considered lunch, though he recognised an old and familiar trait. When he got caught up in the work, he did so in mind, body and spirit. Today had been one of those days.

He kept dinner low key – pub grub and a pint at a chain place right by the East of England Showground. He had to drive by the Marriot hotel, and this caused him to think of Chandler once again. Bliss shook it off. In returning to Peterborough it was obvious that his early days back would light a flame under some memories. Having Chandler there as well for a day had seemingly put him over the edge.

Home was now a rental. At an extortionate rate, Bliss thought. But the place was clean, simple lines, few restrictions, and in a decent neighbourhood. It had been a running joke between him and any colleagues who visited him in his old house that even after four years he had barely unpacked. He had no intention of doing so this time around, either. The majority of his possessions remained in storage. Not his albums or hi-fi, though. Always first out of the packing crates. He put on *Silk Degrees* by Boz Scaggs and cranked the volume up while he put away a second beer. His armchair faced the far wall, which had his old Tannoy speakers in each corner, angled inwards. He sat for an entire album, moving only to flip the record over. Starting to relax at long last, Bliss allowed the booze and the music to envelop him.

*

A minor episode of vertigo meant Bliss took no exercise. His ears were ringing, but that might have been the booze and the music rather than his condition. Whatever the cause, as the clock ticked over into a new day, Bliss knew he would not sleep.

He had never been short of ways to at least try relaxing. The most recent was his meditational exercise sessions. The music and the drink that usually went along with it had also been known to work on occasion. That or a film or TV series he could get his teeth into. Every now and then he pulled his guitar out of its case and ran through a few chords and solo routines. Whenever he did so, Bliss nagged himself to do it more often, to keep the skin on his fingertips hard. But it had been a while since his last session, and once again his strings would now be dull and smell of old copper pennies. Each of these routines had their individual merits. Tonight, however, it was driving that did the trick.

It wasn't speed he craved. Bliss had never figured out what it was, exactly. The motion, perhaps. The night wrapping itself around him, cocooning him inside his vehicle. The focus required on dark back roads, serpentine routes where danger resided on every bend. Whatever it was, Bliss pushed the Vauxhall hard, and eventually felt himself beginning to unwind.

He was into the third day of the case, two full shifts of it behind him. Bliss felt the familiar buzz, one that had been lacking whilst working organised crime. The opportunity to plunge into murder cases again was his sole reason for returning to Peterborough, and he had landed in it with both feet. A world where murder did not exist was not the one he inhabited, and if it had to occur then he wanted to help catch those killers.

Putting the Insignia through its paces helped to release the valve a little. Bliss's thoughts turned once more to the past. When he first relocated back down to London to work with the Serious and Organised Crime Agency he had held on to his house. When he took the NCA posting in Bedford and it became a good fit, he sold up rather than commute. Leaving the area had initially been tough, despite having been there for only a few years, but with no option other than quitting altogether, Bliss had accepted his fate. At the time he had harboured thoughts of a reconciliation with an archaeologist he had met during his previous case in the city, but the move south killed that dead. Instead, in Bedford he began a relationship with a civilian colleague and two months' later moved in with her. A recent divorcee, she had been unable to commit to a relationship, and Bliss had now been single for four years.

He smiled and drummed his fingers on the steering wheel as the city's glow grew large in his windscreen once again. Single had not meant celibate, but Bliss had restricted himself to one or two nights at most with any woman. At times he dated for sexual gratification. On other occasions he sought simple companionship with no strings attached. What he had eventually come to believe was that he no longer desired anything more substantial.

It was not that Bliss believed there was only ever one woman for each man. When his wife was murdered, he did not assume there would never be someone else in his life, that he could never love again. But what he did know was that Hazel had been his soulmate, the one he would always be drawn to, no matter who he was with. The one to whom every other woman would be compared.

As the Cathedral came into view in the distance, lit up like a beacon, Bliss let go a sigh that was almost a gasp of physical pain as he realised that Hazel had been struck from this world and his life seventeen years ago. Thirty-eight at the time, he had got to spend just ten years with the love of his life, the person he had believed he would grow old with. Who could possibly stack up against those memories, those facts?

In truth, no one had come close.

As Bliss slipped onto the Frank Perkins Parkway and headed around the centre of the city towards either home or the station, depending on how he felt by the time he reached the first junction, Bliss was drawn to Joe Lakeham as he had been at the start of what was now the previous day. There was a man who had spent the best part of forty-five years with *his* soulmate. How could a man possibly overcome that kind of loss? Bliss did not think he would be able to go on in Lakeham's shoes, and in addition to strengthening his determination to find this wicked killer, the thought gave him pause for what the man might well do once that happened.

TEN

Waiting was something he did well. Sometimes he thought it might be what he did best. It often felt as if he had spent his whole life waiting for something.

For attention from his father.

Less attention from his mother.

For a girlfriend.

To leave school.

Get himself a decent job.

Everything was a long wait, and so he had grown accustomed to what it took in order to do that one thing well.

This was no different.

Sure, this was physically lying in wait as opposed to mentally coping with the passing of time. A different skillset was required. But the latter could control the former, provided you gave it every opportunity.

And he had all the patience it required.

The area he had selected this time was one of the nicest in the entire city. Close to the college grounds and wrapping around the almost circular park, the average house price had to be around half a million pounds. The property on which he had chosen to wait was being extended and renovated, the owners seemingly living elsewhere while the work was being undertaken.

Abroad, he imagined.

No living in a tin-can caravan during renovations for these sort of people.

Other than a few cursory barriers constructed from scaffolding, a ribbon of tape warning of construction work, some studded tarpaulin, and a scattering of bright orange cones, there was little to prevent a relatively determined person from entering the front garden, which was stacked high with soft building materials such as sand and cement. It was an ideal place for him to conceal himself.

And wait alone in the darkness.

Whenever he heard the initial strains of voices or laughter moving in his direction, he ducked down to secrete himself behind a pile of cement bags until the pedestrians had passed by. If he heard a single set of footsteps he then crept out into the shadows to steal a glimpse of who was approaching.

It had been a busy night, but so far the only people on their own had been two men. At one point he had leaned back against the tower of bags and pressed himself tight against it, as a young couple intruded onto the premises to snatch a kiss and a quick fumble in the dark. His heartbeat thundered in his ears, and his lips became impossibly dry. He risked one sneak peek, smiling to himself as the young man's hands cupped and squeezed the woman's backside whilst grinding his fully clothed groin into her. They were there for no more than three or four minutes, before he heard the woman groan and then suggest they sneak into her grandparents' house to continue.

He smiled at them as they strode away, hand in hand. It was forced and crooked and disingenuous.

A couple of groups followed; first three men, laughing and joking and being overly loud, then four middle-aged women who were even more raucous than the men preceding them.

He wanted to laugh at them. Step out into their path and howl his contempt right in their cackling faces. Instead he watched them all pass by, feeling powerful knowing he was only yards away whilst they remained completely oblivious to him.

Then he heard what he had been waiting to hear.

The footsteps of a lone woman.

Light on her feet, the delicate click-clack of heels echoing through the streets.

He inched forward, eyes bright and wide.

And there she came, striding briskly towards him. Could not have been more than eighteen.

He licked his lips.

Prime meat.

He then pulled a navy blue balaclava which had been sitting on his head down over his face, and flexed his hands inside black leather gloves. It would take him less than five seconds to snatch her off the street.

Five seconds of exposure.

He leaned forward to peer left and right along the street. Saw no one else. Once committed, there was no going back. He had to be certain.

As certain as he could be.

He let the girl pass by, but was already on the move as she did so. He sprang up and forward, raising the hood of his sweatshirt as he moved, but for once the darkness of night was not his friend. This time it was his betrayer. Lying amongst the relative neatness of the building site were a couple of paving slabs, which he failed to notice until he tripped over them, catching his shin and twisting his ankle in the process.

Unable to help himself, he gave a yelp as he spilled out between the two strips of tarp and sprawled face first onto the pavement behind the young woman.

That was when all hell broke loose.

*

For once, Bliss was fast asleep when the phone rang. Bleary-eyed and a little confused, he slid the screen on his mobile to accept the call.

"Traffic have got a live one," Bishop said in a high, loud voice that indicated his excitement.

"Tell me everything."

Bliss set his phone to speaker as he clambered out of bed and began pulling on the previous night's clothes.

"Reports of a man possibly intending to assault a young woman. The eye-witness who called it in said they were coming out of their door to walk the dog when they saw a figure stumble out of the front garden of a house currently having building works carried out on it. The figure fell behind the young girl, who turned, and ran off up the road screaming. The figure picked itself up off the floor and ran in the same direction, but on the opposite side of the road."

Bliss listened with mounting curiosity. Bishop's urgency had suggested a break on operation Moonstone, not Chandler's rape case. Bliss shook his head to clear it.

"Where was this, Sergeant?" he asked.

"By the central city park. So then we have someone else who saw this same figure jump into a van and speed off. Fortunately, they got the plate. It popped up on camera shortly afterwards, and six mobile units were diverted in its direction. I thought this might be DS Chandler's man, so I've put a call in to Sapphire, and I thought I should let you know as well."

"Okay. I happen to know that the SIO on that case is unavailable, so I'm two minutes from jumping in my car. I have an Airwave with me, so I'll listen in to the radio chatter and get over there. You do the same, Bishop."

"Already on it, boss. I'm calling from my own car."

The wheels on Bliss's Insignia spun and he lost a thousand miles of tread on the road outside his door. The Airwave was crackling and humming with activity.

Having been sighted in both Peakirk and Newborough, the van had turned back towards the city, before slanting east and heading out again. Bliss listened intently as he heard the chasing officers describe what was happening and the route they were travelling. Out beyond Oxney Road, in the wide open spaces on the edge of the industrial area, the surface grew more uneven the narrower the road became, until it wasn't much more than a dirt track. As the trail ended, the van did not so much as pause as it slammed into a vast field of wild grass. At this point the driver switched off its lights, and the dark vehicle was lost to view. A helicopter had been requested by Detective Superintendent Marion Fletcher, but it was still twenty minutes away.

A shout went up as the lead chasing car reported sighting the van again, just as it bounced up onto a lane that led towards Thorney. Visual was lost again shortly afterwards, but the six cars were joined by a further four, circling and surrounding the area as much as possible. Several minutes passed, and as Bliss thundered along the B-road that wound its way towards Thorney he heard someone mention Willow Hall Lane. Steering with one hand even at seventy, Bliss punched the road name into his satnav. He slammed his hand against the steering wheel as he realised acres of land lay between him and the chasing pack, and that he had no direct route through to them. Cursing, he pushed on to Thorney, cut back west, and hit Willow Hall Lane from the far end off of the A47.

The road was empty and he gunned the engine as much as he dared, all the while searching for lights, the glint of metal, a fleeing figure. Anything rather than nothing, the blackness pressing against the glass of his windscreen as if leering at him. Through the static once again he heard more excitement, and just as someone mentioned Thorney Dike Drain, he saw the blue and whites in the distance. Bliss stamped on the accelerator and watched the Insignia's long bonnet swallow up the road.

The chase cars were no longer chasing by the time he reached them. They were huddled together on a wide patch of flattened land beneath a canopy of trees. As Bliss stood on the brakes and slid off the road towards them, he saw DS Bishop's Mazda parked up along with them. Right alongside a dark blue Peugeot van.

Bishop came running across to meet him. He was the only one around.

"It looks as if he's hoofed it down along the drain, boss," Bishop said, panting a little. He looked around and threw his arms up in the air. "To be honest, there are so many ways he could have gone from here we're all just guessing. Air support is due any moment, but it may already be too late."

Bliss understood Bishop's apprehension. With large open fields, tree cover, drains and ditches, all compass point were possible.

Unless they got lucky, or the chopper's thermal imaging picked up a lone source nearby, then theirs was now an uphill task if they were going to apprehend this suspect.

"There are a few houses just here," Bliss said. "Let's take a look around."

There were three large properties, plus a collection of outbuildings. As Bliss and Bishop probed the area with their torches, Bliss heard the sky above being cut by blades from the air support team arriving on the scene. The communication was calm as ever, with some minor misunderstandings between those on the ground and those in the chopper. The 500-watt xenon lamp threw down a 15–20 million candlepower beam that lit up the fields, and Bliss knew its FLIR thermal imaging camera would find their quarry if he was within their circling search pattern.

Bliss looked at the beam from his own torch and almost laughed out loud. It was hardly the occasion, but it looked so weak and pathetic by comparison to the light spearing down at the earth ahead of them.

As the search continued, people living in two of the three houses in the same small close came out to question Bliss, Bishop and a uniformed PC who had joined them. Bishop fed the worried householders basic information, and sent the uniform off with them to quickly search their back gardens in order to allay any immediate fears. Out in the fields and along the dike drain the other uniforms were having no luck. Nothing so far from the chopper, either.

"How much of a head start did our man have before traffic arrived on scene?" Bliss asked his DS, as they approached a collection of sheds at the end of the drive where it bordered a field.

"They can't really be sure, boss." Bishop was puffing still, unused to the physical exertion. It was a while since his rugby playing days, and he carried a little excess weight. "He was lost from view for several minutes. Perhaps as many as ten, as few as five."

Bliss tried the door of one shed, shining his torch through its four-pane window. Ten minutes was a massive start if those hunting you down had no idea which way to follow. And if no one went the same way, then further afield there were more properties, a sizeable waste unit, and roads criss-crossing every potential route. Avenues of escape all around.

The final shed searched, Bliss stood his ground for a few minutes, figuring Bishop could do with the break.

"It's a bit of a punt," he said to his DS, "but if our man had it on his toes over open land then the chopper is looking for the proverbial needle. On the other hand, he may not have run at all. He could have chosen to lay low. How about I ask them to focus the thermal on these properties, the surrounding trees and then make their way up towards a stable yard I noticed on my way in. Narrowing the focus makes sense to me."

Bishop wasn't much help. "Your shout boss," he said. "I suppose it's like marking a grid, but from the air."

"Precisely."

As the most senior officer in attendance it was his call, and Bliss thought about it for a further thirty seconds. Then he hit the Airwave and spoke directly to the chopper crew. He told them what he had in mind, and both men up there agreed that it would be a better use of their limited time before lack of fuel played a part in proceedings. Bliss gave the order. He relayed this to the men on the ground and asked them to keep on searching the best they could. Finally, before heading back to the vehicles, he put in a request for more bodies.

Bliss and Bishop walked back out onto the main road and headed towards their cars. At about the same time, both came to a juddering halt.

The Peugeot van was gone.

*

From the control centre back at Thorpe Wood nick, Bishop learned the name and address of the vehicle owner. David Pearson, thirty-seven, lived just outside Peterborough in the little village of Yarwell on the other side of the A1, in a new build on the corner of Main Street and Locks Green. When Bliss and Bishop rolled up outside shortly after one in the morning, the house was in darkness and there was no van parked on its drive. The property had no garage, and a quick check of the surroundings revealed the van had not been left on the street close by, either.

The two detectives walked around the exterior of the house, peered through every window, knocked on the door several times, but they neither saw nor heard any movement inside.

"It was always a long shot," Bishop said, as they stood by their cars afterwards. "He'd have to be a bloody moron to come straight back here."

Bliss agreed. It had to be checked, and he would arrange for a car to sit outside the place until a warrant to enter and search the premises could be signed. But this slick bastard of a rapist had proven to be elusive so far, and there was no way he was dumb enough to think he could bowl up to his own home again without being arrested.

"What do we know about him?" Bishop asked.

"No sign that he's married. No kids. Does alarm repairs for a living. I'll have Short and Carmichael visit the employers first thing. No news as yet about a phone service. Early days, so approaching forty and no family may or may not be significant."

"Any word on the girl from tonight?"

Bliss shook his head. "I've been a little too preoccupied to ask."

He called in, requesting a couple of house-sitters. "Wait here until they arrive," he told Bishop. "Then get your arse home and join me for the briefing at eight."

"I'm fine, boss. I'll come back to the station with you."

"No." Bliss shook his head firmly. "What with the early call on Monday and some late evenings, I want my more senior officers getting some rest. I don't know about you, Sergeant, but my old bones tell me we're not even close to ending our own case, so I want us all to be fit and fresh for that."

*

The canteen at Thorpe Wood was busier than usual, but the mood inside was sombre. The first responding officers were now back at base, taking a much-needed break. Bliss sat with them, having bought them all their first hot drink and whatever type of roll or sandwich they preferred. Here within the city the temperature was comfortable, but out there heading into the flatlands the wind blew hard and cold, with a hint of damp for good measure. They had earned their keep. Despite one of them being in line for a major bollocking at some point.

As he left them to it, Bliss thanked the group of eight men and four women. He then went upstairs to the operations centre and spoke to the night manager, Abigail Cook – a somewhat matronly civilian worker, blessed with a good nature and a dirty laugh from what he had been able to ascertain.

"What more have we got on the van owner?" he asked.

"We're running all the usual checks," she assured him. "But in truth there's not much to know. Your man is not entirely off the grid, not with a salaried job and a fully licensed, fully insured vehicle, but he's not sending up any smoke signals or red flags, either. I'll stick everything in the log as soon as I have it."

Bliss thanked Cook and asked her to pass his gratitude on to her team for him as well. Appreciating those around him had always been one of his strengths. On the other hand, one of his weaknesses was, Bliss suspected, about to be fully tested.

*

Bliss was surprised not to find the DCI waiting for him in the Superintendent's office. He had assumed a dual-pronged anal ripping to be coming his way. But if he thought he was in for an easy ride in Edwards's absence, he was wrong.

"What the actual fuck, Bliss?" Fletcher said, her face pink with what he assumed was nothing to do with the cold night air. She wore a baggy grey sweatshirt and thick jogging bottoms, and her hair was tied up in a ponytail. Her eyes were almost as pink as her cheeks. "Would you care to tell me how both my major crimes team and virtually the entire traffic division somehow managed to let this man escape? In his own fucking vehicle, no less!"

Bliss took a beat. He understood Fletcher's anger. It matched his own when he thought of how their quarry had slipped away right from under their noses. But he also knew that when you had been off the frontline, as Marion Fletcher had been for many years, it was all too easy to forget just how often adrenaline-fuelled human beings could forget their training and basic protocol.

"It was a simple error, ma'am," Bliss replied. He had not been asked to sit, so he remained standing by the chair opposite her desk. "The way I read it, everyone got so involved with the chase, that securing the vehicle was forgotten in their haste to grab this bloke up. In many ways it's understandable, if somewhat embarrassing and a complete pain in the balls."

Fletcher peered at him over a pair of black-framed spectacles that he had not seen before. He guessed the Superintendent used contact lenses, and hadn't had time to pop them back in when she got the call.

"And where exactly were you when this was all going tits up, Inspector."

"I got the call last, I arrived at the scene last. Unfortunately, I had been headed towards Thorney when I learned everyone had stopped by the drain. It took me a while to swing my way around. When I got there, DS Bishop and I searched the nearby properties, whilst the uniforms were fanned out across the open land. Air support arrived eventually, but long after the suspect had made his initial break for freedom."

Fletcher nodded, her face losing a little of its edge. "So it would not have been your responsibility to secure the vehicle."

"It didn't occur to me, guv. We all missed it."

"That's very noble of you to share the blame, Bliss, but was it or was it not your responsibility?"

"No."

"No. It was the responsibility of the first officer on the scene, correct."

"Correct."

"And that officer was..?"

"I don't know, ma'am. Of course, it's not for me to say given it was a uniformed traffic officer, but whilst the result of their oversight is, of course, terrible, the circumstances were harsh enough out there to warrant only a private dressing down rather than any official reprimand, don't you think?"

Fletcher pushed herself away from her desk and studied him closely for a few seconds. "Is that what you would do, Inspector? If it were one of your team to blame for a suspected rapist managing to escape a police chase and search in his very own vehicle even after it had stopped and been joined by half a dozen other police vehicles."

When it was put like that, it did sound bad. Bliss shrugged.

"I can understand someone giving chase in the heat of the moment and forgetting to disable the vehicle or leave someone with it. These two uniforms simply followed their instincts and ran after the fleeing suspect. If it had been me and DS Bishop who arrived first, I can't honestly say we would not have done the very same thing. So in answer to your question, guv, yes that is what I would do if it were one of my team."

Bliss stood there trying not to break beneath Fletcher's scrutiny. It was the first time he had seen this side of her, and he was impressed by it. He had said his piece, and whatever Fletcher decided to do was now out of his hands.

Eventually the Detective Superintendent reeled herself back in to her desk and said, "Very well. I will make my recommendations as to any action taken against the officer responsible. A kick up the backside and no more. For what it's worth, Bliss, I think you're probably right. There is nothing to say this man would not have escaped without the help of his own vehicle. Christ knows what the media will make of it, though. You can bet your pension that somewhere along the line someone is going to prefix the word cops with the word Keystone, but that's for another day. Right now, I suggest you get yourself home and grab some sleep. You look bloody awful."

Bliss grinned. "Thanks for that, ma'am."

"And I apologise for my attitude earlier, Inspector. I realise of course that this is not even your operation, that you willingly gave up your own time to help out your colleagues. I meant no offence."

"None taken, ma'am."

Bliss was dismissed. To say he was surprised by Fletcher's apology was an understatement. She had completely disarmed him. If only all senior officers could be capable of recognising their own lapses of judgement, Bliss thought as he let himself out of her office. He briefly considered chasing up the warrant for David Pearson's house, but decided it could wait for someone actually involved with the op to do the grunt work necessary. At least this time the bastard's attack had failed, and a young girl had been spared the ignominy of being raped. Irrespective of what happened afterwards, Bliss reckoned they should all be thankful for that small mercy.

ELEVEN

It didn't do to be late for your own briefing, but given the night he'd had, Bliss thought the team would forgive him. A few jibes at his expense, perhaps, but nothing he couldn't handle. When he entered the incident room he noticed immediately that he was not the only straggler – DS Bishop was also tardy. It was an understandable lapse, and no shock in the circumstances. What did come as a huge surprise, however, was the presence of Penny Chandler and an unfamiliar sharp-suited man at her elbow.

Bliss decided not to wait for his DS and instead got straight into it. "Good morning all. Apologies for the late kick off. For those of you unfamiliar with the events of last night, there was a break on the recent rape cases, operation Wayfarer. Myself and DS Bishop attended."

"I hear traffic let the suspect escape in his own van, the useless bastards."

"Who said that?" Bliss asked angrily. "Come on, have the courage of your convictions."

A male constable stood, smirking like an errant schoolboy being scolded by a teacher. His shirt was even untucked on one side, hanging down over his trouser pocket. "PC Neil, sir. It was just a joke. But I'm not wrong, am I?"

His final six words hung in the air like a challenge.

"PC Neil, everybody deserves a second chance in my book. That includes colleagues making an honest mistake in the heat of the chase on a dark and windy night when there has just been another attempted attack. It even includes some snotty-nosed copper pouring scorn on his fellow uniforms in a lame attempt to show off. But be warned, constable, one more remark like that in my presence and you're off my team."

"Sir." Neil sat down as quickly as he had shot to his feet.

"Back to business," Bliss continued. "I'm not following up on this incident here with you today. This briefing will focus on our own murder enquiries and operation Moonstone. To that end, I need you lot to bring me up to speed and update me on anything you have discovered since yesterday evening. Any progress made into whether or not our man took trophies? Speak up if you have anything to offer, please."

Carmichael was the first to raise a hand. "I'm following up on Maureen Jackson, boss. It's hard going, as you might imagine, and we've not got around to speaking to everyone identified on our list. That said, unless we're reaching – seeing something that's not there – we may actually have a lead. Several people have mentioned a brooch. Maureen had beaten breast cancer a number of years ago. Subsequently she started wearing a pink bow broach on her coats. I personally went through her bagged-and-tagged possessions and found no such item."

Bliss nodded and pursed his lips. Interesting. "That sounds positive. Have you arranged a search of her house in case the brooch is there?"

"First thing on my list when we're done here, boss."

"Good man. DS Short, you look as if you want to leap in here."

"Yes, sir." Everyone perked up when Mia Short spoke. She just had that way about her; a forceful personality in a petite frame.

"Joan Mitchell habitually wore a necklace with an Akoya pearl. It's not in her possessions pack, and her mother swears blind it's not at home, either. I'm due there with a search team in thirty minutes, boss."

Now the heat was rising. Bliss felt it prickle and creep along his flesh, hairs standing on end at its approach. When the germ of an idea had first formed in his mind it had been nothing more than a hunch, a notion to explore and chase down until it either ran out of steam or gave up its secrets. But this meant something. He was certain of it.

Moving on to Annie Lakeham, there was also progress of sorts. Potentially. According to DC Gul Ansari, Annie's husband had mentioned an old half-crown coin that his wife always had about her person. It had been given to her by her father, in the belief that it was lucky. Annie Lakeham carried it with her at all times because she was convinced it gave her good fortune. The irony was lost on no one. The female detective was someone Bliss had not got around to speaking with as yet, but to Bliss it sounded like a thorough check and report from Ansari.

"Find out what CSI came up with by way of coins at the scene," Bliss ordered. "Might be worth another quick search, just in case."

He paused, surveying the massed ranks before him.

"I know some of you must be wondering why we're bothering. How any of this could possibly take us further. The thing is, people, we don't know what we don't know until we know. Only then can we decide how useful or otherwise it might be. In my view, if we establish that he does take a trophy from each victim, then it makes more sense of the hole he dug over at Ferry Meadows. I suspect he dumps a trophy before he takes the next. I think he was there that night to bury Joan Mitchell's necklace."

Carmichael threw up a hand. "Boss, if that's the case, have you considered that Ferry Meadows might be his favoured disposal site? That Maureen Jackson's brooch might be buried there?"

Bliss snapped his fingers. "Damnit! Well done, Sergeant. Yes, it did occur to me, and then it went right out of my tiny mind. Okay, so definitely worth sending a team back over there. Looking for the coin on the surface, the brooch beneath."

"And what about the necklace, boss?" one of the uniforms piped up. "I mean, he may have gone there to bury it, but we know he never managed to."

"Good, good," Bliss said. He was excited by the depth of thinking going on. It was needed. "I think we have to assume for now that our man still has it on him."

"You don't think he found somewhere else to bury it?" Short asked.

Bliss took a breath. "I doubt it, not after that experience. Would you?"

*

Bliss was more than a little intrigued by the man standing alongside Chandler. When the briefing broke, he made his way directly across to the pair.

"You can't keep away can you, Pen," he said. Bliss smiled with his mouth only. "Must be the fresh air up here or something."

"Or something," Chandler said. Her features had become sallow almost overnight, and her eyes had lost their usual lustre. "My guv and I thought it might be worth being on the patch right now. You and your people came close overnight. You may just have spooked him into making a mistake."

"Your guv?"

Chandler turned to introduce the suited man. It was a good suit, Bliss noted. Sharp maroon tie. Links rather than buttons on the cuffs. A man dressed for success.

"This is DI Perry. Graham Perry."

Cogs began to stir and turn inside Bliss's head as he shook the man's hand. The way Chandler spoke, the hand on the man's arm earlier when Bliss had walked into the incident room, the glances Perry had shot her way. The two were an item. Or had been, at the very least.

"Yeah, I think we spooked him," Bliss agreed, nodding. "As for mistakes, he's made few so far. I believe the Wayfarer SIO, DI Burton, organised someone to pay his work place a visit and they should be there about now. Hopefully they'll come back with some worthwhile information. I was going to send two of my team, but Burton arrived back in the city early enough to oversee things again. The Wayfarer team are going through his financial and other personal data. I imagine by lunchtime today they'll have a full picture of your prime suspect. You're welcome to grab a space in the main unit area until then if you like. Or perhaps have a word with DI Burton directly once she's available."

"Thank you," Perry said. Bliss estimated his age at around the forty mark; a man still young enough to be on his way up the ladder rather than sliding down the snake. "It's a bloody shame he managed to slip the net, but these things happen. The main thing is he's been identified, and that opens up so many more doors that were closed to us before."

"It was an amazing piece of work by traffic to get as close as they did. The area out there is awkward beyond belief at night. With his lights off and so much open space to cover, I'm astonished they located him at all."

"Yes, Penny told me all about the landscape during the drive up. It sounds like a nightmare to try and defend or control. But there's pressure on him now. I reckon there's every chance he'll think about it and come in, try to either bluff us completely or 'no comment' his way through an interview. Thing is, from what I understand the only thing he was seen to do was trip and fall close to the young woman. Without any forensics, he could string it out long enough for us not to be able to charge him."

"If he's as bright as we think, he'll know this won't end well for him if he tries to keep on the run," Chandler said, eyes on Bliss. "So yes, the guv and I have a hunch that this man will either hand himself in for questioning, or just eventually drive home and park up as if nothing had happened."

"Let's hope so," Bliss said. "Save you all a lot of bother. Who knows, he might even just turn up for work this morning."

"Either way, we really appreciate your help last night," Perry said. "It wasn't your case, so we're grateful to you for stepping in and making sure there was an SIO on the ground."

"Not that it did any good."

"Maybe not, but you put yourself out there when you didn't need to."

Bliss liked the man immediately, and for some nagging reason he could not fathom, wished he didn't. The Met DI spoke with a cultured southern accent, a deep timbre from a slender frame. A voice that demanded attention. Acutely aware of how irrational he was being, Bliss flashed what he hoped was an amiable smile.

"Well, I do like to get my feet wet now and again. Anyhow, please help yourselves to our facilities. Hopefully Angie Burton will be available shortly and you can both liaise with her. Pen, hope to see you in the canteen at some point. You owe me a bacon roll."

"I do?" Chandler's forehead creased. "For what reason?"

"Does there have to be one? I'm the boss, remember."

Bliss grinned, shook his head and said to Perry, "These DSs forget their place all too easily if you let them."

"You obviously had her better trained than me," Perry said, chuckling.

Chandler put both hands on her hips. "Bollocks to the pair of you. How's that for training?"

Bliss laughed, feeling pretty stupid now at how he had felt earlier towards the visiting DI. It was none of his business if Chandler and her immediate superior were in a relationship. She was a friend, the best he had, and you were supposed to wish only good things for your friends. Bliss was about to leave them to it when Chandler strode across to the boards on which the murder case notes were either pinned by magnets or written in marker. She stood and stared at them for a few seconds, before nodding to herself and turning to look over her shoulder.

"This is interesting," Chandler said.

"What is it?" Bliss asked, now at her side.

Chandler screwed up her face. "You know you used to tell us there were no stupid questions, no dumb thoughts?"

"Still do. Happy you remember."

"You might change your mind after this."

"Go on. Spit it out."

"Yeah, come on, Sergeant," Perry said, slipping in alongside her. "You're not usually so reticent."

Chandler started nodding. "Okay, well if we exclude the murder of Annie Lakeham because it almost certainly wasn't planned, then the thing that interests me about the first two are the dates. Each of them occurred exactly two days after our first two Wayfarer rapes. Maureen Jackson two days after Carly Morris, and Joan Mitchell two days after Kay Devonshire."

"Are you positive?" Perry asked. He stared at the boards as if they somehow told a different story.

"I am, guv. I remember those dates very well."

"It has to be a coincidence, doesn't it?"

"The acts themselves and the MOs couldn't be more different," Bliss said, more intrigued than excited by the implication of Chandler's words. "It beggars belief that the same man is responsible."

"I'm not suggesting that, exactly," Chandler said, a little less certain now. "More pointing out the facts and asking the question. Is it just coincidence? What are the odds, if so?"

"Shorter than these two investigations being somehow linked, probably," Perry suggested. He stood the other side of Chandler, continuing to study the boards closely. "You have here the murders of elderly women, with no sexual aspect, but vicious and brutal attacks. On the other hand, you have the rapes of two teens. There's also no rape preceding the third murder."

"Penny's right about that one," Bliss said, exploring the possibilities in his mind. "We do believe the murder of Annie Lakeham to be an anomaly because it seems not to be part of whatever cycle he's got himself onto. Close, but one that doesn't quite fit the pattern. I mean, we could be wrong and he could have been waiting for someone to come along on Sunday night. Out of the way in the park, as opposed to a street attack, which is yet another difference. As for the lack of a third rape, I suppose we can't be certain there wasn't one. Many go unreported still."

"So you're giving this credence?" Perry asked, evidently surprised.

"I'm not sure exactly what I'm giving it. On the surface any connection between these two operations seems ludicrous. But now that I am aware of it, the issue of the dates is nagging at me and I can't ignore it. Plus there's Penny's instincts, which have always been spot on. And now that I think about it, whilst the crimes themselves are very different, the means are similar, in that both rapist and murderer move in and out without being seen and without leaving behind any evidence."

The three were quiet for a few moments. It was a lot to digest.

"I'm probably way off the mark," Chandler said eventually, shrugging as she looked between both of them. "But it came to me, so I had to put it out there. It's what I was taught to do."

Bliss was a firm believer in what was often described as a cop's gut. Chandler had felt the twinge, and it sparked her imagination enough to make an outrageous observation. Loyalty alone had not been behind his support of Chandler when speaking to Perry; what Chandler had pointed out was not something they could dismiss without further investigation. However unlikely a link between the rapist and the savage killer seemed, now that the two-day issue had been mentioned it had to be followed up.

"Let's take some time to review this properly," Bliss suggested. "See what we can come up with. However it turns out, this was a good catch, Pen."

Chandler flashed a wide grin. "I hope so, boss."

"Hey, I thought I was your boss," Perry said.

"You're my guv... guv."

He blew out a puff of air. "I guess I'll have to settle for that."

"Come on you two," Bliss said. "If you're quite done, I know just the place to visit right now."

TWELVE

They met in what had once been a training room, but was now the base for the Sexual Crimes Unit. The SCU team only came together when specific crimes, such as rape or sexual abuse took place. It then drew down from a pool of officers, each of whom had undertaken the required courses as prescribed by the regional leadership team. It was true that most officers on attachment to the unit were female; pragmatism had cut a swathe through any gender-related grumblings. To Bliss it made perfect sense that, when the overwhelming majority of victims were female, and the overwhelming majority of those female victims preferred to speak *with* and be counselled *by* females, their wishes were granted. Common sense and policing didn't always go together, but in this sensitive area it prevailed.

It was an hour and a half after Chandler had first raised the question, since when Bliss had concentrated on his own inquiry whilst Chandler and Perry had spent time with the Wayfarer team. Now Bliss had joined them and stood looking at the photographs and information displayed neatly on the array of whiteboards. DI Burton, who had been working on operation Wayfarer since its inception, had offered to take them through the case notes and logs, but Bliss had declined.

"You won't mean to," he said gently, "but you will allow your own prejudices and personal judgements to dictate the way you present your information. I'd prefer it if you let me think and talk my way through what I see here on the boards, what I read in the notes, and you let me prompt for confirmation or otherwise as and when I need it. How does that sound?"

Burton had no problem with working in a way that best suited Bliss. She, Chandler, and Perry pulled up some chairs and allowed Bliss breathing space in which to work.

He cleared his throat a couple of times before beginning his assessment, anxious now to help move this investigation on if he could.

"Your first victim was attacked from behind and was able to provide you with only a sketchy physical description. Your second victim was also attacked from behind, and so also gave you little to work with. What first made you link the two rapes, DI Burton?"

"The manner of the attacks. As you say, both from behind, plus there was a sense of similar build, and the knife used to persuade the girls not to scream."

"That was good work, because it was only much later following a further interview when Penny *confirmed* the same man was responsible. A knife is far from an unusual weapon to use, so you did well putting these two attacks together, Angie. The odour lead may be extremely useful in advancing the operation, naturally, but without the initial link may never have been discovered at all."

Bliss had been studying the whiteboards while he was talking, occasionally glancing down at a set of printed notes clutched in his hand. Now he turned to look directly at Burton. Bliss admired her, both as a person and as a fellow detective. A DC during his previous stint in the city, it was obvious to him then that she was destined for bigger and better things.

"Other than the rape itself, there was no violence," Bliss said. "The attacker on both occasions was carrying a knife, even gestured with it and held it to their throats, but didn't so much as scratch either of the victims. Far from being violent, the attacks were almost gentle; apologetic you might say."

Burton nodded. "That's exactly how it seemed to us. Chandler's interview notes would appear to draw a similar conclusion."

Bliss paused for thought before turning back to the boards. "It took a few weeks before you were able to first connect the two cases and then re-interview both victims. These were young women out walking the streets at night on their own. At any point did you consider they might be prostitutes? That they were not being straight with you about their reasons for being where they were at the time they were attacked? I don't mean to imply that young women should not be on the street alone at night, nor that in doing so we should automatically think the worst of them. I ask only to cover all bases."

"Briefly," Chandler answered this time. "That's one of the reasons why DI Burton and I arranged to set up secondary interviews. It became obvious to me when I read the first interview transcripts that Kay Devonshire was holding something back, and later did so over two further interviews, one of which was at her behest. As a follow-up to that I called her earlier this morning and pressed her hard. Much harder than I was comfortable with, actually. Kay finally admitted that she had joined an on-line community of people who get together for sexual gratification only."

"Sounds dangerous," Perry said. He stood stiffly, hands in his trouser pockets. Bliss wondered if he was concerned about losing his grip on the investigation if a link between the two could be proven.

Chandler shook her head. "It wasn't meant to be. Quite the opposite, in fact. What happens is that you join the group, and you can then select partners you'd like to have sex with. You are advised to meet in a public place first of all, and then if it goes well you do what comes naturally. Many subscribers have specific, individual needs that they can't satisfy in a regular relationship, while others just want to have a sexual encounter without any strings."

Bliss knew all about that lifestyle choice. It had flickered briefly during his own marriage. Ultimately it had led to Hazel being murdered, which was something he had to live with every day. To his mind, the girl he had met and spoken to with Chandler was far too young for such behaviour. Kay Devonshire was attractive enough, and probably considered quite a catch by boys her own age. Why would she need to use such a website? Bliss understood that sometimes it became something that was no longer a choice, more something that drove you. The real question was why you got into it in the first place.

"So, they pick a mate as if selecting from a menu," Bliss said.

"Exactly like that," Burton responded. She looked saddened by the admission. "I suppose it meets a need in this society."

"She's an attractive kid."

"I'd agree. Makes no sense to me, either. It's as if the ritual of dating and getting to know one another first is considered old-fashioned by the people who use these sites."

"I take it the question was also asked of the first victim?" Bliss said to Chandler.

She nodded. "Absolutely no chance that Carly Morris was that way inclined. She was adamant and I believed her."

"For what it's worth," Perry said, "the conversation was on speaker all the while and I agree with DS Chandler. The girl had no idea about the site. She was clearly shocked at it even being mentioned in connection to her."

"And last night's victim? Well, almost victim."

"She's saying she knows about the site but has never used it. Never wanted to, and never would." Chandler spread her hands as if to say it was anyone's guess. "The data team are going to trawl through the various e-mail accounts belonging to our victims and see whether they or any credit or debit card payments were made to the company who run the website."

Bliss nodded at the laptop sitting on DS Burton's desk.

"Show me," he said.

A few minutes later he was looking at Kay Devonshire, the second victim. She posed in a series of photographs that saw her strip down to a pair of white stockings and nothing else. In the final shot she was lying on a bed with her legs spread wide. The text alongside suggested Kay was looking for one-night stands with well-hung older men.

"There's a contact here," Bliss said. "Can you show me his page please."

The profile appeared on screen. The male in the photograph was a prime specimen, oiled from neck to toe, with six-pack abs.

"I take it this Adonis is not actually Darren Moody, the name provided here?"

Burton gave an expansive shrug. "I very much doubt it. But we haven't got around to checking on him as yet. We only pieced this all together within the past hour or so."

"So who did the choosing?" Bliss asked. "Did Kay choose him or did he choose her?"

"He chose her. The way it operates is that the website provides a private messaging address for each member, and they use the messaging service to make contact with other members. Our victim received a message from this Darren Moody, checked him out on the website, and arranged to meet with him."

"So what happened?"

"He didn't show."

"Or maybe he did, only he holds back, having taken a good look at her." Bliss laid it out as much for himself as the others. "So if it's him and victims one and three are part of it but just not letting on, why attack them? These women want sex. Kay Devonshire admits to wanting sex and has gone to meet him for that purpose alone. He knows that before he leaves home. So why doesn't he meet her as himself and just have sex with her consensually?"

"Rape isn't about sex," Chandler reminded him. "It's about control."

"Except that he displayed no obvious desire for that when he raped them," Bliss argued.

"Perhaps he doesn't get off on straight sex. Maybe it only works for him if he takes it by force. The rape itself is all the control he needs. Absolute control over a defenceless young girl."

"Again, isn't that partly what these kind of websites cater for? There must be women who don't mind being involved with the rape fantasy."

Burton shook her head. "I dare say, but it's still acting out a fantasy. Only rape is rape."

They were all silent for a while as that sank in. Eventually, Bliss said, "So how far have you got in trying to track down this man?"

Burton scowled. "Not far, but enough to know it's going to be difficult. The obvious way is to contact the owners of the website and request information. This guy, whoever he is, must have paid with a credit or debit card. Problem is, initial contact has run into a brick wall. It's proving very hard to find out who actually owns the website. And the guys in IT tell me that even if we do, we'll get no joy because the client list will be protected by the Data Protection Act. We're checking with legal, but the word is that they don't have to give us anything unless we can provide good evidence that this man committed a crime or is planning to."

"And your best guesses don't amount to evidence."

"Exactly."

Bliss sighed. "I'm promising nothing, but I may be able to get somewhere with my contacts at the NCA. This website may have crossed their path as being run by someone within organised crime. I'll make a call later. Before I do, what's the feeling here? Is this just a one-off with Kay Devonshire? A blind lead?"

Burton looked at Chandler and nodded. Something passed between them in that single gesture.

"Probably," Chandler said eventually. "I believed Carly when she said she would never consider using such a service. My hunch is that this takes us no further."

"Okay. I'll still make a few calls, see if we can push on with this as a lead. So now I know more about operation Wayfarer. Penny, you also know a great deal about Moonstone. Balls to the wall time, folks. Are these two ops linked?"

"I think the close proximity of the dates in two cases means we have to go along with it as a legit potential lead," Burton said firmly.

"I saw the connection," Chandler said. "And I don't believe we've ruled it out as a possibility."

"That leaves you, Graham" Bliss said, turning to Perry.

The DI shook his head. "If it were my case I'd exclude it. I'm sorry, Sergeant, but I'm just not seeing it. I don't think the dates connection is a good enough reason to waste resources on chasing it down."

All eyes were now on Bliss. He felt their scrutiny, but did not waver.

"Apologies, DI Perry. I'm siding with the women on this one. For now. But there'll be no official correlation between Wayfarer and Moonstone. Not at the moment. There may be something here, but not enough to go public with. We each follow our own ops, but we also keep in mind the potential overlap. That good enough for everyone?"

He knew it would be. It was a punt. With the van owner, David Pearson, now associated with the rape inquiries following the car chase, operation Wayfarer had more traction than Moonstone right now. They did not need this lead as much as Bliss did. He and his team now had to assess how and where it fit, and if it helped their case at all. They badly needed Pearson to be caught and questioned, which alone would be a positive step. Bliss was reluctant to face Edwards without something solid to appease her; one serious leap forward. Bliss shuddered involuntarily at the thought of his next meeting with the DCI.

Which was precisely the moment when DC Carmichael burst into the room and said, "Sir, there's an ex-cop on the phone who says he's seen this MO before?"

Bliss turned. He felt his chest tighten. "Which MO? The murders or the rapes?"

"Well, that's just it, boss." Carmichael frowned. "He says both."

*

Rocking back and forth soothed him.

Usually.

Sitting alone in the dark, knees pulled up to his chest, arms tightly wrapped around them, pivoting on his backside.

Rocking away all his cares and woes.

But today it was having no effect. The mistake he made with the hole paled into insignificance compared to the one he had made last night as he lunged for the girl.

And a lunge was precisely what it had become.

The previous two girls had not been aware of his presence until he had them under his spell; wielding a knife as opposed to a wand. On those two occasions he had been stealth personified. Graceful, silent, every limb a perfectly synchronised movement.

A Swiss watch.

A human bullet train with laser tracking.

Last night he was chaos, he was mayhem and he was an uncoordinated clown. It was humiliating to recall his arms flailing and flapping uselessly, the stumble so ungainly and inelegant.

And almost devastatingly costly, of course.

He would not forget that in a hurry.

If not for the buffoonery of the police he would now be sitting in a jail cell.

He jerked his head up at the thought. Stared vacantly at nothing for what felt like an age as his thoughts first cascaded and scattered all around, before assembling themselves in neat, manageable piles.

Sure, the idiocy of the police had opened a door for him, but as unexpected as it was he had nonetheless recognised the route out. Perhaps he was being too hard on himself. After all, it was a misstep that had caused the initial problem, nothing as shameful as poor planning. A simple trip and fall, something that could happen to anyone at any time.

But getting away… that was all him.

Returning to his vehicle and fleeing in it after the police believed they had him cornered: him again.

When put into context, more things had gone right than had gone wrong. He needed to bear that in mind rather than flagellate himself.

Now, and in the future.

And saving the best for last, the small matter of him still being free.

Free.

Free to try again.

The very thought made him sigh.

What was that saying about there being plenty more fish..?

THIRTEEN

William Baker, fifty-eight, once a sergeant with the Cumbria police, now retired and living with his American wife in San Diego, California. That was how the caller introduced himself to Bliss. He sounded calm and reasonable, but there was also the vague hint of excitement of a man who had something to contribute again.

"Thank you for calling, Mr Baker," Bliss said. "I understand you have some information for me relevant to both my murder inquiry and another on-going investigation in the city. Is that correct, sir?"

"It is. And call me Bill, please. To get right to the point, Inspector, whilst I ended up stationed in Cumbria I was born and raised in Peterborough. Because of that I browse the *Telegraph* on-line pretty much every week. I read about the serial murders, and as I was scrolling down the page I just happened to catch sight of another article that mentioned a rape case with two victims so far. I was not a detective like you, but I experienced stuff. You know? I have to tell you, Inspector Bliss, seeing both of those reports on the same day almost stalled my breath."

"For what reason exactly?" Bliss asked. He kept his tone neutral.

"Having experienced a lot of different crimes, even though it was a few years ago now, I'm aware of how different the profiles would be of a rapist compared to a murderer. You'd never put the two crimes together unless they were one and same incident, right?"

"Right." *Not quite,* Bliss thought. But he wanted the man to continue. Baker was taking his time to set the scene. And why not? He had a captive audience.

"So seeing the two like that, seeing they were both running at the same time, and that until this week's murder there had been two of each, reminded me of a case I'd seen before."

Despite himself, Bliss felt a chill settle at the base of his skull. "Was that when you were stationed up in Cumbria, Bill, or here in Peterborough?"

"Neither."

"Neither? So where, then?"

"Out here, Inspector. Right here in California."

Bliss felt the air being sucked from his lungs, the sad last balloon tied to a post following a street party. He put back his head, cursed silently. For a few moments he had dared to believe. Now he felt his interest wane.

"I see. In the US. So, Bill, what makes you think they are in any way connected to our investigations?"

"I suppose the irrationality of it. Ironically. I know that sounds crazy, and I guess you haven't even considered making a connection between the crimes back there. Why would you? But you might want to look into it now. See, around fifteen or so years back there was an investigation over here that just about drove law enforcement and the FBI nuts. Rape and murder. Young women raped, elderly women murdered. Separate cases. Until they weren't. Turns out, the Feds' ViCAP computer system spat out three things that were shared between the two: shoe size, physical description, and a rank body odour."

Bliss lurched forward and then froze. An itch raced between his shoulder blades and the bottom of his stomach seemed to fall way.

"Okay, I'm with you so far," Bliss said, far more calmly than he felt. "These rapes and murders were linked to a single perpetrator. You say it was some time ago, Bill. Do you happen to know how it ended? Was the perpetrator caught?"

"That's just it. That's one of the reasons for my call. See, this is such an unusual combination of crimes for a single unsub that it sticks out. I saw it here. I reckon you have it over there. And no one was ever charged for it, so could be the reason he was never caught is because he hightailed it across the pond."

Bliss ran it all through his head. The foul odour was the stinger. No way could that connection be ignored. Yet, still something bothered him.

"You say this happened around fifteen years ago," Bliss reminded Baker. "Did the FBI and law enforcement out there have an age range in mind for their unknown subject profile?"

For the first time, the ex-cop paused when spilling out information. "Hmm, now that I can't really recall," he said. "Thirty-to-forty rings a bell."

"Which would make him at least forty-five now, possibly so much as a decade older."

"I guess. That fit in with your line of thinking on your case, Inspector Bliss?"

Bliss was grateful to William Baker for having made the call, but was not about to allow the man inside the case. Ex-cop or not.

"I can't respond to that, Bill. For operative reasons, you understand. But you have certainly given me a lot to think about. Look, I will need to chase this up with the authorities out there. Can you recall any of the names that were reported at the time. Victims or FBI?"

"Actually, I can. The SAC was a guy by the name of Lewis Claybourne. ASAC was Sandra Grant."

Bliss made a note of the names for both the Special Agent in Charge and his assistant. "And in which specific area was this please?"

"I can't be sure on all of them. One was definitely near Palm Springs. Another might have been Reno, or perhaps Fresno. I can't be sure right now as I always get the two mixed up. I'm pretty sure one case came out of Long Beach, or that general area at least. My wife and I had just moved to LA at the time, so we saw a lot of that investigation on the TV news and such."

"Bill, you have been a massive help," Bliss said. "I'm not saying our two separate cases are connected, nor that they have any correlation with what happened out there. However, you've provided us with a new line of inquiry and I'm going to put that to my team right now. I can't thank you enough."

"Think nothing of it." Baker sounded pleased with himself nonetheless. "I've been out of the game now for nigh on twenty years, and I still want to see these bastards nailed to the wall."

"You and me both. Right now I'm going to switch you through to someone who will take down all your details. Thanks again, Bill."

As Bliss punched a button on the phone his mind was alive with possibilities.

Given the one thing Carly Morris and Kay Devonshire had seemed certain of was their attacker's physical strength and presence, it did not seem likely that the man who raped them had also raped and murdered women out in America fifteen years earlier. Even so, if the FBI profile was off by a distance, and the man responsible here was even a little older that suspected, then it might not be beyond the realms of possibility.

Bliss nodded to himself. He would take that.

*

The four walked slowly along the embankment beside the fast-flowing river Nene. Bliss had bought them each a coffee from Nero's and, despite the cool day chilled further by a bustling breeze, suggested they take a walk. Jackets on and fastened, collars pulled up, they strolled by the water's edge.

"Didn't you once live around here?" Bishop asked Chandler.

She nodded. Pointed to a yellow-brick tenement building on the other side of the river. "I still own it," she said. "I didn't know if I'd be coming back here when my secondment to Sapphire was over, so I let it out for a year."

"Nice location," DI Perry remarked. "Right in the centre of the city."

"It is, and it isn't. On match days when Peterborough are playing at home it's jammed solid with football fans and cars. Plus there are events throughout the year and the noise can be a pain sometimes. But I need to make back what I paid for it, so it's mine for a while yet."

"I used to run along this embankment when I was training," Bishop said, treating them to bit of on-the-spot jogging.

"Judging by the belly, that was a few years ago now, Ian."

"Ouch. That hurts, Penny. I think I'm still a fine figure of a sportsman."

"Yeah, Sumo wrestler, maybe."

This reduced the four of them to tearful laughter. "You and I were pals when you were stationed here, Penny" Bishop said. "What happened?"

"Shit," Chandler replied, still smiling. "Because shit happens."

Bishop turned to Bliss. "So what a turn of events today, boss. I'm not sure what to make of it."

Bliss grunted. "Neither am I, if I'm being honest. I thought it best to get out of the station mainly because I didn't want anyone getting wind of this until we've made a firm decision. Carmichael will keep schtum if he knows what's good for him. And he does."

"I was struggling with the whole rapist turns murderer thing," Chandler admitted, with a shake of the head. Her nose had turned pink. "The two-day deal was hard to ignore, and I was happy that we were unofficially considering the potential of a connection. I was never convinced it was more than that. But now this call from the States has really put a rocket under it."

"And then some. That's the other reason why I wanted to get out of there. The thought of trying to explain this to the DCI or Super didn't bear thinking about."

"A connection of sorts is undeniable now though," Perry said. "The body odour reported out there as well seals the deal in my book."

"Agreed. I'm just not sure how. We're looking at someone who was doing the same thing back in the early noughties all the way out in California, then went dark, and for some reason started up again in our humble little city. On that basis alone it's not outlandish, but for me the age issue grates. It doesn't sit right with me."

"Me neither," Bishop said. He shook his head as if to emphasise the negative.

"I think we all see that as a sticking point, boss," Chandler said. "But then you go full circle, list the pros and cons, and you keep coming back to odour. Might not be a fingerprint or DNA, but in its own way it really stands out from the jumble of information we have. No way that can be a coincidence."

Bliss knew Chandler was right. One coincidence too far. There were still plenty of missing pieces, but now they had something real to work with. That sparked a thought, and he reached for his mobile. He pressed a number and asked to be put through to the operation Wayfarer team, and was fortunate enough to land with Burton. Bliss thumbed the speaker button.

"Hi, Angie. It's Jimmy. I was wondering if there was any update on David Pearson."

"Nothing major, I'm sorry to say. Two members of my unit spoke to his employers. By all accounts he's a good, hard worker. He wasn't at work today, but then they were not expecting him to be because he is officially on annual leave. Looking at his schedule for the past few months, he's been near or near enough to the rape attack locations, but they're hardly out of the way so that means nothing. The van is his own. Word is he takes a few private jobs, but the company don't care provided he doesn't steal clients already on their books. No sighting at his house as yet. And yes, we're still awaiting the bloody warrant because the judge is debating with legal. I think we'll get it, but we happened to pull a right hand-wringer of a judge."

"So nothing going our way, but nothing going against, either."

"I suppose that's a positive spin, Jimmy. I never had you down as a glass is half full sort. More a case of 'my glass is half empty so fill the fucker up' sort."

Bliss chuckled. "I keep telling people, Angie, I'm a changed man these days."

"Well, I barely knew you last time you were posted here. I take people as I find them, though. Which is good for you, because by all accounts you were one grumpy bastard last time."

"Maybe *because* I was here. Did you ever consider that?"

"Either way, you're okay by me. So the upshot is, we're not much further advanced. I hope to be ransacking his house by late afternoon, though. You want to have DS Chandler and that cute DI join us?"

Bliss glanced across at Perry, who, to give him his due, pretended he had not heard the compliment. "I think they would like to," he said. "Particularly Graham, and especially now. Please give me a bell when you get the nod. They are both with me at the moment."

"Please tell me you don't have your phone on speaker, Jimmy."

"I don't have it on speaker."

"You lying fucker. Well, that's me colouring up right now. And don't worry, Jimmy… I think you're cute, too."

Bliss shook his head as he killed the call.

"If we land this David Pearson character, or he gives himself up to us, are we agreed he's in the frame for it all if he stinks to high heaven?"

"I'd say so," Chandler said. The other two nodded.

"So then that's one strand to pick and pull at. Locating that fuckwit is a prime objective. However, so far all we have is intuition and the word of an ex-copper now living about five-and-a-half thousand miles away, to even suggest that operations Wayfarer and Moonstone are somehow tied together. We are in agreement that the issue of bad odour is a major lead, one that seems to link investigations in the US and our rapist here and now. There is no obvious connection between the US murders and our three here, however. Given that's the main weakness of the new theory, I think myself and DS Bishop need to look harder at that aspect. We can contact the FBI, the various police departments involved, and then we look for one more commonality. That's all it might take."

"That remains another avenue for us to explore also," Perry said. "The rape cases on both sides of the Atlantic have a clear tie-in. Perhaps we can help each other explore that line of inquiry until news of our escaped suspect comes in."

"If you're sure. I thought you might fancy working alongside DI Burton."

Bliss grinned, and noted Perry blushing as he glanced across at Chandler. Now Bliss was certain: there was or had been something between the two of them. And he was keen to find out more.

*

Even a university as old as Cambridge ebbs and flows with the times. The Institute of Criminology, founded in 1959, was now located in a modern, box-like four-storey building on the Sidgwick part of the campus. As Bliss and Chandler made their way from the crowded car park to the smart entrance, students spilled both in and out ahead of them. Perhaps even the wise men who had foreseen the need for such a faculty subject, had never envisaged its popularity.

It had been Bliss's idea to come, and for Chandler to tag along. Their only viable suspect was nowhere to be found, DCI Edwards was said to be haunting the corridors looking for him, and he was sick of having his mind turning in ever decreasing circles. Bliss had consulted with the institute before, when heading up a human trafficking investigation. Then he had wanted to get inside the skin of a man who thought nothing of shipping over hundreds of women from China, Thailand, Russia and several parts of eastern Europe in steel containers, and condemning them to existences of sexual slavery. Today he wanted to stop a headache and get off his arse to take a punt, and having called ahead to make an appointment, decided Bishop could babysit DI Perry for a couple of hours.

The two detectives found Professor Robert Gillingham on his hands and knees in a small and cluttered office, looking anything but his usual composed and thoughtful self as he tossed files and folders around the room without any apparent care. Although the walls of the room were painted in a standard neutral cream colour, the rosewood bookcases, cabinets and desk gave the office all the splendour it required. When Bliss rapped on the open door with his knuckles, Gillingham beckoned them in without so much as a glance in their direction.

"Make yourselves comfortable," he said, a deep, guttural voice belying the slight, fragile frame. "I won't be a moment."

Bliss smiled at Chandler and nodded towards a set of leather Chesterfield-style armchairs with scroll wingbacks, arranged around an oval wooden coffee table. They sat down with a respect befitting the furniture, Chandler demurely crossing one leg over the other as the chair appeared to swallow her whole.

"Can I get either of you a drink?" the Professor asked, still sifting through what to Bliss looked like the wreckage of an explosion in a stationery department.

"No, thanks," he replied. "I can see you're busy, Bob. I don't want to take up too much of your valuable time." *Or mine*, he thought, second-guessing himself now that they were actually here.

"Sure. It's really no bother. I can have– ah-ha." He looked up at them for the first time, beaming now, clutching a blue folder. "Found the bloody thing." As he got to his feet, the cartilage in one of his knees popped as if a thin bone had snapped in two. He slapped the folder down on his desk, then walked across to join them.

"Good to see you, Bliss," Gillingham said, holding out a hand. The two men shook, before the Professor did the same with Chandler as she was introduced. Then the man fell into a chair and stretched out his legs, pushing his fringe back with both hands. Gillingham was in his mid-forties, and looked even younger. Trim, he wore a suit well. He shook his head and glanced pointedly at the mess on the floor. "Just when you think you have a system..."

He sat upright and his narrow face seemed to crumple as he gave a broad smile. "So how are you, Bliss, old man? Still the scourge of hardened criminals?"

"I do my best, Bob."

"Which is all we can ask of ourselves." Gillingham nodded sagely. "So, tell me how I can help."

Bliss shifted uncomfortably. "Okay, well I know what I'm about to discuss isn't exactly standard procedure, and I don't think you're going to be too impressed with me, but I'm hoping you'll understand once you hear me out."

"Hmm." Gillingham clasped his hands as if in prayer and touched them to his lips. His eyes gleamed behind a pair of frameless spectacles. "Now you have me intrigued, of course, so I must let you continue. Good psychology, Inspector."

Bliss laughed. "It wasn't planned that way. Look, Bob, the situation is this: while I may require an in-depth profile from you at some point, I'm also looking for something more off-the-cuff. Some immediate thoughts, based on information and crime scene photographs."

Professor Gillingham was one of only half a dozen criminal profilers used by police forces in the country. Having worked with him on two previous occasions, Bliss valued the psychologist's insight. He watched the man struggling to come to terms with the request.

"You know I'm not fond of instant evaluations, Bliss. I'd hate to steer you in the wrong direction simply because I haven't had time to digest all the facts and evidence."

Bliss shook his head. "I'm not looking for that. This is different. Today I'm going to tell you what I think and I want your opinion. What I need is your immediate thoughts on a couple of things, and then if necessary you can follow that up with your usual thorough report."

Gillingham pursed his lips and gave a slight nod. "Why don't you tell me what you have, and I'll consider what to do with it. No promises."

Bliss glanced at Chandler and shrugged. "What do we have to lose?"

The DS nodded and fixed her eyes on the Professor. She opened up a thick folder and pulled out a set of photographs and typed documents fastened together with a staple. "Let me begin by showing you these and running through the cases."

Gillingham took the photos from her hand and began sifting through them. "Explain to me what I'm seeing."

"Two young women. No more than girls really. On their own, walking down the street. Jumped from behind, large-bladed knife used to prevent them from screaming or struggling, clothing below the waist lowered, raped, left where they lay. Same MO, same perpetrator."

The Professor looked at the images one more time, then shifted his gaze. "And what do you have for me, Inspector?"

Bliss withdrew a similar looking bundle. "Three women. Aged between fifty-eight and sixty-four. Stabbed many times. Massive sharp-force wounding to the vulva in the most recent incident, but no injuries to either face or breasts on any of them. Each victim was also missing all ten fingernails."

Gillingham took his time studying the crime scene photographs. When he finally looked up, his eyes were narrowed. "Let me guess: despite the acute differences in MO and choice of victim, you're asking yourself if you might be looking for the same perpetrator?"

"We are. Yes." Bliss nodded and eased forward. "How can you possibly know that?"

"If it were anything simple, you would have no need for my input. There are two of you, two cases, I put two and two together."

"It took us a while to contemplate any sort of link. Frankly, we're confused about the different psychologies involved."

The Professor moistened his lips with his tongue. "Let's look at the rape for a moment. Tell me, DS Chandler, were these attacks started and finished within just a few minutes?"

"Yes. In both cases they were over very quickly."

"And there was no binding, no brutality beyond the act of rape itself?"

"No. Once the man was finished he just ran off and did nothing else to harm them."

"Interesting. As I'm sure you are aware, such cases are usually about control; the man subjecting the woman to an ordeal of power and dominance as much as the sexual violation itself. But I don't see that here. My observation, for what it's worth at this early stage, is that the perpetrator is unused to sexual contact, that the rape was a means to an end and therefore the act itself was the entire reason for committing it. This is a man who may have even been a virgin until he raped the first victim, and quite possibly seeking to move beyond mere masturbation in order to achieve sexual gratification."

"And the murders?" Bliss pressed.

"The exact opposite of the rapes, in that they are typical. An obvious mother fixation. Good old Oedipus rearing his ugly head once more. Your man is very angry with her, but also loves her a great deal."

"Can you explain that in a bit more detail, Bob?"

"Of course. The brutal and frenzied attack reveals his anger, and the terrible wounds in and around the vagina imply the mother fixation. He deliberately avoids the face, however, implying deep feelings for the real target of these attacks, and leaving the breasts untouched also steers me towards his mother, the nurturer and sustenance-provider. Essentially, he's doing to these women what he'd like to do to his mother, yet a deep-rooted love won't allow him to harm her."

"Okay. So, as unlikely as it may seem, do you think these cases could be connected? Is it possible that we are looking for one man?"

Gillingham took a look at the documentation for each set of victims. Details were sparse, but included all the necessary items.

He nodded. "I take it the main reason you think they are linked is because of the dates of the first four attacks?"

Bliss spread his hands. "Penny here saw it first. There's nothing else there to draw anyone to that conclusion. Or even to consider it, for that matter."

"Yet you are pursuing that line of inquiry."

"The dates may be the only potential connection, but they're crucial. One such coincidence we could ignore. Two means we cannot."

"So tell me what you think is happening here."

"Bob, I need you to keep in mind that I'm an amateur. I know I said earlier I'd walk you through it and let you deliver a verdict, but I don't want to muddle your own thinking."

"You won't. My mind is already made up. So run through the scenario for me."

"All right. I see a mummy's boy, living at home even though he's probably in his thirties or older. I see a life of repression, a home where girls were not welcome, where sex was never mentioned, or if it was the act was condemned. I see a man who has vented his frustration on a real female, and then within a couple of days becomes so angry with his mother for creating the situation he's now in, for creating the emotional environment that caused him to act that way, that he feels the need to vent the inner rage. Only this is his mother, so he has to choose an alternative. A surrogate, as it were. Afterwards, the pattern is repeated."

"But if this is all about his mother, why are young girls chosen for the rape? Why not the older women?"

"Because he doesn't want to kill the girls. He wants to have sex with them, therefore he wants them to be both physically attractive and also easily intimidated."

The Professor sat back in his chair and clapped his hands together a few times. "Bravo, Bliss. Excellent. My on-the-job tuition paid dividends."

"You think I'm right, then?"

"Oh, I didn't say that. The psychology was decent enough, though. I was willing to make an observation regarding the rape cases, and I agree with much that you've said about your suspect in relation to his life and the way he feels towards his mother. As for whether the cases are connected, and therefore that you have a single perpetrator, I'm afraid I have to give that a lot more thought based on a lot more detail than I have here."

"I guessed that would be the case. And I do appreciate why you won't commit yourself so quickly on such a serious matter. But can you give us an inkling. Nothing we'll hold you to, I promise."

Gillingham sniffed and got to his feet, pacing slowly across to one of two tall windows in his office. He stood for a few moments staring outside, fingers laced behind his back.

"Very well. You bared your soul, I'll bare mine. Whilst highly unusual, I don't think it's impossible that this is the same offender. I'm guessing you wanted my view because you don't want to waste time and resources on it if I don't agree with you. Also, knowing you, Bliss, you're looking to get your bosses off your arse."

"Oh, that's good work, Professor," Chandler said. "You've got Bliss sussed, at least."

Bliss ignored her, other than a roll of the eyes. "So whilst you're not able to say for sure one way or the other, Bob, you wouldn't rule it out."

The man turned back to face them and nodded. "That's about the size of it, yes. It's improbable, but not impossible."

"One more thing then, Bob. From what you've seen, how old would you say this man is?"

On the drive down the A14 to Cambridge, Bliss and Chandler had agreed to make no mention of the potential connection to the US. However, Bliss did want an opinion as to their deviant's age, as the disparity still bothered him.

"I would suggest anywhere between twenty-five to thirty-five. And I mean in both cases. I would be extremely surprised if he were outside of that range."

Bliss nodded. The verdict was as expected, but still he felt disappointed. He was about to respond, when his mobile rang. Bliss apologised and accepted the call. When he was done he immediately sprang to his feet.

"We have to go. Thank you so much for that, Bob."

The Professor walked back across the room and they shook hands once more. "A break in the case?" he asked.

"You could say that," Bliss said. "Our prime suspect just walked into Thorpe Wood nick."

FOURTEEN

By the time they got back to Peterborough, David Pearson had already been interviewed and asked to remain at the station for further questioning. To the surprise of everyone, the suspect had agreed, and even more baffling had not yet requested a solicitor. The place was buzzing when Bliss and Chandler walked back into the nick, smiles on the faces of every suit and uniform, but Bliss had only one question for Burton when he reached her office.

"Does he stink?"

Bliss caught the glance between Burton and Perry, who sat in a chair on the other side of the DI's desk.

"Fuck!" Bliss said. "He doesn't. I can see by the look on both your faces that he doesn't."

"It means nothing," Burton said defensively.

"It means everything if that's the only damned thing we have against him."

"The body odour detected by both Carly Morris and Kay Devonshire means he smelled on those days. Perhaps it was the body's reaction to extreme stress, or excitement. Fear, even. Or guilt, for that matter. You know body chemistry can do that, Jimmy. Today he's not out raping, so today he doesn't smell. It could be just as simple as that."

Bliss hung his head. Drew in a deep lungful of air. He was standing in the doorway, and Chandler squeezed into the office around him.

"So how did the interview go?" she asked.

"Not great," Perry admitted, a sour look on his face. "On a positive note, Pearson's work repairing alarms includes time spent

134

working in schools. Checks are on-going, but he may well have spotted his rape victims there. He has no alibi for either night, so that's also something in our favour. He was home alone, watching TV, and would not have spoken to anyone on the phone. He spent some time on Facebook and even made some posts, but they could have been done from his phone, or even a tablet. The suspect can't prove he was at home, but on the negative side at the moment we can't prove he wasn't."

One aspect of that concerned Bliss more than any other, especially when it came to the possibility of linking the two very different crimes of rape and murder. He decided to keep it to himself for the time being.

"And here's the even worse news," Burton jumped in. "Pearson claims his van must have been stolen. He says he was away on a fishing trip, and when he arrived home today the van was gone."

"Wait a minute," Bliss said, jerking upright. "If there was a car sat on his place, how is it he handed himself in? Why wasn't he snatched up the moment he arrived home?"

Burton shook her head, jaw jutting and set firm. "They were pulled off the house. My DCI says if the warrant had come through he could have justified having a crew there, but that it was a huge waste of resources having a car tied up doing nothing."

"Your boss sounds about as fucked up as mine appears to be."

"Don't be so hard on them, Jimmy. They have a difficult job to—"

"And anyone who sides with them is fucked up as well," Bliss interrupted, his voice louder than he had intended. "Penny-pinching politics allows these pricks to slip through the net time after time, and I for one am fucking sick of it and sick of the people who sit back and allow it happen and say nothing about it."

Bliss back-heeled the door hard enough to slam it closed, then stood there feeling his hands become fists, heart battering away at his ribcage. Felt three pair of eyes on his. There was silence for several moments. Then DI Burton said, "Your new relaxation techniques are paying off, I see."

That broke the tension. Broke them up as well, each of them laughing hard, Chandler weeping through what looked like convulsions as her hands clutched the pit of her stomach.

"Oh, fuck you, Angie," Bliss said eventually. "You ruined a perfectly good rant there. And how the hell do you know about my relaxation techniques?"

Burton looked up at him, her laughter relaxing into a broad smile. "Seriously? You think you could waltz back in here without us knowing what you've been up to recently, the current state of your mind?"

"Yes. It's called privacy."

"Well, if you believe in that around here then you're a piss-poor detective. The moment word spread you were being posted back, the grapevine went into full production overdrive. We know all about the mind health, all about your floozy in Bedford."

"Never mind me," Bliss snapped, switching track. "Let's get back to David Pearson. He arrived back from a fishing trip, discovered his van missing, and then came here to report it. So he didn't come here to hand himself in, as I was told. But none of that explains how he managed to go on a solo fishing trip and then come over here without using his van."

"I'm afraid your blood pressure might not be able to stand what I'm about to tell you," Perry said. "But I'll chance it. Unfortunately, the van is not Pearson's only vehicle. He has his own estate car as well."

This time Bliss did call on his new mental exercises. He began the countdown in his head, allowing a time delay from thought to reaction. "And this was not picked up why?" he asked once he felt more composed.

"I'm afraid, in all the ruckus last night, no one thought to run a search for a second vehicle."

Bliss touched a hand to his scar, and then brought the other up and tugged both down the sides of his face.

"That one is one me," he said. "I was the senior officer last night. I should have actioned it."

"No one is blaming you," Burton insisted. "Even if you'd thought about it, I'm sure it would have been way down on our list of priorities. He was using a van. Our lot chased a van. None of us here thought to question whether he might have a second set of wheels."

"Well I should have. What's more, if I remember correctly, a witness thought they saw a dark estate near the scene at the time of the attack on Annie Lakeham. What colour is Pearson's motor?"

"Dark green. Sorry Jimmy."

Bliss probed his cheek with his tongue, shaking his head. "Thanks, Angie. I appreciate your support. But it was my miss. My error. I'm big enough and ugly enough to take it."

"Ugly enough for sure," Chandler said, provoking another round of laughter.

"Hey, what is this? Have a pop at Bliss day?"

"That's every day, boss."

"Look, Jimmy," Burton said. "I know your DCI is being a bit of an ogre on your side of the fence, so I'm entering into my log report from earlier that you and I discussed the possibility of a second vehicle, and that we both thought the other was handling it. It happens when investigations and investigators cross. That way we spread the blame."

Bliss shook his head throughout every word. "No way. This was my cock-up and I'm the one who falls by it. Nothing to do with you."

"You don't have a say in the matter. It's going into my log, so if you don't tell your boss the same as I'm telling mine then we're both in much deeper shit."

"But why? Why would you go out on a limb for me?"

Burton smiled at him. "Because you were treated badly last time you were here. Because some people don't want to listen to the good you did, only the bad. And because you deserve a break. That enough for you?"

"I'm sensing a moment here," Chandler said. "You two want some time alone?"

"I don't think that will be necessary, Penny," Bliss said, flashing her a look of affected contempt. "And thanks, Angie. It's appreciated. Let's see how things go when I speak with Edwards. There's so much going on inside my head right now it's spinning. Anyway, I think it's time I had a word with our suspect. Let's see if he was home alone when my three victims were being murdered."

*

As it transpired, David Pearson was not at home alone on two of the nights in question. To Bliss he both looked and behaved sullen and resentful throughout the questioning, but that was perhaps understandable if the man was innocent. Pearson's dark brown hair was long and unkempt, and he sported a few days' worth of stubble on his face. Beneath the stubble both cheeks were pockmarked from old acne scars. Other than a slight musty smell from the man's clothing that he may well have been wearing for a couple of days, the suspect had no evident odour at all. Certainly not the vile stench described by both rape victims.

Bliss introduced himself and Bishop. Upon hearing the title of their unit, Pearson frowned. "I spent more than an hour answering questions earlier," he said. His accent was local. "I don't know what else to tell you. I only came here because my van was stolen, and now I'm facing all kinds of questions about nights when I was sat at home watching the box."

"I'm not here about those nights," Bliss told him. "I want to talk to you about two other nights. Specifically, August 25th and September 15th." Bliss had decided not to mention Sunday night; he thought that slipping something anomalous into the mix was unnecessary. "Where were you on those nights, Mr Pearson?"

The man's brow creased, forming a deep furrow in the centre of his forehead. "That's two nights after the dates your colleagues asked me about."

"Precisely."

"I had trouble enough thinking about those two nights, now you ask me about these. Why won't any of you tell me what this is all about? I'm trying not to be a prat about things, and I do want to help if I can, but I'm wondering if I need a solicitor."

"Not if you've not done anything wrong," Bishop said.

"Yeah, right." Pearson puffed out his lips. "Now I know you're kidding."

"Is there any reason why you're reluctant to tell us where you were on those two nights, Mr Pearson?" Bliss asked. He kept his eyes on the suspect. He knew just how to scrutinise a man being questioned.

"I'm not reluctant. I'm having trouble remembering."

"Or you don't really want to say you were at home on your own again, so you're trying to think of where else you could say you were that can't be disproved."

"If I was, I was."

"Speaking of which," Bliss said. "Do you live alone all the time, Mr Pearson?"

"Yeah. What of it?" Pearson squared up his chest.

He was becoming belligerent now. Bliss knew they would lose him soon, that the suspect would demand a solicitor rather than merely consider contacting one.

"No big deal, Mr Pearson. I just wanted to be absolutely clear as to whether on any nights you shared your home with someone else. A girlfriend, say. Or if your mother lived with you or stayed with you at times."

This was the aspect that had concerned Bliss earlier. The profile they had been building relied on their suspect being very attached to his mother. Such characters usually still lived at home, or their mothers lived with them in their homes. Pearson living on his own was yet another aspect that did not quite gel and Bliss wanted to dig a little deeper.

"My mother? Why would you mention her of all people?"

Bliss controlled his facial expressions. The man's reaction was interesting, but Bliss did not want to give anything away to Pearson.

"I'm trying to help you," Bliss said. "You're struggling to recall where you were on specific dates. I thought that maybe someone may have been staying over on those nights, and that it could, perhaps, jog your memory."

Pearson was an average-looking man of average height with average features. But when he grew serious things changed. Focus brought with it dimension and character, especially in and around the eyes. He was not a man to take lightly. Bliss noted the change and stored it away in his mental safety deposit box.

"I'm just not sure why you would mention my mother is all. But you know what? Now that I think about it, I reckon I might have been fishing on those nights."

"On your own?"

The man nodded and smiled, sat back with his arms folded across his chest. "That's right. On my own, as I always do."

"So nobody to verify your whereabouts in other words."

Pearson regarded him closely. Bliss felt the strength of the man's scrutiny. He was being weighed up. His words were being considered. The man was about to either get up and walk out or make that request for a solicitor. Bliss decided to suspend the interview hoping to delay either of those two actions.

Rising swiftly, Bliss said, "Thank you so much, Mr Pearson. I do apologise once again for keeping you here. I understand that you came here merely to report your vehicle stolen, but as has been explained to you, that same vehicle was involved in a pretty serious crime. Rather than have you traipse back and forth to the station, or have officers dropping by every five minutes when we have further questions, I thought it best that we try and tie up all the loose strands in one visit if we could. You understand, right?"

This time the man was like a rabbit caught in headlights. The flurry of words had thrown him. Bliss hoped that despite any irritation Pearson felt at being detained longer than he may have wanted, he also saw the sense in what Bliss had said. Irrespective of his guilt or innocence, Pearson would not want to return for further questioning, and certainly would not relish the police showing up at home or at work.

For what seemed the longest time, Bliss and Bishop stood waiting for a response. Pearson looked up at them, and Bliss could see a sharp glint in the man's eyes that told him there was a lot of thinking going on. He had no real feel for Pearson as a suspect at the moment, but very much wanted a second crack at speaking with him without a solicitor being present. The break was necessary for that. Just when he began to believe he had misjudged the situation, Pearson sighed, nodded and sat back in his seat.

"Don't be too long," the man said. Folding his arms. "I do have a home to get to, and I'd also remind you all that I'm the bloody victim here."

*

A small team assembled in the incident room. In addition to Bliss, there was Short and Bishop from his squad, plus Burton, Chandler and Perry. As Bliss had called the meeting, he also chaired it.

"Pearson is getting jumpy," Bliss explained. "To the point where I don't quite know what he'll do next, only that he will do something. I was about to ask him about his job, about his work in schools, but as we can find that out from his employer I made a decision to back off. I think we need to discuss what, if anything, he can be arrested for at this juncture. Realistically speaking, at best he is in the frame for the rapes. You can tie the van to the attempted attack last night, and the van to him. On the other hand, you may find it hard to prove attempted rape based on what happened last night, and you also can't yet prove Pearson was the attacker. If you look at what there is at the moment from a detached perspective, if you even managed to place him in that van last night then you have him fleeing the scene of what exactly? A stumbling close to a young girl. No way will that fly. And that's if you can even place him there."

"So what are you suggesting?" Burton asked. "I spoke to him earlier and I agree he's not going to willingly sit there answering questions until we can build a case against him. But what's your thinking?"

"Unfortunately, my thinking is that there is currently more to suggest he's not your man, and therefore not our man either. However, the fact that we can't find anything yet to prove his innocence leaves the door open as far as I'm concerned. He's not fazed by us, but he is irritated. He may even have something to hide; I'm just not sure what that might be."

"I agree," Bishop said. "There is something not right about the man. But that doesn't make him a rapist, let alone a rapist and a murderer."

"The rape is the only thing on the table at the moment," Bliss said, looking at DI Burton. "That makes this a decision for you and your team, Angie."

Burton rolled her eyes. "Great. With what we have – which is pretty much zilch – I'm not sure we can lay a finger on him."

"Equally, you wouldn't want to let him go just yet," Perry said.

"Which brings us around in a full circle," Chandler observed drily.

Bliss gave it the time it deserved. Irrespective of whether the attack last night could be proven, there was no doubt in his mind that whoever had fallen and then fled, who had then led the chasing police vehicles a merry dance, before eventually escaping, was the rapist. The question he was unable to answer was whether that man was David Pearson. Bliss could not begin to look beyond that right now, to spend time wondering if the man was also a serial killer. That would only muddy waters already far too sullied to see a clear way though.

Too many questions, not enough answers. Bliss mentally took a step back. When a case squeezed together like this you had to reset your focus. This clearly was not a time to ponder all the things they did not have on the man, rather what they did. At this stage it might only be one single thing. And that one single thing in this case was the van. Unequivocally, David Pearson's van had been involved in the incident. The team had no real evidence of attempted rape, but the van had fled the scene and, more importantly, the chasing police vehicles. Bliss understood there was no proof at the moment that Pearson was the driver, but he was the vehicle owner and had offered no conclusive evidence that he was not involved. Not that he had to; the onus was on the police to prove he was. But that had to start somewhere.

"Charge him with failing to stop," Bliss said finally. "That's my advice."

"What? A motoring offence!" Perry scoffed. "That's ridiculous."

"It's all you can pin on him right now. You can go for the rapes if you think that's best, Angie, and Graham is right when he says my suggestion is a ridiculous charge to put up. On the other hand, I don't think you have enough to charge him with rape or attempted rape, and if the Superintendent shoots it down then the minor offence will appear even more ludicrous if sought afterwards, perhaps even gratuitous and spiteful, and she may toss that as well. However, if you go for the failing to stop from the beginning and explain to Fletcher that you need twenty-four hours to build a different case based around it, she will perhaps see it as less frivolous and grant it."

Chandler gave a soft whistle. "Blimey, boss. That's a bit of a reach."

"I know it is. Let's be clear, if you speak to him again without any sort of charge he'll react negatively. None of us want to see him walk out of here today. That means you have to arrest him. The actual charge you want to nail him with can come later, but the initial arrest of the motoring offence will keep him here right now. Yes, his solicitor will kick up a stink. Who gives a shit? You have to persuade Marion Fletcher. I think she'll buy this, but you know her better than anyone else here, Angie."

"And in the end it's my call," Burton said, shaking her head. "Fucked if I do, fucked if I don't."

"You've never been so well fucked."

Burton smiled at him. "And how would you know that, Inspector? You been peeking at my diary?"

Bliss winked. "I bet that would be an eye-opener."

"Oh, shit! What a call to have to make. How about a vote, or is that passing the buck?"

"I think it's a viable option," Chandler said. "You're the one who has to make the final decision, but seeking opinions is a good thing, not a bad thing in my view."

"I agree," Bliss said. "And you know my vote."

"I'm with the boss," Bishop said.

"I'm against it," Perry said. He shrugged. "Not sure if I even get a vote, but I would arrest the man for rape. You get a day either way, so I'm not sure what you would lose."

Chandler sighed. "It's a tough one. I know Fletcher, and the boss might be right. She may not appreciate an overreach, and may prefer this approach. It's not just about the actual arrest, either, but also how it plays out in the media. That will be on her mind. We go for rape and she has to somehow make that sound plausible to them. We go for a motoring offence, they won't bat an eye. I don't like it either way, but I vote for the failing to stop."

Burton took a deep breath, her already ample bosom swelling to great effect. When she let it out she said, "I'll try it. There's probably no right or wrong way to do this, only in retrospect once we have our answer. But this'll buy us time."

Bliss was happy enough at that. It put them all against the clock, but sometimes that was exactly what an investigation needed.

FIFTEEN

DCI Edwards found Bliss tucked away behind his own desk. He had ignored three of her mails requesting his attendance in her office *'immediately'*. He had also ignored a verbal message passed on by Short. Bliss realised that by sitting alone catching up on reports he was merely delaying the inevitable, but he wasn't prepared to throw himself to the wolves quite yet. They would have to come to him.

And come to him one had, although at least he had been spared the pack.

Edwards wordlessly entered his office and closed the door behind her, standing with her back to it as if attempting to prevent his escape. The DCI's cheeks were pinched, and her eyes blazed. Briefly Bliss wondered if that look was normal for her, or used only when he was around. He couldn't decide if there was anger in them, hatred, or a heady cocktail of both.

"You think I'm going to meekly go away if you ignore me, Bliss?" Edwards asked. She folded her arms beneath her breasts, fingers drumming against her ribcage.

"Ignore you, boss?" Bliss shook his head as if he had no clue what she was talking about.

"I sent a number of emails. A message was delivered personally by DS Short."

"Sorry, boss. DS Short did pop her head in to tell me something, but I wasn't really listening as I had a lot going on at the time. And I've been way too busy to even check my inbox today, let alone respond to anything."

Bliss hoped DCI Edwards would not call his bluff and take a look for herself, because there were a few open mails either side of hers in his list.

"I see." Her tone suggested that she did not. "Let's skip that for now then. Instead, why don't you tell me what you have been so busy doing."

There was no question of stringing this out. There were too many loose strands, and with this woman any lies he told her pertaining to an investigation would have serious consequences for him somewhere down the line. Better to bite down now and accept the reaming.

Bliss explained, in as collected a manner as possible, everything that had taken place since the two had last met. The lack of movement on operation Moonstone, his late-night involvement on Wayfarer, the theory of a possible link between the two cases, his and Chandler's visit to Cambridge, and finally the interviews with their prime suspect.

Edwards nodded her way silently throughout. Her expression never once altered. Bliss thought she would make a great poker player should she ever turn her hand to it. When he was through, he sat and waited for the DCI to digest it all and then hit him hard.

He did not have to wait long.

"So, let me see if I'm getting this right," Edwards said, in a voice oozing contempt. "First you bungled the pursuit of a suspect; then you ordered the use of valuable assets on a case on which you are not the SIO; you unfeasibly connect two entirely separate investigations together, based on an odour and the unverified ramblings of an ex-detective; neglected to run a simple vehicle ownership check on a suspect; employed an expensive outside psychology expert; and finally you falsely detained an innocent man. Is that the sum of it, Inspector? Or have I omitted anything? It would be easy to do so, given the lengthy list of wrongdoings."

It sounded bad. But it also sounded wrong. Different mind-set or not these days, Bliss was not about to let Edwards get away with that.

"When you put it that way, it's a long list," Bliss said. "But most of what you just said was bullshit."

"I beg your pardon."

"Sorry. Most of it is bullshit, *boss*. Let's take them one by one. I was the last to get a call and the last to arrive on scene following that pursuit, so I'm not sure how I could possibly have bungled it. I followed up on the case because the SIO was not available and I was the senior officer. The odour was not the reason the investigations were linked, that happened due to the close proximity of the incident dates. Those ramblings from an ex-copper are unverified only because I haven't had five minutes to myself since I spoke with the informant, but they can be easily verified – or not – and will be – or not – in a single telephone conversation with the FBI. As for not running the vehicle check, that one is my fault and I will happily cough to that minor indiscretion. My friend at Cambridge spoke to us at no cost to this department unless I should request a written report. And last of all on the charge sheet, given David Pearson was sitting in a room having already been interviewed by the time I arrived back from Cambridge, and had voluntarily remained here, I find it difficult to see how I somehow managed to detain him illegally.

"That said, I will hold my hands up to the fact that our suspect managed to escape last night. I was the senior officer, so I am accountable. But you can't have it both ways: either I am responsible, and so had the authority to do everything else that followed, or I am not and so can't be blamed for any of it."

Bliss sat back in his chair, folding his own arms now and matching his DCI's fierce glare of hostility.

Edwards fumed inwardly for a few seconds, and Bliss watched as her cheeks turned from florid to pale again before she spoke up. "If I had my way, Bliss, you'd be investigated for every stage of this fiasco. But as it happens, the Detective Superintendent has confirmed that the officer responsible for the escape of your suspect has been spoken to and no further action is to be taken. She is also quite happy that, as the most senior officer available, you followed protocol and made decisions relevant to our intelligence at the time. She has asked that you speak to the relevant US authorities as soon as you are able, and to consider the possibility of the two operations being linked. In short, you are being given some rope, Inspector. Personally, I hope you take just enough to hang yourself with."

"Your full support is much appreciated, boss."

Her glare became all the more spiteful. "Do not push me, Inspector. You may have earned yourself a reprieve from Fletcher, but if there is any more insubordination from you I will have you suspended. Do we understand one another?"

"Boss, I'm actually not convinced that you understand me at all," Bliss said wearily. He took the edge from his voice. "But I'm hearing you loud and clear."

"Good. Then you're on a final warning."

He shook his head. "Yes. That much I know. Only, given everything we just discussed, everything I said, everything the Superintendent appears to have said, I'm really struggling to understand why."

Fletcher shot him a withering glare. "It's your attitude, Inspector. You feel you can ignore my instructions, that you can act with impunity and never have to ask permission or answer for your mistakes. You seem to believe that you can do as you please, without informing me as to your progress, and as your superior it is my job to either tame you or move you on."

"I've been here five bloody minutes." Bliss got to his feet, staring hard at Edwards. He held up a hand and spread his fingers to emphasise the number. "But it didn't need even that. You were at my throat right from the beginning. I realise you wanted this case, but I didn't take it from you, it was given to me. If I have ignored your instructions at times it's because I have regarded them as vindictive and petty, and not in the least bit professional. I cannot do my job if I have to run every little detail past you first. I'd remind you that I have a murder investigation to manage and we are on a clock against there being another victim, so if you tie my hands and legs together, then I cannot function."

"Is that so, Inspector?"

"Yes, it is. In fact, let's you and I go and speak to Detective Superintendent Fletcher right now and have her adjudicate on this."

Bliss felt his heart racing after that. There was a queasy sensation in the pit of his stomach, and a dull throbbing in his temples. At this precise moment he didn't care for internal politics, nor did he care for his own job. There were three victims in need of justice, and whilst the killer remained at large other women were at risk.

Judging by the expression on the DCI's face, Bliss thought that maybe Edwards was chasing those same thoughts down her own particular rabbit hole. The simmering anger in her face and fury in her eyes appeared to diminish. Neither entirely evaporated, but they were clearly reduced when she next spoke in a more temperate voice.

"I do not require lessons from you as to the importance of this operation, Inspector. However, it was never my intention to impede you, and if you believe that's what is happening here, then I will take a step back."

Bliss nodded, yet could not let it go. "With respect, boss, you've suggested that much before. Yet the litany of allegations you just read out against me was almost entirely without merit. Other than being given this investigation over you I really can't see why you should have it in for me."

Edwards swallowed thickly. "Your reputation preceded you, Bliss. A reputation for insubordination, for going your own way, for swimming upstream, and for bringing down a house of cards. I was not about to allow that to happen again. Not on my watch."

Bliss was conscious of his team working just outside the office, and through the pane of glass in the door he could see faces turned towards the two senior officers. He took a breath; his colleagues needed solidarity and leadership, not petty squabbling. It was time to walk it back a little.

"I accept those first three allegations. The fact is, there was a time when I only respected my superiors if they earned it, not simply by virtue of their rank. There's probably a little of that still in me, but I have changed in the past twelve years. I still speak my mind, I certainly don't suffer fools gladly, but I am more in control of my issues. As for bringing down the pyramid that was here back then, as I mentioned once before there is only one regret I have and that is the loss of Flynn, because he was a good man and a fine leader. Unfortunately, when you remove the stones beneath, the capstone falls as well. I couldn't prevent that, but it doesn't mean I was wrong. People died, Chief Inspector. Cops here covered that up, were complicit and corrupt, and some were even responsible for murder. Should I have ignored what I discovered?"

"No." The DCI shook her head. "That's not what I'm saying. But perhaps it would have been best had you not uncovered it at all."

"Better for who?" Bliss asked. "Not the victims, that's for sure. Nor the surviving families. Look, boss, the other day we met in your office and I thought we had reached an understanding. It seems I was wrong. I'm not asking you to like me, I'm not asking you to approve of the way I go about things. I'm just asking for a fair shake."

Edwards made no reply at first. Finally she nodded and said, "You'll get it, Inspector. But that does not mean you have carte blanche. There are still lines of communication, channels you need to go through. I will continue to challenge you when I see fit. However, I will monitor in a more hands-off manner until I see a definite need to step in. As far as I'm able, that is. We both have our own methods, Inspector."

Bliss nodded. Edwards turned and left his office without a further word. Bliss let go a long sigh of exasperation and relief. Superiors were rarely anything of the sort other than in name.

He decided to visit the incident room for an update. Having left his office still inwardly fuming, the last person Bliss would have wished to run into as he headed towards the canteen was the bulbous figure of Sergeant Grealish. As before, the big man stood in his way. Bliss closed his eyes for a moment then stared hard at the officer.

"I'm in no mood for this," he said. "Really I'm not."

Grealish nodded. "I can understand why you'd think I'm here to give you grief. Fact is, Bliss, it's the very opposite. I heard what you did on behalf of the traffic officers responsible for letting your suspect get away from the scene. That was a very decent thing to do."

Before Bliss had a chance to respond, his mobile rang. He raised a hand and answered the call. "Excuse me," he said. "This may be urgent."

It was Chandler. She spoke and he listened. "Give me ten minutes," he said. When he killed the call, Bliss looked across at Grealish once more. He stuck out a hand. The sergeant did the same and the two men shook.

"I have to go," Bliss explained. "They found the van."

*

When Bliss arrived at the scene, DI Burton pulled away from a couple of CSI operatives and marched across to him wearing a puzzled frown. Her hair was being whipped by the breeze, and her battle to straighten it was a losing one.

"I know," he said, raising his hands defensively. "I'm gate-crashing your case, and I apologise. I still harbour thoughts that our two operations might be connected somehow."

Burton nodded. "That's fair enough. I thought you'd have your hands too full for this."

"I guess that depends on what this is," he said.

They were at the far end of First Drove near Crowland, close to the bank of the river Welland. Only wheat fields surrounded them, long since harvested. The sky was still low and grey, a cold wind blew in from the east, but at least the rain was holding off. The van was a burnt-out shell. Bliss could still feel heat emanating from the wreckage, and the air around it shimmered in a fine multi-coloured haze. There was no sign of fire brigade vehicles. Even if they had attended they would not have lingered beyond putting out the flames and making the area safe; cars were being burnt out all the time for one reason or another.

"I'll bet my left nut the clothes he wore went up inside there as well," Bliss said. He glanced around at the flat lands, the city seeming far away in the distance. "Picked a good place for it as well."

"I think your left testicle is safe, Jimmy. We'll find nothing of value here now. And yes, it's a good place for setting light to an abandoned vehicle, but I am left to wonder one thing."

"How he got from here to wherever he went next."

"Precisely. You're good. Ever thought of becoming a detective?"

Bliss grinned despite himself. The defeats were mounting up, and each one took its toll.

"No way he walked back," Bliss said. "It's too bloody cold and windy for one thing. So either he had help or he got a ride somehow."

"I'll have someone call every cab company and ask about pickups anywhere near here."

"That's going to be a long job. We're in South Holland here. If he was headed back into Peterborough he might have called a city firm, but we're in Lincolnshire and close to Deeping, Bourne, Spalding. Could've used any of them."

Burton sighed and bit on her bottom lip. She was cute, Bliss thought, with high cheekbones, and the cupid's bow of her lips was alluring. Burton stood only a little over five foot, he guessed, and had a full figure to be admired. He was a single man, Burton was divorced. There was nothing wrong in his book with appreciating a woman, provided he was not also objectifying her. Angie Burton was attractive, and that was that. Though not necessarily when she was troubled and windswept, as she was now.

"The timing is close," Burton said. "We don't have an idea yet as to exactly when this van was set alight, but whether Pearson had time to fire it up and then drive over to Thorpe Wood is… well, it's going to be tight."

"Perhaps that's why it was done during the day and not overnight," Bliss suggested. "Had to provide himself with an alibi."

"That's a thought."

"Yes, it is."

"What's your overall impression about Pearson?" Burton asked him bluntly, hands stuffed deep inside her coat pockets. The steady wind continued to play all kinds of tricks with her hair, and she moved from foot to foot to keep them warm.

"I don't feel it," Bliss replied. She would understand what he meant.

Burton nodded. "Nah, me neither. But some fucker was driving this van last night, and I want to nail the son-of-a-bitch!"

"Yeah, me too. Nice wellies, by the way. That shit brown colour really suits you. Gucci, are they?"

"Jimmy, if I could be arsed to take my hand out of my pocket I'd flip you two fingers. So instead I'll just say, go fuck yourself."

He grinned. "If I could do that, Angie, I'd be in a circus."

"If you could do that, I'd drag you into bed and never let you leave it."

Bliss's phone sounded off. He turned away to take the call. He had forgotten that before leaving the station he had asked Short to place a call to the Los Angeles FBI field offices and to make enquiries about the information received from their ex-cop. So he was surprised to now be speaking with Special Agent-in-Charge Derek Ferguson. He spoke to the man for just shy of fifteen minutes, and when he was done he turned to Burton.

"Good news?" Burton asked.

"I'm not sure," Bliss said, thinking hard about the conversation he had just finished. "It looks like I'm off to California."

SIXTEEN

Robbie Newman was not exactly the tall, dark, tanned and somewhat arrogant man Bliss had imagined him to be. In fact, Robbie Newman wasn't a man at all.

On the sheet of paper he had yanked from the printer back home in his study, a single paragraph informed Bliss that he would be met at the airport by a Robbie Newman. Bliss had almost seen the chiselled features, standard FBI uniform of black suit, white shirt, black wingtip shoes with a shine you could see your face in. The person holding a card with his name on as Bliss emerged into the arrival lounge at Los Angeles International airport, however, was a small, slender woman in a powder-blue trouser suit. She looked to be in her mid-thirties, though in wearing her fine blonde hair pulled back in a ponytail, she may easily have been knocking five years off her true age.

Bliss hoisted the holdall strap over his shoulder, and extended his hand to the woman. "Robbie Newman?" he asked, forehead corrugating.

Newman smiled broadly and shook off a further few years. "That's me. You must be Inspector Bliss. So where are your bags, Detective?"

He turned his shoulder, indicating the holdall. "I travel light. That way nothing will be lost, and I get through arrivals quicker if I don't have to stare at suitcases going round a carousel for an hour."

"Good plan. Wish I could do the same, but somehow that never seems to work out."

"It's good of you to meet me. And you're clearly better informed than I am. I must confess that I thought I was being met by a male agent."

They started to walk, Newman's gait easy and confident as she led the way. "I get that a lot. I prefer Robbie to Roberta, which is my real name, but I guess it kind of makes things like this a little confusing."

"Not that I'm disappointed," Bliss hastened to add. "But you build up a mental image, and you're… well, not at all what I was expecting."

"Whereas you're exactly what *I* was expecting." Newman laughed as he frowned and threw her a sidelong glance, then added: "Solid, tough-looking, determined. Dependable."

"You make me sound like a bulldog."

Newman laughed. "Oh, and I'm not an agent, either. I guess that's something else they neglected to tell you. I'm a detective. Just like you."

Looking at this blonde, stunningly attractive fellow law-enforcer, Bliss thought Robbie Newman might be many things, but just like him was not one of them. The detective reminded him of DS Short, and that was no bad thing at all. If Newman had even half of Short's edge, then he was in good company for the next few days.

The arrivals lounge was bustling with activity, luggage trailing behind travellers like faithful pets; eager, weary people looking to end their voyages. On the other side of the flimsy barrier, shiny faces beaming in welcome. Newman weaved her way through and across the general flow of human traffic, heading towards a side door marked *Official Personnel Only Beyond This Point*.

"I like that crack about the bulldog," Newman said over her shoulder. "I can see we're going to get along just fine."

"You thought we might not?" Bliss asked. He heard the door snap closed behind him, the lock slamming back into place. They were now in a narrow corridor, Newman leading the way still. Bliss's voice bounced off the pale green walls.

"I wondered. I was in training one time with a guy from Scotland Yard, and he was… well, I think you Brits would call him a 'stuffed-shirt'."

"That sounds like someone from the Yard."

This caused Newman to laugh again. Bliss decided he liked the sound. It came easily. As he followed her around a series of corners, he couldn't help but study Newman. The suit fitted her well, the jacket unfastened, and her behind looked neat and compact. Bliss could not remember a time when he hadn't taken every opportunity to look at a woman's backside, and he hoped the days when it meant nothing to him were a long way off yet. *You could admire,* he told himself, *without it meaning any more than that.* He knew women appreciated a washboard stomach – a six-pack – and a well-developed chest, so where was the harm in eyeing a firm bottom, or a nice pair of legs? Even these days in a world full of so-called safe spaces, where freedom of speech came with a caveat and greater tolerance was preached to a hand-picked audience, admiring the other sex was simply human to Bliss's mind.

He and Newman moved through another door out into an underground car park. The detective indicated her Ford parked only yards away, unlocking the doors with a press of her key-fob. Bliss tossed his holdall onto the back seat, then buckled in beside his escort. It was a large saloon, with a roomy interior and comfortable bucket-style seats. Newman's slender frame appeared smaller still behind the wheel, which she had to sit close to.

"You have a good flight over?" Newman asked as she settled in.

"As good as any twelve-hour flight can be, I suppose."

"You not a happy traveller, Inspector?"

"Please, just call me Jimmy. And no, I'm easily bored. Plus, half a day is a long time to be cooped up in a small cylinder with your knees pressed up against the seat in front of you."

"I guess. Shame they didn't fly you business class."

"With our budget I should be grateful they didn't stick me in the luggage compartment."

Newman laughed aloud once more. She was ridiculously easy to please he thought. Or perhaps she was trying too hard.

"So you're a detective," Bliss said. "From Los Angeles?"

"I've been loaned out," Newman admitted with a small nod. She glanced across at him and winced. "Sorry. You really should have been informed by the FBI. A breakdown in communication, I guess."

Bliss wondered who had been behind the decision to partner him with a cop rather than an FBI agent as expected. He had no idea whether Newman was a capable detective or not, but he imagined that whoever signed the order to send her had seen it as a sign of their contempt for his business there. Bliss knew from speaking to SAC Ferguson at the Los Angeles field office that the Bureau were not keen on providing assistance in what to them was a cold case. Nevertheless, he had expected a better level of co-operation, and certainly more respect. It was discourteous. Perhaps they were concerned that he would discover something they had overlooked.

Within ten minutes they had wound their way down onto Interstate 105, and were heading east, Bliss noticed. He had expected this, having checked Google maps prior to leaving home. It was a little after four, and a glorious afternoon was somewhat marred by a ribbon of smog that hung over the city like an ever-circling flock of brown birds. Still the sun managed to pierce the layer of pollutants, and Bliss felt the heat toasting his hands through the windscreen. The Ford swept past the low buildings of downtown Los Angeles, tall desert fan palms swaying gently on the pavements, before bypassing the high-rise business section at Century City and turning away from the city centre.

They made their way north for a few miles on I-5, before getting back on track on I-10, which would take them all the way to Highway 111. As they made their way across towards the low desert, Bliss and Newman chatted amiably. He found her to be an extremely affable companion, with a ready wit, and though he had spent less than an hour in her company, Bliss felt comfortable sitting alongside the LA detective. They slipped down into the canyons, through the San Bernardino Mountains, leaving the urban sprawl behind in their mirrors. Traffic flowed easily on the eight-lane freeway, and the detective drove well.

"Have you ever visited Palm Springs before?" Newman asked, switching lanes to ease past a truck. Bliss had never quite got used to the fact that in the United States, overtaking was allowed either side of a vehicle.

"No." He shook his head. "I hear it's a nice place."

She nodded. "It's real nice. Hot, though. This time of year is usually not so bad, but I hear it's been in the high nineties lately." She turned her head and smiled at him. "I've brought factor five-thousand sunscreen with me."

Bliss laughed. "It was hot in Vegas when we visited a few years back, and we drove through Death Valley, so I know how hot it can get over here."

"Let's hope the air-con keeps on working."

"I'll fan you if not. You know, the desert is quite strange out here."

"How's that?"

"Oh, I suppose I expected it to be… well, more sandy. It looks to me just like dry dirt."

Newman nodded. "Which it is. Yeah, I guess if you aren't aware of it, you might expect something more like the Sahara but with a lot of vegetation."

As they slipped through the town of Banning, Bliss noticed a cluster of buildings ahead and to his left, a single tall structure jutting up towards the sky like a finger pointing towards the heavens. Moments later they drove past a sign and he turned to Newman, frowning.

"Did that just say 'Morongo Casino'?" Bliss asked.

"Yeah. Big casino and spa resort right there."

"I thought gambling was illegal in California. That's why people here head out to Vegas and Reno."

"Ah, the mysteries of California State law. Some card room gambling is allowed, and of course you also have race tracks and the lottery. But casino gambling remains illegal. This land around here, however, belongs to the Morongo tribe – Native Americans. For reasons I've never been able to figure out, the laws governing reservations aren't quite the same as for everywhere else, and they're allowed to have casinos. Something to do with the reservation being their own private land. It's kind of a nation within a nation, you might say. Of course, we assume mob money is involved somewhere, but it's a close-knit community, and it's a way for the Native Americans here to make a decent living."

"That reminds me of an argument I had in a pub back home with a visiting American police officer. We were playing pool, and the conversation had already started to get on my nerves. You know, how the US saved us from German tyranny, how our food is awful, our beer warm and our teeth are black. And then he went off on one about how us Brits should give Ireland back to the Irish. I told him we would, round about the time the Americans gave the US back to the Native Americans."

Robbie Newman's mouth popped open. "Oh, my. I bet that went down real well."

Bliss chuckled at the memory. "Like a turd in a punchbowl. I might not have been as brave had we been in Boston."

A little over twenty miles further on, they swung right on 111 towards Palm Springs, where they headed down Palm Canyon Drive. When Newman pulled into the Hyatt they were immediately met by a smartly dressed porter, who was pushing a gold-coloured baggage cart.

"If you'd like to check in, ma'am," he said to Newman, "I'll bring your bags in and the valet will park your car for you." He flashed a toothy smile.

It was a little after six, and though the heat had died somewhat, Bliss realised how good the air-conditioning inside the Ford had been. Unlike Florida, where the heat was like stepping into a sauna, here it was dry and more like an oven. He followed Newman into the foyer, and was even more impressed than he had been with the initial service. The six-storey atrium was lavish, with thick carpeting and more gold-coloured metal on all the handrails and up the side of the glass lift. He stood gazing around while Newman checked them in. Minutes later he felt a tap on his arm.

"The rooms are ready," she said to him. "But they suggest a drink out by the pool while we wait for our bags to be taken up. I don't know about you, Jimmy, but I sure could do with a cold one."

"I was just thinking the same thing." Bliss smiled. "Ice-cold beer in a frosted glass."

Newman's eyes sparkled. "I can't promise the frosted glass, but will a Bud or a Coors right out of the ice-box do you?"

Bliss licked his lips. "Oh, yes. I'll get them in."

"Uh-uh. This is on the tab, and as the Feebs will be picking it up, the cold ones are on them. Just like the valet parking."

The pool was smaller than Bliss had imagined, but there were plastic beds laid out for the guests – many of which were being used – and tables were dotted around the sundeck close to a small outside bar that went by the name of Spritzes. Bliss sat in the welcome shade of a canopied table, while Newman ordered their drinks. When she joined him, the cop took off her sunglasses and blinked in the harsh light.

Newman had a narrow, slightly upturned nose, and lips that reminded him of Angelina Jolie. Bliss wondered if the detective had to work harder because of her looks. Mia Short had always complained of just that issue back home.

"We'll be hooking up with Officer Brian Leary tomorrow," Newman told him, fingering the indentations left behind by her shades. "He was the investigating officer here, and he figured you'd like to meet with him at the scene."

Bliss nodded. "Sounds good." It was ideal, but what was perfect was the beer when it arrived. Ice-cold, and in a frosted glass, too. It almost burned Bliss's throat as he drank the amber liquid straight down. When he finished, and let out a satisfied breath, he was amused to see Newman's glass empty as well.

"I needed that," she explained, wiping her mouth with a paper serviette. "I told them to leave it five minutes then bring over two more, but I think I underestimated our thirst."

Bliss smiled. He looked around, feeling hot, yet comfortable in the shade. "I could get used to this. I can almost forget I'm here to work."

"Well, you can definitely forget about it for tonight, Jimmy. Nothing either of us can do until we speak with Leary, so let's just chill. D'you want to eat here later or head out and see what we can find?"

Bliss thought about it for a moment, then said, "How about we freshen up in our rooms, then take a walk. If we spot something nice, we'll eat out. If not, I'm sure the food here is as good as everything else about it."

They settled on Woody's Palm House just a short distance from the hotel. During their walk, Bliss had noticed how clean the streets were; not a scrap of litter in sight. People smiled, acknowledged strangers with nods, and the atmosphere in general seemed like that of another world entirely. Bliss had to remind himself that he was here to learn more about a rape and a murder. In the restaurant they first ordered a beer each, then both decided on the house speciality cheeseburger, cooked medium-rare. Bliss spoke in glowing terms about the suite, and the hotel in general, marvelling that it had its own mall attached. They spent a couple of hours eating, drinking and talking, almost as if they were a couple enjoying their first date.

By the time they had checked in at the hotel it had been too late to call Chandler: the eight-hour time difference meant she would be in bed asleep. Bliss briefly wondered if she was doing so alone, but quickly thrust the thought from his mind. It had no place here. No place ahead of rape and murder inside his head. Perhaps no place full-stop.

"Where do you keep going?" Newman asked him. She cut a slice of apple pie with her fork, mixed it into a mound of melting vanilla ice-cream, and popped it into her mouth.

Bliss frowned at first, then caught on. "Sorry," he said. "I'm being rude. I'm a little tired. Plus, my mind is still partly at home."

"Missing your family already?"

"No family." He gave a tired grin. "Just this bloody awful case. Well, *cases* perhaps."

"I read up on it before meeting you at LAX. Mostly about what took place here, but a little about what's happening over in the UK as well. They do sound awfully similar."

"That's why I'm here. It's a stretch, though. I think you Americans would call it a 'Hail Mary'."

Newman laughed, the sound catching at the back of her throat. "Well, they do come off from time to time, Jimmy. That much I know."

Fatigue then settled on Bliss like a physical weight, and he decided to head back to his room. He didn't want to push the boundaries of his condition management even further than he already was. Bliss expected his body to pay for the flight, the drive, the long hours kept wide awake. He needed his medication and a decent sleep in order to curb the cumulative effects. Newman told him she'd take another walk and explore a little.

"Good night, then, Robbie," Bliss said, slipping out from behind the table. "It's been a real pleasure spending time with you. Thanks for making me so welcome."

Newman smiled and waved a hand. "Some people make that easier than others. Get a good night's sleep, Jimmy. I've requested seven-thirty wake-up calls for both of us. Breakfast at eight?"

"Sounds good."

For a moment, Bliss wondered if he should shake Newman's hand or give her a quick, friendly peck on the cheek. He did neither.

"Sleep tight," Newman said. Her eyes held his for a moment longer than they had so far.

"You too." Bliss smiled, turned on his heels and headed back to the hotel, wondering what, if anything, that look had meant.

SEVENTEEN

"How high up is it exactly?" Bliss asked as the aerial tramway moved through the fourth supporting tower, rocking back and forth several times before lurching and climbing on towards the final pylon away in the distance.

"Are you anxious about heights?" Newman asked him, the merest hint of a smile playing across her face.

"No. I was just wondering."

It wasn't the height, rather the motion at each station that bothered him. It was like being temporarily caught in a small boat on an open sea during a gale.

"That's good, because it's about a climb of 6,000 feet from the station down in the valley. It's a long way up, Jimmy. At that altitude the temperature can differ by about thirty degrees, which is why I suggested you bring your jacket."

Bliss peered ahead at the San Jacinto mountain range looming before him, and could only wonder at its majesty, the sheer face implacable and awe-inspiring. A tramway guide above his head told him that as they ascended they might spot Desert Bighorn sheep, deer, foxes, bobcats and even mountain lions. It was impressive to think of those creatures living below his feet; all the wild animals at home walked on two legs.

"It's beautiful," Bliss said to Newman. "Every bit as stunning as you promised it would be."

They had met for breakfast in her room. Prior to that, Bliss had been in touch with Thorpe Wood the moment he stepped out of the shower. Nothing had changed for the better during his short absence, which only increased his frustration. Pearson, their only viable suspect, was out on bail having been charged with failing to stop. The bogus charge had held him, but he had requested legal representation and the duty solicitor had protected his client. Newman called Bliss just as he was about to head down to the restaurant in the atrium. When he knocked on her door, he wondered if she would be fully dressed or in her robe. When she opened up wearing a denim shirt, maroon jeans and black Nike ankle-high boots, he couldn't decide whether he was relieved or disappointed.

What were you hoping might happen? Bliss asked himself silently. The robe parting accidentally as Newman casually draped herself across the bed, or perhaps falling open completely? This wasn't some awful eighties porn film. And what did the notion say about his current state of mind? Robbie Newman was attractive with an extremely pleasant personality, and he had enjoyed her company immensely the day before, but these were immature fantasies and they had no place inside his head.

Bliss chided himself silently. This was a part of his nature that he had yet to control, but he was working on it.

For breakfast, Bliss chose bacon and eggs, while Newman settled for an omelette and hash browns. The food was hot and tasty, and there was plenty of it. While they ate, Newman fed him a few more details about the murder case that had dragged him out there, as well as filling in a little background on the man they were about to meet. The murder had caused quite a stir locally, and while the cop they were going to see had not been in charge of the investigation, it had nonetheless affected him deeply. Bliss understood; an unsolved of this nature could never be forgotten.

*

Leary was in his late fifties and stood straight-backed at well over six feet tall. Beneath a baseball cap that bore the Palm Springs PD insignia, his hair was cut close to the scalp, and what there was of it was silver. He had a long, oval face. His moustache was neat, flecked with grey, and piercing brown eyes suggested warmth and subtle intelligence. His skin was tanned and leathery – the result of working out in the desert sun for too long. The creases around his eyes, mouth and neck were white, like a network of scars. Leary wore a thin brown leather jacket over a grey ribbed sweater, stonewashed denims and boots with toes that came almost to a point. Bliss was almost disappointed not to see and hear spurs jangling as the cop walked.

Newman introduced herself and Bliss, who felt his hand swallowed up by the larger man's. "Pleased t'meetcha," Leary said, his voice a slow drawl, made deep and harsh by a combination of cigarettes and booze, Bliss guessed. "You have a good trip over, Detective?"

"I did, thanks. Bit tired this morning, but from previous experience I know the jet-lag's worse going the other way."

Leary nodded thoughtfully, staring down at his own feet. "Never been out of the US of A m'self. All set to go to the first Gulf war when that went belly-up, and never had the inclination to vacation abroad." He turned to Newman then, smiling and squinting in the sunlight. "And it's a treat to put your face to the voice, Robbie. You're every bit as pretty as I'd imagined you to be."

Bliss could only admire the ease with which the man ingratiated himself with them. They could easily have been three friends about to set out on a hike. He was all set to go, but Leary suggested they grab a coffee from the Top of the Tram restaurant before visiting the site.

"I have a colleague cordoning off the grid as we speak," Leary explained as they sat at a table by a huge, sweeping window that overlooked Palm Springs itself and the desert stretching for miles beyond. They might as well have been looking down at it from an aircraft. "Had to get permission from the manager of this facility, and that took a little longer than I'd reckoned on."

"Turning on the charm didn't work for you, then?" Newman said, her eyes smiling.

Leary laughed, a deep, resonant sound. "Some say money greases the wheels, but I think a few well-chosen words can do the same." He shrugged. "Just not always."

"It's a staggering view," Bliss said, staring out of the window. He could appreciate it more now that he wasn't locked up in a small box strung high above the desert by a thin line of cable.

"Takes my breath away every time I see it," Leary said, nodding appreciatively. "On a clear night you can see the lights of Vegas, more than two hundred miles away. Mind you, the way we're headed today is very pretty, too."

Beyond the restaurant, aerial tramway station and the vista points overlooking Palm Springs, lay dense woodland and mountainous terrain, through which hiking trails were neatly woven, one leading to the very summit of the San Jacinto mountain itself. Leary took out a small map and jabbed a long finger at a circled area.

"The crime scene was some way off the closest trail, and if it wasn't for an amorous couple looking for somewhere to canoodle, we may not have found this victim at all before the creatures had their fill."

Bliss was thinking back to the mailed murder book precis he'd read, the details of which had been sketchy at best.

"I saw the casino on the way here yesterday. Robbie tells me it's not the only reservation close by. Now I know why, when you saw the feathers on and around the victim's body, you suspected a Native American."

"I know why you're here, Detective," Leary said, meeting his gaze. "But we still believe the man responsible for what happened here came from that Morongo reservation."

Bliss sucked in a deep breath, suddenly feeling a little light-headed. The altitude, he hoped. He'd enjoyed an uninterrupted sleep, but that had come after a dizzy spell lasting twenty minutes or so. He did not want to waste time out here being laid low by his health, and steered the notion to the back of his mind.

"Which is why the FBI showed an interest, I guess. But if you're right, Brian, then I've had a wasted journey."

The big man smiled and got to his feet. "Now, Detective, how can it have been wasted when you got to meet a honey like Robbie, here?"

Bliss shot a glance at Newman, wondering if she might seethe at the *honey*. But the LA detective seemed not at all put out by Leary's over-familiarity. Bliss knew women back home who would have sued the service for blatant sexism at the use of such a term, but even in this land of rampant litigation, reason appeared to win the day. It was an individual issue, he supposed. If Robbie Newman didn't mind, why should anyone complain on her behalf? The argument went that some women were too daunted to voice their concerns. Bliss got the impression that Newman had not been intimidated by a man in a very long time.

*

They walked for twenty minutes, taking designated paths, then Leary pointed towards a cluster of oak away in the distance. He headed up a natural slope of grey rock towards them, and swiftly disappeared over the other side. Newman followed, Bliss bringing up the rear. As she stepped onto the rock she turned to him and said, "Interesting guy, huh?"

"Oh, yes. Has a way about him, that's for sure."

"You think I should have said something back there when he called me 'honey'?"

Bliss was surprised. Newman must have caught his glance after all. The LA detective was sharper than he had given her credit for. He pondered her question for no more than a couple of seconds before shaking his head.

"That's entirely your call, Robbie. Me, I'm not a politically correct beast, nor a man of the millennium. Some people think I pre-date dinosaurs. I reckon it's okay that he feels comfortable speaking that way to you. I also think it's nice that you don't feel overawed or somehow belittled by it."

As they climbed over the peak and then down again into some dense vegetation, Newman was nodding. "Nothing wrong with a little old-fashioned charm. I may not have taken it in quite the same way from a younger man, but Leary is old school. Even a dumb LA broad can see that, Jimmy."

Bliss laughed. There was nothing dumb about Robbie Newman.

By the time they caught up with him, Brian Leary was squatting, fingering the dirt on the floor. They had ducked beneath the tape used to cordon off the area, and Bliss felt a familiar gnawing in his stomach that always came upon him at the scene of a crime such as this.

"We used tape to grid out the area," Leary explained to them, without looking up. "Dropped a numbered card wherever we found something. Did it all by the book." Now he glanced up at Bliss. "Y'all do something similar back home?"

"My teams pin string in a yard-square pattern, stretched taut, but it's the same good technique. You wouldn't believe the way they used to run scenes of crime back home, Brian."

"Same in these parts, I reckon." Leary took off his cap and scratched his head, wiped the rim of the hat before replacing it. "A Lieutenant from San Francisco spent some time here many years ago, and he set us all straight in how to process a crime scene."

"So this is where Pam Kite's body was found," Newman said, hooking a thumb into the pocket of her jeans. Her eyes scanned the area, though of course nothing remained of the crime scene itself.

"Yup. Right on this very spot." Leary unzipped his jacket, took out a large brown envelope. "You might want to take a look at these photographs."

Bliss, huddled inside his navy fleece with its England rugby union logo, took the envelope from Leary and withdrew a dozen or so ten-by-eights. The quality was good, the subject sickening. Sixty-year-old Pam Kite was lying sprawled on the dirt with her hands stretched out over her head. She was naked, her discarded clothes lying nearby. One of the shots revealed a light covering of grass and plant life spread across the woman. There was evidence of mutilation over much of her body, apart from the face and breasts, but the real debasement had been carried out on her fingers with the removal of the nails. Bliss knew from his summarised murder book that identification had been from partial dental records and a small tattoo on the victim's upper arm, and now he could see why. Pam Kite had no recognisable features, her nose, cheeks and jaw having been eaten away by scavengers. Instead of a face she had a fleshy, bloody pulp. No open casket here.

Putting together the photos and the basic report he had read on the flight over, Bliss took a few moments to take a good look around and consider the evidence. There were only two real issues that correlated to the victims back home: the taking of the nails, and the lack of wounds to the same two areas. But those two things were plenty.

"Run it through for me please, would you, Brian?" Bliss said.

Leary straightened, blew out his cheeks and checked his boots again. "Like I said, a couple of lovebirds stumbled 'pon her, ran back to the main station and called it in. I was first officer on the scene, which I immediately secured. The case was then taken over by Sheriff Leroy Tyler. Had a coupla G men here for a day or so as well, but they mostly observed rather than use FBI muscle to stake a claim. Other than some footprints that matched some of the marks left on Pam Kite's body, which we later ascertained were from a size twelve boot, worn by a man standing a little under six feet and weighing in at about a hundred-and-ninety pounds, the only real evidence we found were the feathers. The placement of them on the body told us they were left by her killer."

"What type of feathers?" Bliss asked. "I mean, what species of bird?"

"Hawk."

"Indigenous to this area?"

Leary nodded. "Oh, sure. Plenty of 'em around here right now if you care to seek 'em out."

"I gather the investigation led you to learn that Pam Kite had been a regular visitor to the casino, and from that point on the working theory was that whoever killed her may have initially spotted her there."

"That's about it. Tyler fixed on that notion right from the get go, and he never saw too much to change his mind. In the end it was pretty much narrowed down to one of two men, far as Tyler was concerned. But though both were questioned, they stayed silent. Had no choice but to release 'em."

"And Sheriff Tyler never looked elsewhere?"

"Nope. Over a beer and a burger in his back garden, he told me he knew who it was, but that sometimes we don't get our man and the likes of Pam Kite don't get justice." Leary narrowed his gaze. "You about to do some Monday morning quarterbacking here, Detective?"

Bliss was familiar with the expression. It was one he liked. He shook his head abruptly. "I'm not about to second-guess the moves made here based on what's been discovered since, no. Hindsight is twenty-twenty, but I'm looking at this as a fresh case. My initial area of focus is to figure out if my killer could be the one who did this."

"And?" Newman asked.

"And I'd have to say I'm pretty certain now he had nothing to do with it. On the other hand, I do believe there's a good chance of them being connected."

"And just how would that be?" This from Leary.

"Possibly a copycat. I came over here as much to speak to the FBI's main suspects as I did to get a feel for the murder scenes themselves, and I will still do that. Right now, my every instinct tells me that the ages of the person who carried out the attacks here and the ones back home are approximately the same. And that's just not possible with a fifteen-year gap between them."

"I see that, Detective. So where the heck does that leave us?"

"If I'm right, it leaves us both with unsolved investigations and two different perpetrators possibly still out there somewhere."

"Possibly?" The Palm Springs detective frowned at him and peered over the top of his sunglasses.

"Well, people who commit serial crimes tend not to just quit of their own volition. So, when it comes to your perp, there's every chance he is dead or he's in jail."

"Of course. And it just so happens one of the prime suspects is dead and another sitting in jail right now."

Bliss held out the photographs in their folder. "How keen are you to nail the man who did this, Brian?"

Leary eyed him closely. "I was first man up here, Detective. I saw what that vicious bastard did to Pam Kite. How keen d'you think I'd be?"

"Good." Bliss turned to Newman, who was also watching him. "How about you, Robbie? You want to sit down over a cup of coffee and see if we can work this out?"

Newman smiled. "It'd be a pleasure."

"Good. Then how about we head down this mountain back to an altitude that doesn't suck all my breath away, find a place that serves good coffee, and put our heads together?"

"You got an idea, Detective Bliss?" Leary asked, setting off back towards the tramway station.

"One or two, Brian. One or two. And once again, please call me Jimmy."

They made their way back, sun beating down relentlessly, its heat kept at bay up there at more than 8,000 feet above sea level. It was a beautiful place, Bliss thought, but tainted now by what had happened all those years ago.

"You enjoy your trip up Crocker's Dream?" Leary asked both detectives. When he saw their raised eyebrows and looks of curiosity, he chuckled and said, "Francis Crocker was the man responsible for getting this tramway built. Planned it all out in the fifties, first ride was in September of sixty-three. A man of vision."

"It's very impressive," Newman agreed.

Bliss nodded. "Yeah. I doubt he ever envisaged murder taking place up here, though. You'd think there were enough places for that down in the desert without it ruining this pleasant spot."

Leary agreed. "The desert's a big place, Jimmy. Plenty of room out there. I've often wondered about that m'self."

As they climbed towards the tramway station, Bliss looked back over his shoulder, wishing his visit had been under better circumstances.

"Nowhere is sacred anymore," he breathed. "Nowhere at all."

*

The coffee was good, the doughnuts even better. The café was located in a rectangular courtyard just across the street from the Hyatt. It was cool, clean and virtually empty. The lack of patronage allowed the three to discuss the case pretty much as they wished, pausing only when their young waitress both took their order and then brought their drinks and food. In the far corner an elderly couple were working their way through two of the largest sandwiches Bliss had ever seen. The woman was pale, her hands shook on every bite, and she had a headscarf wrapped over white hair. By contrast, her companion was nut brown and wore a Ping cap, suggesting he might spend time on one of the local golf courses. They hardly spoke to one another, but neither were they going to overhear anything said.

"Talk to me again, Jimmy," Leary said, both hands wrapped around the steaming mug. "Tell me how you see things from your fresh perspective."

Bliss took a drink from his own mug, then set it down on the table. They had left Newman's car in the hotel car park, and Brian Leary had parked the police cruiser in a street just behind the café. As he and Newman walked across the street, Bliss had felt the full force of the day's heat. An almost physical presence, enfolding him in a fierce embrace. The café's air-conditioning had come as a welcome relief.

Bliss considered carefully before responding to Leary's words. "The US attacks have been with me only for a day or so. I can see why all four suspects were high on the list and made the final cut. The crime scene photos convinced me that there was some kind of link between yours and ours. My guess is that the removal of the fingernails is a signature the cops and FBI would have withheld from the public in order to weed out the kooks who want to confess to crimes they did not commit.

"However, we all know information like that can leak or be bought from one of the many people involved in such cases. So, either that information is out there somewhere where our killer back home picked up on it, or our killer and yours have been in touch."

"You're definitely ruling out the single perp theory?" Newman asked.

"Not conclusively. But I am setting that to one side for now. I think it's much more likely that we have two killers, and it makes sense therefore to focus on who they might be and how their particular deviances were shared."

Leary was nodding his head throughout. "I can buy that, Jimmy. It sounds plausible enough. Two killers, shared information."

Bliss sipped some more coffee, finished off his apple doughnut. Wiped his hands with a serviette before continuing. "There are plenty of possibilities. Could be it's on the internet somewhere. May even have been exposed by a newspaper article. The US perp could have talked, and it spread from there. Potentially the two could even have spent time together."

"Now that's a thought," Newman said. "That makes a whole lot of sense."

"There is just one thing that I keep coming back to, however. And it's that which makes me believe the two do know one another."

"The body odour," Leary said, snapping his fingers and then pointing at Bliss. "If it's not the same perp, then your guy is somehow replicating it."

Bliss nodded. "That's the way I'm thinking, yes."

"Tell me something, why did you choose to come out here to the Springs of all places? Of the four original suspects, Raymond Andreas, our local Native American, is the only one who is deceased. Seems like a strange choice coming to the scene knowing you can't interview the guy."

"This murder was the first," Bliss said simply. "The rape took place in Banning two days earlier, but whatever intuition I have is reserved for murder. The killing of Pam Kite is the starting point for me, and I thought I owed all of the victims the time it would take to visit and see what sense I could make of it."

Leary leaned forward, resting his elbows on the narrow table. "Jimmy, I'll be as straight with you as I can be. It's good to see someone putting some real thought into this. I don't like to bad-mouth a colleague, you understand, but Sheriff Tyler never stretched beyond his first impression. I get the idea you don't do that sort of thing."

Bliss thought about how his attitude and temper often caused him to act almost like a spoiled child at times. "I wouldn't be so sure about that, Brian," he said, shaking his head. "I think we all occasionally have our weaknesses in that area."

Just at that moment, Bliss's phone rang. He checked the display. It was DS Short. That could only mean one of two things: bad news, or a break in the investigation. He excused himself and stepped outside to find some space away from earshot.

"Go ahead, Sergeant," Bliss said.

"I'm sorry to disturb you, boss. But we have another one."

His gut clenched. "Rape or murder?" Bliss asked.

"A rape."

Bliss closed his eyes. "Shit! I don't suppose David Pearson is still under surveillance is he, Mia?"

"No, boss, he isn't. And wasn't at the time of the latest attack, either. DI Burton worked hard to arrange some form of obs on him, but there simply wasn't enough evidence against him to back it up."

"Understood. What's the name of our new victim, Sergeant?"

"Tania Evans. Eighteen."

Bliss nodded to himself. Burton knew her job and would follow up by speaking to Pearson again, querying the suspect's whereabouts at the time of the fresh attack. Bliss could do nothing for Tania Evans, but what caused pangs of anxiety in his stomach was the notion that if their theory was right, the clock had just started ticking down to the next murder.

They had less than forty-eight hours.

EIGHTEEN

The interior of David Pearson's home was exactly as Burton had imagined it to be. The furnishings were meagre, and what there was of it looked cheap and tatty and uncared for. Clothes, packaging, containers, dishes and cutlery lay scattered around the floor. Food had congealed, hardened, gone rotten. Filthy and torn net curtains hung at a couple of windows, but the rest were bare, the glass panes equally grubby. Everything looked second-hand, perhaps even once dumped and now salvaged. The air was musty and stale, with a sweet undertone that Burton didn't care to dwell upon. She saw nothing to suggest Pearson did not live alone.

The suspect was not exactly thrilled to receive a visit from the three detectives – Chandler and Perry having joined her for the interview before they headed back down to London.

"This is coming close to being harassment now," Pearson complained. "I should have a solicitor here."

"Do you have your own solicitor, sir?" Burton asked him.

Pearson sighed and rolled his eyes. "No. You lot have to provide them if I ask, though."

"If we question you formally back at the nick. I'm perfectly happy to do that if you wish. I thought we'd keep it low key and just ask a few questions here in the… comfort of your own home. It's entirely up to you, Mr Pearson."

The man plumped himself down onto a threadbare sofa that looked as if its better days had occurred in a skip. A cloud of dust rose into the air around him. He pointed towards an equally shabby sofa of indeterminable colour. Burton declined, as did her two colleagues.

"So what do you lot want this time?" Pearson asked. "Who am I supposed to have attacked now?"

"Thank you for getting to the point, sir," Burton said. "And as you've asked… are you able to tell me where you were last night?"

The suspect gave a huge sigh and shook his head. "Dog with a bone, you lot. Look, of an evening I tend to be doing one of two things: watching the box or fishing. Last night I wasn't fishing."

"Are you able to recall what you watched, and when?"

Pearson smirked. "Yep. My *Breaking Bad* box set. All night until I went to bed."

"Anyone able to verify that, sir?" Perry asked. He wrinkled his nose in obvious distaste, though whether at the man, the state of the house or the peculiar smell, Burton was unable to tell.

"Let me think now." Pearson made a show of considering the question, even going so far as to stroke his chin. Eventually he tired of his game and shook his head. "Now that you mention it, detective, I was on my own all evening and all night."

"No sleepovers then?" Chandler asked.

"No, love. Nothing like that. Though I have a vacancy if you're interested."

"Not even if it was a choice between you and my electric toothbrush. Tell me, Mr Pearson, do you see your mother often?"

Now the man leaned back and fixed his narrow gaze on Chandler. "What is it with you people and my bloody mum? What the hell has she got to do with any of this?"

"It's a straightforward question, sir. Why are you avoiding answering it?"

"Because I don't see what business it is if yours."

"You don't need to. I'm making it my business by asking the question."

"And I'm refusing to answer until you give me a better reason why I should."

"You do seem awfully protective of your mother, Mr Pearson," Burton said, shuffling from foot to foot. "The fact is, we're not fully satisfied with what you've told us about your movements on the days you were previously questioned about. Nor last night, for that matter. That makes us suspicious. If we can't get answers from you, then we tend to look elsewhere. Your employer, your family and friends. We may need to talk to your mother. Better all-round if you just tell us what we want to know now, that way we may not need to bother her at all."

Pearson was silent for a while. Burton could almost hear the man's mind turning over. Finally he nodded and said, "Fine. My mum lives just around the corner. We see each other a lot. I didn't tell you that before because I didn't want to involve her. She'd be terrified with you lot jackbooting your way into her home."

Burton ignored the jibe and spread her hands. "There. That wasn't so bad, was it? So then, is there any chance that on the evenings in question you were with your mother?"

"I have no idea. And neither would she, for that matter. I wasn't with her last night, that's for certain. As for the others, I can't remember."

"And you're saying your mother wouldn't recall, either?" This from Perry.

"Correct."

"Are you telling us this because you don't want us to interview your mother for some reason, Mr Pearson? Or because you're afraid of what she might tell us if we do?"

Their suspect huffed, sat forward on the very edge of his seat and glared at each of them in turn. "Neither. I'm telling you that because it happens to be true. My memory is just poor, but my mum is losing it a bit upstairs. I'm lucky if she remembers who *I* am half the time."

"I guess we'll just have to put that to the test," Chandler said. "Appreciating the lateness of the hour, if you give us the address I'm sure DI Burton and another colleague won't mind popping over to see your mother in the morning."

Pearson grinned. "Please do. Not that you'll find her in. My mum is away at the moment. Coaching holiday in the Cotswolds."

"At this time of year?" Burton scoffed.

"Other than her mind slipping, mum's pretty healthy. She enjoys checking out nice villages, stopping off at hotels, putting away a few cream teas and playing a bit of darts and bingo. The cold or rain don't bother her at all."

Burton sniffed. It was starting to feel awkward with the three of them standing, looming over the man. If he'd indicated any signs of being intimidated by it, that would be one thing. But he clearly wasn't, and now it merely felt uncomfortable.

"We're going to need details, sir. Name, address, contact numbers, e-mail, even social media platforms used. I know all about silver surfers."

"You can have the first three. I doubt my mum has ever used a computer."

"We'll have that off you then before we go. Meantime, Mr Pearson, I'd like to know how close you are to your mother. Do you spend a lot of time together, especially as she lives close by?"

It seemed that the suspect had decided enough was enough. He got to his feet, his clean and relatively new-looking attire of sweater and grey cargo trousers a striking contrast to everything else within the house. Pearson folded his arms across his chest.

"Your mother fixation is your problem. I have no clue what my relationship with her has to do with these rapes and murders you keep banging on about, and to be honest with you I am sick and tired of listening to you about them. So, either arrest me or go harass some other poor sod. We're done here."

Burton sensed he would not backtrack, and she had no desire to drag him in. Nodding, she said, "Very well. If you'd just let me have that information you promised us."

Less than a minute later they were back outside the house, walking down the path towards their vehicles. The three of them stood by Perry's silver Audi. The night air had grown colder, and a hoar frost looked on the cards.

"What d'you think?" Burton asked her colleagues.

"I don't like him," Chandler said.

"For the attacks or as a person?"

"Maybe a bit of both. He's clearly slovenly, and a bit sleazy if his remark to me is anything to go by. But Bliss has always insisted that the clever killers, the ones who do not want to be caught, don't leave anything to chance. If Pearson's mother is that easily confused, then why isn't he telling us that on at least one or two of the nights in question he was with her?"

"That's a fair point. But he remains your most viable suspect," Perry said. "I would usually agree with Bliss's point of view on that particular issue of the good ones leaving nothing to chance. However, in this case I'm not sure that we can draw such conclusions based on whether square pegs slide effortlessly into square holes. There's something off about this man. He's nervous about more than just having to talk to us."

Burton put back her head and gave an exasperated sigh. "Which leaves me nowhere because I agree with the pair of you. I don't get the feeling that Pearson is our man. Neither do I believe we can rule him out. Not at this stage. It was his car used by the rapist, his job fits the bill, and he can provide no verifiable alibi. That's three strikes against."

Chandler agreed. "You have to keep monitoring him. Even have another crack at him. And certainly speak with the mother."

"Will do," Burton said. "You think we still don't have enough to get a full surveillance package agreed?"

Burton realised she was on uncertain ground. A full twenty-four observation request demanded three teams of two officers per day. With funding the way it was, the brass were looking to cut costs wherever possible. These rapes and murders were about as despicable as crimes can get, but it all came down to the evidence they had on the subject being observed.

"If it helps, we'll support the package request," Perry said. "I'll also check if we can help with any funding shortfalls, given this forms part of our own Sapphire operation."

Relieved, Burton smiled and shook the hands of her two fellow detectives. "Let's go for it. Our victims deserve nothing less than our best efforts."

NINETEEN

An interview with FBI suspect Jake Willett, the first of the three Newman had arranged on Bliss's behalf, was due to take place the following afternoon in the San Fernando valley. Until then, their time was their own. With little else to do for the remainder of the day, Newman drove Bliss out into the desert, where they hiked around hot springs and in amongst the unique and spectacular Joshua trees. The spiky yuccas were extraordinary, and the smooth rock formations a joy to explore as the descending sun painted them a sandy red. Bliss and Newman each put away a beer and a steak sandwich at a roadside diner, then headed back towards their hotel at around five-thirty. While they were busy seeing the sights, Bliss had felt completely relaxed for the first time in as long as he could recall. As for Robbie Newman, she remained great company, and extremely knowledgeable about her home state.

On the outskirts of Desert Hot Springs, with the sun having plunged into the Pacific, for a while the sky looked as if it were on fire. A short while later, as dusk swiftly wrapped around them, Bliss felt Newman tense by his side, and he noticed that her gaze kept flicking to the rear-view mirror. A few seconds later the inside of the Ford was illuminated by dazzling white light. Bliss turned in his seat to look out of the rear window, but was momentarily blinded.

"They came out of nowhere," Newman said. "One moment there was nothing, the next we got a thousand watts aimed at us."

Bliss could hear it now, too. The muscular grunt from a large petrol engine. Some big V-8 aspirating away behind them.

"Probably just kids," he said. "Slow down and let them pass."

Newman eased back. The two-lane blacktop was clear as far as the eye could see on a long, straight road, but the vehicle behind them refused to go by. After a few seconds, she stamped hard on the accelerator instead, the car automatically shifting down a gear before hurtling forwards at speed. Whatever followed them easily kept pace.

"I'm going to pull over," Newman said, glancing sideways at him. "Let this asshole move clear. Fucker might be drunk for all we know."

"You sure that's a good idea?" Bliss asked her. "This is a lonely spot."

"Has to be better than having him on my ass all the way until we reach our turn."

Newman slowed, tapped the brake to warn the driver behind them that she was about to stop. Then she indicated, slowed to a crawl and pulled off the road and onto the desert dust, tyres crunching on the baked dirt. Initially keeping close to the Ford's rear end, all at once there was a massive roar from a tweaked exhaust and the vehicle blew by them, rocking the saloon as it passed within inches. Bliss noted that it was a pimped-up GMC truck, lights affixed to anti-roll bars and on the cab's roof. It took off like a bat out of hell.

Bliss and Newman glanced at each other and exchanged nervous laughs. "That was fun," she said.

"Oh, yeah."

"Good job we're two brave, no-nonsense, hard-ass cops, or that might have been a little intimidating."

Bliss shook his head. "Nah. It was nothing. I was completely confident."

"You were?"

"Sure."

"Why?"

"I had you in the car with me."

Newman shook her head, dug an elbow into his ribs, and let the truck disappear from view over a rise in the road before releasing the footbrake and slipping back onto the blacktop. Two minutes later, Bliss noticed something up ahead. He pointed beyond the windscreen.

"What's that up there on my side of the road?"

The shape was vague at first. But as their car hit a slight incline on the road, the silhouette of a truck sitting just off to the side became more apparent. Bliss glanced at Newman.

"You ever see Spielberg's first film, *Duel*?" he asked.

Newman nodded. "I was just about to ask you the same thing."

Right then the truck's lights blazed once more, and to Bliss's astonishment it crept forward to block the way ahead. Newman could easily have navigated around it without any mishap, but this was clearly a challenge.

Newman slowed the vehicle yet again. This time she shot Bliss a sidelong glance and said, "You ever had any firearms training, Jimmy?"

"I have, yes."

"Pistol?"

"Yes."

"How about a shotgun?"

He shook his head.

"Well, that's okay. You pretty much just aim, fire, pump and repeat."

"Okay."

"Climb into the back seat," she told him. "Push up the armrest and turn the lever anti-clockwise. That'll release the back of the seat. Pull that down and that'll let you into the gun compartment. Take out the shotgun. It has one in the chamber."

Bliss was already on the move. He did exactly as Newman had instructed. He was in her country, her jurisdiction, and this was her situation to handle. They could have sped by, or turned around, but instead Newman had opted to take matters into their own hands. Bliss approved. By the time he clambered back into the front seat, the two vehicles were only fifty or so yards apart.

"When I stop, I'm going to open my door, climb out and wedge myself in the jamb," Newman told him. "You do exactly the same. Keep the shotgun lowered at around a forty-degree angle; ready to raise and fire, but that way if you accidentally pull the trigger you won't harm anyone."

Again, Bliss followed Newman's lead as she stopped the Ford and exited the vehicle. The night air was sweltering, and immediately Bliss felt himself begin to sweat. The truck was angled across the road, nose on, lights preventing Bliss from seeing little else.

"Driver," Newman called out. "Kill your lights. You have ten seconds to comply, or we open fire." She ducked, turned her head to Bliss and whispered, "Wait for me. I may be bluffing."

She was. Ten seconds became twenty. Then thirty.

"Driver. That was your one chance. Believe me this time when I say that if those lights are not extinguished by the count of ten, we will fire on you. My partner and I are Los Angeles Police detectives. We will use lethal force if necessary."

Bliss got ready, his pulse racing and throbbing in his neck. Newman sounded in control, but this was an armed situation and he knew that just about anything could happen from this point on.

Newman started the count once more. She was on nine when the night went dark. It took several seconds for Bliss's eyes to adjust and starlight to reveal three figures in the cab of the truck and three more now standing in the flatbed rear. All but the driver were holding rifles. Critically, however, not a single one was pointed at either Bliss or Newman.

"What do you want with us?" Newman adjusted her stance as she called out, her weapon aimed in the direction of the truck's windscreen.

Bliss steadied himself, the shotgun feeling slick and heavy in his hands. He had never fired a weapon at anything other than a training target, but he was prepared to do whatever was necessary depending on how his this played out. He had a partner to protect. As his eyes settled further, he saw that the men were Native Americans.

When no answer came, Bliss hissed across at Newman. "You think they're drunk?"

She released one hand from her weapon and held it up as a caution against him speaking again. "Driver, if you don't have business with us then I suggest you move on your way. Go on now. Go about your evening before this kicks up a notch and becomes serious for everyone involved. I will use lethal force – I shit you not."

The truck had been idling. Bliss heard a gear shift, followed by a rasping, gurgling sound as the vehicle rolled backwards. Then the truck turned, its lights sprang on again and it headed away from them at no more than average speed. We're going, but not running, was the implied message.

Bliss licked his lips and blew out some air. "Well, now that was not spooky at all. What d'you reckon that was all about, Robbie?"

Newman walked around to his side of the Ford and took the shotgun from him. Bliss saw tension in her shoulders and written all across her face. "Someone, possibly Leary, would have informed the reservation police about our visit. A courtesy, plus you might have decided to pay them a call for all anyone knew. My guess is that bunch either found out or were told we were here and didn't want us to go digging around into their man."

"Even though he's dead?" Bliss remarked, as Newman slotted the shotgun back into its rightful place. Her own weapon was now holstered.

"Probably family members, some friends as well, maybe. They claimed his innocence all along, and don't want that to change."

Bliss nodded. It made some sort of sense. "What were their intentions do you suppose?"

"If they'd meant to harm us those rifles would have had us in their sights from the moment we stopped. No, I figure they wanted to put a scare into us, nothing more."

"Then they failed big time where you're concerned." Bliss chuckled. "I'm glad I had Annie Oakley on my side."

Newman looked at him over the roof of their vehicle. She grinned. "If only they'd known I can't shoot for shit."

On the drive back to the Hyatt, Bliss silently checked himself out. No tremors. His heartbeat had dropped back to something approaching normal. He seemed in good order. Even so, the run-in with a group of armed men was another worry for him. Stress was such a trigger for his condition, and often a delayed one. Another good night's sleep was needed.

As soon as he stepped out of the car and Newman tossed the keys to the valet, Bliss felt the full burden of failure dragging him down once more. The mountain range in the background seemed to mock him. He had come a long way for no reward so far, whilst back at home another young girl had been raped. Bliss felt foolish and defeated. When Newman asked him about dinner he patted his stomach, told her he was full and was just going up to watch some TV and turn in early. He sensed the detective's disappointment, but Newman nodded and smiled anyway.

In his room, Bliss made use of the hotel's wi-fi to summon up his remote access into the computer system back home. He called up the logs from the past two days. The squad were mopping up after David Pearson, but had formed no new leads. Davina Ball, the young girl who had narrowly avoided becoming the attacker's third rape victim, had failed to add to their weight of intelligence. She had not noticed the odour, but then the attacker had not got anywhere close to her. Other witnesses described a man slight of build, average height, dressed all in black, wearing a hooded top. High probability he was Caucasian, but that was it.

The poor kid who had become the latest victim had provided nothing more, either. Tania Evans had been attacked in the Fletton area of the city. Her statement gave up the same MO, same odour, same result. Their only viable suspect had been subsequently visited and questioned. Once again he was unable to provide a satisfactory alibi. According to the input from DI Burton,

Pearson had become agitated this time, and was now being both belligerent and obstructive. They were getting nowhere with him. Bliss checked to see if Chandler and Perry were still around, but saw they had returned to London. He felt disappointed not to have had more time with Chandler, who increasingly felt like his only anchor to the job.

When Bliss ended the connection he felt both isolated and anxious. He was the lead investigator on a triple murder case and was stuck thousands of miles away playing a hunch which, if it went wrong, might easily cost him his career. The more he thought about the next few days, the less he felt sure of himself. Detective Newman was great to be around, and seemed like she knew her job especially having taken on a truck-load of angry and armed men, but she was still a relative stranger to him. He needed grounding.

He needed Penny Chandler.

Without pausing to second-guess himself, Bliss placed a call to New Scotland Yard and the Sapphire extension. DI Perry was not available given it was not quite six in the morning UK time, but by chance he landed at the desk of Perry's superior, Detective Chief Inspector Westcott. Bliss explained who he was, where he was and why he was there. He outlined the theory in place, and was surprised when Westcott bought into it. At that point he felt he had nothing to lose, so suggested Chandler join him as a seconded member of the operation Wayfarer team. Initially sceptical, the DCI then suggested it might be better for someone at inspector level or above to be involved. Not wishing to be stuck with Perry, Bliss explained his prior working relationship with Chandler and how that could only help matters on a short excursion in a foreign country. To his immense relief, Westcott eventually agreed, and said he would get her out there on the next available flight.

An hour later, just as he was settling down for the night, Bliss's mobile chimed. A text from Chandler, informing him that she was booked on the noon flight from Heathrow and he was to meet her at LAX. Pleased with himself, Bliss lay back in the bed and wondered how he would begin telling Chandler about his strange evening encounter.

*

His father wasn't calling him useless now.

His mother wasn't calling him insignificant now.

Oh, no.

Now he was use*ful*.

Now he was *significant* once again.

And he was being treated for his labour.

He had targeted Tania Evans specifically. He had not done so before, but he was learning, growing – improving. He had spotted her whilst working one day. He was in a sixth form centre at one of the schools he worked at, checking on some cable close to where Tania and her little gaggle of friends hung out. He learned her name from them as they spoke to her, but by then had already become fixated upon her. She was simply beautiful, with a little pixie face and elfin body, and a great pair of legs which he happened to catch sight of when her navy skirt rose high as she sat down. When he sneaked glances – which was often – he could occasionally see all the way between them up to her white panties.

From the moment he decided he had to have her, the rest could not have been easier. He had waited for her to leave school that afternoon, and had followed her all the way home. He made sure he was one of many people travelling in the same direction, so she had never suspected the presence of her stalker. After that it was a matter of following her again until the right moment came along.

He only had to wait a day.

The pleasure was indescribable.

So much more intense than sex with a girl who had come along by chance.

This time he already knew his victim intimately, the cadence of her voice, the charm of her laugh, curves of her face, fullness of her lips.

This time he got to wrap his fingers around breasts he had previously noticed and lusted after.

This time he got to remove the panties from and explore what lay beneath on the real-life girl who had already featured in several of his masturbatory visions.

This time he had cried when he came.

The best part was knowing that, in visiting plenty of different schools in order to earn his meagre living, there would be no shortage of similar choices in the future.

Having returned from his successful attack on Tania, his mother had visited him in his room and immediately sat him down to rake through his hair with her nails. His treat for a job well done. He closed his eyes and curled his toes and shuddered throughout.

"Do my nails for me now, please," he said afterwards.

His mother was more than happy to. He knew that by tomorrow she would start eating into his brain once more, that his pleasure was temporary at best. But to enjoy that pleasure you also had to appreciate the pain. No one knew that better than he.

TWENTY

Jake Willett had old teeth. Teeth that belonged in the mouth of a man closer to eighty than the fifty Willett had been alive. Sick-looking things they were, a few twisted or leaning, all yellowed and riddled with plaque and disease. Bliss knew it was wrong of him, but he could not take his eyes off them when the man talked.

And boy he could talk.

Born and raised in the Ohioan flatlands, the second son of a farm labourer and store beautician, Willett had seen his future disappearing over the horizon in a sea of corn, tombstoned by rusting John Deere tractors, a waitress for a wife, and a pick-up truck full of rug-rats. He had fought it in his head, but settled for it in his heart. Then out of nowhere he had enlisted into "this man's army". That lasted about as long as it took for reality to settle in. By then, many a woman – and even a couple of guys – had told him how good looking he was. "Like a movie star" they had said. Willett took them all at face value, and no sooner had he quit his base in Arkansas than he was on a Greyhound to Los Angeles and the bright lights of Hollywood.

This much Willett told them as he busied himself tossing back a whole four-pack of Bud.

"Would I know you from anything?" Bliss asked him.

"Are you seeing this crap-hole I'm forced to live in?" Willett asked, taking it all in with a panoramic sweep of his head. "This look like the home of a man you might have seen in a movie?"

"Or TV?" Bliss offered.

This earned him a look of rebuke from Newman. Bliss didn't really care; he was only feigning interest to kick-start the man talking. The home was one of those mobile sorts with no wheels, that had never been anywhere and never would. Standing on a bed of breezeblocks, the long, rectangular wooden structure needed a paint job the way its owner needed a dentist. There were a hundred more just like it in the same densely-populated downtown region, dusty kerbsides filled with beaten-up trucks and one-eyed dogs. The interior was a riot of blonde wood and chintz in garish colours. The three of them had to clear newspapers and magazines off the chairs they were offered in order to sit down, but the place looked like a health hazard and Bliss didn't care to imagine what the stains on the upholstery might be.

Willett closed his eyes. Shook his rectangular head with its stubble at both ends. "Did some extra work on a *Law and Order*. Had one line in some hospital drama; could've been *ER* for all I know. Maybe *Chicago Hope*. Whatever."

He popped one eye open as he scrabbled around for another four-pack.

"So, don't you believe all that Bull. Shit. about how any guy with a handsome face and a buff body can make it in Tinseltown. You gotta talk as well. And you're hearing my voice right now."

It was a thin, reedy voice with a nasal edge. It reverberated, and it grated. The man opened his mouth and the spin cycle on a washing machine started up. For a well-built man the voice was puny, the reason for Willett's thespian failings all too clear. *Might have helped had you brushed your teeth occasionally,* Bliss thought all the same. Though to be fair, a regular intake of crystal meth might have had something to do with that sad array of enamel railings.

It was Chandler who steered them back on track by asking Willett about his time in Glendale.

Earlier, Chandler had exited LAX like a woman lost in another world or a different time. The twelve-hour flight had done her no favours, and she looked as if she was more prepared for sleep than an interview. Chandler appeared flustered when introduced to Newman, and the look she gave Bliss caused him to wonder if he had dragged her out here against her will. What should have been a thirty-minute drive straight up the I-5 to San Fernando took more than an hour due to roadworks and traffic congestion. By the time they entered the valley, Chandler had found her second wind and was wide awake. She and Newman chatted like old friends, which Bliss found less than amusing, as their conversation veered towards diagnosing his many apparent flaws. He would have preferred it if their focus had remained on Jake Willett.

The big man squirmed a little in his chair, not liking the shift in gear from Chandler. He yanked the ring off his fifth Budweiser and drank from the can as if it were his first. Cuffed foam from his lips before responding.

At least you spared us the belch, Bliss thought.

Willett belched and said, "You people treated me like shit, that much I can tell you. Tossed me into jail with a bunch of fucking gangbangers and faggots, sweated me in that tin box of an interview room. Violated my civil rights." He sat back, folded his arms, beer can still gripped in his meaty hand.

"Mr Willett, you were a prime suspect in a double rape and homicide investigation," Bliss reminded him. He was glad of the ceiling fan because the sweltering day had kicked up a notch or two during the day. "It's no surprise if the police and FBI treated the matter seriously. The reason we're here today is because you were never cleared, and the case remains unsolved. Now, I believe we're showing you respect by coming to your home rather than dragging you in to the police station, so I'd be grateful if you would forget what happened before and simply answer our questions. That sound okay to you?"

Willett gave that some thought. Bliss could see where the man might once have been handsome and fit, but the booze, drugs and too much bad food had wrought havoc with the man's looks and his bulk. The man chewed on his bottom lip, and Bliss felt like slapping him.

"Mr Willett?" He looked hard at the man, drumming his fingertips on the Formica table top.

"Well okay, Mr Brit Copper, I'll tell you and these two skanks what I told the cops and Feebs way back when: I did nothing wrong. I have no clue what I was doing on the nights in question, so I have no alibi, either. I can't prove where I was, but you can't prove where I wasn't. And I wasn't anywhere near no rape or murder."

Bliss was no fan of double negatives, but that statement had him perplexed. He flicked a glance at his colleagues. The two skanks, apparently. That would warrant a few comments on the ride home if he had a say in the matter. Newman nodded. Chandler shrugged. In his experience, people who kill more than once tend to have an alibi all worked out. Newman was confirming that Willett was sticking to his original statement, made some fifteen years ago. Chandler was sitting on the fence as to whether he came across as guilty or not. Bliss did not care much for the man, but neither did he believe Willett to be guilty.

"Why do you think the police and FBI looked so hard at you, Mr Willett?" Bliss asked.

"I'm sure that must be written in one of them files you people keep."

"It is. But how about you humour me."

The one-time actor sighed and set his beer down on a small table overflowing with cans and bags of corn snacks. A puddle of garbage lay on the floor beneath, shoved off to make room for fresh refuse.

"They said it was because I knew Betsy Flowers. She was one of the girls got raped. That was it. That was their entire reason. They brought me in and treated me like I was Ted Bundy or some such, and all because I knew one of the victims."

"You didn't just know Betsy, though, did you? You tried very hard to get close to her."

Willett shook his head, his cheeks becoming as florid as his nose. "Ain't nothing wrong with a man wanting to get to know a woman better, is there?"

Bliss shook his head. Crossed one leg over the other, adopting a more casual pose. "Except that you were thirty years old, and Betsy was half that."

The man snorted. "You wouldn't have known that to look at her. She would've easily passed for twenty at least."

"I can't fault you there, Mr Willett. Betsy was a fine-looking girl. Mature for her age. Physically, at least. I can see why you might have tried to get close to her."

Bliss waited for Willett to relax his own posture before continuing.

"But then how do you explain continuing to attempt a relationship with Betsy once you knew how old she was? Are you a paedophile, Mr Willett?"

As heavy and out of shape as he was, Willett sprang to his feet with a lot more agility and vigour than Bliss had thought possible. The big man stood just inches away, glowering, hands clenched, a heavy vein in his neck livid with colour.

"How dare you? How the fuck dare you? That girl was my one moment of weakness, and I have paid for it every day since. You think other people don't see things the way you do? You think I haven't had to live with the whispers, the pointing, the accusations? Betsy's brother attacked me with a baseball bat. I fought him off and who d'you think the police took away and threw into a cell?"

Willett stood there, chest heaving, face creased. He kicked out at the trash lying on the floor, scattering the cans like tenpins. Then, as if he were a balloon and someone had let the air out through a pinhole, his shoulders sagged, his legs buckled, and Willett fell into his chair which moved a good six inches backwards. Then he leaned forward, put his head in his hands and started weeping.

"I would never have hurt Betsy," Willett said through his sobs, tears flowing now. "Never. I made a mistake. But not one that should have cost me any chance of a decent life afterwards."

Willett paused to run a hand across his face, looking up at the three of them. "The worst thing for me was that they never cleared me. Never caught anyone else."

"The worst thing for Betsy was she got raped. That changed her life as well, Mr Willett."

"You think I don't know that? I couldn't be more sorry for the poor girl. But I didn't do it. And nothing any of you could say or do can ever change that."

*

They were five miles away heading back down to LA when Newman asked Bliss if he had meant what he'd said about Betsy Flowers. Bliss turned his head, eyes narrowed.

"You mean about her being mature and attractive for her age? Are you serious? I was baiting the man."

"Good. Because there are plenty who do think she had it coming, the way she looked and dressed."

"I'm not one of them. And fuck you for thinking I might be."

Newman's mouth fell open. Then she started to laugh. "Oh, my God! The famous British stoicism slipped there, Detective Jimmy Bliss."

This time he turned in his seat to face her. "You can't ask me something like that without expecting a hostile response." Bliss was relieved that Newman was treating it lightly, but still he bristled.

"Noted. It won't happen again." Newman gave a mock salute.

"Good." Bliss managed to smile. "Now find me a really good burger bar. I'm famished."

"Don't worry about him," said Chandler from the back seat. "He always gets cranky like that when he's hungry."

*

Bliss and Chandler had a drink in the hotel. He was booked into the Sheraton by the airport, and even the refreshments there were on the FBI. Fat mirrors behind the highly-polished wooden counter made the bar appear much larger than it actually was, but it was still a sizeable room. Even so, it was crowded with people and bustling with noise and activity. Apart from their table, which was unnaturally quiet. Bliss could not quite figure out Chandler's mood, so he decided to rewind a little.

"DI Perry seems like a decent bloke," he said. "A bit of a clotheshorse maybe, but a good detective and boss to work for from what I can tell."

Chandler nodded. She had chosen a cocktail by the name of El Gordo, with a tequila base. She had taken only two sips and already her eyes had a gleam in them. "He's great," she said. "By far the best boss I've ever had, actually."

Bliss chuckled. "Really. I would remind you that just the other day you thanked me and said you had learned everything you knew from me."

"Right. How to piss people off. How to alienate people. How to irritate, annoy and anger people. How not to deal with the media. How not to deal with superiors. Need I go on?"

"No, I think that about covers everything. My hard work clearly paid off. Okay, so Perry is a great bloke and a great boss. Is that it?"

"Is that what?"

"Is that it as far as Perry is concerned? You have anything else to say about him?"

Chandler narrowed her gaze. She tilted her head just as the bar's sound system switched to an Eagles track. "Such as?"

"Are you aware that you answer questions with a question?"

"Do you know you're doing exactly that same thing right now?"

"Do *you* know you're avoiding the question, and in doing so are making me wonder if you have something to hide?"

Chandler edged forward on her chair to face him. She met his gaze. "If you want to ask me something, Jimmy, go right ahead and ask."

"Do I have to?"

"You do."

"But you know what my question is going to be."

"Yep. But you still have to ask. I'm not going to volunteer."

Bliss swallowed. Took a hit from his beer. "Is your relationship with Perry more than professional?"

"Why does that matter?"

"Here you go again with answering a question with a question."

"Why does it matter, Jimmy?"

"It doesn't."

"Well then?" Chandler shrugged.

He looked into her eyes. "I still want to know."

"Okay. Then the answer is yes."

Nodding slowly, Bliss wanted to look away. Walk away. Forget he had ever asked. But he had. And here they were. "Is this an old relationship or is it still going on?"

"It's not old. But it's not current, either."

"Is it over, or are you... on a break?"

"I think it's over."

"I'm sorry if it's painful to talk about," Bliss said, looking down at the table. "I never meant to intrude."

"Yes you did." Chandler turned to face herself in the mirror behind the bar. "And I wish I knew why."

*

Robbie Newman rented an apartment in Brentwood, west LA, within spitting distance of Sunset Boulevard. It was part of a thirty-unit complex with shared utilities and a pool. The poolside chairs were all being used when Bliss and Chandler arrived for dinner at eight-thirty, but they were happy to be inside and out of the heat that lingered long after the sun had dipped beyond the horizon.

Newman was now wearing a purple sleeveless top and blue jeans. She fit her clothes really well, Bliss thought, watching her slink around her own home like a cat.

"Nice place," Bliss remarked. He wasn't simply being courteous; the pale yellow walls created a spacious effect on what was in reality a small living space, with an open-plan kitchen, but it was sparsely furnished so there was no clutter to emphasise its dimensions.

Bliss noticed an array of framed photographs on one wall. Newman in some. One showed her surrounded by two men and a woman at Newman's police department passing out parade.

"Your family?" he asked, indicating the photo.

"My mother and father."

"And brother?"

Newman shook her head. "Unfortunately not. That's my husband. Ex-husband now. Sadly, if I want to show the photo I have to have that creep in it."

Bliss was surprised. He had Newman down as a career cop, with no time for a long-term commitment like marriage. "Why a creep?" he asked. "He cheat on you?"

"Jimmy!" Chandler gasped the name, clearly shocked.

"What? Me and Robbie are homies now. We're tight. Ain't that right?" he grinned at Newman, hoping he had not misread their relationship.

Newman grinned right back at him. Nodded at Chandler. "It's fine, Penny. Clearly your friend has no filter. And no, my ex didn't cheat on me. Well, he may have done, but that's not why he's a creep. He beat me. Just the once, but once was enough."

Bliss regarded the man in the photograph. A full twelve inches taller than Newman, and about twice as wide. The thought of him wading into Robbie made Bliss feel nauseous. He blew out some air.

"I'm so sorry," he said. "Me and my big mouth. What a great start to the evening. Can we come in again and pretend that conversation never happened?"

"It doesn't matter," Newman told him. "It was all a long time ago."

"No, it does matter. What I said was tactless irrespective of what happened between the two of you. The truth only makes it worse. I apologise, Robbie. Please forgive me."

Chandler gave a low whistle. "I'd snap his hands off if I were you," she said to Newman. "A Bliss apology is a rare thing indeed. I'm marking it in my diary."

That seemed to settle them. Newman turned out to be an excellent cook, and the chicken pasta dish she put together was so tasty Bliss went back for seconds. Over dinner they all relaxed more, talking in generalisations and steering clear of the interviews. Nobody wanted to bring those intrusive shadows into play during down time. They had each agreed upon this at the outset. For Bliss it was a tough call as to when work time ended and down time began, but dinner in the home of their LA police detective host seemed an appropriate place to begin.

Newman revealed more about her marriage, how it had been lust over love, and a desire from her point of view to maintain the kind of stability she had known all her life. Her father had been a cop, mother a high school teacher. Discipline was very much ingrained into her, and from childhood she sought an orderly life of service. Marriage had felt like the logical extension of education and career-building. Only by the time Newman realised neither she nor her husband were in love, they had taken their vows and were attempting to hold things together. The physical violence had been the final straw for Newman. The price her husband paid in exchange for her not pressing charges was a quick divorce, free of lawyers with the exception of the paperwork being drawn up and lodged in records. Sometimes, Newman admitted, she wondered if he had hit her because he knew of no other way to say goodbye.

Chandler's dip into the familial pool was tentative. A toe in the water followed by a brief flurry of inconsequential information was about its extent. Bliss did not draw his friend into discussing her daughter, despite Newman's easy-going demeanour and apparent sympathetic nature. He admired Chandler for being taciturn when it came to that particular aspect of her life, much as he mostly was when it came to discussing his wife and her murder.

So by the time things inevitably swung around to Bliss, he instead spoke about his parents. He had missed them enormously when they first uprooted themselves from London and moved to Spain, but had also been both proud and thrilled, because over there they had thrived rather than stagnated the way some couples do as they enter their senior years. Bliss neither skipped over his father's death, nor dwelled upon it. His grieving was over, but a fond memory was never far away whenever he thought of the old man, and always seemed to trip him up into shedding the odd tear.

"So your mother remained in Spain?" Newman asked.

"No. Not for long, anyway. She sold up both the business and the house, bought a little place in Ireland, and has now made that her home. She refers to it as her final resting place, and I constantly have to remind her what that actually means."

They laughed at that and Chandler raised a glass. "To the esteemed Mrs Bliss. We forgive you for lumbering us with your lump of a son, and wish you all the very best on this latest stage of your great adventure."

"Aw, thank you, Pen," Bliss said. "Part of that was quite charming."

"I'm sure she'll kick on and thrive again."

Bliss nodded. "She's made a start. Got herself involved with an on-line community of widows. She tells me they are extremely supportive, and that it helps her to get things off her chest. She spent an evening recently ranting about my dad, blaming him for robbing her of more time with him by not living more healthily, not relaxing like he was supposed to. Apparently, she ended up contradicting herself after about three hours by saying how he would have curled up and died much earlier if she had changed him in that way."

"There's a lot of truth in that," Newman said. They were on the coffee course, and she had put together three decent Irish lattes. "It's the difference between being alive and living. They sound like a great couple."

"They were." Bliss nodded, smiling fondly as he saw his parents together in his mind's eye. "And I have done my best not to mock this coven of widows when I speak to my mum."

"Ooh, you rotten sod!" Chandler said, swatting his upper arm. "I'm sure they are all just lonely women looking to help each other acclimatise to being on their own after all those years."

He laughed. "I know. I was only joking. A coven needn't be a bad thing."

"Bullshit," Newman said. "It's derogatory and you know it. I think what your mother is doing is quite sweet."

Bliss raised a hand to surrender. "I do, too. Hey, I'm me. I take the piss."

Newman screwed up her face. "Do you mean you're sarcastic? Is that what that means?"

"It is."

Newman nodded appreciatively. "I like it. I might use it myself."

"Jimmy follows his version of the Descartes mantra," Chandler chimed in. "I'm DI Bliss, therefore I'm sarcastic."

Newman set her cup down on a coaster. She looked between them, the edges of her lips curled upwards. "You two have such a great relationship. If you don't mind me saying, it's more like siblings than lovers. Is that what went wrong between you?"

Chandler frowned. She glanced at Bliss, then back to Newman. "What do you mean, Robbie?"

Newman's brow creased. "You two had something going, right?"

Bliss put back his head and laughed. It came out stronger and louder than he had intended. "Me and Pen? You think we were… Oh, Robbie. What on earth gave you that idea?"

Newman's face turned crimson. She put a hand to her mouth. "I am so sorry. Truly I am. There's just this chemistry between you that tells a different story."

"And that story is me and Penny hooked up, didn't much like it as a couple, and now enjoy some weird brother and sister vibe?"

"Something like that." Newman bit her bottom lip and then smiled.

"Sorry, Robbie," Chandler said. "Your radar is way off this time. You seriously think me... and... him... ?" She shuddered theatrically.

Bliss jabbed a finger at her. "Hey, that's hurtful. You could do worse you know."

Newman regarded Chandler and nodded enthusiastically. "He's right, Penny," she said. "You really could."

TWENTY-ONE

It was a ninety-minute flight from LAX to San Francisco. It took them half an hour to claim a rental car, and a further hour to drive from the airport to San Quentin state prison. Bliss had never been able to relax whilst flying, but the journey was a necessary irritant. Given the round-trip drive time was about twelve hours, he suffered the flight in silence.

"You're quiet, Jimmy," Chandler said to him at around the halfway point on the journey.

"Prisons are not my favourite places. Convicted killers are not my favourite people."

"Understandable. But at least you get to ride with two babes on your arm."

Bliss laughed. He couldn't help himself. Chandler had always been able to find exactly the right way to soothe him. "I'm sure Detective Newman just loves being referred to as a 'babe'," he said.

"Actually, I'm fine with it," Newman said from across the aisle. Chandler had snared a window seat, so Bliss was trapped between the two of them. He sensed a conspiracy taking place.

"Of course," he said. "Just as you were charmed by being called a honey."

"I'm shallow like that. What can I say?"

Bliss turned to Chandler. "And Pen... really? Babes?"

She elbowed him in the ribs. "Chillax, Jimmy. Loosen up, dude."

Bliss rolled his eyes. "I know we're in California, but ease up on the surfer speak. You're from East Anglia not Newport Beach."

"But you just said it yourself, it *is* California, Jimmy. Home of the Mouse."

"And home to the only state prison that still maintains a death row."

Chandler blinked. "Bummer. Someone's been doing their homework."

"Actually, it's only nominally a death row these days," Newman pointed out. "There hasn't been an execution in California since Clarence Ray Allen back in 2006. You know, he was seventy-six when he was killed by lethal injection, having spent twenty-odd years on death row. Oddly enough, for murders he didn't even commit. He ordered them whilst in prison serving life without parole for several other crimes, including murder. What goes around comes around, I guess."

"Sounds like a real charmer," Bliss observed.

"But the death penalty still exists here, right?" Chandler asked.

Newman nodded. "It does. But the US District Court ruled that it's unconstitutional due to the delays, and I suspect that the furore over Allen's execution has played a part in none happening since."

"Why, what happened?"

Newman sighed. "Oh, well the man was frail and in a wheelchair, mostly blind. At one point while he was on death row his heart stopped and they resuscitated him. Imagine that – keeping him alive just in order to kill him."

"It's a tough call," Bliss said. "It seems to make little sense in a case like that where they could have done it a couple of decades earlier. I take the point some make that an eye for an eye creates a society no better than the people it executes. But I also understand that in some cases the only way you can be certain they never kill again is to do just that."

"I agree. I think it's often easy to make judgements when you're at a distance. Those who insist it should never happen might take a different view if it was their partner, sibling, parent or child who had been brutally murdered."

"That's revenge, though," Chandler said, leaning across as if to emphasise her argument. "If you want a person dead because they murdered someone close to you, that's revenge. If you want to do so because it takes that killer off the streets for good, that's another matter entirely. I can see that. I'm only glad we don't have that decision to make."

Bliss nodded. "Take our man back home. He's murdered — savagely and horrifically — three women. He'll do so again, have no doubt about that. Say you have a gun, you have him in your sights. You can arrest him, give him the chance to evade life in prison because of some forensic mishap, or perhaps be released in ten years because some psychologist says he's a changed man or found God. Or you can pull the trigger. What do you do, Pen?"

Chandler shook her head. "I don't know. The right thing is to give him his day in court and let it ride."

"No. That's the legal thing. Is it really the right thing?" Bliss turned to Newman on his left. "How about you, Robbie? You actually have a gun. Do you use it given the same scenario?"

The Los Angeles Detective did not even pause. "I would put him down. Put him down and then turn away without a second thought. I see a difference between that and injecting an old man barely able to cope with taking his next breath."

"I'm with you," Bliss said. "I'd be happy enough if our killer never got to see the inside of a courtroom. On the other hand, I don't care for state-sponsored murder, either."

"Speaking of killers, any word from home?" Chandler asked.

"Not really." Bliss had called in before leaving for the airport. "Burton's team are sifting through CCTV footage near where Pearson claims to have fished. He's offering no help as he says he can't remember which route he took or which location he chose, other than it was somewhere north of Deeping. Forensics came up short with the burned-out van. On the bright side, no follow-up murder victim as yet."

As the wheels came down ahead of landing, they agreed to focus on the positive aspect. Their drive took them through the vast, tall and absurdly hilly city of San Francisco, before heading over the Golden Gate Bridge, blowing by the tasteful haven of Sausalito and on to the prison itself. San Quentin, now more than 160 years old, stood on over 400 acres overlooking the San Francisco bay. A glorious view offered for those who could see it. At the gates, Newman badged her way in. She had no firearm to check as it was forbidden for even serving law enforcement officers to carry weapons on flights unless transporting prisoners. Bliss and Chandler showed their passports and police warrant cards. Twenty minutes later, after much clanking of steel doors and barred gates, they were seated at an interview table in a small square room opposite Lucas Delaney.

He was a bear. A raw, animalistic savagery dwelled in his eyes. Delaney was easily six-four, and well in excess of 300lbs. His beard was thick and bushy, grey and white. The slabs of meat that passed for arms were sleeved with ink; ghoulish images of graveyards and skeletons and misshapen creatures from some kind of hellish imagination that Bliss was glad he had no part of.

Delaney was one of around 700 San Quentin inmates currently on death row.

"It says in my file that you were convicted of shooting to death a man who barged into you and spilled your drink in a coffee house," was how Bliss chose to begin the interview.

The bear sat and studied him for a moment, before nodding silently.

"Did you do it, Lucas?"

The report said Delaney had waited out in the parking lot for thirty-year-old Ashley Rider, had then followed the man home, before shooting Rider as he exited his vehicle on the driveway in front of his home in Merced, about a 140 miles from where they now sat.

"Not me, sir," Delaney growled in a voice entirely suited to his enormous frame.

Bliss shrugged. "Well, you're in here now. You may not ever be executed, but life without parole is the most you can look forward to if not. Thing is, Lucas, it strikes me that a good Christian man like yourself would probably want to meet his maker with a clean conscience. Am I right?"

"Yes, sir. And I will. Like I said, I'm innocent."

"Of shooting Ashely Rider? Maybe. No, what I'm referring to, Lucas, are the rapes and murders you were questioned about a number of years ago."

Delaney eased back in his chair, which was bolted to the concrete floor. It groaned in protest beneath his bulk. "My lawyer said I could talk to you, said you could do me no harm. I figure he thought you wanted to talk about the Rider shooting."

"You can have your lawyer present in the room if you wish," Newman told him. "But we're just talking here, Lucas. You will never leave San Quentin, so you could admit to anything without adding a single day to your time."

The bear gazed at her. Kept it there for an uncomfortable amount of time. Then turned it back on Bliss. "I got nothing to say about rapes or murders. I never raped a girl in my life, and I told them that back then."

Interesting that Delaney chose not to include the murders in that statement, Bliss thought. He decided to press the prisoner.

"But Lucas, you were never able to tell the police or FBI agents where you were on the nights in question. The girl who was raped spoke about a big, strong man. You were living in Merced at the time, so you could easily have driven down to Fresno and back. It's one straight road. A witness claimed to have seen a black Ford truck nearby, and you owned a black Ford truck at the time. You see where this is heading, Lucas."

From the man's file, Bliss knew appearances in this case were deceptive. Delaney might look like a big, dumb ox, but he was in fact fiercely intelligent. He just had an uncanny knack of disguising it.

"I see where you are *driving* this," Delaney said. "It's not a crime not to remember where you were, a whole year afterwards. This is America, so there are plenty of big, strong men around.

I reckon there must be about quarter of a million men living in Fresno. And Ford trucks are what this country was built on, so I'd say there was more than one of them around, too."

Chandler leaned forward across the table. She looked up into his grey eyes. Half the man's size, she nonetheless held her fix on him. "You said you never raped a girl in your life. You said a lot. But you never once said you did not murder those two elderly women. Did you murder them, Lucas? Did you? Your God would like to know the truth."

Lucas Delaney was the only child of Kathleen and Patrick, two church-going Catholics whose appearances at their son's trial were infamous. They had led a picket of the courthouse, part of which they tried to inject into the trial itself. Every time a witness spoke against their son, the defendant's parents made slit throat gestures, spitting and cursing at anyone close by with a bad word to say about their God-fearing son who would not hurt a fly. It was Newman who had hit upon the notion of using religion to open the man up.

Bliss studied the prisoner. Apparently he did not reserve his glare for American detectives, the full poisonous glower aimed at Chandler for daring to speak. When Delaney made no move to answer her question, Bliss filled the silence.

"You don't like women much, do you?" he said to Delaney. "What's up with that, Lucas? Mummy issues?"

"You leave my mother out of this."

"Did I touch a nerve?"

"Just let it go, man."

"So I did strike a nerve. She treat you badly, Lucas?"

"What did I say?"

The bear's voice grew louder this time. His wrists were cuffed and chained to a thick steel bar set into the table at which they sat. The room was a twelve-foot square box, and the rattle of the chains was loud as the man moved his hands.

"No. I bet it wasn't badly. I bet she treated you really well. Maybe even too well, eh? Your mummy have the hots for her baby boy, Lucas?"

There was just a flinch this time. The slightest rattle of chains. Bliss saw the man's immense frame move, and then settle. Happened in an instant. Same thing happened to Delaney's face; rage creasing the flesh around both eyes, and then smoothing out again. Bliss was impressed with the prisoner's self-control. He wasn't quite sure what it all meant, but whilst the prisoner was not adverse to violence – his killing of Ashley Rider was about as clear-cut as you could possibly find in such a case – Bliss wasn't sure he had looked into the eyes of their man, either.

"Sorry about that, Lucas," Bliss said. "I get a bit carried away sometimes. Tell me, if you did not rape two women, what do you think of the man who did?"

Delaney gave that some thought. Then he said, "I think he should burn in hell."

"Good answer," Bliss said. "Now I think we are getting somewhere."

The door opened without warning and a corrections officer came in with a tray containing four dark drinks in glasses. Delaney chugged his back in a couple of swallows and cuffed his mouth, after which the officer took the empty glass and left again without a word.

"Table service," Bliss said with a smile and a nod towards Delaney. "Now that I wasn't expecting."

"Lawyer arranged it."

Bliss took a sip of his drink. Semi-flat cola of some description. He winced and set the glass aside. "Ugh. Not great."

"You wouldn't have wanted mine, either. It's an acquired taste."

"It looked like cola. What was it, root beer?"

"My special lemonade. We death row prisoners enjoy our treats from time to time. You want something cold and fresh you have to buy it from a vending machine out in the snack room."

Bliss nodded and got back into it. The interview continued for a further hour. At no point were they able to break the man and have him admit to the rapes and murders. Not that Bliss had anticipated they would. The prisoner had been grilled by experts. What he was hoping for was a slip, an observation or word out of place. The closest they got to it was when Delaney asserted that he had never met any of the teens or elderly women. This had been the major barrier for the FBI, because whilst they suspected Delaney had met Darlene Schwartz when he worked for the telephone company, they had never been able to put the two together on any specific date or time. It was Newman who pushed him on this matter.

"Thing is, Lucas," she said. "We know you helped install a new phone system in the Lexington building, which is where Darlene Schwartz worked during that period. Can you really be so certain that you two never crossed paths?"

Delaney sighed as if expressing frustration at a particularly dense child. "I never said I didn't work in Fresno. I never said I didn't work on that project in that building. I think you'll find I never even said I didn't come into contact with the Schwartz woman. What I did say, and will say again now, is that if I did run across her or meet her at any point, it didn't register with me. I must have been in an elevator, walked along a corridor, been in various rooms with dozens of people, maybe a hundred or more who worked there during those weeks. She may have been one of them. If she was, I didn't know because her face meant nothing to me. Not then. Not now."

"So again, you can't definitively say you never met?"

"No. And you can't definitively say I did. I spoke to plenty of people there. Perhaps I even spoke to her."

"That's interesting," Chandler said immediately. "According to your records, you claimed you didn't recall talking to any women while you worked there. Are you now saying you did?"

Delaney paused, and Bliss thought he saw the man's lips curl upwards. "Do you even hear yourself?" the prisoner asked. His eyes became slits. "Do you? Are you a DS because your DCI had a quota to meet? Look at the records again. I said I did not *recall*. Do you know what that means? It means I do not remember.

So if I don't remember, then I cannot say one way or the other. Now, let me make it clear for the morons in the room: Darlene Schwartz and I were in the same building at the same time. That's it."

The man was edgy about it, but Bliss did not think there was anything there. No links between Delaney and the other three victims were discovered. There was no evidence to suggest the man had ever been in either Banning or Palm Springs. No credit card use anywhere nearby. As repulsed as Bliss was by the man, Lucas Delaney was a tenuous suspect at best.

Bliss sat back in his chair and folded his arms. His signal that he was done. Ten minutes later they were back on the road.

TWENTY-TWO

O n the flight back to LA, Bliss realised he had overlooked two potentially valuable resources on this visit. So far he had spoken to two suspects and had one more to go. He had spoken to one cop who had investigated one murder and rape, and had another to go. He would be speaking to the FBI SAC at the time, now retired and residing in a beachside place called Morro Bay. But not one of those people – other than one of their suspects, perhaps – were there whilst any of the crimes were being committed. So intent on discovering their murderer, Bliss had forgotten all about the rape victims; as they probably had been ever since being attacked, he thought, and felt shamed by his own omission. Thing was, they were not merely victims.

They were also survivors.

Bliss asked Newman to set up interviews in between those already arranged if at all possible. The detective said she would do everything within her power, but reminded him that the women might not wish to dredge up something so horrific from their distant pasts. Bliss told Newman he understood entirely, and that he would not pursue the matter if that was the case. The women had to be willing if he was to learn anything valuable from them.

By the time they landed and had cleared out to Newman's vehicle in the LAX parking lot, Bliss had his answers. Rape victim Charlotte Johnson was now living in Fort Lauderdale in Florida, and wanted no part of it. But victim number one, back where it all began in Banning, was still in the state and agreed to talk provided it was later that same afternoon. While she still had the courage.

"This may be the time for you to step forward, Pen," Bliss suggested as they settled into the Ford and waited for the air-con to wash the interior with cold air. "Your specialism might draw something out of this woman, or at the very least you might see or hear something we don't."

Chandler made no reply for a full few seconds. Then she leaned forward and rested her hands on the back of their seats. "Would you mind if I don't? I understand what you're saying, Jimmy. But not only is my head not in the game right now, I've also had my fill of rape and the torment it brings into lives, the havoc it wreaks. I wouldn't be an asset at the moment, and it sounds as if you have one shot at this. I think it best if you two do this one on your own."

Not for the first time, Bliss felt a pang of regret at ever recommending the Sapphire unit to his friend. He felt responsible, as if he had pushed Chandler into an area that obviously affected her deeply and was not without fallout. He thought Chandler was a perfect fit for this particular interview, but refused to push her on it. He knew he could, knew she would buckle if he applied a little pressure. But Bliss would not do that to his friend.

Newman dropped Chandler outside her hotel, then pressed on towards the coast and Laguna Beach. It took them about thirty minutes along the 405, which was relatively clear being a Sunday. The house was on Cliff Drive, overlooking a place signposted as Recreation Point. The residence was stone-fronted, with a tall and wide chimney stack that ate its way through the gabled roof. A triple garage squatted to the rear of the property.

"They must be minted," Bliss said as Newman parked in a bay opposite. He got out to look at the Pacific which seemed close enough to touch, while Newman fed the meter.

She peered at him over the roof of the car. "Does that Englishism mean they must have money? If so, then you'd be right. This is some prime real estate right here."

Palms swayed and rustled in the breeze coming in with the waves crashing to shore. Bliss tilted his head back for a moment.

The light wind felt good on his face, together with the heat from a sun that now plunged towards the ocean in a cloudless blue sky.

"Come on, Jimmy," Newman said. Her voice carried the weight of what they were about to do. "Let's get this over with."

Maddie Biasi was a week shy of her nineteenth birthday when she was raped. Her family lived in Banning and worked in Palm Springs. Her father was a golf instructor, her mother a concierge at the Hilton. Maddie had an older sister and a younger brother. She had spent the afternoon at the Galleria with four friends in nearby Riverside. She then hung out with her boyfriend and two of his pals in Lion Park, before the couple got into an argument and Maddie stormed off on her own. Between there and home, Maddie got snatched up and dragged down onto the dry and dusty river bed, where she had a kitchen knife held to her throat whilst the man who had grabbed her up raped her from behind.

Now in her mid-thirties, Biasi was a stunningly attractive women, slender, tanned and healthy-looking. She wore her jewellery tastefully, and her make-up was applied to enhance rather than conceal. After welcoming the two detectives into her home and pouring them both a chilled glass of homemade lemonade, Biasi showed them into a living room overlooking the ocean front.

"You have a lovely home," Newman said, glancing around appreciatively. The décor was simple, yet everything in it was effective. From the long row of oak bookcases, every shelf stuffed with hardbacks of varying ages and conditions, to the stained-glass bowl that took pride of place on an oak chest that was being used as a coffee table.

"Thank you." Biasi tucked strands of streaked copper hair behind her ears. "My husband is a movie producer. I worked as a make-up artist on a studio lot, where we met. I would not be living in Laguna otherwise, I can tell you."

Bliss liked the woman's modesty. And her poise. Some rape victims fall off the edge of the world, but not this woman. And as she went on to tell them all about her ordeal, without faltering or so much as a strain in her voice, Bliss came to admire Biasi. Yet, as with every other victim or lead so far, this one was also going nowhere.

"I didn't see him, I'm afraid. Felt him. Big and rough. Calloused hands. Smelled him, too."

"According to your statement," Newman prompted, "it seems the odour was the one notable thing about him. That set him apart, I mean."

Biasi nodded. "Yes. It was awful. Pungent. It made me feel sick."

Bliss edged forward on the soft leather chair. "Mrs Biasi, do you mind if I ask you something a little more personal?" he said.

She flicked her gaze at him and gave a tight sardonic smile. "More personal than being raped you mean?"

"I'm sorry. That was tactless of me. I didn't know how to phrase it better."

She waved her hand. "Don't worry about it, please. It's a part of me, who I am. But it's more a part of my past and who I was. I won't pretend it doesn't hurt occasionally still, but I was always determined he would not take me inside my head the way he did that other part of my body. So yes, please ask whatever you like."

"How long did the act itself last?"

Biasi seemed surprised by the questions. "I've not really thought about it in some time, Detective. But I would say it lasted no longer than a couple of minutes. If you mean the actual physical penetration."

"I did, but I didn't want to lead you," Bliss said. "And other than the rape, there was no actual physical violence, either before or after?"

"No. None. He got what he wanted and that was that."

Bliss smiled. "Thank you."

"I think what we were hoping for here," Newman said, "was something new, something you forgot to mention in your witness statements that came to you long afterwards. Perhaps that our visit would jar something loose. Unfortunately, it doesn't look as if that's the case."

"I'm sorry," Biasi shook her head. For the first time since their arrival she looked uncomfortable.

"No, please. I'm the one who should be apologising. The Palm Springs and LA police, plus the FBI all let you down, Mrs Biasi. On their behalf, I am so terribly sorry for the fact that the man who raped you was not apprehended."

The woman looked down at her hands, now clasped together in her lap. "That's very kind of you, but you were not one of them. And I have to be honest and say they were so good to me and did their very best."

"I have to ask one more thing," Bliss said. "You must have been aware of the four suspects who became the primary focus of law enforcement. You may even have been asked about them, shown photographs perhaps. I wonder, Mrs Biasi, was there one of them who just… felt like he could be the one? One who stood out more than the others, for whatever reason."

Their victim and witness gave that some time. Took a deep, long breath. Released it through her nose. "I *was* spoken to, by both the police and FBI, on a few separate occasions. And yes, I was shown a number of photographs and there was an awful lot of detail thrown at me. I was always drawn to the Native American man. Andreas, I believe he was called. But I was still just a teenager when it happened, and when I look back I think my focus on him may have been because he lived nearby. I really had nothing more substantial than that to go on."

"So his photograph and physical description meant nothing to you?" Newman asked.

Biasi shook her head. "No. None of them did."

"But you did consider him to be the more likely of the four."

"I did. I just can't point to any conclusive reason why."

"And later? Now? Any insight since?" Bliss asked the question, knowing full well that he was reaching, but this woman was the only victim they were able to talk to and they had to make the most of it.

"If I ever do think about it, it's only ever briefly," Biasi whispered. "And even then it's more about what happened than who did it to me."

Bliss looked across at Newman. She nodded. They were done.

As they walked back out into the evening heat, the ocean breeze stirred the tall palms once more and its caress was welcome. Bliss looked back over his shoulder. Maddie Biasi was standing by the window. He raised a hand and smiled. She did the same. Bliss felt humbled by Biasi's strength and dignity. He was glad he had thought to include the surviving victims, but at the same time could not help but feel grubby for doing so.

TWENTY-THREE

"Did your father love you, Robbie?" Bliss asked Newman. He was staring out of the windscreen as the Los Angeles streets flashed by in a blur of motion, but he was looking deep into the past.

"He did. Still does as far as I know."

"Mine too. Still would if he could."

"And your point is?" Newman asked.

"We both turned out okay, right? Our fathers loved us, and we turned out well. I read all about the home lives of the four suspects. Their fathers didn't give a flying fuck about any of them, and look how they ended up. You think cause and effect might be in play here?"

Newman glanced across at him. "Not every man hated or abused by his daddy turns out like that, Jimmy. You must know that."

"Of course. I'm just saying, sometimes it goes that way. I'm not suggesting they would all have gone on to be fine upstanding citizens like the two of us if they'd had our fathers. Just – maybe their fathers didn't set them up well to handle everything that life can throw at a person."

"That may be true. Doesn't excuse them."

"I'm not suggesting that, either."

"Then what the hell are you on about, man?" Newman hurriedly shifted her hands on the steering wheel. She was a conscientious ten-to-two driver he noted, even when agitated.

Bliss chuckled. "Should I turn the air-con up, Robbie? You look a bit hot under the collar there."

Newman gave a low growl beneath her breath. "You talk in riddles, you strange, twisted Englishman. Look, I get the whole psycho-babble shit about kids who are treated mean often turn out to treat others the same way. No denying that. I'm just saying it isn't always true, that it need not go down like that."

"I get it. I do. I think what I am trying to say, in my own inelegant way, is that whilst not all victims of childhood abuse turn out to be abusers, the majority of abusers were themselves abused. They did what they did because of what was done to them. And on goes that particularly appalling circle of life. I'm not saying we should give them a break, sing 'Hakuna Matata' and all hug one another. I'm just saying that vicious circle has to be broken, or else we're all fucked."

"Oh, well if that's the point you're making then I'd say we're all fucked."

Bliss nodded. "You know, Robbie, I think you may well be right."

*

They met up with Chandler for drinks and dinner back at her hotel. No one particularly wanted to go out anywhere, the day's exertions catching up with each of them. Before their drinks order had even arrived, Chandler was wanting to know how the interview had gone. Bliss explained that they had drawn little from it, other than Biasi's feeling that Andreas may have been her attacker, and his own sense that this victim at least had moved on and left that awful moment far behind her.

"You know," Bliss said, "I would rather we got nothing from a woman who has come to terms with what happened to her, than a lead from a woman broken by her ordeal."

Chandler's eyes widened. "You really mean that?"

"I do. I was impressed by Maddie Biasi. Happy for her that she was in a good place."

Chandler reached out and gave his hand a squeeze. "You still have it in you to surprise me, Jimmy. You just may be a modern man after all."

Bliss laughed. "I'll take that. You call me a metrosexual, though, and we'll have words."

Newman was looking hard at them, a grin splitting her face. "Are you sure you two have never…" She let it go unsaid.

"Don't start that again, Robbie," Chandler said, shaking her head. "Jimmy and I know where the line is, and we'd never cross it."

"If you say so." Newman was clearly dubious.

"We do," Bliss said firmly, hoping to put a lid on the subject once and for all. "Now can we please move on to another topic."

"Okay. So tomorrow we have a very busy day. We're in the Valley again to see our final suspect. Then up to Ventura to speak with the detective who worked the rape of Charlotte Johnson. After that it's our FBI agent further up the coast. Long day. Lot of driving. I suggest you get all the rest you can tonight."

Bliss nodded. He felt his shoulders fall, his chin dragging down with them. He started breathing through his mouth, as if oxygen had become hard to find. Quite how he had avoided a bad case of the spins so far on this trip he did not know. Given his energy depletion, the absence of them was welcome.

"And the following day we have agreed to meet with your boss to provide feedback, right?"

Newman nodded. "You got it. It was part of the deal for the FBI footing our expenses. You provide feedback to us, we provide feedback to them."

"I don't have a problem with that. Fact is, I think he'll be pleased. We've not uncovered anything that was missed. We've confirmed a few things, got a feel for where our own cases began, but other than that we're leaving it all relatively untouched."

"Why do you think he'd be pleased?" Newman asked.

"Because the cops didn't screw things up."

She pursed her lips. "I think he'd swallow that in exchange for knowing who killed and raped those women."

"Good. Then hopefully when we find our man back home in the UK, we'll be able to ask him."

"You think your guy knows our guy?"

"I'm sure of it. And I think I may just be able to use that knowledge as a lever. I think if we…" Bliss allowed his words to tail off as a thought occurred to him out of the blue.

"Jimmy?" Chandler was staring at him.

Bliss checked his watch. "Sunday has come and gone back home," he said. He smiled at the two women. "Two days since the last rape. Two days have come and gone and no subsequent murder."

"That we know of," Chandler said.

"No, they would have called me immediately, Pen."

"I don't mean that, Jimmy. I mean, a body might not have been discovered yet."

Bliss let go a loud sigh and dropped his head once more. It felt so heavy, he just wanted to rest it on a pillow. "Of course. Bloody idiot. I'm not thinking clearly."

"You okay, boss? You need to rest?" Chandler's look of concern was immediate and unrestrained.

He looked up and nodded. Relief at there having been no murder had been flushed away in an instant. He had not been thinking straight. His mind was unclear. It was a trigger warning, one he had to take notice of.

"Yeah, I think I do. I'm a bit woolly at the moment. I'm going to head off."

"I'll come with you," Newman said, rising from the table. "No sense in taking two separate cabs."

But Bliss shook his head. "No, you take your time and leave when you're ready. Sorry to be a party-pooper, but I think I just need to close my eyes and heal for a while."

Bliss felt his head spinning now. He seemed to have little control over the words he was using. He had learned that when his brain became fatigued at having managed to keep him both upright and lucid for long periods, it started to go into some form of hibernation. That meant it carried on doing the important stuff, but the minor miracles were set aside. The human form of a reboot was required for him to regain some sort of equilibrium, and his body was insisting that he allowed one pretty soon.

Nodding his goodbyes, Bliss walked away and went in search of a cab. Somehow he made it back to his room in one piece.

TWENTY-FOUR

Lorenzo Pines was dying. Lung cancer had visited him at the turn of the year, and before its end it would carry him off into the good night. By all accounts he had never been a huge man, but now he looked rail thin and shrunken. *It was as if he was ageing backwards,* Bliss thought. *Like Brad Pitt in that shit movie.*

"Got a smoke?" Pines asked as the three of them took their seats.

The Valley Vista nursing home was a single-storey structure, its external stucco painted pale blue, the interior walls pale green. Pastel shades for a twilight world. Vivid colour came in the form of paintings and photographs, each in frames made from driftwood, set a foot apart along the corridors.

Not where the aged and-or infirm residents can sit and contemplate them, Bliss noted. Not where something visual might prompt a cerebral response and stir the imagination. That would never do, not here in the eternal departure lounge. Both the area where they first encountered Pines, and the family room where they now gathered, were bare and cheerless places perfectly matching the fading lights of the inhabitants.

Bliss made a show of patting down an imaginary breast pocket before responding to the man's request for a cigarette. "Afraid not. I hear they're bad for your health."

Pines reared back as if he had strayed into the middle of a rattler's nest. "That's harsh," he muttered, in a low, brittle voice. "You do know why I'm here, right?"

"Karma?" Bliss suggested, adding a breezy smile.

"What the hell? Karma for what, man?"

"Well, you did rape and murder several women, Lorenzo. Some might say you're getting off lightly."

Pines hacked a cough into his fist. It was both weak and wet, much like the man himself. He started to rise, using a stick to help lever himself up.

"You know, I agreed to this interview against my lawyer's advice. But he was right, I was wrong, and you Detective Bliss, are a real piece of shit!"

Bliss sensed he had lost the interview. *Bad Bliss. Bad cop.* And look who we have here waiting in the wings to take over. Two good cops. Two good female cops.

"I'm so sorry, Mr Pines," Newman said, interjecting just as they had rehearsed in the car. "Please ignore this dumbass Brit. Now, how about myself and the delightful Penny here persuade you to sit back down. We know our place better than this jerk, and we would love to hear your side of the story."

It was Chandler who had come up with the idea. She thought it would be useful to see how Pines reacted to the dichotomy presented by two women who were both powerful and in control, yet at the same time fawning and conspiratorial with him. Chandler believed it would create an interesting dynamic with this particular suspect, based on his background. Newman had loved the idea and jumped at it. Bliss thought it inspired. He had recovered well overnight, and had waved away the concerns of his colleagues when they met for breakfast. The reboot had done the trick.

For the longest moment, Bliss wondered if he might have pushed too hard. Pines wavered, looking between them. But eventually the man eased himself back into his chair. He jabbed his stick at Bliss.

"You keep your tongue and I'll speak to these two fine ladies."

Bliss raised both hands. "They are welcome to you," he said. He sat back and stared out of the window into the home's rear garden, where stones and trickling water sought to comfort daunted spirits.

"So, Mr Pines," Newman began. "You became a suspect in these awful crimes because you knew one of the victims. Is that right?"

Pines licked his lips. A lizard-like flick of the tongue. "It is. I was a janitor at Cal State. Collins taught English Lit there before she retired."

"And Mrs Collins made an allegation against you, is that also correct?"

"Yeah, a bullshit one."

"Tell us about it," Chandler urged him gently. "Because I can't understand why the police became involved at all."

"You got that right. That bitch had it in for me because I didn't jump every time she snapped her fingers. Damn teachers and professors are like surgeons the way they treat blue collar workers. She told the vice president of the university that I was spying on girls in the changing rooms, that I entered without knocking, that sort of shit."

"That's surely something they could have kept in-house. An internal investigation only. After all, you were the janitor and you had a job to do in those changing rooms. You had every right to be inside them. The only issue here is one of timing. Mistakes happen. I'm sure anything that occurred was accidental."

"Yeah. It's easy done when you have so many other things on your mind."

Interesting, Bliss thought. The way Chandler had phrased the question lured Pines straight into a trap. He had previously denied everything, yet he had just all but admitted some form of intrusion.

"But Mrs Collins and the VP didn't see it the same way, it seems." Chandler shook her head and made a show of looking across at Newman as if their thoughts were in sync. "Sounds to me like a simple misunderstanding that they blew up out of all proportion."

"No wonder you were angry with Sarah Collins," Newman said. "Her complaint led to the university police talking to you, and then an interview with Long Beach officers. You must have felt dreadful, Mr Pines."

"You know it." He nodded furiously. "That bitch would've cost me my job if it weren't for my union stepping in."

"So you had every right to be pissed with her."

"I did. She deserved everything that came her way."

Bliss felt a catch in his throat. They had reached a critical point much earlier than he had expected. Pines had been grilled by experts, and had never once swayed from his expressions of innocence. Having him even hint that he had taken revenge on Sarah Collins would tilt this entire investigation on its axis. *Slowly, detectives,* he thought. *Ease the man into it.*

"Including being murdered?" Chandler said, a pained expression on her face. "She sounds like a horrible women, but I'm sure you wouldn't have wished that on her."

"Well, no. Of course not that." The man looked uncertain, beads of sweat now dotting his brow as he attempted to appear sympathetic. There was no sympathy that Bliss could see, yet neither was there any contrition. Either Pines had not murdered Sarah Collins, or he was unashamed at having done so.

"And, of course, the police and FBI just assumed you were responsible," Chandler prompted, her tone gentle and smooth.

Pines nodded. He glanced across at Newman. "That's right. For no reason."

"Other than the fact she spread rumours about you that almost cost you your job."

"Yeah."

"And that you made threats on her life."

"Yeah." Pines frowned, and he shifted on his seat. "I was angry. We all say shit when we're angry."

"I agree. But see it from the perspective of the police if you can, Mr Pines. There's this woman who pissed you off enough for you to say you would cut and kill the bitch, and then shortly afterwards she is cut and killed. You can see why they looked at you, yes?"

"I guess. But they came at me hard. They kept coming, too. My lawyer said it was a disgrace the way they kept coming back at me."

Pines appeared genuinely indignant. Not that this meant anything. Bliss had lost count of the times he had witnessed nailed-on guilty criminals complain bitterly at what they perceived to be victimisation.

"Mr Pines, there is no doubt in my mind that you were badly treated," Chandler said. She fixed him with her most understanding of smiles. "Both by Mrs Collins and then the police and after that the FBI. But that was a long time ago, and circumstances have now changed. You've got only a short time to live, and I think we can make it work out that you go out on top. You'd like to stick it to them, wouldn't you, Mr Pines? Those cops and agents who plagued your life for so long."

Pines nodded. The lizard-lick tongue darted again. "I would. I surely would. You think you can make that happen?"

"I do."

"How."

"Confess, Mr Pines. Imagine the faces on all those cops and agents, the people where you used to work, anyone in fact who believed you to be guilty. You tell them now that you did it, and exactly how, you will ruin their lives. They won't believe how you blew them off and got away with it for so long. You unwind your middle finger at them all and show them how you had the last laugh."

Pines blinked. Looked across to Newman. Even to Bliss. Then back to Chandler. Then he laughed. He laughed hard and long, and just about hacked up what was left of the good part of his lung in the process. His eyes squeezed out some tears, and his cheeks took on colour they had probably not seen in years. When he was done, Pines wiped his eyes with the palm of his hand and leaned back in his chair. Sipped from his plastic no-spill tumbler of water.

"Thank you," Pines said. "I needed that. Been a while since I laughed so hard I damn near wet myself. Darlin', you really think if I was guilty that would've worked on me? I got cancer, not brain damage. Now, if you don't mind, I need my rest and I'd be obliged if you would all just get the fuck outta here."

*

The cop who had worked the remaining rape case had cancelled on them, so they headed north-west towards the coast and blew through Ventura rather than stopping to try and persuade the man. Bliss did not think he would offer any further insight, and was happy to have a less busy day.

A life of service was all Don Connelly had ever wanted or known. First as a marine, then a Maine homicide detective, and finally an FBI agent. He had served all three with pleasure and distinction, before putting in his papers at the age of sixty. An east-coast boy, his FBI posting to California had given him a taste for the climate and terrain on the other side of the country, which is why he chose to live out his retirement by the ocean.

Every police officer or FBI agent saw plenty of investigations fall by the wayside without achieving a successful resolution. They first became open-unsolved, then plain old unsolved. Most are just cases; they come and go on the breeze. But every officer or agent also has one case above all others that stays with them. Haunts their dreams. For ex-Special Agent-in-Charge Don Connelly, the three rapes and three murders that came together to form a single investigation, was the one he found impossible to let go of.

Morro Bay, a few miles to the north and west of San Luis Obispo, was the largely unspoiled coastal town to which Connelly had moved when he left Los Angeles. By then he had buried both his wife and son – the former to a heart attack that stopped her from breathing even before the ambulance arrived, the latter to a sniper's bullet in Afghanistan. A fit, good-looking senior with his own place by the sea, a decent head of hair, and most of his marbles remaining, attracted many suitors. But the ex-agent chose to remain alone.

"But not lonely," he assured them, a shy smile adding warmth to his eyes.

They sat outside by the pool, shielded from the worst effects of the sun by a canvas awning that whipped and cut through the breeze with a crack from time to time, like a ship's rigging. Newman and Chandler sipped iced tea, but Bliss had gone with a chilled bottle of Anchor Steam beer to match the one Connelly had been drinking when they arrived.

Once they were settled, their host took them through his side of the investigation. Connelly revealed that, by the time it dropped on his desk, the rapes and murders had already been linked. The behavioural sciences team out in Quantico had fought against that decision all the way, but eventually even they admitted that freaks existed, and not everything could be wrapped up neat and presented with a pretty bow on top. Occasionally, people stepped outside the boundaries of explicable and predictable behaviour. The dates, the odour, and the investigative instincts, suggested that had happened here.

"Exactly the same as our operations back home," Bliss said, feeling an immediate bond with the pleasant and friendly retiree.

"But we're not talking about it being the same unsub, right?" Connelly said. "The age gap wouldn't work, I'm guessing."

"We can't know for certain, but it's extremely unlikely. I'm getting the sense of a completely different physicality as well. Your perp here is a relatively big man, whereas ours is slight."

"So... what are you thinking? A copycat? Of an obscure, relatively unknown, certainly uncelebrated crime?"

"You're right to be sceptical," Bliss said. "But I don't know how else to explain it. Same MO. Same odour. The two-day gap between rape and murder. That can't be a coincidence."

Connelly took a final pull from his sweating bottle. Shook his head. "No. No, you're right about that. But you mentioned the odour. Are you suggesting that your suspect has in some way manufactured a smell in order to complete the full replication?"

Bliss drank from his bottle before responding. "I haven't really given it much thought, but once again if you follow the logic then you come to that conclusion, yes. If it's not the same man, then it's a copycat. If it's a copycat, then the odour is part of the signature only, and therefore manufactured."

"It makes sense when you say it out loud, I guess. So, if you don't mind my asking, Jimmy, what exactly is it you're still looking for out here if not your own unsub?"

"Conviction." Bliss replied without pause.

It was a good question, and one he had wrestled with all along. He glanced from face to face around the table before continuing.

"I knew it. Or at least, believed I did. It would have made things so much easier if I was wrong. But I also wavered, and in doing so I managed to dissuade myself away from that instinctive certainty. So yes, I wanted to regain all that. And I have. But I also badly needed to clear my head and start the process of rethinking everything. Usually that means starting at the beginning. In this case, the beginning was here."

"But you just agreed the same man could not be responsible." Connelly frowned at him.

"I know. But whatever kick-started our man back home, began here. In Banning, to be precise. A rape, followed two days later by a murder. And something about them, plus the other rapes and murders, ignited a similar spree some fifteen years later over 5,000 miles away. The origins of our investigations are here, and here is where I believe my answers can be found."

They had another beer and more iced tea. Chatted a while. About things other than crimes. But then it came around again – as it always does when law enforcement gathers together.

"So, did you ever have a favourite suspect?" Newman asked Connelly. "One who stood out more than the other three?"

Connelly barked a bitter laugh. "Oh, that's a long, hard road that leads to dark nights of the soul, young lady. I chase my personal demons down that road to hell all the time. Now, my predecessor, he didn't look much beyond Raymond Andreas. Said he was convinced of it because both the first rape and murder took place in the same general location, and so that's where the unsub was also most likely to live. That spelled the Native American to him, naturally."

"It's not a terrible line of thinking," Chandler said.

"No, it's not. Often it's accurate. And shared by the Palm Springs PD at the time, too. What was that great line in *Silence Of The Lambs* about first coveting what we see? That's a good fit in this case."

"So for your predecessor, the case died when Andreas did."

"Yes, ma'am. Killed it stone dead in his heart."

"But not in reality. In reality it had to continue. And you still haven't hung your hat on anyone I notice, Mr Connelly." Chandler gave an easy grin.

He matched it, creasing his tanned face and neck. "Okay. I'll tell you what I've told plenty of other folk since. My money at the time was on Pines"

"He have the body odour problem back then?" Bliss asked, looking up sharply.

"Not that I noticed."

"You would have, by all accounts. But that's certainly one thing all four suspects shared: the *lack* of body odour. How did you explain that?"

"We didn't. Only in that a great deal of time passed between the crimes and us being able to talk to any suspects. I think it was assumed the unsub had cleaned up his act by then. Anyhow, it had to be one of them." The man shrugged.

"Did it?" Bliss asked. His thoughts had recently taken him down a different path. "Only if the rapist-killer was one of the four suspects who made the final cut. What if it wasn't?"

Connelly paused, bottle to lips. He took a breath and set the beer to one side. "It's not that we didn't consider that possibility. We did, of course we did. It's just we were convinced that those four from everyone we spoke to were the only suspects who could have conceivably been at every crime scene. Believe me, we went through a lot of potential suspects before we managed to narrow it down to just four. DNA gave us nothing, so there was no magic bullet to chamber for our hunt. But like I say, we did always wonder if the unsub had never made the original list." He shook his head, and rubbed his mouth. "I guess I don't really even want to think about that possibility anymore."

"I've seen nothing wrong so far with either the police or FBI investigations," Bliss said quickly, hoping to allay Connelly's fears. "Sometimes you just have to accept it's not going to happen. If he'd gone on longer he might have made a mistake. But then another young girl might have been raped, another elderly woman murdered. If not getting your man is the price you have to pay for no more victims, it's one you live with."

Connelly's head came up. His eyes brightened and a smile touched his lips once more. "You know, I never looked at it that way before, Jimmy. I thank you for that, I surely do. But yeah, if that's the price then I would pay it in a heartbeat. It gets to me still. When I'm alone sometimes and I get around to reflecting on the past, this damned case will yank on a few hairs at the back of my neck. Sets a cold feeling in my gut for days. But it melts away after a time and I get on with my life. Only thing to do. But you're right, Jimmy. It's a fair price."

"Only for us it goes on back home," Chandler said. She tossed back the last of her drink. Shook her head. "Isn't that a cheery thought."

TWENTY-FIVE

Bliss sat alone in his hotel room. It was one-thirty in the morning but sleep eluded him, although he was weary beyond belief. His condition was predictable in only one sense: when he had a vertigo attack one day, it would be followed the next by fatigue. It was also cumulative, so too many attacks – no matter how minor – left him feeling it deep in his core. Adrenaline only got him so far.

At least his mind was occupied. On the long drive back to LA Bliss had thought of something that might provide the additional insight they were looking for. He had asked Newman to contact her FBI liaison and have them produce as much digital information relating to all four suspects as they could. He wanted mail, signed deliveries, social media exchanges, posts on forums, anything and everything. He knew it would take time pulling it all together, but Bliss was hoping that tucked away within that data they would find some form of contact between the US perpetrator and their own twisted psychopath. Bliss was particularly keen to read through any fan mail from a Lucas Delaney acolyte. There had to be a trail, he was convinced of that.

The first batch of information came through quickly. Data mining such personal material was generally a bureaucratic nightmare wrapped in red tape as thick as a man's thigh. But that was not entirely the case with the incarcerated Delaney. Not only was his capacity for such exchanges vastly diminished due to the amount of time he had spent in prison, but it also provided easy and relatively instantaneous access. At the very least it might eliminate him from further investigation.

A similar case could be argued for Andreas. The man was dead, which was something for the Bureau to explore. They promised to dig deeper, but were able to transmit a great many files relating to the man on death row.

Bliss had downloaded the data files to his laptop, which he took down to the hotel's office services room, where he hooked it up to a printer. It churned out 137 sheets of paper in total, and Bliss put the cost on his room's tab. For the past ninety minutes since returning to the room he had been sifting through the hard copy records, at times scanning when the details were of no relevance, at other times squinting hard in concentration.

When his thinking became woolly, Bliss decided to get some fresh air. He left the Sheraton and on impulse turned right, heading nowhere in particular. It seemed to be never completely dark in LA, especially close to the airport where the night sky took on an amber glow. The area was choked with hotels and airport parking lots, feeding the frenzy that was LAX. Bliss drifted by a huge 24-hour open car park, marvelling at the sheer volume of vehicles standing silently in the night. As he approached a car rental complex, Bliss felt the prickle of something scuttle across his neck.

He was not alone.

Bliss turned, ready to confront whoever had sought him out.

He was astonished to recognise the man who stood there now, only two yards away.

"Pines?" Bliss said, his eyebrows scrunching together. "What the hell?"

Back at his nursing home, Lorenzo Pines had not looked as if he had the strength to stand, let alone leave the building to track Bliss down here. Unshaven and scrawny-looking, the man appeared to offer no real threat. Not until he pulled a gun out of his jacket pocket. That got Bliss's attention, who then heard the steady approach of a vehicle, which drew up to the kerb. Pines waggled the gun.

"Get in," he said, his voice dry and ragged. "Let's take a ride."

Bliss did as instructed. As he opened the rear door to the long and wide saloon that had stopped alongside them, he asked himself how he had got it so badly wrong. There was no doubt in his mind that Lorenzo Pines was a piece of shit. A waste of skin, blood, sinew and bone. Bliss was convinced that the man was perverted, that Pines had indeed spied on young girls as they showered and changed. It was also a pretty safe bet that Pines had given Sarah Collins a hard time after the teacher had made a formal complaint about him. Bliss's gut, however, had told him that Pines was not their man. He came across as the seedy type who would get his kicks from hard-core voyeurism, but that when it came to the real deal and actual physical contact, he would slink back beneath the stone from which his kind so often emerge into the fading light.

On the two or three occasions that he attempted to speak during the drive, Bliss was shut down by Pines raising the revolver and jamming the barrel against the side of his head. It brought back some terrible memories, of a man he had once trusted and stood shoulder to shoulder with. A fellow cop who had first betrayed him and then tried to kill him.

That had been a situation he had controlled.

This was very different.

Pines only spoke to the driver a couple of times, calling him Stan. The car had turned around and headed in the direction of route one, following it through onto Lincoln Boulevard. They cruised through Mar Vista, Santa Monica, Pacific Palisades, and then on the edge of Topanga State Park the driver slipped off the slick surface of the Pacific Coast Highway onto a dusty, rutted road that started climbing into the hillside, the Pacific Ocean dark and brooding as it glistened behind them. Every 100 yards or so there were signs warning of undeveloped surfaces and no exit. The hillside seemed to lean in to brush against them, soil and roots jutting out like skeletal hands attempting to grasp them and prevent further passage. The road wound its way up higher into the hills until it ran out of steam, a wall of trees preventing it and them from going any further.

"Out," Pines ordered as the car came to a halt.

He and Bliss were joined by the driver. Pines moved ahead, walking across to a small clearing that sat pointing at the ocean, the canyon falling away steeply beneath them. Bliss peered over the edge and saw nothing other than darkness below. His every nerve-end was jangling, senses acutely heightened, but his mind was churning. He was not certain of Pines' endgame here, and during the forty-minute drive had decided to wait it out until waiting was no longer an option. It looked as if they had reached that point.

Stan was a lot bigger when he stepped out of the car than he had appeared stuffed into it. A black man, tall and wide and round, the driver seemed uneasy with his own bulk as he moved. His side-to-side gait used up a lot of energy getting him not very far at all. He brought up the rear, and after only thirty or so paces was breathing heavily, like an asthmatic. He wore a massive white T-shirt sporting the Adidas logo, equally huge knee-length shorts and black sneakers that to Bliss looked twice the size of his own.

"You busted my chops when you came to talk to me," Pines said to Bliss. He was also wheezing, and were it not for the gun in his hand Bliss would have considered the whole thing absurd. "You allowed those two bitches to dominate the conversation, but I could tell you were the one pulling the strings. I guessed you might have figured me out, so I thought it best you and I had a pow-wow. I brought Stan here along for protection, given my state of health. I think he's enough, don't you, Detective?"

Bliss nodded. "I'd say so. The gun in your hand helps as well."

Pines hacked a laugh, spat a wad of phlegm out into the dirt at his feet. "You don't say much, Detective, but what you do say counts. I like that about you."

"So why don't you do the same, Pines. Tell me how you did it? I walked away from our interview believing you were not the right fit. How did you manage to convince me, the police and the FBI of that?"

The gaunt, narrow man cackled again. An ugly moist sound. "And there was me thinking you were Dick-fucking-Tracy. Damn. You got me wrong all over again, fellah. Did not kill that bitch Sarah Collins. Sure, I'd've fucked her over with a two-by-four if I didn't think the bitch would've enjoyed it. I didn't touch her, though."

Bliss glanced across at Stan, back to Pines. "So what's this all about then? Why are we all here."

Pines shook his head, slow movements that looked as if they gave him pain. His pink tongue worked its way in and out of his mouth.

"Man, I thought you'd figured me out. I watched those girls just like Collins said I did. Sometimes I'd walk in on one of them while they were changing. I'm no paedophile, right, cause them girls were of age. Let's get that straight between us. Man, that was some fine, sweet-looking young pussy, though. Tits so firm you could bounce a coin off them. I'd walk out of there with a boner like you wouldn't believe. One girl wearing only a towel almost collided with me one day as I turned to leave, and I brushed my dick right up against her thigh. Fuck. I nearly shot my wad there and then on the spot. Thing is, couple of times I did more than look. Coupla times when I was lucky enough to trap a girl in there on her own, I grabbed myself a feel. Didn't fuck 'em, but I got myself a good handful of those big, round titties and knuckle-deep in their twats."

Bliss was repulsed by this confession, and Pines must have seen it in his eyes. "What? You never fancied yourself slipping into some young cooze? I'm not talking kids, Detective. These are legal teens, man."

"Don't you bracket you and me together," Bliss said, his "wait and see" policy now out of the window. "You think me casually admiring a young woman's body from afar is the same as you copping a feel of some terrified teen? What did you do, threaten them with something if they told on you? They didn't speak out so you must have done something."

Pines idly waved the revolver around. It was a big beast, and Bliss imagined it would probably take his head off at this distance. He wondered how stable it was. Perhaps when Lorenzo Pines came to pull the trigger the bullet would backfire and explode in his hand.

"I did what I had to do," Pines acknowledged. "They moved on. No harm done. It was a quick feel, that's all. They were all getting much more than that from their boyfriends on a Saturday night I can tell you."

"A quick feel which they did not give permission for."

"Hey, I could've fucked 'em."

"Yeah, you spared them that at least. You're a real stand-up guy, Pines."

This time the gun was pointed straight at Bliss's face, its barrel just a couple of feet away. Bliss took an involuntary step back, which made Pines laugh. His narrow shoulders jerked as his chest went into spasm for a couple of seconds.

Stan had said nothing since they had all got out of the car. Bliss threw him a sidelong glance, weighing up his options now that Pines was starting to lose his cool. The large black man was not staring at Bliss, however. His attention was all on Pines, and by the look on his face he was not pleased about something he had heard. Stan opened his mouth as if about to speak, but the moment broke when there was a snap in the air and a harsh rustle of scrub out in the darkness of the trees that stood by like dark sentinels.

"The fuck was that?" Pines said, spinning around and almost stumbling as his body turned.

"Coyote," Stan told him.

"For real?"

"Fuck, yeah. Coyotes gotta eat don't they?"

"Fucker comes for me I'll make that coyote uuugggleee." Pines waved the gun in the air and cackled at his own joke, a wet abrasive rasp.

"Be cool, man There be three of us and only one of him."

"How the hell you know there's only one of those motherfuckers out there?"

"Cause I gotta brain, man. Coyote don't hunt in packs."

"Well, there'll be only two of us soon enough, so you better be right."

Stan flexed his shoulders and puffed out his chest. Bliss looked on hoping the pair would turn on each other and forget all about him. It was clear that Pines intended to kill him up here in the hills.

"What?" Pines snapped at his partner in crime. "The fuck you gettin' all pussy about?"

"Forget the damn coyote man," Stan said to Pines, putting some weight behind his words. "The only animal around here I care about is you. You touched girls? You really did that, man? You asked me to snatch this guy up, drive you out here, back you up if things got outta hand. You never said shit about touching girls."

"They were young women," Pines said, shooting him an angry glare. "Eighteen, nineteen or so. Nothing to get bent out of shape about, Stan."

"But you didn't ask them first. They never said you could."

Pines whirled, the gun weaving tiny circles in the air once more. "What the fuck do you care, Stanley?!" His voice was weak and hoarse, but it was filled to the brim with venom and now starting to overflow. "You drive and you help me with this prick. That's it. That was our deal. Who the fuck asked you to comment?"

He shook his head angrily and pivoted back towards Bliss. The gun came around with him.

There was a sharp crack, and Pines' right eye disappeared inward, the back of his head exploding in a glut of bone and brain and gore. Stan stood there looking on with little apparent sympathy or horror when Lorenzo Pines fell to the ground as if his legs had been chopped away beneath him. Bliss felt his jaw drop and his mouth fell wide open, shocked by the casual violence and fearing he might be next. Only Stan was not holding a weapon.

They came in heavily, then, loud voices calling for Stan to get on his knees and to put his hands on his head. Bliss turned to see dark figures emerging from the deeper blackness around them. Wearing what looked like black motorcycle helmets, and armed with high-powered semi-automatic rifles, the Los Angeles SWAT team descended upon Bliss and Pine's driver with swift assurance. Bliss sank to his knees also, not wanting any trigger-happy team member to see him as a threat and take him out accidentally.

Bringing up the rear of this charging mass of testosterone, a familiar figure.

Detective Newman.

Newman strode purposefully across the dirt and helped Bliss to his feet, smiling warmly. "You okay?" she asked, appraising him closely.

Bliss nodded, feeling his chest tighten, pulse racing hard. "I am now. How the hell did you find me?"

A hefty figure dressed in a suit beneath his body armour stepped forward. "Ah, that would be me you'd need to thank," he said.

Bliss warily shook the man's offered hand. "And who might you be?" he asked.

"Lieutenant Brandon Mills."

"And you're responsible for finding me?"

Bliss knew he ought to be sounding more grateful right now, but from the corner of his eye he could see Newman looking down at the ground, scratching the toe-end of her boot in the dirt, and he got a sense he was not going to like what he was about to hear. Some coyote, he thought.

"Well, I am the person who gave the order to have your phone traced from the moment you landed at LAX, so you might say I just saved your life, Detective."

Bliss considered that for a few seconds. Then shook his head. "I don't think so," he responded defiantly.

Bliss glanced across at the giant of a man having his hands cuffed behind his back, surrounded by half a dozen cops aiming their weapons at him. The barrage of noise that had accompanied their entrance had all but died away, but the movement remained constant, and lights flashed and flickered all around them.

"I have a feeling Stan there was about to step in and put Pines down."

The driver looked up and over at him. "I woulda broke his damn chicken neck. I don't like no perverts and I don't let no motherfucker talk to me that way."

Bliss nodded and turned to Mills. "And you... You tracked me without my permission?"

"Didn't need it. This is my city, Detective Bliss. I couldn't let you run loose over here while you were looking into our cold cases. That wouldn't have been due diligence on my part. I just wanted to keep track of your movements, that's all."

"That's all, Mills? You ever heard of something called professional courtesy?"

"Yeah. Usually from people whining because they didn't get their own way. Not often I hear it from someone who really ought to be more grateful."

It took all of Bliss's inner strength not to take a swing at the smug prick. The man had stepped way over the line and thought he deserved praise for doing so. Instead of reacting, Bliss breathed slow and steady through his nostrils. Looked across at Newman.

"Any chance you could take me back to my hotel?" he asked.

"Sure." Newman did not even pause to check if it was okay with her boss.

As Bliss was about to turn, he steadied himself. Looked back at the black man, who was being hauled upright, his rights being read to him. "That's a nice car, Stan. What is it?"

"Pontiac Leman. 1985."

"I hope you get to drive it again soon." Bliss felt no animosity towards the man. He didn't believe Stan had any idea about what Pines had in mind when he offered to drive him around and act as muscle for him. "Say nothing, get a lawyer. I'll put in a good word for you."

The big man gave a nod that told Bliss he knew the system was stacked against him and he would be doing time for as long as the LAPD could enforce.

"Come on, Jimmy," Newman said, taking hold of his arm. "Let's get you out of here."

TWENTY-SIX

Dawn had come and gone, and Bliss had not slept at all. After waving Newman goodbye at the drop-off point outside the hotel, he had started sifting through the data files again the moment he got back to his room. He couldn't quite believe what had happened, and it was impossible to stop seeing the way Pines had bowed out, no matter how often Bliss tried to wipe the memory away. He found himself speculating as to how close he had actually come to being murdered. His initial assessment of the situation had been that Pines was acting like a tough guy handing out a warning. A beating, perhaps, and certainly leaving Bliss up there on the hillside afterwards. But Pines had become unglued pretty swiftly, and in the end Bliss had believed the man was going to kill him.

Bliss was unbalanced again and a little fuzzy around the edges; the spins were mild this time, but more frequent. Stress. He didn't think he had more than another day in him, which was fine as they were due to head home tomorrow anyway. Bliss so badly wanted to find something, though, some nugget to take back with him. It existed, and now their search could at least be narrowed down because Lorenzo Pines was not their culprit.

Whilst poring over a list of Delaney's physical post – every one of which had been scanned to PDF – and a number of miscellaneous items delivered to San Quentin in his name, Bliss had the overwhelming impression that he had missed something. The harder he tried, the more it swam out of view. Bliss was beat, his eyes were raw, but if he was ever going to find the missing piece it had to be now. In that moment something occurred to him. Bliss used the hotel phone to request a number and to be put through directly. After a few minutes of back and forth he managed to get through to a supervisor at San Quentin, whose remit covered the correction officers on death row.

Bliss explained that he had been part of the trio of law enforcement officers who had met with Lucas Delaney. "I'm interested in the drink he received during the meeting," Bliss said. "It was black in colour but wasn't a cola or anything like that. The prisoner told us it was his special lemonade. I was wondering if you could tell me more about it."

"I'm afraid not," the supervisor responded immediately. "That right there is protected information, due to privacy laws. I can't divulge that information over the telephone."

"Privacy laws. Concerning what he likes to drink?"

"More like *has* to. That's all I'm prepared to say."

Even more curious now, Bliss started sifting through the data he'd received with renewed vigour. Twenty minutes later a bulb lit up inside his head.

First there was a single paragraph about the prisoner requiring a glass of Black Magic every hour when in stressful situations or when exercising. Bliss ran a search and discovered the black drink Delaney had been given was an activated charcoal, which was often used to cleanse the body of toxins. Bliss wasn't sure why anyone would need that when in certain situations, but decided it was probably nothing and certainly not worth spending any more time on.

On the same sheet of paper, further down the page, was the section that really ignited the bulb. Once a year, Delaney received a package sent from the UK. The only detail provided suggested the package contained a toiletry item by the name of Clinirol, a quantity of four items in the package. Bliss frowned, and stared off into empty space for a moment. Why would Delaney have to resort to ordering anything from the UK, let alone a toiletry item? Bliss's impression was that if they did not have something in the USA then it probably did not exist.

He booted up the laptop again, loaded Google and ran a search. What he saw on the screen next brought a gasp from the back of his throat. Bliss felt numbed. He knew his mouth was hanging open, eyes wide and round, stomach suddenly roiling, but he was incapable of controlling any of it at that precise moment. It could not be this easy, he told himself. Yet the home page of this website suggested otherwise.

It had been sitting there all this time. Waiting for someone to come along and ask the right question. Nobody had. Not even him, as this discovery had been landed as part of a mass trawl in a large ocean rather than a single hook in a small pond.

Bliss swallowed thickly and picked up his mobile which was sitting on the bed beside him. He called Chandler's phone. It rang five times before it was answered.

"This better be either Jimmy Bliss or a heavy breather at this time of morning," Chandler said, her voice dry and distant.

"I've found him."

The silence that followed lasted so long that Bliss felt compelled to repeat himself.

"I've found him."

"I thought that was what you said, but I was busy slapping myself awake. You found who, Jimmy?"

"Our rapist-killer. Correction, *their* rapist-killer. I found the man who began this whole sorry mess."

"I almost daren't ask," Chandler said, composed and alert now by the sound of it.

"Lucas Delaney."

"I don't believe it."

"Me neither. He only made it in at third on my list."

"Behind Andreas and Pines, right?"

"Right. But it's Delaney, and the truth has been there all the time, Pen."

Bliss explained how he had combed through data search results, the masses of information he had printed out.

"So I noticed the annual package from the UK, located the description of the items they contained, then I Googled Clinirol and there it was on my screen."

"What was?"

"The answer. Clinirol is a heavy-duty antiperspirant. The kind of stuff they don't sell at Boots or Walmart. It's so powerful you use it only every two or three weeks or so. It's used in the treatment of excessive sweating and—"

"Body odour."

"Indeed. And you remember the drink they gave him? It's activated charcoal, and it can help to control the excretion of toxins in the event of excessive sweating brought on by exercise and, among other things, stressful situations."

"Fuck, Jimmy! Fuck!"

"I know. Fuck indeed."

"But why order in from the UK?"

"That's puzzling me as well. Fancy an early start to the day, Pen?"

"Order in some coffee from room service. I'm on my way."

"I'll order for three. I have to call Newman."

*

There was no way Bliss could get around telling Chandler about Pines, so he just plunged straight in at the deep end. She sat on the edge of his bed, her eyes widening and tension etching itself into her features as he walked her through it piece by piece.

"Those fuckers!" was what she said when he was done. "They're tracking us?"

"Well, me I know for certain. You as well would be my guess."

Chandler shook her head. "You can't trust anybody these days. Especially you, Jimmy Bliss."

He knew he was in trouble. Chandler only ever used his full name when she was livid with him. Despite her size she could be fearsome when riled. What she lacked in bite she more than made up for in bark.

"What did I do?" he asked.

"What did you..? You were abducted, whisked off into the hills and almost murdered. Most people would have opened with that when they placed a call to their partner."

Bliss wanted to argue, but Chandler was right. As she always seemed to be. He shrugged a little hopelessly. "I was excited. I found something concrete. Or, perhaps the ingredients for it anyway."

Newman arrived moments later. She entered the room hesitantly. "I come in peace," she said, giving her widest smile.

"Only if those bloody traces are not still running," Chandler said, her tone suggesting a thawing frost.

"Not my call. However, I did make my feelings clear on the matter. For what it's worth."

Bliss watched Newman closely as she took a chair at the circular table by the window that ran the width of the room. "So you knew our phones were being tracked then?"

Newman nodded. Her ponytail bobbed. "I did. I'm sorry. The decision was made above my pay grade."

"I have to say I feel a little betrayed. We are not here looking to cause anyone any trouble. I doubt any of our past cases would stand up to close scrutiny years after they took place, and that is understood at all levels, which is why cold case squads exist at all."

"I understand that, Jimmy. Really I do. But *you* have to understand that at a certain level within our law enforcement structures, people are elected to their posts. They are extremely protective of them, even long after they have moved on or retired. Fact is, they didn't much like the thought of you digging around and they decided to keep track of you. It's not nice, hardly in the spirit of co-operation, but neither is it the worst thing to have happened since you arrived."

"Yes, well I just heard all about that," Chandler said. "I'm still in shock I think."

"Especially after our run-in with armed Native Americans in the desert on our second night."

"Your what with who and where?"

Newman pulled a pained expression. "Ah. Jimmy didn't tell you about that."

"No. No, he didn't."

Bliss cleared his throat. "All right," he said. "Clearly we could discuss a lot of things here this morning, but I think it's time we got back to the reason you're both in my room right now."

*

Bliss had pieced together all four sides of the puzzle, the hard edges that framed the bigger picture. With the help of both Chandler and Newman, they completed the entire image just as the sun crept out from behind its early morning cloud cover over Los Angeles.

Lucas Delaney suffered with a condition by the name of Trimethylaminuria; a rare metabolic disorder, also known as TMAU-Syndrome. It had nothing to do with personal hygiene, which blew their original working theory out of the water. The odour could be controlled by specialist roll-on anti-perspirant. According to his records, Delaney had tried products available across the USA, but an allergic reaction to certain chemicals used by American manufacturers brought him out in an irritating rash. The prisoner's lawyer had fought to have Clinirol imported from the UK, and the single annual delivery provided enough of the roll-on to last Delaney a year.

"I can't believe this was missed," Newman said as the details became clear. "It's an oversight of immense proportions."

She, Bliss and Chandler were seated around the low wooden coffee table in his room. Two pots, both now empty of the hot drinks they had carried, stood on a tray together with their three equally empty cups.

"It is an oversight, but it's an understandable one," Bliss said. "No one involved with the investigation would have had any idea that Delaney had this condition, that he used the product, or that he was having it imported every year. It's described as a clinical product. Even if an investigator had read the information, it would have been discarded. Same with the charcoal. Delaney's lawyer would know more, but to anyone else it's just a drink to help with toxins. It's only really when you put the two together that you start to wonder. You'd have to be looking for it. "

"Yeah. So why wasn't anyone doing just that? The rape victims described the smell. None of the suspects smelled. That was dismissed too easily. Somebody ought to have focussed on why that might have been."

"If I hadn't been there to see him take that drink, I doubt I would ever have become curious," Bliss said. "That alone caused me to start looking at specific information."

"The boss is right." Chandler rolled her neck muscles. "Robbie, when you're dealing with something as big as rape and murder, minor details that seem insignificant slip through the net. I'm not saying the odour aspect itself was insignificant, only that the details about Delaney's annual order of a clinical item was. As was the fact that he used a drink designed to flush out toxins."

Newman shook her head. "I feel as if we screwed the pooch here. Exactly what my bosses did not want to happen."

"We all missed it," Bliss said.

"You didn't."

"I did. And then I discovered it by accident. I wasn't looking for a reason why these men had no odour. It was blind luck."

"I have a question," Chandler said. She was squinting at a piece of paper. "If I'm reading this correctly, Delaney had his lawyer petition to have this Clinirol product imported."

"That's right." Bliss nodded, wondering where Chandler was taking them, given they had already established this fact.

"So how did he know?"

"How did who know what?"

"How did Delaney know the UK product wouldn't irritate him in the same way?"

Bliss pondered that for a few seconds. He then shrugged and said, "I suppose he looked for a product lacking the chemical or ingredient that the US ones had."

"You think? Did Delaney strike you as the sort of man who would know that?"

"He's no fool," Newman chipped in. "He could have asked. Researched."

Bliss was staring at Chandler. By the look on her face, something was churning inside her head. He had grown to trust that look.

"Tell us what you're thinking, Pen," he said.

"I'm not quite sure. It's just a crazy notion right now."

"You know me: I love a crazy notion. Come on, spill. It was you who first suggested the possibility of a connection between the ops remember."

Chandler swallowed. Regarded the two of them thoughtfully. Seemed to reach a decision. "Okay. How easy would it be to find out if Lucas Delaney had ever been out of the country?"

Bliss had one leg crossed over the other, his laptop open and running on his lap. He sat up straight, one hand holding the laptop to prevent it falling. The sensation he had experienced when laying eyes on that website for the first time was back with him. Now he knew precisely where Chandler had been leading this.

"You mean home," Bliss said. "The UK."

Chandler nodded. "We have been asking ourselves how the specific details of both the rapes and murders were passed on from the US perp to ours in the UK. What if Delaney was there to do it in person? And remember his dig at me during the interview? He seemed to know how UK police ranks worked. Sure, he could have read it somewhere. But equally, he could know because he spent time there."

Bliss's eyes flicked back to his laptop monitor. Something Chandler had just said chimed with the medical condition information he had been reading. There was something he was missing, and it linked in with Chandler's idea. He shook his head as he read the information again. No, not Chandler's idea exactly. More the way she had expressed it. Bliss thought back: what exactly had she said?

He ran it back. And again.

"Jimmy?" this from Newman.

Bliss raised a hand. Chandler had mentioned how the specific details had been passed on. That was the phrase that now gnawed at him. Where could there possibly be a link with what he was reading? He blinked and read the relevant paragraph again.

Trimethylaminuria is a metabolic enzyme defect. An uncommon—

"Fuck!" Bliss said. Something solid and heavy appeared inside his chest and lodged there like a cannonball. His temples throbbed, and his skin prickled. He felt as if his head was on fire.

"Jimmy?" Newman's tone was more insistent this time.

Bliss looked up at them. Chandler and Newman regarded him with concern. He pulled saliva into his mouth before speaking.

"What if he didn't just visit the UK? TMAU-Syndrome is a rare genetic disorder. It's carried in the *genes*. It can be *passed on* in the genes. What if we're not looking for just a wannabe copycat or some acolyte that met with Delaney? What if we're looking for Lucas Delaney's son?"

TWENTY-SEVEN

At eleven-thirty that morning they were sitting in the office of Commander Adrian Harris at the LA police headquarters on West 1st Street. Harris was the chief for the Cold Case Special Section. Although Harris was not Detective Newman's direct line manager, he had been responsible for seconding her from Robbery-Homicide for this one-off task. A neat, tidy man with a neat, tidy moustache, Bliss guessed he was about forty. As he stood to shake their hands, it was apparent that a desk job might be causing him to thicken around the middle. Gaining weight seemed to come with gaining a star and a better suit.

The four sat in the quiet, air-conditioned office on the second floor of the building, reviewing the visit. Glass walls provided visible access to accompany an open-door policy. Each of five four-drawer filing cabinets supported a plant of some kind, providing a splash of colour and appeal. The Commander, jacket worn and tie knotted tight into the shirt collar, seemed to revel in his transparency.

With the introductions over, pleasantries dispensed with, Bliss manoeuvred Harris through every stage of their investigation so far. He was not allowed to refer to it as such, because officially only city-employed cops were allowed to carry out investigations. Unless you had a private investigator licence, which neither Bliss nor Chandler had, of course. Instead Bliss had to refer to it as their assessment.

Harris nodded and smiled his way through it. Right up until the moment Bliss mentioned his discovery in the records furnished by the Federal Bureau of Prisons. At that point, the previously relaxed Harris sat forward, hands clasped together on his desk. Forewarned by Newman over breakfast, Bliss was watching the Commander closely. The change in body language was both immediate and obvious.

"Are you saying this office missed that information?" Harris asked when Bliss was through explaining.

"Not at all." Bliss shook his head. He smiled at the man. "I'm not suggesting anybody missed anything. I am merely informing you that the information was there. I stumbled upon it by pure chance."

"How about the FBI, did they miss it?"

Bliss narrowed his gaze. "Commander Harris, I don't think you understand what I am telling you. Nobody missed an obvious lead here. This was no smoking gun left in plain sight. It was a snippet of information that I happened to be reading. I wasn't looking for it because I hadn't thought to. So there should be no blame attached anywhere. Not to the LA police department nor the FBI."

The smile slipped back into place now that Harris understood no criticism would be headed his way. A fleck of lint on his trousers that seemed to have been bothering him now appeared to have vanished.

"So you're saying you requested data records of everything that went in or came out, and in amongst all of that you just happened to pluck out a juicy detail that now ties our prisoner with events back in the UK."

"That's about the size of it, yes."

Moments later, Harris lowered his voice, leaned in towards Bliss and said, "I find that hard to believe, Detective. And more than a little convenient. I wonder whether you might have known more from the very beginning than you were willing to share with Detective Newman."

Bliss inclined his head a little and met the Commander's suspicious gaze. "If you are questioning my integrity, Commander, then I object in the strongest terms. There is not a single scrap of information or evidence that I have withheld. Every thought, every idea, has been discussed openly. I requested the information as we drove back from Morro Bay. I printed it out and sifted through it when I was at the hotel. Could just as easily have been Robbie who found the link, or Penny. It happened to be me. By chance."

"Yet, as you say, you were the one who had the idea that somewhere in that data was a link between our perp and your own. You're telling me that was also by chance?"

Bliss shook his head. "No. That was me being thorough. That was me believing the connection was there somewhere, me following that conviction through because, to be perfectly honest, I was desperate. If you are now suggesting I knew all along what I was looking for, that I already had the answer and all I had to do was find the critical piece of evidence to confirm it, and used you people to do so, then you're wrong. And I resent the implication."

Harris's features became rigid; clearly a man unused to having his authority challenged. He continued to glare at Bliss, who did not blink or falter. Without uttering a word Bliss was now challenging the Commander to repeat the accusation. The silence between them was broken by Newman.

"Sir, I realise it's not my place, but I have to tell you that both Detective Bliss and Detective Chandler have been nothing less than fully cooperative. If you could have seen them in action for yourself over the past few days you would know that they excel at what they do. I've rarely seen such single-minded determination, and, in all honesty, I'm not surprised that Bliss was the one who found the information we needed. He's one of the best police officers I have worked with, and, in my opinion, we ought to be thanking him. Thanking them both."

Harris looked up at her. His expression did not alter. "You're absolutely right, Detective Newman: it's not your place."

"I've had enough of this," Bliss said, getting to his feet. "I was perfectly happy to come here today in order to provide you with an update. It was the least we could do in exchange for your hospitality. I would have thought you would be pleased to clear a cold case, irrespective of who paved the way. You still have to prove a case against Lucas Delaney, but at least you can now focus your investigation on him. It's not my place, either, but you would be doing yourself a huge favour if you allowed Detective Newman to continue on this. She is an example to the LA police department, and you're lucky to have her.

"That said, Commander, I find your line of questioning offensive. I don't have to sit here and take it, so I won't. Anything else will be followed up by my team when we return home. My own report will be sent to your mail inbox within twenty-four hours."

Bliss jerked his head at Chandler, who also stood. She raised her eyebrows at Newman. Bliss turned and headed for the door. "We'll catch up before we leave, Robbie," he said to Newman. To Commander Harris he said nothing more.

*

On balance, the meeting could have gone better. Bliss recognised that. The subsequent conversation with DCI Edwards, however, never stood a chance. Clearly fuming, Edwards laid into him for letting down the entire UK police service by disrespecting a Los Angeles division Commander. It did not seem to matter to her what Bliss said in his own defence. Edwards dismissed Harris's veiled accusations as if they were unimportant, and instead lambasted Bliss for his lack of diplomacy and professionalism in walking out of the meeting. Bliss kept both his tongue and his temper as he listened to Edwards rant. He discerned genuine fury in her tone, and could imagine her face creased with contempt for him. Concluding the call, Edwards demanded he contact Harris to apologise.

"I won't be doing that," Bliss told her.

He could have agreed and then just not done it. But he did not want to buckle, not when he believed he was in the right.

"Both DS Chandler and Detective Newman agreed with me about this specific point. Harris implied that I had used the LA police department, that I had known all along what we were looking for, and had simply wanted to use their systems to gain access. That's not the way it went down. I won't apologise for doing my job."

"The apology is not related to how well or otherwise you did your job, Inspector." Edwards was firm about this. "You need to apologise for walking out of that meeting, showing complete disregard for Commander Harris's position, and for doing so whilst in the presence of a more junior detective."

"He left me no option," Bliss argued. "The man questioned my integrity. Are you okay with that? Should I be okay with that?"

Edwards did not respond immediately. When she did, her voice was a little more measured.

"What is it with you and authority, Bliss? You fail to recognise that it doesn't matter what Commander Harris thought or said. He has a rank that demands respect. He doesn't have to be right. He doesn't have to be pleasant. He can make accusations without a scrap of proof to back them up. And he can insult your delicate senses, Bliss. Why? Because he has earned the right to do so. Should he? Of course not. He's a shit for doing so. But he did, and you should have sat there and took it and ended the meeting with his pride intact. You had the opportunity to be the bigger man, and you failed to take it."

Bliss made no reply this time. He couldn't, because the words would have choked him. Edwards was right. He did have a problem with authority, if that authority was abused. Commander Harris had, in Bliss's view, abused his position by making unfounded allegations without allowing Bliss to defend himself. Bliss believed he had the right to stand his corner, but also realised this was not the case when it came to rank and seniority. He ought to have reacted in precisely the way DCI Edwards had indicated. It did not mean they were right or he was wrong. It was just the way things were done, and had been done ever since people had differentiated between levels of command.

"I'll call him," Bliss said.

"To apologise?"

"Yes."

"Are you just fobbing me off, Bliss? To get off the phone?"

Bliss smiled. "No. I considered that earlier. But you make a valid point, boss. I need to apologise to him and make things right before I leave."

"Well… That's good. I'm glad. I know you won't like doing it, Bliss, but it is the correct thing to do."

"Yes, boss."

"And well done out there, Inspector. Exceptional work tracking down that evidence."

Bliss didn't know what surprised him more: his own acquiescence and surrender, or a word of praise from Edwards. Either way, he had pride to swallow, and that required something alcoholic with which to wash it down.

*

Whilst DS Burton had not been able to convince her superiors that a full obs package on Pearson could be justified, she did get the go-ahead to mount an 8.00pm to 8.00am watch on the suspect's home. Calls to Pearson's mother had led only to voicemail, so that was one avenue they would have to stroll down another day. Burton had been happy enough with the twelve-hour monitoring, considering those were the hours during which the attacker had always struck.

A detective from Burton's team and a uniform had been tasked with the job. DC Henry despised stakeouts. Hour upon hour trapped in a small space with sour breath and stale farts, wedged into uncomfortable seats, eyes fixed on a building in which nothing ever seemed to happen, were not high on his list of enjoyable ways to pass time. The boredom factor was a major issue, and he hoped to persuade his colleague for the night that taking turns sleeping was the way to go.

"You want to play *I spy*?" police constable Barron asked as the clock ticked toward the hour mark of their shift. He grinned and shrugged playfully.

"Yeah, why not?" Henry responded as he continued to stare straight at Pearson's house. "I'll go first. I spy with my little eye, something beginning with..." He turned his head to look at Barron. "D."

"You mean 'dickhead', don't you."

"Got it in one. You win. Game over."

"Look, we've got another eleven hours or so of this, so let's not waste it bickering, eh?"

Henry puffed out his cheeks. Nodded. "You're right. This is no one's favourite gig, but the money's good, so sure, let's make the best of it."

While the two were in conversation, neither were in a position to see the back door of David Pearson's home open, a figure dressed in dark clothing slip through the gap from the kitchen into the garden, and the door then close again behind it. There was no back gate or alleyway beyond, but the wall that provided the perimeter was only six-foot high, and easily scalable to a man using an overturned plant pot to stand on. All of this would be discovered much later on.

*

Grub was on the corner of Seward and Barton. This was to be their last meal together before Bliss and Chandler flew home, and Newman had persuaded them both that the Grub brunch was the best in LA. South Hollywood was no longer the best of neighbourhoods, but the attractive, single-storey restaurant had carved out a niche for itself if the volume of customers was a reliable sign.

Bliss ordered the French toast, Chandler the same, whilst Newman requested pancakes and bacon, fruit on the side. Their waitress was young but short and heavy, panted a lot, smiled even more, and was a ball of fun and information.

"How full are you?" Chandler asked Bliss.

"Why do you ask?"

"Because your pride is sizeable, and, if you swallowed the entire package, I don't see you being able to cope with that French toast on top."

Chandler laughed at her own lame joke, and Newman joined in. Bliss grinned and held up both hands in mock surrender. "It's all good. I said my piece. Harris said his. We won't be sending one another Christmas cards, but I salvaged things. I hope."

"He came on too strong," Newman said. "I don't want to appear disloyal, but I think he was a little embarrassed that you discovered more in a few days than the LA police department had in years."

"You heard me, Robbie. I explained how it happened, that I got lucky. He didn't want to listen. Anyway, water under the bridge and all that."

"So what's your next move?" Newman asked.

Bliss turned to Chandler. "Pen, what's the latest from home?"

"Nothing more from Tania Evans, the third rape victim. And no, no news on a fourth murder as yet, boss."

Bliss nodded and looked back at Newman. "Then in answer to your question, once we're home we find out if, when and where Lucas Delaney lived and hopefully what he did during his time in the UK. If we are right, during that period he fathered a child. First thing, of course, is to look hard at David Pearson to see if he could be the man's son. If not, then we widen the investigation and put the word out. It won't be easy."

"Should your people be watching this guy if you now think it's possible he's Delaney's son and therefore your only suspect?"

"Oh, they're watching him closely anyway. Have been since the rape on Friday."

"And you, Robbie?" Chandler asked. "Jimmy has hooked your man for you, but can you reel him in?"

"I'm sure we will. Jimmy was kind enough to really push for me to run with it, but even if I'm allowed to, the Feebs are bound to take the lead." Newman shrugged. "You know, I'll be happy enough to be a part of it. It was never my case, but I've grown into it over the past few days."

"We're all part of the solution, not the problem," Chandler said.

Bliss glanced at her, nodding. "If only our superiors recognised that part, life would be so much better."

Their flight was not until late afternoon, but Newman had to head back to her office. They said their goodbyes outside the diner.

"How did you like your first visit here?" Newman asked Chandler.

"Well, it was work. But it's a great place."

"Come back for a vacation. I'll show you the sights."

"I might just do that. But at least I can tell my friends I saw the Pacific Ocean."

"And what will you say about it?" Newman asked.

"That it was blue and wet."

Bliss gave Newman a hug, and in return she pecked him on the cheek, wiping away a trace of lipstick with her thumb.

"It was a genuine pleasure, Jimmy. Look me up if you're ever in LA."

"I'll do that. You're a credit to your police department, Robbie. I recommended you complete our work here because I think you'll do a great job. Thanks for making us both so welcome. In amongst all the darkness, you also made it fun."

Bliss waved as Newman drove away. He had enjoyed her company enormously. Watching her leave was more than a professional wrench. Since Hazel's death he had found relationships hard work, even relatively long-term ones. With Newman he had felt relaxed in a way that surprised him. Perhaps being so far from home had allowed him to become so. He hoped it was more than that. He hoped the callouses on his heart were becoming softer.

"She's great," Chandler said, as if reading his thoughts.

"Yes. A great cop."

"Oh, Jimmy. What are we going to do with you?"

Bliss grinned. "Nothing," he said. "I'm great as I am."

She turned to look at Bliss. "I've decided something. Something significant."

"Okay."

"I don't want to complete the final three months of my secondment, so I'm going to ask to be relieved of it."

Bliss flashed a look of concern. "Where will you go?" he asked.

"Hopefully nowhere. I want to re-join the team, boss. If you'll have me."

"You want to come back?" Bliss had imagined Chandler would spend her year down with the Met and decide that was where she wanted to be.

"I do. I decided just now."

"What persuaded you?"

"A number of things. But I know I don't want to spend all my time working rape cases."

"You'll need to interview with potential bosses," Bliss said.

Chandler frowned awkwardly. "I sort of figured I'd just slip back in with your unit."

"But I don't want you back."

"You don't?"

"No." Bliss shook his head firmly. Chandler's look of astonishment was a picture that made him smile. "Penny, you need to be heading on to bigger and better things. You are a rising star. You stay with me and all I'll do is hold you back."

Chandler turned square on, her eyes fixed on his. The pavement around them was busy, but they remained right in the middle with pedestrians swarming either side.

"I have to do this, boss, and I don't want to hear about futures or careers. I want to be happy doing my job again. And no, you will not hold me back. I can only ever learn and grow by working with you. I want to join the squad again. It's the only place I want to be. What's more, I belong there."

Bliss had to admit it felt good hearing Chandler's words. During his first spell as her DI back home in Peterborough they had seldom seen one another outside of work or during a post-work drink, which often included other members of the team. Since coming out to California they had spent many more hours together, and their connection had become tighter. Bliss had started to think of the two of them as a real partnership again. Despite his surprise, and a genuine desire to see his friend improve and develop, he decided there and then to do everything in his power to bring Chandler back into the fold.

"Yes," Bliss said eventually. "You're right, Pen. You do belong there."

TWENTY-EIGHT

Bliss had only been gone a few days, but in his absence winter seemed to have sent autumn scuttling off for good long before it was done. He imagined it was something to do with the shift in temperature between Los Angeles and Peterborough, but the day felt cold and damp and miserable when he arrived back in the city.

Unable to sleep on the long and uncomfortable flight home, Bliss understood his out-of-kilter internal time clock required a day or two to settle. The easy way out would have been to steer clear of the office rather than facing up to matters. He had earned a break. But the thrill of solving a case out in California in addition to providing a major lead in his own operation had been short-lived, because a lot had changed during the time his mobile had been switched off on board the Virgin Atlantic flight.

When he had turned it off back at LAX, Bliss believed the worst thing he had to confront upon his return was a fresh rape victim and an investigation still going nowhere. The first thing he did when landing was switch the Samsung back on. In the eleven hours in between, he had acquired five missed calls and thirteen text messages.

As well as his second murder victim – the spree's fourth in all.

Chandler had been unable to get the same flight, so Bliss had arranged for DS Bishop to collect him from the kerb outside Heathrow arrivals. They took three separate motorways, before cutting across to the A1, bypassing Bedford along the way. It was slow going. Bishop filled him in on the two attacks that had occurred during Bliss's absence. He knew about Tania Evans, but the body of Carol Payne was discovered less than an hour after

Bliss had boarded his flight. She was sixty-four and lived with her husband Derek in the Orton Goldhay district. She had taken the short walk home from a function at the church hall, something she had done at least twice a week for the past nine years.

It was to be her last.

Bliss asked himself what the chances were that David Pearson, their alarm specialist suspect, could find no alibi for any of eight separate evenings. The odds must have been staggering. On the other hand, Pearson lived alone, seldom socialised, and fished often. Perhaps it was not so outlandish after all.

No further leads had been forthcoming. Yet Bliss was returning with information from the States that might just blow their own operations wide open. Before leaving LA he had requested information on Lucas Delaney from all UK data sources. None of his fresh batch of voicemails and texts had concerned this search, so Bliss placed a second call himself. He was told that his request had yet to be actioned, but was rising higher up the requisition list and that he should expect to hear back within the day. Bliss hoped that by the time he was ready to stand up in front of his team again, that information would be in his hands. If he could provide absolute proof that Delaney had fathered a child in the UK, then expanding the logic to a genetic link between the killers would be an easy sell.

The first thing Bliss had to take care of was briefing both Detective Superintendent Fletcher and DCI Edwards. He called Fletcher's PA from the car to arrange an appointment, and was almost ten minutes late by the time Bishop had negotiated mid-afternoon traffic. Bliss brought his superiors up to date with what had happened in the US, and was pleased by their reaction when he dropped the bombshell about Delaney having spent time in the UK.

"I take it all the dates tie in?" Fletcher said, pushing herself back into a more relaxed pose.

"They do. According to US records, Lucas Delaney was over here from 1985 to 2001. If he fathered a son during the early stage of that period that would put the son within the age range we are looking at for our own suspect. His UK exit time is one year before the first rape and murder in southern California. In addition to any and all information on Delaney during his time here, I have also requested any crimes with a similar MO committed during that sixteen-year timeframe. Once we narrow down where Delaney lived and worked, we can also narrow down our search parameters."

"How confident are you that this Delaney person is our suspect's father?" Edwards asked.

"My confidence is high. The metabolic condition from which he suffers is potentially genetic. Put it this way: it makes a lot more sense than a copycat."

"Yet that remains a possibility still."

Bliss glanced across at Edwards. "Of course. And we have not dropped that, or any other angle. It remains a strand within our overall investigation."

"So the father–son… strand may actually be nothing at all."

He knew exactly what the DCI was doing. Downplaying what he believed to be the most significant lead they had, whilst at the same time attempting to hang him with it should the lead take them nowhere. It was subtle rather than overt, leaving a path open for her to claim a leadership victory if things went in their favour. It was clever. It was politics. And it disgusted him.

"It may be everything, it may be nothing," Bliss admitted, looking back at the Detective Super once more. "I believe it's the former."

"And what of our latest victims?" Fletcher asked him. "My understanding is we still cannot rule this Pearson chap in or out as a suspect."

"That's my understanding as well. I'll be getting updates on everything as soon as I meet up with my team again. The issue I am most concerned about now as a matter of priority is confirming Carol Payne's estimated time of death, and then discovering whether Pearson was under observation during that window. Or if he has any other kind of alibi this time."

Edwards shook her head and rounded on him. "Which forces me to ask, DI Bliss, do you not think these women would have been better served had you remained here investigating, as opposed to gallivanting in America?"

That barb got under his skin. Bliss choked it back down before it had a chance to foment. "If you're asking me whether my being here would have prevented Tania Evans being raped or Carol Payne being murdered, then I suppose only time will tell. If I'm right about the father–son aspect, then clearly my presence here would have been irrelevant and my presence out there crucial. If I'm wrong, then I fully expect you to remind me of it when the time comes."

Edwards seemed to bristle at his response. "I think somebody needs to consider asking the question, because I'm certain the media will get around to it and it's something we will need to get ahead of."

"A lot of ifs buts and maybes, Chief Inspector," Fletcher said dismissively. "I understand your desire to pre-empt, but let's at least wait until we know for sure which way this new lead will take us before tearing it to shreds. I sanctioned the Inspector's visit to the US, and, Jimmy, I think you did some remarkable work out there."

"Thank you, ma'am."

"For what it's worth, I believe you have something with this new lead of yours. Of course, the timing could have been better, so the media are likely to try and make something of your absence at a critical juncture. However, you solved a long-since cold case of theirs in California and came home with a potentially valuable lead, so no one can say it was a worthless trip. In point of fact, we should be making some good publicity out of its success. And Edwards, if I read or hear the term 'gallivanting' by any journalist I will know where it came from and I will not be best pleased. Now, thank you Inspector Bliss for your hard work. The Chief Inspector and I will chat for a few more minutes whilst you go and catch up with your team."

As Bliss made his way downstairs to the incident room, he was smiling to himself. In rebuking Edwards prior to ending their meeting, Superintendent Fletcher had both shown him her support and warned off the DCI all in one comment. What's more, it gave him the breathing space he sorely needed.

*

After the expected round of jocular comments about Bliss having disappeared on a jolly whilst his minions got on with the real work, he held up his hands and calmed the chatter.

"It was a lovely place, with lovely weather, lovely food, and lovely company," Bliss said. "And yes, I did happen to solve their case for them. But believe me, it didn't take long for reality to settle in once I landed back at Heathrow. So, please bring me up to speed with everything you have on the latest two attacks."

Short had been liaising with DI Burton on the rape case. Her report did not take long. Other than to confirm that the MO was exactly the same, and that David Pearson remained the prime suspect, that was it. It was stalled, despite both a failed attack and the rape, they were getting no further.

It was Bishop who brought him up to date on the murders. Sadly, his report was as limited as Short's had been. One fresh murder, no additional leads. Pearson had been under observation at the time of the murder, but upon being questioned the detective concerned admitted that neither he nor the uniform with him had spotted Pearson even once during the entire shift. A light had remained on in the living room the whole time, but there had been no sign of movement. Disappointed, but unsurprised, Bliss opted for being positive and upbeat, though it was difficult to rouse a team who felt so deflated. The few forensic leads they had would help if they made an arrest, but were wholly ineffective in leading them to a suspect.

"Please tell me we now have a twenty-four-hour watch on David Pearson," Bliss said. "Tell me that at least."

DS Bishop nodded. "Affirmative, boss. Full package was applied as soon as news came in about the murder. He is under plainclothes surveillance."

"Any word from the pathologist on TOD?"

"Still waiting for Doc Drinkwater to get back to us, boss. Currently she says her original estimate is probably going to be accurate within thirty minutes either way."

"Okay, chase them up again would you, please. I want to rule Pearson in or out and any change between estimated and official time of death may well do that for us. Also, DS Short would you please speak to whoever is running the observation team sitting on Pearson. I want their log mailed across asap."

"Will do, boss." Short made a note on the pad sitting on the desk in front of her.

"Any further possible links with victims?" Bliss asked. "We know Pearson worked in schools occasionally, so may have initially encountered one or more of his rape victims there. Are we really still waiting for his employers to pass across their records?"

"Not exactly," Bishop replied. "We have some. They say they have the jobs on their systems, but that the alarm specialists they use are on paper only until the job sheets are handed in. Apparently, there were so many last-minute changes, all of which caused mayhem with their financial system, that they stopped recording the names of the engineers until after the jobs had been attended. That is being collated as we speak and we've been promised access to it today or tomorrow."

"Make it today, Bishop. How about anything connected with the communities where some of his murder victims lived?"

"Nothing so far. The company don't have a contract with the housing association, so we can rule that out. Someone like Pearson can earn well off the books, so we're checking other alarm companies. Oh, and I know it was a shot in the dark, but those plastic baggies of items you collected from the Stanground murder scene came back with no positive results."

Bliss shook his head. Five minutes back in the UK and already he was exhausted. The eight-hour time difference was dragging him down. He wondered what Robbie Newman was up to at that precise moment.

"We push the Pearson angle as far as it can bend until it breaks," Bliss said. He looked around the room. Every face was glum, and all betraying the same weariness he felt.

"I know you're all at your limit right now," Bliss said. "I want to thank each of you for all your efforts, especially in my absence. I have asked for everything you have, and everything you have is what you have all given me. But I'm going to ask for more. This sick bastard is not on any kind of cycle, but we should expect him to take a break for a week or so at least. However, we can't allow that to make us slack. I need your very best, and I need it at all times. We can sleep when this prick is banged up. And he will be."

Bliss's mobile chirped. He took the call because it was coming from records. "Please tell me you have something positive," he said. "Because I'm not the only one feeling the pinch right now."

The civilian who had interrogated the HOLMES database system was a twenty-seven-year-old female from Birmingham, and the Black Country was evident in her every word.

"I have information for you, Inspector. Whether it's positive or not depends very much on what your expectations are right now. I'm sending you everything in a single file, but I thought I would call with the highlights. Lucas Delaney lived in both Chelmsford and London. We have a work record for him, financials, credit reports. There is no evidence he married, but we can attach two offspring to him. One male, one female. I am seeing two rapes and two murders in Chelmsford that would appear to fit the bill, plus a couple of items from his time in London."

Bliss put his head back and punched the air. "Yes!" he cried. "I could kiss you."

"A simple thank you will suffice, Inspector."

Bliss thanked the woman and killed the call. He related the information to his team. There was a moment of silence before the room erupted. This was huge. Delaney was in the vicinity of similar crimes here in the UK, but the best news of all was that he had fathered a son. Before now, Bliss had only had a generous measure of faith in this lead. Now he knew it to be true. Knew it deep inside where it could never be questioned again.

The son was their man.

Bliss calmed the troops, whose faces were now unquestionably joyous. "Bishop, you find me a link between David Pearson and Lucas Delaney if one exists. If he is that monster's son then there will be a trail somewhere. Short, you look into everything else that I am going to forward you as soon as it comes in. If Pearson is not the son, then someone else is."

His phone made a different sound, this time signifying that a mail had dropped into his inbox. Normally Bliss had that tone switched off, but today was a red-letter day. He swiped and scanned, swiftly absorbing the general details of case reports and data. Then something snared his attention, and Bliss could feel his blood drain away as if he had severed an artery.

He looked down at his phone as if it had grown teeth and bitten him.

"Everything all right, boss?" Short asked him, as she strolled by towards a desk with a computer terminal on it.

He shook his head. "No, Sergeant. Everything is not all right. One of these files is telling me that in addition to hits on cases involving a similar MO at around the time he would have been living in Chelmsford, Lucas Delaney's name actually popped up on a case report from the Met in London."

"Well, that's good. Isn't it?"

"Yes and no." Bliss swallowed. "There was an investigation into the rape and murder of a young girl. Delaney was not only a suspect, he was also the girl's father. He was later ruled out by the DS who assessed the interview."

"So why the long face, boss?"

Bliss leaned back against the wall. Closed his eyes and shook his head. "Because I was that DS," he said.

TWENTY-NINE

"I can't believe I missed this," Bliss said, a sick sensation in his stomach. He wasn't feeling sorry for himself yet, but was damn close to it.

Bliss had not interviewed Lucas Delaney in connection with the rape and murder of Delaney's own young daughter. That task had fallen to a fellow DS from the same team. He had asked Bliss to listen to the recorded interview and to offer an opinion. Bliss had seniority, and understood the DS would be guided by his more experienced view. Bliss had clapped eyes on the suspect just once, briefly, and then only from a distance as Delaney was led away by uniformed officers.

The man he had seen for all of twenty seconds during the last month of the last year of the millennium was a big man, Bliss remembered. But he was no bear. A clean-shaven man, above average height, muscular build. Did that man, glimpsed only fleetingly, have the capacity to become the one Bliss had spent time with in that San Quentin interview room? It was almost two decades between the two events. A lot of brain cells lost in that time. Could he really be faulted for not recognising a man he had never met and only listened to eighteen years ago? *Probably not,* Bliss decided. Yet he would and he did blame himself. Not just for the man, but for the case. And the subsequent victims.

Bliss's recommendation not to press charges had released a man who, in all probability, had raped and murdered his own daughter and would later go on to rape and murder again. Bliss blinked. Let it sink in. The ghosts in his field of vision were now legion.

"What about the name?" Chandler asked.

After arriving at Heathrow that afternoon she had been travelling straight to her office at New Scotland Yard when her phone rang and she was instructed to divert north to Peterborough instead. Chandler called ahead, and they had arranged to meet for a drink.

Charters was a converted Dutch barge, tethered to the river Nene just yards from the city's oldest bridge. The vessel was now 110 years old, and had worked the rivers of Holland, Belgium and Germany right up until 1990. The barge was made of riveted steel, and was 176ft long. A year after it retired from transporting cargo, it was hauled across the North Sea and opened as a bar. The bar itself was below deck, and at shortly before five-thirty was already gearing up for a busy night.

"What did you say?" Bliss asked. An outbreak of raucous laughter had drowned out Chandler's question.

"I asked about the name. I can understand your mind missing the transformation in the man himself, perhaps even slipping the name Lucas Delaney, because it's neither interesting nor uninteresting. It just is. But seriously, Jimmy, when you put the name together with the man and the murder inquiry back then, how is it possible for you not to recall a connection?"

Bliss was taking pulls from a cold bottle of lager. He felt like having something stronger, but was starting the evening slowly.

"I'm certain that if it had all happened last week, last month, last year, or even last decade, damnit, I would have put it together. But when I saw him this time it was in a completely different context. He must have easily been a hundred pounds heavier, had that bushy wild beard, his flesh all crisped up and wrinkled from the sun. Physically there was no comparison. As for the name, Delaney is not so rare as to make it unforgettable."

Bliss took out his phone, scrolled through the file he had been sent and pulled up a photograph of Lucas Delaney which had been provided to the police at the time of the investigation on which he had been DS.

"Look at him," he said, showing it to Chandler. "You met him. Would you have ever believed that was the same man? Even if someone had told you so before you went in there? I saw him for a few seconds and listened to his interview for a couple of hours nigh on two bloody decades ago. Are you telling me you would have spotted it, Pen?"

Bliss watched closely as Chandler's eyes scoured the photo. Finally she gave him the phone back and shook her head. "I now know it's the same man and I still can't see it. Bloody hell, what happened to him?"

Bliss raised his eyebrows. "He grew up, Pen. Up and out."

"Is it even important?" Bishop said. Bliss had asked both him and DS Short along, but Short cried off due to a prior engagement she could not pull out of. "Remembered or not remembered, it helps us how? Boss, I understand if you feel you let something slip through the net, but that's ancient history right now. We have to find Delaney's son. That's all that matters."

Chandler patted Bliss on the arm. "He's not wrong, boss. I know you'll beat yourself up about this, but keep your self-flagellation for when this is over. We are close now, and that's because of you. Focus on that instead. We are so close I can taste it. Take the win first, then I'll talk you out of your funk."

Bliss smiled. Drained his bottle and ordered them all another. Chandler was right. Bishop, too. He had fucked up. He would have to deal with that at some point. But not now. Not yet. There were more pressing concerns requiring his full attention. He took out his phone and made a call.

DC Carmichael was the only member of the team available, and the call was switched to him up in the Major Crime unit. Bliss asked Carmichael to check to see if there were any results in as to whether David Pearson and Lucas Delaney were related. Bliss felt his heart racing during the silence that followed as Carmichael did as he was asked. Bliss took a few deep breaths. All they needed was this one break. If Pearson was the San Quentin prisoner's son then everything else would fall into line.

Bliss heard a scratching on the other end of the connection, followed by Carmichael's soft west country accent. "It's in, boss.

Just this second. Sorry, but no joy, I'm afraid. David Pearson's heritage can be traced back to his biological parents, and the father was not Lucas Delaney. We are still waiting on DNA results for final confirmation, but it isn't him I'm afraid. Pearson is not our man."

Hugely dispirited now, Bliss thanked the DC and was about to kill the call when Carmichael spoke up again. "Oh, and boss, I realised how low you were feeling earlier so I thought you would want to know this. Another reason why you may not have put two and two together with the Delaney of 1999 and today's Delaney is because during the time you investigated that case he wasn't even going by that name. He was using his mother's maiden name, so you would have known him as Hardie."

"Hardie." Bliss uttered the name as if partially consuming it to assess its flavour. He began to nod, slow at first then faster. "Yes. Yes, now *that* name is familiar. I remembered the case as soon as it was mentioned, but absolutely nothing concerning the name Delaney. I guess that's one sliver of light at the end of a very long tunnel. Thanks, Ian."

Bliss outlined the conversation to his two companions. They were pleased for him about the name, but more than disappointed to learn that Pearson was not their man.

"In truth, he only ever looked a reasonable bet at most for it, boss," Chandler said. "Other than the use of his van, we never really had anything solid on him. Whoever our actual guilty party is must have stolen Pearson's van after all. Now I feel bad about what we put him through."

"He could have been more honest with us from the beginning. But you're right, it can't be nice to be falsely accused."

"For fuck sake!" Bishop snapped, making a fist as if preparing to punch the side of the barge. "Why is everything going against us on this bastard case?"

Busy rubbing his eyes, Bliss was at a loss as to what to say. They were having to work so much harder than usual to make even the slightest of inroads into these operations, and as Bishop had suggested, it was starting to feel as if everything was set against them. On the other hand, Pearson had always been an outside chance. The news Bliss had just received did not take them any further away, just no nearer. All the same, there was no succour to be found here.

"We regroup again in the morning," Bliss said on a sigh. "We rest, we sleep, we gather ourselves and we go again. And here's a challenge for you both: I want one fresh approach from each of you by the time morning briefing begins."

Chandler pulled a face. "That's hardly fair. I'm not even part of your team."

"Will you be at the briefing?"

"Yes."

"Then you're part of the team."

She grinned. "Fair enough. Boss. Looks like my much-needed beauty-sleep regime has gone for a burton."

"Aw, I don't think you need beauty sleep at all, Penny," Bishop said. He cracked open a bag of salted peanuts and popped a handful into his mouth, grinning at her all the while.

"Thank you, Sergeant. There is at least one gentleman at the table."

"Hey, I was going to say the same thing," Bliss complained. "He just beat me to it."

Bliss's phone rang. "Probably more bad news," he muttered, swiping the screen to answer. DC Carmichael again.

"Boss. Thought I'd better bring you up to date with news just in. The reason we had problems tracking down the woman Delaney lived with is because she was divorced when she met Delaney but hadn't changed her name, so our records had her as Marjory Porter."

"Now her I do recall. I interviewed her over her daughter's murder. That's the name she was using at the time. So she then changed back to her maiden name afterwards I assume?"

"She did, boss. Only we have no trace of her under that name, either. So, I'm wondering if she changed it by deed poll, either because of what happened to her daughter and perhaps she wanted to go back beneath the radar, or maybe even because she didn't want Delaney finding her."

"Good thinking, Ian," Bliss said, nodding appreciatively to himself. "Go ahead and get that looked into."

"Wheels already in motion, boss."

"Top man. Leave word to have me alerted the moment that comes in, and get yourself off home. Nice work, Constable." Carmichael was a promising detective, and a little encouragement couldn't hurt.

Bliss updated Chandler and Bishop. "You know," he said, "I am starting to remember more and more about that case. I don't believe I ever saw the son, but I saw photos of the daughter, of course. From what I remember she was a lovely-looking kid. The mother, Marjory, was as distraught as you'd expect any mother to be who had just had their teenage daughter raped and murdered. She was never adamant that her live-in boyfriend was responsible, but she suspected him. As I recall now, we would never have looked into him too hard beyond the obvious were it not for her pointing the finger in his direction. I know as a rule we always look at family first, but there was nothing about the man that set off any distress flares."

"Don't worry about it, boss," Bishop said. He screwed up the empty bag of nuts and drained his glass. He then wiped his salty hands on his suit trousers. "If you made a decision in good faith, based on all the information available to you at the time, then your conscience is clear. We can all be perfect with the benefit of hindsight. As for Delaney, not recognising him has had zero effect on the case, so forget it."

Bliss nodded. "You're right. I know you're right. And I'll get there in the end. I just need to work my way around to it is all. It's a process. I don't have your sunny disposition, Sergeant. But thanks."

Bishop was another good cop, and a good man as well. There was a damned fine team at Thorpe Wood, and Bliss felt as if he owed them one.

His ring-tone sounded again. Bliss rolled his eyes. "Bloody hell. I've never been so popular. This must be what being a drug dealer feels like."

He answered the call.

"Boss, it's DC Carmichael again."

"I thought I told you to go home, Ian."

"I know. And I will. But I thought I'd give it a few more minutes, see if anything crucial came in."

"And the fact you're calling me again suggests it has."

"Oh, yes. Big time. And boss, this is what we've been waiting for. I have back the details on Marjory Porter. These days she goes by Marjory Thompson. She lives with her son, Malcolm. And we have an address."

THIRTY

The semi-detached bungalow in the village of Sawtry, a ten-minute drive south of Peterborough, was the only unkempt property on the road as far as Bliss could tell. Its paintwork was faded and peeling, strips curled back on themselves, large blisters on the point of bursting. The front garden was wildly overgrown, in stark contrast to the manicured lawn of its attached neighbour. Drab nets hung in the two bay windows to the front of the property. The bottom panel of the front door had been replaced by a sheet of plywood.

Bliss cast his mind back eighteen years, recalling the visit to Marjory Porter's home, a second-storey flat. It, too, had been in a similar state of neglect and disrepair. It did not appear as if age and a change of name had improved the woman's character. Bliss recalled her as surly and quick to anger, but then she had just suffered an unspeakable tragedy and allowances were made. He wasn't sure what might lie behind that battered front door now, but he would not have to wait long to find out.

The advance team were gathering just around the corner, together with armed officers. They would plan their entrance into the property, ensuring all exits were also covered, should Malcolm Thompson be at home and decide to make a run for it. A dog handler and his canine partner were also standing by. The advance team would attempt an orderly entry first, by knocking and making a request of whoever opened the door. Should that be refused, they had a warrant and entry would then be forced, the armed team stepping forward at that point.

Bliss, Chandler and Bishop were parked close by in the unmarked Vauxhall. Once the house had been made safe and anyone inside secured, the three of them would be called in. Bliss would like to have had more time to prepare, and also to ensure that both mother and son were inside the property. That preference had to be weighed against the chances of Malcolm Thompson slipping away to carry out another attack.

It was a no-brainer.

The residence had been placed under immediate surveillance, and a single light had been reported as being on in what was thought to be the living room. No activity reported from anywhere inside the house. Bliss had presented the facts to DCI Edwards, together with his recommendation that they go in as soon as possible. Edwards signed off on it without so much as a squeak of protest. Her wings had been clipped by Marion Fletcher, and she would not try to fly free so soon afterwards.

There was a flurry of movement in the street, and seconds later a dozen police officers approached the bungalow. Bliss felt the usual surge of excitement, and could only imagine how those leading the advance team were feeling right now. The first officer both rang the doorbell and rapped on the door. He repeated the process without pause. From his vantage point, Bliss saw the door pulled open, but could not see into the property. A conversation ensued, and to his surprise the team then entered the bungalow. Bliss had expected a breach to be required, and his guess was that this swift and apparently agreeable entry meant the son was not home. Bliss just had to hope they would not discover that Malcolm Thompson did not live at home after all.

Less than five minutes later, the tension inside the Insignia increasing rapidly, Bliss received the call telling him they were safe to enter the property.

*

"Oh, I fucking remember you well," Marjory Thompson said when Bliss identified himself. "How could I not with a name like that? Bliss? Is that any sort of name for a copper? Not that you were much of one. You're the cocksucker who let a murderer go free."

Thompson sat at the kitchen dining table. She wore a threadbare dressing gown over a thin nightdress of indefinite colour or age. Unlike her ex-boyfriend currently residing in San Quentin, the woman had gained no weight at all as far as Bliss could tell. In fact, she had possibly lost some, but in fat only because she was lean and firm for a woman her age. It might have been a long time ago, but Bliss was absolutely certain that the woman he had met back then had been soft and out of shape. Her hair was just as greasy now as it had been in 1999, face blotchy and pasty. The only colour was the network of red veins that spread out from her nose and across her cheeks. *A drinker,* Bliss thought. *Or once had been.*

"Where's Malcolm?" Bliss asked, ignoring Thompson's outburst.

"That man fucked our daughter and then stabbed her to death and you let that fat fuck walk away."

"Where's your son, Marjory?"

Thompson threw an arm out wildly. "I told them other soapy fuckers that Mal doesn't live here anymore."

Bliss shook his head. "But that's not true is it, Marjory? Before I came in here to talk to you, officers informed me that your second bedroom appears to have been slept in recently, with male clothing in the wardrobe and chest of drawers. There are two toothbrushes in the bathroom. And I noticed a letter addressed to Malcolm on the counter by the kettle."

The glare she gave Bliss was filled with hatred. "You got no shame? You going to apologise for not giving my Maisie justice? She was barely thirteen fucking years old."

"I'm not responsible for killing your daughter. But yes, if we're right about this now then I am sorry for the mistake I made back then. It was a genuine error, if so, but an error for all that."

"I should fucking sue you."

Bliss shook his head and sneered at her. "You could try. Right now, your only concern needs to be telling us where Malcolm is."

"Why, you want to ruin his life as well do you?"

"It's interesting, Marjory," Bliss said, never once taking his eyes off Thompson. "But that's the first time you've actually questioned our presence here this evening. Most people would have asked that before allowing the police inside. Certainly, they would have asked before now. It's almost as if you were expecting our knock on the door at some point or another."

The woman glanced away. Gathered herself. She took a cigarette from a pack on the table and lit it with a disposable lighter. After a couple of puffs she pinched something from her bottom lip and tapped her fingers on the table.

"I'll tell you this, Bliss: your apology is worth fuck-all to me. You fucking destroyed me the day you let that miserable sack of shit go free. Me and my son. And you're wrong about him. You hear me? Whatever you want him for, he didn't do it. He couldn't have because he was with me. Whatever hour of whatever day, he was with me."

That was the moment Bliss decided he would arrest Thompson as well and bring her in for further questioning. Malcolm's mother had just unwittingly confessed to providing an alibi for her son irrespective of whether it was true. A part of him tried to locate genuine sympathy for her, for whatever his decision eighteen years earlier had contributed to her miserable existence since. But spending time with Thompson now had reminded him of what an awful person she had been back then. The impression he had taken away from his initial encounter with Marjory Porter was of a woman who cared more about being the centre of attention than she did her murdered daughter. He did not believe for one moment that his decision to release Lucas Delaney without charge had damaged her in any way. And if she knew what her son had done, what he was capable of, then Bliss would punish her for attempting to shield the man.

Thompson's tapping on the kitchen table had drawn his attention, however. Everything about her reeked of neglect, apart from ten things: her nails. They were perfectly manicured and shaped, painted and polished to a high gloss sheen. If Bliss had not been certain of Malcolm Thompson's guilt before entering the property, he was now. The pristine nails on this slovenly woman told him everything he needed to know about the origins of their suspect's signature.

Changing his approach, Bliss said, "What does Malcolm do for a living?"

Perhaps caught unawares, Thompson answered him. "He works with computers."

"Whereabouts?"

"In schools mainly. Local company sends my boy out to them when they need stuff fixed." She uttered the words proudly.

Bliss glanced at Chandler and Bishop in turn. The nods he received indicated they had picked up on it as well.

Just then, a uniformed officer stepped into the kitchen. "Inspector, we found a mobile phone hidden away inside a drawer full of sweaters. The device belongs to Mrs Thompson. Sir, there's something you need to see."

The uniform handed the phone to Bliss. On the screen was a text message, sent to Malcolm at just about the time the police had knocked on her front door. It contained two sentences: THEY ARE HERE. YOU KNOW WHAT YOU NEED TO DO.

Bliss read the message one more time then passed the phone to Bishop, his eyes returning to the woman sat across the table. "What is it he needs to do, Marjory? I'm sure your son will have understood the message. Now I need to."

Thompson leaned across the table. She beckoned Bliss closer with one slender finger, its nail gleaming in the harsh kitchen light. He edged forward. Then she smiled at him and said, "Go fuck yourself and the horse you rode in on, Inspector-fucking-Bliss."

Bliss took a breath. Nodded. Got to his feet. "Sergeant," he said, turning to Bishop. "I need to go home and scrub myself clean with a wire brush. Please arrest this woman."

"With pleasure, boss," Bishop said, above Marjory Thompson's strident protests. "What charge?"

"Any and all you can think of," Bliss replied. "And if you can persuade her into resisting arrest so much the better. Set the dog on her and don't pull it back until it's had its way with her down to the bone."

Bliss left the room without a backward glance. It seemed to be a habit he had acquired lately. He decided he could live with that.

THIRTY-ONE

The next twenty-four hours flew by as if someone had activated a fast-forward button on their lives. Given the nature of the charges against her, they had Marjory Thompson for a day. The only legitimate charge she faced was one of attempting to pervert the course of justice, which covered Thompson's statement of intent to alibi her son irrespective of the truth. The CPS informed Bliss that they would not seek charges against her for failing to provide details of Malcolm Thompson's whereabouts. Bliss was aware that even the one charge was spurious, as she could argue in court that it had all been a joke, perhaps a stalling tactic. On the other hand, Bliss thought he might get lucky if he requested a further twelve-hour extension when the time came.

The first interview was a cursory one. It was designed to cover little more than the reasons for detaining Thompson, and for Bliss and his team to ascertain how the woman would approach matters. Thompson demanded and received a duty solicitor, and the clock began to run down. After a brief discussion with her legal representation, Thompson denied the charge against her, citing a misunderstanding on her part due to being in a confused mental state.

Bliss asked Thompson once again to reveal the precise meaning of the text message she had sent to her son. Thompson declined to comment. Bliss left it at that until more evidence could be gathered and sent the woman back to her holding cell.

The teams from both Major Crimes and Sexual Crimes combined to work the evidence, search the property in Sawtry – including both front and back gardens – and to continue ploughing through records.

Tech-IT leased a small unit on a minor business estate on the edge of Sawtry village. Shortly after eight-thirty on the morning following Thompson's arrest, Bliss and Bishop visited the premises to speak with Malcolm Thompson's employer. Vincent Hope was in his mid-twenties, had contracts with a number of schools within a thirty-mile radius, and employed on a freelance basis ten people ranging from basic technicians to certified IT engineers.

When asked, Bliss declined to reveal why they were looking for Thompson. But he knew exactly what his own first question was going to be.

"Is Malcolm Thompson due to be working today?"

"He was scheduled to," Hope replied. "Texted in sick yesterday."

"You have his home address I assume."

"He lives in the village. At his mum's place."

Bliss sighed. "And that's the only address you have for him?"

"Yes. Look, if you tell me what this is all about maybe I can help. Has one of the schools complained about him?"

"Why would they do that, Mr Hope?"

Hope shrugged. "I don't know. You hear of things happening around kids. Not that anyone had a bad word to say about Malcolm."

Bliss narrowed his gaze. He detected a change in inflection, a slight raise in timbre that suggested some form of anxiety. "Are you certain about that, Mr Hope? I will be asking for a full list of your clients, and we will speak to them all. It'd be a shame if something had slipped your mind just now which we later assume must have been a deliberate lie. You could lose your right to work in schools at all. That would be a big chunk of business to lose."

The man took a breath. His shoulders sagged. He was sitting in an armless office chair at a desk on which stood an array of three monitors all hooked up to a single base station. Eventually he nodded, as Bliss had suspected he would.

"All right. All right. I didn't want to get Mal into trouble over something so minor. Look, all that happened was in one school in Huntingdon a teacher complained that Mal lingered around the sixth form girls a little too much for her liking, and that he was a bit... creepy. He made her nervous. She reported him to her principal, and we were asked not to send him there anymore."

"And what did he say when you asked him about it?"

"How d'you mean?"

"You questioned him, I assume. Asked him about the report. What was his response?"

Hope swallowed and licked his lips. "Well, thing is, I didn't question him as such. I just told him they were being arsey and I was sending someone else there in future. I didn't think it was a big deal."

Bliss ran a hand over the scar on his forehead. "You take your duty of care seriously, I see."

"It was nothing. Really."

"Mr Hope, given your employees work in schools, you must have them CRB checked, yes?"

Hope screwed his face up before answering. "That was a Criminal Records Bureau certificate. Now they use the Disclosure and Barring Service."

"They use? Are you saying you don't certificate your employees, Mr Hope?"

"Technically they aren't my employees. They sub-contract and so are self-employed, and are therefore responsible for their own certificates."

"But a self-employed person can only obtain a basic certificate. I'm pretty sure that's insufficient to work in a school."

"Look, schools don't ask about DBS types, so we don't question. A certificate is a certificate."

"I doubt that, but let's move on," Bliss said. "So you would have had sight of them, yes? Taken photocopies, or scanned them to PDF perhaps."

Hope raised an eyebrow, and Bliss smiled and said, "Yes, I know a little bit about technology. Even an old Luddite like me.

So, I would like to see a copy of Malcolm Thompson's DBS certificate."

"It might take a while to dig out," Hope said, clearing his throat. "I'm not the best record keeper. Any chance I could pop it into the station tomorrow?"

Bliss stared him down. "You mean tomorrow after you've tracked Thompson down and got him to hand it over, because you don't actually have a copy of it. Am I right, Mr Hope?"

"Mal said he had one. Couldn't lay his hands on it because things were a mess after moving back in with his mum. I gave him time and then... I suppose I just forgot about it."

Bliss looked across at Bishop. "Anything?" he asked.

Bishop shook his head. "I'll stay on here for a chat with Mr Hope if you want to get back, boss. I'll call up a car when I'm done."

"Good. I want that list of clients. I want a list of the sub-contractors. And I want copies of all their DBS certificates. Have someone contact every school where Malcolm Thompson worked. I want to know if the school in Huntingdon was the only one with suspicions about him. And I want to know if he ever worked in the schools attended by our victims."

Bliss left Bishop to it, glad to have someone to whom he could delegate important matters without worrying whether the job would be done well. Back at HQ he bumped into his old friend, Kaplan.

"How are you doing, Lennie?" Bliss asked.

"Not as well as you. I hear you got a result."

Bliss spread his hands. "Sort of. Time will tell. But put it this way, I'm hoping to free up some time for that curry in the very near future."

"Good man. I hear you put the Yanks in their place as well."

"You hear a lot, mate."

Kaplan tapped the side of his nose. "I keep my ears open. Which reminds me, how close did things come with that suspect who wanted to shoot you?"

Bliss rolled his eyes. Chandler. Probably told Short, who in turn told someone else, who in turn...

"Close enough that I could have done with a change of underwear," Bliss admitted. "I think the bloke originally set out only to scare me, and his own psychosis did the rest. I guess we'll never know."

"And how about this female cop you were hanging around with?"

"Ah, Detective Newman." Bliss smiled at the memory. "Yeah, she was nice. Good cop, too."

"Anything there we can get into when we meet up for that meal?" Kaplan asked, a grin cutting a thin line across his face.

Bliss patted his friend on the arm. "I'm really not sure about that, Lennie. It was probably nothing more than just a moment in time, you know? Anyhow, let me put this bloody case to bed first."

Kaplan winked. "You nail their arses to the wall, Jimmy. Fuckers deserve everything they get."

Back in the Major Crime area Bliss walked in on a minor squabble between DCs Hunt and Ansari. His presence interrupted their bickering.

"What's going on?" Bliss demanded to know, staring down the two detectives.

"Nothing, boss," Ansari said. She shuffled some documents on her desk.

"Nothing, boss," Hunt agreed, his hand resting on the computer keyboard at his own desk.

"It didn't look like nothing. Didn't sound like it, either."

From the few words exchanged with some venom between the two as Bliss had entered the unit, he guessed Hunt was trying to palm Ansari off with some of his own tasks. Hunt was the more experienced officer, and probably considered delegation as a perk of the time he had put in. Bliss wasn't standing for it.

"Whatever it was, kill it now. I realise there's a time pressure, and we're all stressed, but this is the point at which we hang together. We pull our own weight, understand?

"Yes, boss," they both said in unison.

"Good. Anyone unwilling to do that can come and see me and I'll find them something else to do. Something a long way from here."

Bliss looked at them. They looked at each other. Their nods were genuine enough, Bliss thought.

"Good," he said. "Get on with it, then."

It was nothing unusual for the tension to get to the team. If they were not good at their job they would not be part of the investigation, but they were also human with human frailties. Emotion tended to rob even those with the very best of intentions of their manners. Before the operation ended there would be other fires to stamp out, but Bliss knew Hunt and Ansari would be fine. Bliss suspected that within five minutes they would both be huddled together and bad-mouthing him instead. The thought brought a smile to Bliss's face as he headed to his office.

*

Every time Bliss checked his watch or a clock on the wall, twice as many hours had elapsed than he would have guessed. It was always this way when you had someone in custody. Unless they had committed a serious crime, twenty-four hours was the limit for detaining them without charge. As things stood, Marjory Thompson would walk. The Pissed-o-Meter now stood at *ballistic*, and Bliss could not disagree.

With the duty defence brief by her side, Thompson "no commented" her way through the first three interviews. Bliss watched those he did not take part in. In the first he had partnered up with DS Bishop. Then he had let Bishop and Chandler give it a go, believing his own presence in the room served only to antagonise the woman. For the third interview he sent DS Short in with DI Burton, hoping two females might draw something out of Thompson.

The proverbial blood from a stone would have been easier.

The thing about Thompson was that, despite appearances to the contrary, she was no dummy. Her personal hygiene and habits, choice use of language and voluble nature made it easy to infer that she was a poorly-educated women of little substance. Whilst Thompson was no Oxbridge graduate, her education and employment records were surprisingly good. The woman was not a fool, and she certainly had no intentions of backing down.

Thompson's expression scarcely faltered, irrespective of either the content or tone of the interviews. By the end of the third session, Bliss and his team had used up more than half of their allotted time. Long before then, Bliss knew she would not give up her son. They would have to find him without his mother's help, but she could sit and rot right up to the end of the twenty-fourth hour for all Bliss cared. As he made his way from the interview room observation suite to the incident room, he felt sluggish and laden by guilt. None of this needed to have happened. If only he had prosecuted Lucas Delaney eighteen years ago, perhaps a host of young women would not have had their lives ruined by falling victim to a rapist, nor a number of elderly women lose their lives. The pressure to end this, and end it now, was increasing with every passing minute.

Bliss struggled to find the words he would use with his team. It was hard to see how things could get any worse.

*

He was finding it very hard to make sense of all the scrambled thoughts inside his head. It had always been that way; as far back as he could remember he had been the boy everyone else avoided unless they were teasing him or bullying him; sniggered at from afar by the brainiacs and completely ignored by the girls. There was so much going on inside his head, but he had never been able to make sense of any of it.

The voices he heard were just thoughts.

Just stray, malignant thoughts. Not real at all.

He knew that. And yet…

His mother's voice was the loudest, the most strident. The false mother; the bitch mother. She was the one who pushed his buttons, got him all confused and his head spinning in circles.

His actual mother would never treat him like that.

She was kindly and comforting and supportive and ran her fingers through his hair, made sure his nails were strong and sculpted despite their unusual length. She took care of him.

The one whose voice he heard more often was much harsher, so much more judgemental, and the way she mocked him and ridiculed him about the girls made him want to…

Well, best not to think about that.

When he got to thinking that way, it was his father's voice that took over. He hadn't seen his father in a long, long time, but he had never forgotten the gruff-sounding voice, deep and booming and powerful. You did what he told you to do without question, or there would be a heavy price to pay. He had learned that lesson when just a small child.

With his mother's voice (*just thoughts, Malcom,* he told himself, *just thoughts*) going on and on and on to the point where he wanted to scream but instead ended up doing exactly what she wanted him to do, and then his father pitching in and insisting he react to what he had been forced to do, a third voice entered the fray and attempted to make some sense of it all.

That was his own voice, he thought.

His core speaking up.

At least, he hoped it was.

Only it was never strong enough, never forceful enough, and it lacked the strength and conviction to do battle with the other two. They were his mother and father at the end of the day, and what kind of disrespectful son would ignore a parent's wishes?

So now the police were with his mother. They had come to the house. His mother had sent him the text.

THEY ARE HERE. YOU KNOW WHAT YOU NEED TO DO.

He and his mother had talked about what path he should follow if the police should come. Although, when he thought about it now, it was really more a case of his mother had spoken and he had listened.

She had not asked for his opinions.

They had not discussed any of it.

She had simply instructed him.

It was the first time as far as he could recall that his actual mother and the false mother (bitch mother!) had demanded the same thing of him. He wasn't at all sure whether that made things more or less confusing, but it did make those thoughts all the more powerful, louder in his ears, so loud it made him want to scream. When it got like that there was only one thing to do in order to release the searing agony of it all.

He had to do what his mother's voice told him to do.

He looked around, blinking in the dim light.

How had he got here?

How had been able to drive here?

There had been no conscious thought, he had no memory whatsoever of the route he had taken.

Why was he even here at all?

It wasn't the kind of place he would normally come to. But there had to be a reason. A good reason. His mother had told him what needed to be done. If that meant it had to be done right here, then that's how it would be.

He was dressed for the occasion, too. How had that happened? When had that happened?

Focus, he told himself.

His own voice?

You have a job to do.

No, not his own voice after all.

Then he saw her. Walking between a row of parked vehicles. He knew he could reach her before she got anywhere close to where she was going.

"Do it!" his mother said, in a voice so loud he thought it might cleave the world in two.

He stepped out of the relative safety of the car, pulled down the face mask and yanked up the hood of his sweatshirt. Then he started walking, the comforting feel of a carving knife in his hand where just moments before there had been nothing.

*

Having ordered his team and Chandler home for some much-needed down time, Bliss decided to follow his own advice. His house was a jumble of boxes, some open and spewing up scraps of clothing or household items, most still sealed with brown tape. In his living room he had taken time to set up his TV, Tivo box, Blu-Ray device, and the hi-fi system. His pride and joy was the Rega turntable – all two grand's worth. Bliss sat in the room's only armchair, leg support extended. He sipped sixteen-year-old Royal Brackla whisky from a crystal tumbler, and listened to Muddy Waters playing some blues.

The hi-fi system sat in front of sliding glass doors that stretched from one wall to the other. From where he sat, Bliss could see out into the illuminated garden. This was exactly what he needed. The chair, the single-malt scotch, the music, and that view. It brought him a peace unlike any he had known before. He needed this time and space in which to gather his thoughts and make them more orderly. He had become ragged again with his thinking during this investigation, allowing himself to be distracted by Detective Newman, Chandler, and even DI Burton. It was never a good idea to insinuate personal issues into the work environment, but police work in particular demanded that level of professional detachment. Bliss realised he had to work his way back to that.

The young girls and women demanded his best. Their names fluttered about him like moths around a naked lightbulb. Annie Lakeham most of all. Her face, her ruined body, was the only one he had seen close up. Her husband the only victim family member he had met. He planned to visit Derek Payne, the husband of murder victim Carol, the following day. Not that he expected the visit to lead to anything new, to add to the few lines of inquiry they were already following. It was just the right thing to do.

Before moving back to Peterborough, Bliss had decided that life was about balance. He wanted to live rather than merely exist, but he wanted to live in harmony with the world around him. His life had changed in so many ways, and he did not consider his current path to be some sort of fad. His readings had taught him that life was best enjoyed from being centred. Yet this case had him consumed, ignoring everything he had so far learned about relaxation. Bliss mentally rapped himself for that. He had not ignored everything; suggesting otherwise was overly harsh. But he had strayed, and that bothered him.

He was about to replace Muddy Waters with Albert Collins, when his landline rang. So far only one person had used that number, so he could guess who it would be. Bliss smiled as he answered.

"Hi, Mum. How are you doing?" he asked.

"How did you know it was me? You have that caller ID thingy on your service?"

"No, but everyone else I know uses my mobile number."

"I'm not even sure if I have that, Jimmy. Anyway, how are you settling in? I've been watching things on the news about all kinds of things going on in Peterborough. Is that you investigating that?"

"I'm involved, Mum. But don't worry about it. Tell me how things are with you."

"Good. You remember I told you about that group of people I've been talking to on the computer?"

"Yes. The Moonies. You're a hippy now, right?"

"No, you silly sod. The Afterlife group. You know what, Jimmy, this is the best thing I've done since your father passed. I've met so many wonderful people. Some of them live here in Ireland. And we're going to arrange meetings in the future where all of us can get together at one time."

Bliss remained sceptical. The name suggested all kinds of religious connotations, and his atheistic bent caused some concern that his mother might be getting involved with a bunch of charlatans. He knew of groups who organised themselves to fleece the recently bereaved, having them shell out their pensions and savings on nonsense related to spiritual contact with those who had passed away. It was his mother's life, though, and her own spirits had certainly been lifted in recent weeks. Bliss did not have the heart to dissuade her from the way forward she had chosen. Though he would have this organisation checked out.

"That all sounds great, Mum. I'm really pleased for you. I was worried you'd be isolated out there, but I guess with the internet you can at least feel as if you're part of something. The meet-ups sound like a good idea as well. Be nice to meet new people."

A couple of minutes later they touched upon his own health. The flights had not bothered him as much as he thought they would, and a condition triggered by stress was hardly ideal for a Detective Inspector hunting a rapist and sadistic murderer, but he was coping. Which was what he told his mother before they ended the call.

He felt a little more upbeat after hearing how less sorrowful his mother sounded. He decided to go with a Stevie Ray Vaughan album, beginning with the track "Pride and Joy", which felt ridiculously appropriate at that very moment.

Halfway through, his mobile sprang to life. Bliss let out a groan and thumbed the receive icon.

"Inspector Bliss, this is Superintendent Fletcher."

"Ma'am. What is it, have we caught a break?" Bliss could not imagine what circumstances would induce his Superintendent to call him directly when he was officially off duty. Perhaps they had their man at last.

"Inspector, you need to get back to the station right now."

"Of course. What's up?"

"Bliss… I'm sorry, but DS Chandler has been abducted by Malcolm Thompson."

THIRTY-TWO

"Hello, you prick," Marjory Thompson said to Bliss when he walked into the interview room. Her face was puckered with spite and rage.

Bliss took a seat opposite the woman, whose eyes never left his. Upon his arrival back at Thorpe Wood station, the Detective Superintendent had informed him that a text message had been received on Marjory Thompson's mobile, in which her son had indicated the successful abduction of DS Chandler. Subsequent checks by a couple of uniforms out on patrol had discovered Chandler's car in the hotel car park, her keys lying next to it in a puddle. Chandler was absent from her room, her mobile was offline, and CCTV footage confirmed the attack which, whilst indistinct, was enough to convince Fletcher that the text message was the real deal. At that point Bliss insisted that he have one final crack at Marjory Thompson, determined that he could squeeze something from the woman that would help them find her son.

"Hello, Mrs Thompson," Bliss responded, without a flicker of emotion. The interview room reeked of nervous tension. "I think it's about time you handed your son in, don't you?"

Thompson laughed. For some reason that disturbed Bliss more than he could explain. "I should? I can't think of a single reason why."

"Before we continue, please confirm for me whether you want your solicitor here for this interview."

"Am I going to need one?"

"That's not for me to say." Bliss shifted his head to one side and winked, out of shot of the camera. "I suppose it depends on how innocent you are. Or perhaps how brave."

The woman glared at him, before shaking her head. "No need. I can handle you."

"Very well. Tell me, do you love your son, Mrs Thompson?"

"What a stupid question." Thompson frowned, regarding him with suspicion now. "Of course I do."

"Really? Only the murders of those elderly woman suggest your boy absolutely detests you. And if that's the case, you have to wonder why. Did you mistreat Malcolm, Mrs Thompson? Is that why he hates you? Why he pictures you when he kills?"

"Never!" Thompson sat forward and leaned across the table. "I would never hurt Mal. I take care of my son. I look after him. Always have."

"Maybe too well at times, huh? There are different kinds of abuse, you know."

"You're sick."

Bliss smiled. "Oh, I'm the sick one."

Thompson shuffled back, sitting stiffly. "You won't get to me."

"What makes you say that?"

"Because you're a failure. You failed me, Bliss. You failed my daughter. You failed my son as well. When all is said and done, you helped make him what he is today."

"I made a mistake based on evidence at the time. I couldn't have known."

Thompson continued as if Bliss had not spoken. "But that wasn't good enough for you was it? No. You failed my daughter and my son and now you want to take him away from me."

"Because he's a monster. That's why. He needs locking up and the key throwing away."

"You heartless pig-fucker. That's my flesh and blood you're talking about."

"Mrs Thompson, it's quite clear to me that you knew what your son was doing all along. Yet you did nothing to stop him. Young girls have been raped, older women brutally murdered. Is that not heartless? Tell me where I can find him. You owe it to the victims."

Bliss had decided not to reveal at this stage that Thompson's son had snatched Chandler. In his opinion, that would exacerbate the situation and serve only to make the woman all the more determined not to reveal Malcolm's whereabouts.

"Not a chance!" Thompson cried. "Not even with my last breath. You think you're so fucking clever, but we'll see about that. Oh, you have no idea what kind of a shit storm is coming your way, Bliss."

"Idle threats," Bliss said dismissively. "Look, you need to think about this more clearly. It's in your best interests to tell us where we can find your son so that we can end this before things get so much worse for him."

"My boy," Thompson said, again with a hint of pride. "He has his habits. But I can't let you take him away from me, Bliss. I really can't. I would do anything to prevent that from happening."

"You may not want to help me, but you can't stop me hunting him down like a dog. And whilst he has his 'habits' he broke the pattern last night. Went for a slightly older woman this time. Or younger, I guess. Depends on what he intended doing to her I suppose."

"Oh, he's going for broke this time, Bliss. We decided you had to be punished. We decided we had to make things personal, as you have done for me and my family. So, Mal would've started with the rape of your colleague, and he'll end it by killing her and then bringing me her ten shiny nails."

Bliss felt the hair on his arms rise, a chill touch his blood. "Are you telling me you knew what he was going to do? That you conspired with your son to abduct DS Chandler?"

"You just don't get it do you, Bliss? You think you're so clever, but you're just incredibly stupid. I realised what Mal was doing. Of course I did. He's my son, and his father's son in more ways than one. It repulses me to even think about it, but he's my only child now, so what's a mother to do? And then when I saw you were back in the city and had been put in charge of the murder investigation, I wound him up like a clockwork toy and let him go. You can't imagine how delighted I was when I discovered you were here, and having you work on the murders was the cherry on top. In my wildest dreams I never imagined that happening. One of those things that is both unpredictable and inevitable at the same time, I suppose. Sometimes fate just opens a door for you."

Bliss had listened to Thompson with mounting anger and outrage. "You are one sick and twisted individual. So you admit you unleashed your little boy on my friend?"

"What difference does it make now? Yes, that was his part in paying you back."

"Paying me back for what? For not giving your daughter justice? Or for trying to convict your son for being a rapist and murderer?"

"Both of those things, Bliss. Both of those things and more. What started out as one reason became another. Either way it was only right that you pay a hefty price."

"But your own daughter was a victim to both rape and murder. How can you possibly justify setting your son on someone in order to subject them to that same fate?"

Thompson hiked her shoulders and snorted. "He was already on that path. There was nothing I could do to prevent it from happening again. All I did was... point him in a different direction."

"I don't believe that. I don't believe he started all this without some influence from you."

"I am what I am. He is what he is. Mal reacted to how things are between us. I tease him a little, I slap him down when he needs to be, but we always make up in the end. I never asked him to rape, never told him to murder. Well, not until I let him loose on your friend."

Swallowing hard, Bliss thought quickly. "You say Malcolm is his father's son in more ways than one. Do you know about Lucas, Mrs Thompson? Do you know what he did when he went back to America?"

The woman smirked. Her baleful eyes mocked him. "Do you really think I would ever forget what that man was capable of? I was never absolutely certain that he killed my Maisie, but I strongly suspected him. Once he left I lost touch for a long time, but then I saw a documentary on TV about death row prisoners in California, and Lucas's name was mentioned. I was aware that he had once gone by the name of Delaney, and I knew right away it must be him. They mentioned that he had been investigated for those rapes and murders in California. So when they started happening here, of course I knew it had to be Mal. That acorn definitely did not fall far from the tree."

Bliss took a long, deep breath. He could not decide which of the two was the more despicable: Malcolm Thompson for raping and murdering, or his mother who not only did nothing to prevent further attacks, but actively encouraged her son to continue and then aimed him in Chandler's direction. Bliss felt sick to his stomach.

Finally, Bliss nodded and said, "Mrs Thompson, I'm going to ask you one last time to tell me where we can find your son and my detective. Before you answer, let me just say this. If you tell me, I promise you that we will do everything in our power to take Malcolm down with the least possible force appropriate to the situation. If you don't, our armed unit will be given a shoot to kill order."

Thompson started chuckling at him. "Oh, Bliss. You think I can be bought by that little speech. Whichever way you find him, you'll kill him. Even he knows that, and he's prepared for it. But I'll tell you what, if you turn off the tape and video recorder, I might just give you a little something to be getting on with."

Bliss narrowed his gaze and stared deep into Thompson's eyes. There was a gleam there now that had not existed only moments before. It might be something, might be nothing.

"We're done," Bliss said, getting to his feet. "Wait here and I'll have someone fetch you and take you back to your holding cell. You're playing games with me now, and I've had enough of them."

Bliss pressed a button on the recording device which stopped the tape from rolling. He then left the room. Thirty seconds later he returned.

"You have less than a minute," he told Thompson. "I've turned off the camera. If you have anything worthwhile to say to me, say it now. This is your last opportunity."

For a moment, Bliss thought she had been yanking his chain after all. That it had all been mere bluster. But then Thompson nodded and said, "If I were you, I'd be the one holding my mobile when Mal texts in again. I know he will have sent one already, and there's every chance he will send another one soon. See, you prick of a man, sometimes the pain of loss, of knowing what happened and also knowing you could do nothing about it, isn't anywhere near as bad as witnessing it all. I'm not certain, but I think Mal might want you there to see your friend suffer. If he does, he'll send another text. This time it will be for you, Bliss. Just you."

*

Bliss was pacing the floor like a wounded animal searching for a way out of a cage. He was aware of his team watching him, perhaps even growing concerned about his reaction, but he could not stop himself. Chandler was about to become Thompson's fourth rape victim – that they knew of. She was also about to become another of his murder victims. With nothing further from Marjory Thompson, and no clear indication so far as to where her son might have taken Chandler, Bliss was reduced to waiting for a text message that might never come.

He had decided not to tell anyone about his final exchange with Marjory Thompson. For the time being, at least. What he *had* done was volunteer to keep her mobile with him, even if he left to go home. Bliss claimed he wanted to be the first to answer the phone should it ring. Nobody questioned this, and there was no good reason why they should. Bliss realised he was on shaky ground, but figured he still had time to make a final decision and perhaps change his mind once the text came in.

If it came in.

Bliss reasoned that he was not preventing the hunt from going forward by keeping the conversation from his team. The alert for any GPS location on Malcolm Thompson's phone was still active. It was unlikely, however, that the few seconds it would take to send a text would provide a specific location. At that point, the content of the text would dictate Bliss's next move.

"This can't have been a chance encounter," Bishop said, snapping Bliss out of his reverie. "There may be coincidences, but none on that scale. He had to have been lying in wait for Chandler. Therefore, he had to have known where she was staying."

"Which means he had been following her," Short said, jumping in. "Or followed her on that one occasion at least."

Bliss thought about it. "He could just as easily have called all the city hotels. He would have known her name from media reports. Penny was mentioned in at least one newspaper report that I saw. All he had to do was ask for her by name."

"I worry about what he might do now," Carmichael said. "He'll be in a high state of agitation."

"We have all the patrols out we can drum up," Bliss said. Then he nodded. "But I agree, it may not be enough if he's already secreted himself and Chandler somewhere."

"I still can't believe it wasn't David Pearson," Short muttered, shaking her head wearily. "My money would have been on him all day long."

"Yeah, and did you hear about him?" Hunt said, looking around at the team. "He was caught sneaking back into his house. The obs team had no idea he'd slipped out. This time, though, he coughed. You know why he was being so secretive? He's a bloody poacher. He thought we'd bang him up, leaving his mother on her own and in the lurch."

"Fuck him!" Carmichael said. Something on which they could all agree, Bliss reckoned. It made him think of Chandler, how she had expressed her regret at what they had put Pearson through. So typical of her. She always sought the higher road.

Bishop sighed and said, "Boss, I hate to do this, but I need to remind you that Marjory Thompson is now due for release. I know you requested a further twelve hours, and with her admission you're bound to get it. Equally you could now charge her for aiding and abetting. New charge, clock reset. On the other hand, if we let her go we may get lucky and Malcolm might try to contact her. Perhaps we should consider doing that and then sit on the house and monitor all calls."

Bliss could see the logic in the suggestion. Yet releasing Thompson would require him to yield the mobile phone. Right now it represented his only potential method of receiving personal contact from Malcolm Thompson. He could not give that up.

Shaking his head, Bliss said. "Thanks, Sergeant. But I think I'm going to stick with keeping her here for as long as we can. If we get the extra twelve we take them. Then we recharge. We can't know what those two cooked up between them before we hit the house, and I feel safer with her right under our noses. Besides, I don't see DCI Edwards agreeing to putting resources on another twenty-four-hour observation and monitoring job."

"Are you sure about that?"

"You disagree, Sergeant?"

Bishop nodded. "I do, boss. I think you're wrong on this one."

"Well, if I am then I'll take responsibility for it. I have to make a decision now, and I've made it. Please note your disapproval for the record if you feel the need, but let's move on anyway."

Bishop accepted the decision with no further argument. Instead it was DS Short who spoke up. "Once Thompson knew we'd raided the house and would most likely have taken his mother into custody, perhaps all he wanted to do was take out his anger on someone from the team. DS Chandler was mentioned in an article, as you say, so it could just be rage that drove him rather than his usual… whatever lust spurs him on normally."

"That sounds plausible, Sergeant. We have to hope so for DS Chandler's sake. If you're right, he may not harm her immediately. He may try to use her as leverage somehow. As things stand, we can't know, and all we can really do is wait for a decent break in our search for him. And we need that bit of luck quickly, because I dread to imagine what thoughts are running through his head right now."

*

He had never found licking his own wounds to be an easy task. His failure with Davina Ball was embarrassing enough to still burn his checks whenever he reflected upon that night, but there had been a sound reason for it, given the accidental fall he had taken. Yet still he had felt an overwhelming desire to redeem himself in a way that the subsequent rape and murder had not been able to satiate.

Trust his mother to come up with just the right suggestion.

First of all she had excited him, then calmed him again whilst attending to his nails. When he was at his most relaxed, his mother had dropped a hand grenade into his lap: she knew about him.

All about him.

About the rapes.

About the murders.

He listened impassively as his mother gently chided him, before she stepped up a gear with her usual mockery and degradation. He swallowed it all down like the most acidic bile imaginable, before finally his mother began to roll it back. There was to be no final gut punch, no stab to the heart. This time she led him somewhere she had never taken him before: mutual understanding.

This was no mere forgiveness. This was her acknowledgement of what he did and why, indulging him, sympathising with his desires and their origins. Not that she once veered towards allocating blame to herself; that was too much to expect. But this was a side to his mother he had not even dared to hope existed.

And then she had suggested a slightly different path for him to take. His head filled with humming and high-pitched whistles, he listened intently to what his mother had to say. Initially he felt some internal resistance. This police detective was not the kind of young girl who had ignored him all his life, she was a woman who meant nothing to him. Neither was she the kind of woman he would happily slaughter in place of his own mother, for no matter how closed his eyes were and imagination open, he simply could not see this much younger woman as a proxy for the woman whom he loved and despised in equal measure.

Yet the more his mother spoke, the more she ate her way into his mind.

This time it would not be for the usual reasons, which is why nobody would expect it.

This time it would be to inflict pain on someone else, and perhaps help his mother at the same time. Should the need arise.

This time there would be a genuine reason beyond that of desire and rage.

And all he had to do was wait for that first text.

Now, their plans in place and under way, he could not take his eyes off his phone. He did not understand why his mother wasn't calling him, or texting him. That didn't seem right.

He didn't know if she would be angry with him now, and he really didn't care. He had played his part from the moment he received that initial text telling him that the police had come after all, and that he knew what to do next. He had known. And he had obeyed, following her instructions to the letter. Yet still she had not contacted him since. It didn't matter if she was annoyed with him. He just wanted his mother to hold him.

To stroke his hair.

He wanted to feel those nails on his scalp.

Burrowing into his flesh.

If his mother wasn't contacting him there had to be a damned good reason.

He could think of only one.

Which meant it was time for the final act.

THIRTY-THREE

*D*ark Night of the Soul is the title of a piece of work by the sixteenth century Spanish poet St John of the Cross. Its common usage refers to times of utmost despair and loss of self. Bliss considered this as he experienced just such a night in the hours that followed the secretive conversation with Marjory Thompson.

Having returned home a little after 2.00am, Bliss slumped onto his chair and stared out into the night. As much as he desired the kind of escape only alcohol could provide, he did not fetch a beer from the fridge in case he had to drive somewhere in a hurry. After a while he opened a tin of creamed rice and ate his way through half of it, before shoving aside the first food he had consumed in many hours. He tried to stretch out and find some peace, but constantly found himself perching on the edge of the recliner with his head in his hands contemplating all the terrible indignities his friend might be suffering at the hands of a psychopath. Bliss tried hard to summon up a positive frame of mind, but every thought had become dark and bleak and utterly without hope.

Shortly before dawn, with Bliss gnawing at his knuckles by this time, came the text he had been waiting for. It told him where to go, it told him what to do and, more importantly, it told him what not to do.

Two-and-a-quarter hours after receiving the text from Malcolm Thompson, Bliss nosed his Insignia into the small village of Happisburgh, which nestled on the Norfolk coast approximately halfway between Cromer and Great Yarmouth. The latter part of the journey had been perilous, with rain and fog obscuring the way ahead. Bliss had tempered his speed only by a little, and on more than one occasion a bend had sneaked up on him out of nowhere, causing a moment of alarm and a wrestle with the steering wheel.

Bliss found navigation easier without headlights on full beam, but still his view of the road was reduced to only twenty feet or so, the fog aided by rain in its attempts to blind him. The further east he drove the more he felt the car buffeted by high winds. It was only when he saw a bright light occasionally piercing the wall of haze ahead that he realised he was close to the shore. Bliss strained his eyes until a slight break in the grey veil allowed him to see the very tip of the lighthouse away to his right. At that point he had to stamp on the brake, almost missing the turn that would take him to the meeting point.

Guilt and fear drilled into his head. The text had insisted he come alone. That the first sign of another vehicle or person would result in Chandler being both defiled and killed. Bliss had adhered to the instruction.

He was all too aware of the repercussions should he fail to get Chandler back unscathed, let alone alive. Not the fact that it would mean the end of his career, nor in having to confront the scorn and anger of his colleagues. Bliss feared what it would do to him as a person, the effect upon his mind. He did not know if he could cope with the loss of his friend, but he was absolutely certain he would not survive being responsible for it. Following the instruction to come alone was a gamble, but one Bliss believed he had no choice but to take. He would accept whatever punishment his superiors deemed fit afterwards, provided Penny Chandler was returned safe and well when it was all over. Nothing else mattered to him.

Killing the lights as soon as he reached the lighthouse itself, Bliss turned the car around, facing it back down the single-track lane, and left the engine ticking over. He doubted the sound of the engine on idle could be heard from more than twenty paces away. As Bliss opened the door it was almost swept from his hand by the high wind. He exited unsteadily, raised the collar of his heavy winter jacket, and gave himself up to the elements. As he closed the car door behind him, rain beating down, the chill air almost thick enough to touch, Bliss noticed something deep into the mist. A vague shape, darker than anything else around it, yet impossible to identify. With no clear plan in mind from this point on, he made his way towards it, and within seconds realised it was another vehicle.

Bliss forced himself to slow down. He wiped rainwater from his eyes, blinked rapidly. Approaching from the rear of the vehicle, Bliss edged his way towards the driver's side door. Step by step the amorphous object coalesced into something more distinguishable. He could see no one inside, but that did not mean they were not there. Bliss reached the car, paused only briefly, then grasped the door handle, tugged back and wrenched the door open.

The car was empty.

As he straightened, Bliss thought he heard something. He looked ahead, the wind stepping up a notch, rain decreasing slightly as it did so. A trade-off, it seemed. Something fluttered close by, out of sight and out of reach. Bliss sensed it more than saw it. Something he felt shifting the air around him rather than anything he heard or could identify. Almost close enough to touch, yet invisible to him. Some kind of apparition, an unseen presence all around him. The thought chilled his heart.

The sound came again, and although it appeared to be far off and he knew it was being distorted by the weather conditions, Bliss was convinced it was a voice. Ignoring the eerie sensation of an unwelcome presence, the choking claustrophobic conditions, and the danger that lay out there in the grey, moist mass, he moved towards it.

From what Bliss could remember from his brief view of the area on Google maps, he was pretty sure he knew where he was headed. If he had not been turned around by the fog, Bliss felt certain he was shifting towards the edge of the cliffs. He could see the way ahead only so far as to feel confident that he would not stumble over the side, but that also meant he could not move as quickly as he would have liked. Bliss assessed the distance and reckoned he still had maybe thirty or forty yards to walk before the drop, but he did not want to rely on memory alone.

The sound came again. Bliss jerked his head up.

A voice.

Definitely this time.

Given the density of the fog and the lashing rain, the sound could have been close by, but it seemed to Bliss that it was still some way off in the distance. It felt as if it came from ahead and to his left, which would take him towards the entrance to the beach and the village itself. The voice had been high-pitched, and it might have been his imagination but Bliss thought it was calling his name.

Penny. Please let it be her, and please let her be safe.

Fog shifted effortlessly across the land towards the water, spilling over the edge in a foamy white torrent as it met the inclement weather coming in the opposite direction. Bliss had to lean into the wind coming in off the North Sea. It was almost as if it was trying to blow him backwards, away from the danger. It drove rain into his unprotected flesh, stinging like a shower of needles. Each gust, however, parted the fog as if it were a barrier of off-white curtains momentarily being pulled aside. This gave Bliss a much greater perception of depth, and he realised he was closer to the cliff edge than he had initially believed. Thunder rolled across the cliff tops. When it continued, but then ebbed and flowed, Bliss understood he was wrong. What he could hear was not thunder but rather the sea, waves booming against the angled cliff face and rocks below.

"Jimmy!"

Clear this time.

Still distant, but a woman's voice calling his name. It remained indistinct enough that he could not tell for certain if it was Chandler, but he knew it had to be. His heart raced and breathable air was suddenly hard to find as he trudged on.

The further he got from the lighthouse the more he became aware of its beam pulsing, momentarily slicing through the mist ahead of him before winking out as if it had never been there at all.

Bliss stopped walking, gathering himself. He wiped rain and ocean spray from his face, salt stinging his lips. Another sound reached his ears, and in recognising it he also realised what the flitting ambiguous shapes were that he had seen earlier: hovering birds, disturbed by the gusts and complaining bitterly, caught out by unwelcome currents of air. Not wraiths, as his imagination had earlier briefly suggested. Just seabirds.

The question for Bliss now was whether to respond to whoever was calling his name. If he could not see them then neither could they see him. It was not clear to him whether this was advantageous, nor to whom. Logic suggested that the longer he went undetected the better, possibly affording him the opportunity to surprise Malcolm Thompson. Yet stumbling upon him and Chandler did not feel right, either. And in this ever-thickening fog, that was the most likely outcome if Bliss continued to blunder on aimlessly.

That or miss them altogether.

Which was a genuine possibility out here right now. He could walk within ten paces of them and not know they were there. Yet neither could he stand and wait like a tethered goat.

Bliss hunched forward and continued to walk as steadily as possible, as firm of foot as he could manage, easing his way in what he hoped was the direction of the voice. He did not reply to it, choosing instead to be guided by it when it came again.

Seconds later it did. This time there were two words in addition to his name:

"Help me!"

THIRTY-FOUR

Bliss didn't know if it was mounting panic or terror stabbing hooks into his heart, but he thought the voice sounded closer. More clear, yet weaker at the same time.

He had to fight his every natural instinct in order not to shout out a response. Instead, he adjusted his direction slightly until he believed he was walking north along the edge of the cliff. It felt as if the wind had him trapped inside a funnel, for no matter which way he turned it wrapped around him, the damp tangy air seeping into his lungs and forcing him to him cough it back up. He imagined this was what it might be like to be caught up in an automatic car wash.

"That's far enough, Bliss!"

Bliss looked left, right, straight ahead. An indistinct dark mass emerged from out of the pale grey shifting fog. A standing stone, perhaps. Or maybe two people. It was impossible to tell for sure, but Bliss continued to inch his way towards the nebulous form. No way Thompson could tell if he was still approaching, not at that distance. Bliss remained silent, but on the move.

"I said that's far enough!"

And this time it was. As rain swirled and battered against him, Bliss could now see it doing the same to both Thompson and Chandler, whose hands were thrust behind her back – lashed together, he guessed. He could not yet make out the details of his colleague's face, but she was barely 125lb and not a woman built for this baleful weather, so Bliss could only imagine she was suffering. The intermittent sweep of the lighthouse torch created a vague slow-motion strobe effect through the fog as they all stood motionless, casting shadows that appeared to flicker and dance.

"Are you okay, Penny?" Bliss called out, blinking away the rain, the wind jabbing at his eyes. Standing still was the worst thing he could do under any circumstances; his balance always under greater duress when motionless. Now he felt himself rocked back and forth by the elements. Some of the gusts were so fierce he thought one might pick him up and deposit him onto the rocks and into the sea below.

"Fuck her!" Thompson shouted. "It's me you have to worry about."

Charmer's just like this mother, Bliss thought.

"I need to know that my sergeant is all right."

"And I need you to damn well focus on me."

"My sergeant tells me she's okay or I walk away."

"That's a risky tactic, Bliss," Thompson said after a slight pause. "Do you really want to fuck with the only person keeping your colleague this side of the cliff edge?"

"I just need to hear her tell me for herself. Then you have my full attention."

He heard a muffled muttering, and then Chandler's unsteady voice saying, "It's me, Jimmy. I'm fine, boss."

Bliss could have broken down and wept right then. Relief and rage tore through him. His emotions were all over the place, and anger was fast becoming the dominant force. Were it not for the presence of Chandler, Bliss felt as if he might rush at Thompson, wrap his arms around the man and take them both out into the void and whatever waited for them below. But to his right he saw the land fall away, Chandler no more than two paces from her own oblivion.

"Tell me what it is that you want, Thompson?" Bliss asked, his breathing ragged as the moist fog ate into his throat once more.

"You know what I want. For you to suffer. You get the choice, pig. I can throw this bitch over the cliff now, or I can have a bit of fun with her first while you watch."

"You might have misjudged this, Thompson. I'm sure my sergeant would rather go over that edge than be subjected to a vile intrusion by the likes of you."

Thompson laughed. "Yeah, except that I know you will both want to stretch this out just in case I make a mistake, to see if you can somehow save her. So I've misjudged nothing."

"You know you're mad, don't you?" Bliss said. "Stark raving mad. Knowing what I do about you now, I can't help but wonder if your mother drove you to carrying out those despicable acts, or if the depravity was lurking inside that demented brain of yours all along."

"Do you want me to push her off the cliff, Bliss? Do you? I will, you know."

"You do and you lose your leverage, Thompson. There would be nothing stopping me then from hurling you down there to join her."

There was silence for several moments, other than the faint cries of the birds and howl of the wind, waves battering the rocks far away. Bliss had been debating whether or not to tell Thompson about his mother, that she was in custody, charged with aiding and abetting both rape and murder. It was a tough call, but he opted to play the only card he had.

"I have a bit of leverage myself, Thompson," Bliss said. His eyes constantly flicked from Chandler to the man who held her, hoping for one chance to intervene. He could tell by his colleague's eyes that she was close to breaking down. "We have your mother in custody. She confessed to everything. She will be charged, and she will do time and plenty of it."

"No!" Thompson shook his head furiously, taking a step behind Chandler now as if using her as a shield. "My mother would never do that. She would never break."

"We didn't need to break her. In fact, she volunteered the information quite happily. She seemed very proud of herself."

"You're lying."

"Think about it, Thompson. I know that she realised you were responsible for the series of rapes and murders, after which she encouraged you and then sicced you on my colleague here. How could I know all that if your mother hadn't told me?"

For several seconds only the wind and rain and sea heaving somewhere beyond and below them could be heard. Bliss tried to draw Chandler's gaze but her eyes were glassy and inattentive. She was shutting down, weakened and seemingly accepting of her fate.

"If you're not lying," Thompson said, "then we can trade. You free my mother, I free this bitch."

"Don't do that, Jimmy!" Chandler cried out, and then squealed sharply.

"Don't you speak again, bitch!" Thompson snapped. "Or I'll twist your arm even further back next time. Bliss, you get my mother freed. You do that, your colleague gets to live."

Bliss cuffed moisture from his face and licked his lips. Chandler's outburst told him she was not quite done. The wind howled and the rain beat down with relentless abandon. He was caught this way and that, swaying unsteadily. He widened his stance and dug his heels in. Things had changed around. Suddenly he really did have some clout of his own. Only now he had to make the most of it.

"And how do you see that working out exactly?" Bliss asked.

With every other word, Bliss took a small step. Creeping his way closer to them.

"How do you think I can contact the rest of my colleagues from here? You think a mobile is going to work out here in this weather? I'm not even sure one would work on this shore at the best of times, but in this thick fog...? What kind of a masterplan was this, Thompson."

Bliss realised the man had opted for the dramatic over the practical. It must have seemed like such a good idea at the time. Remove both him and Chandler from the familiar. Drag them out here into an area of clear danger and opportunity for even accidental harm. He could not have counted on the weather playing such a massive part, but the cliff edge was intentional. Thompson was nowhere near as dumb as others had imagined him to be, but he did have one thing working against him: he was crazy.

"What are we doing out here anyway?" Bliss called out. "Why this place?"

"We came here a few times on holiday when I was a kid. My gran had a caravan nearby. Me and Maisie used to go fishing for eels. This was… this was the last place I ever saw my sister happy."

Bliss nodded to himself. Now the location made some sort of sense. Thompson's sister was still reaching out to her brother from the grave after all these years.

He took another half step closer.

Now Bliss could see the fatigue and strain written large on Chandler's face. Despair in her eyes. Fear, too. It was quite possible that his friend believed she was about to die, and Bliss could see she was on the verge of melting into shock. He recognised that in her mind the situation they were in had no good ending. He glanced at Thompson, who was now peering angrily at his own phone. Seeing no signal bars, Bliss guessed. He knew he could not advance a great deal further before Thompson sensed the shift in proximity. Yet he was still too far away. No matter how quickly Bliss moved he would not reach Chandler in time if Thompson decided enough was enough. No time even if he made the decision to rush the man instead.

The situation began to feel hopeless. Bliss felt choked and crushed by the thought that he might lose Chandler after all. He had to avoid that at any cost. No matter what the risk to himself. But before desperation set in, he had to try one last time to turn things around.

"Let's all go back and head into to the village," Bliss suggested, as the beam of light swung around one more time to brush up against them. "We can call from there. I'll make the call, Thompson. I can't guarantee they will let your mother go in exchange for Chandler, but they might for me instead. I can at least try. You can sit there alongside me in the same vehicle and listen to every word we exchange."

Bliss tried his best to sound reasonable, though he felt anything but. Deep loathing and hatred for this man burned like molten steel in his heart.

"You think I'm falling for that bullshit?" Thompson sneered, slowly shaking his head.

"Falling for what? How is it a trick? You still hold all the cards even after we take this back to the village. I can't call from here, you know that now, so what do you suggest we do?"

After a moment, Thompson said, "You go back. You go alone and make the call. Do whatever you have to do. Then you bring me answers."

"That's no good. How will any of us confirm when your mother is free if we have no phone signal out here? I can't keep driving back and forth to ask. And how will you know I am telling you the truth if you don't hear it for yourself?"

Bliss noted Thompson inclining his head as he tried to work things out. Deep in thought, Thompson was paying less attention to Chandler, which had been Bliss's strategy all along. He wanted to try and isolate just the two of them now: him and Thompson. Try to remove his colleague from the equation.

"How about this," Bliss said, as if an idea had just occurred to him. "I stay here with you. Just me. You let my sergeant go. She makes the call for me, explains what the situation is. They set your mother free, DS Chandler drives back and tells us when it's done."

Thompson's face twisted and curled as he considered the suggestion. Bliss swayed as the wind took hold again, curls of fog drifting around his legs like fat, white snakes. He willed the man to go with it. It was the longest of long shots, but he had to get Thompson away from Chandler and these cliffs.

To Bliss's horror, Thompson gripped Chandler's arms tighter still as he first eased her away to arms' length and then shuffled them both back six inches closer to the edge.

"I may be crazy according to the likes of you, Bliss, but I am not fucking stupid. The only thing keeping you from killing me here and now is the fact that I have this bitch alongside me."

"Then tell me how," Bliss snapped back, hearing the desperation in his voice. "How do we do this without being able to call anyone. How, Malcolm? How?"

"All right, all right, all right! Let me think, fuck you."

"It can't be done unless we go elsewhere. Doesn't have to the village, but it does need to be somewhere we can at least get a phone signal. You have to see that. You must be able to recognise that, Malcolm!"

Bliss was desperately trying to hurry him now, hoping to confuse Thompson into losing his composure. He felt it was the best way to get the man to listen, to accept what he was being told. It wasn't a lie; there could be no resolution in the way Thompson wanted whilst they stood out there enveloped by the fog and the rain with no communication possible. The fact that Marjory Thompson was never going to be released from police custody was a bridge that would have to be crossed as they came to it. Hopefully, if he did manage to call HQ, then whoever he spoke to would be savvy enough to play along. For Bliss, the immediate concern was removing Chandler from this perilous situation, one that was getting all the more precarious with each second that ticked by.

Something occurred to Bliss then. Something that would depend on Chandler being sufficiently alert despite her predicament and the shock that was beginning to settle upon her like a cloak cast from concrete. He decided it was worth a gamble.

"How's your ankle holding up, Penny?" Bliss shouted across. "When we spoke yesterday you told me you'd sprained it. I wondered how it was handling this uneven terrain. I wouldn't want you to stumble on anything and make it worse."

Chandler had told him no such thing.

"It's not good, Jimmy. I'm struggling a little."

Bliss smiled to himself. Though clearly frightened and in terrible danger, Chandler still had her wits about her. He hoped that was enough.

"Will you two shut the fuck up and let me think damnit!"

Thompson was unravelling. Bliss knew arguing with him was a risk, and he had no intention of pushing the man so far that he broke. He just needed Thompson to bend.

At that moment something triggered in Bliss's memory. Not long ago he had read about increased coastal erosion. Bliss was aware that these cliffs felt the weight of rain often throughout the year, every year. The cliff edge was where the soil was at its weakest, and therefore the most vulnerable to shifts. He looked at the placement of Chandler's feet, and in that instant feared for her life. Not at the hands of a madman, but to the tragedy of a stupid accident caused by the ferocious weather. As if to hammer home the point, a fierce wet gust swept in and caused them all to reel. Still the spinning shaft of light sporadically punctured the ever-shifting wall of fog to bathe them in an eerie glow.

"Come on, Malcolm," Bliss said, loud but not severe. The use of the killer's first name was deliberate. "Even if we move away from here you still have the upper hand. I'm sure you don't have the cliffs as your only deterrent. That you have a weapon of some kind. You're in control. But you must understand that I cannot free your mother from here. That's just the way it is."

Thompson shook his head. Bliss could tell from the slump in the man's shoulders that he was weakening. The killer grasped Chandler's arm and interlocked it with his own. He pulled her tight, and took a step forwards and to her right – away from the point where the earth fell away. The moment they moved, Chandler slid her foot out from beneath her and fell forward, her weight and momentum dragging Thompson with her.

Bliss had felt his muscles coiled, tensing, waiting for the moment when he could spring forward. He did so the moment he saw Chandler's leg start to move. Bliss hit Thompson at precisely the moment when the killer's grasp slipped away from Chandler's arm. For that instant Thompson stood alone, unbalanced. Bliss slammed into him shoulder first. His pace, weight and momentum were superior to the killer's, and despite Thompson's natural forward movement he was knocked backwards. As his arms flew up in the air, his left foot got caught in the sodden turf. Thompson's body twisted, his arms flailed, causing the fog to swirl around him as if an ethereal ribbon were tied to his wrist.

The two of them hit the ground hard at just about the same time, the intermittent beam from the lighthouse briefly washing them with its light. Bliss found himself on his knees, arms outstretched in order to regain his balance. Thompson' face was only inches from his own, and Bliss saw his eyes were round and wide and terrified. A glance further on told him why: Thompson's legs right up to his upper thighs were hanging over the edge of the cliff, thrashing around in the air seeking to attain a purchase they could not possibly find.

Several seconds passed. Bliss first thought about the frightened little boy whose sister had been so brutally torn from this world, and then the kind of man Malcolm Thompson had become. Was he worth saving? Bliss didn't think so. He thought the world would be better served if Thompson suddenly ceased to exist. Only that same world did not revolve around what Bliss thought was best for it. So in spite of his loathing for the man, he reached out to grasp both his hands.

For a moment, Thompson resisted and fought Bliss off, screaming obscenities at him. The movement served only to drag him further backwards, further over the cliff edge. The next time Bliss attempted to hold on to him, Thompson let him, the sudden realisation of his hazardous situation etched into the man's horrified features. Their hands locked for a second, then slid away, the rain on their flesh making it difficult to form a strong grip. They reached out again, fingers clawing. Some sort of hold was obtained, but Bliss felt it was still too weak. He wanted to release and try one more time, but if he did so he could not be certain of making it.

Thompson begged for help, still thrashing around like a distressed fish on a hook, heaving his body from side to side.

"Stop struggling," Bliss screamed at him. "You're only making it worse. You have to calm down and lie still."

Either Thompson did not hear him or he ignored Bliss's advice, for his wild movements continued unabated. If anything, they increased as his panic intensified. Clearly the man was terrified, half of his body now hanging out in open space, a sheer drop into a raging sea waiting below to swallow him whole if he could not be pulled back.

Bliss tightened his grip.

He thought he had a better hold this time. Believed it was strong enough to enable him to haul Thompson back onto firm and secure land. He started to tug.

And then the earth gave way beneath them.

Bliss felt it, the shudder of a massive vibration beneath his chest. Thompson must have felt it, too. His screeching grew louder, his every movement became more violent. Thompson was bucking now, this way and that, squirming to regain some footing, some sort of hold. The effect of the lighthouse allowed Bliss to see Thompson's terrified features before the view was mercifully snatched away again.

The jolt from below came once more. Bliss felt his chest being thrust up into the air as the soil raised and broke away beneath him. It was as if a demonic mouth with jagged teeth had opened up in the earth, seeking a sacrifice. The upward surge caused Bliss's arms to raise from his prone position, and every inch they elevated weakened his grip on Thompson's hands. It had the exact same effect on the killer, and with that joint motion Bliss felt their fingers slip away from each other before finally parting.

"No!" they cried in unison as the cliff edge gave way.

Bliss would never know how much anguish he truly felt at that moment. But he would never forget the sight of Malcolm Thompson easing away almost in slow motion at first, falling backwards on a huge wedge of soil, before being sucked down into the grim void below where the rocks and the sea waited. The fog danced and parted around the flailing figure, then regrouped again to form its substantial barrier. Thompson was gone, as if he had never been. Bliss thought he heard the man cry out one last time. It did not so much recede as simply die.

THIRTY-FIVE

Five days later, Bliss huddled together with Chandler beneath a canopy of overhanging tree branches. They had opted to walk around the lakes at Ferry Meadows, and a downpour had caught them unawares. Despite being wrapped in warm, heavy clothing, they shivered in the freezing shower of rainwater that made its way through the meagre protection. Bliss didn't mind at all, though he kicked up a fuss and blamed his colleague for forcing him outside in such awful weather. Chandler gave as good as she got. As she always did. He was happy to have her back, the secondment to Sapphire having been cancelled just as soon as Bliss had been able to make the call.

"This seems like a sunny beach in Bermuda compared to what we went through on that cliffside," Chandler said, rubbing her upper arms to get some warmth into them. She stopped suddenly, glanced up at him and winced. "Sorry. I don't suppose you want reminding."

Bliss shrugged, staring off into the distance across the lake. "I survived, you survived. What's not to like?"

"Now that's a first. Someone died and Jimmy Bliss doesn't want to take on the burden of guilt for it. And rightly so. If there's any blame going around it should fall on my shoulders. You were on the ground, helpless really in your position. I just sat there on my backside and watched. I froze. Choked. Maybe if I had–"

"Don't do that to yourself, Pen. You tell me off enough for wallowing, so heed your own advice. You'd just escaped with your life. You were in shock. Your hands were tied behind your back. Nobody could think straight in those circumstances. And what could you really have done?"

Chandler gave a stiff nod. "I suppose."

"Malcolm Thompson had it coming. I doubt even his mother will truly grieve over him, not deep down where it counts. She despised and loved him in equal measure. He became the product of her insanity."

"But he's still responsible for his actions, right?"

"Of course." Bliss nodded as he turned to face her. Chandler was a staunch believer in accountability. "Pen, at the time I would have been happy to have her there as well and see them both go over that cliff together. I suppose in many ways the old me would have held on to that. I have a different perspective these days. To a certain degree, at any rate. He *is* responsible, and he *had* to be held to account. But he was also a victim of sorts. Not in the same way as his own victims. They were entirely innocent and he doesn't deserve to be thought of in the same way. But we can't know what kind of person Malcolm Thompson would have turned out to be were it not for his mother's influence. It's likely he had his own warped mind – just look at who his parents were. Still, as she told me herself, his mother wound him up and let him go towards the end there, and I wonder if part of her had always been doing something similarly repugnant."

"I understand what you mean," Chandler said. "And I don't disagree. It's hard to disassociate the factors behind an act from the act itself. I think if you drill down deep enough every person who ever committed a crime would have one of those causes to point at and say 'That's where it all began, that's where I started to turn.' Society can't afford to look at it that way, though. If we did, no one would go to prison, not even for murder."

"I'm with you, Pen. Don't think otherwise. It's just that I can also see the other side of the coin these days. Ultimately, the only result that matters to me is that you and I walked away."

It had taken Bliss three full days to clear things up with both DCI Edwards and Detective Superintendent Fletcher, to ensure no charges were going to be brought against him. Currently he was in the middle of some down time from his troubles back at Thorpe Wood, and so he was allowing his mind to run loose.

No ceilings, no walls, no boundaries whatsoever. Beneath it all there was no angst tearing him apart. That Thompson had died whilst he and Chandler had lived was something he was comfortable with. He had tried to save the man. Done all he could, given the awful conditions. Bliss felt that Mother Nature and Mother Earth had combined to consume Thompson, providing their own form of justice. Who was he to argue with that?

Bliss coughed up a laugh and took a long, deep breath, removing himself deliberately from his reverie. Those deep levels of soul-searching could wait for the Occupational Health therapist.

"Bloody hell it's cold and damp out here," he said, rubbing his hands together. "Whose bright idea was it to take a walk on a day like this?"

"Don't get me started."

"Not that I don't enjoy the cold and rain occasionally. I just don't recommend it when it's wrapped inside a thick fog on the edge of a sheer drop is all."

Shaking her head, Chandler said, "What a mad pair of bastards those two were. So, she manipulated her son into coming after me specifically so that you would eventually be sucked in and end up suffering. How does a person even begin to conceive of a plan like that?"

"I spoke to my friendly Prof over in Cambridge. His best guess is that over the years her own guilt at the loss of her daughter manifested itself into anger and that she felt compelled to direct her increasing desire for retribution against someone other than herself. I reckon for some time that may have been aimed at her son. Next in line was me, probably because I represented the official service that let Lucas Delaney get away with it. It's likely that she had been tearing down her son's self-esteem from an early age, which built up his growing resentment towards her. But she would have held all the power in that relationship."

"Did he have any further thoughts as to how the rape and murder desires spilled over?"

"He did, yes. He felt it likely that after carrying out the rapes, which were genuine lustful yearnings, Thompson subsequently beat himself down again afterwards, with a lot of help from his mother. And because he blamed her but could never find the strength to take it out on her directly, he chose surrogates in order to vent his anger."

Chandler shivered. "Speaking of mothers, how was yours when you told her what happened?"

Bliss smiled. He had called his mother to let her know much of what had taken place, mainly because he did not want her to find out first by reading a newspaper article or watching an item on the TV news.

"I tactfully negotiated my way around how close I was to being dragged off the edge of that cliff with Thompson," Bliss admitted. "She didn't need to have that image fluttering around inside her head."

Chandler turned to face him. "One day someone should tell your mother what a bloody hero you are, Jimmy."

"I'm no hero. I was bricking it out there with that wind almost forcing me over the side."

"You're a hero to me. And to others who know the truth. You risked your career and then your life for me, and I will never forget that."

Bliss nudged his friend with his elbow. "Oh, stop it. You're embarrassing me."

"Deal with it. There's a lot more fawning where that came from."

"Listen, if the Professional Standards Department get called in, just speak up on my behalf. That's all I ask of you."

Chandler narrowed her gaze. "You think they might? The Super seemed to be on your side."

"She was. Even Edwards came down in my favour to a certain degree. But I broke the rules. And not for the first time. If it had gone the other way and I'd lost you, Pen…" Bliss shook his head. It did not bear thinking about.

"You did what any of us would have done. Not a single member of the team spoke out against you. Every one of them said that, if asked, that's exactly what they will say: that they would have handled it in exactly the same way."

Bliss was touched by the support he had received from everyone at Thorpe Wood. Even Grealish had made a point of slapping him on the back and congratulating him. Despite the shadow still hanging over his head, Bliss was starting to feel as if things had changed for the better.

It had been an eventful few days.

Robbie Newman had mailed him to say that she had been allowed to take part in the re-questioning of Lucas Delaney, and she also took time to reiterate her willingness to show him around her city if he ever got over to LA again. Bliss did not hate the idea. His team was nicely moulding itself into something he could feel proud of, and in Bishop, Short, Carmichael, Ansari and Hunt, Bliss felt a bond had been formed that would endure. Chandler coming back into the fold was, of course, the icing on top. And even DCI Edwards had found her humanity it seemed, for she had been only warm and congratulatory following events on the coast.

Those were the silver linings.

As for the remorseless clouds, David Pearson was now attempting to sue them for harassment, but Bliss knew that would go away in time. Chandler had been right about that: the team had put the man through the wringer, the force of which must have been terrifying. Malcolm Thompson was dead, but the trail of misery and mayhem left behind in his wake would resonate down the years for so many innocent people. His father would by now have been charged for multiple counts of rape and of murder, but it could hardly impact on his death row existence. Marjory Thompson was on remand having been charged with aiding and abetting a number of crimes including the abduction of a police officer. She wasn't going anywhere in a hurry, but lives had been both lost and wrecked, and for what?

"So much misery," Bliss said softly. His shoulders slumped. "Where will it all end, Pen?"

Chandler shook her head, damp hair flapping in the strong breeze. "It won't, boss. That's the thing about our job. Tomorrow's another day."

"Today's not over yet. Who knows when the next call might come in and what it might bring?"

Just a moment or two later, his phone rang. The two looked at each other for a moment, and then each shook their head. Astonished at the timing, Bliss reached inside his jacket and took out his mobile.

"DI Bliss," he said.

"Fancy a drink, boss?"

It was Chandler. Bliss looked up to find her laughing as she stood with her phone to her ear. She had obviously thumbed his speed-dial number whilst her phone was still in her pocket.

"You think you're funny?" he asked.

Chandler nodded. "Actually, yes I think I am."

"Tell me why I'm welcoming you back on my team?" Bliss asked.

"Because I'm cute and cuddly and a genuine pleasure to be around."

"No, that doesn't sound right at all. Try again."

"Because I'm bloody good at my job."

"Nope. That seems entirely wrong."

"Okay. You asked for it. You want me back because you can't cope without me."

He said nothing for a moment. Then he gave Chandler a sidelong glance, smiled and said, "That's the one, Pen. That's the one."

Bliss then put an arm around his sergeant and led her away.

THIRTY-SIX

"**Y**ou kept your word to me, Inspector," Joe Lakeham said to Bliss. His eyes were red-rimmed, cheeks dappled with tears, yet still he managed to force a grateful smile as the two sat once again sipping tea in Lakeham's living room. "And I truly thank you for that."

Bliss nodded. "I'm not sure I believe in closure, exactly, but this is probably the closest you're ever going to get."

Lakeham shook his head. "Oh, no. No, that will maybe come when the man's mother has been convicted and sentenced."

"She's as good as in my book. Nothing is going to go wrong with this prosecution, Mr Lakeham. I'm as certain of that as I have been about anything in all my years of service."

"That's good to know. Even so…"

"I understand," Bliss said. "You won't accept it's a done deal until she's serving time."

"Exactly so, Inspector."

"And what then, sir?"

Lakeham looked up at him. "What do you mean?"

Bliss paused. He felt there was unfinished business still to discuss.

"Mr Lakeham, I've been where you are. I know what it's like to come home to an empty house. I know that it feels like when you walk into empty rooms. There are mornings when you never want to drag yourself out of bed, nights when you never want to get back into it. I never had the pleasure of sharing my life with Hazel for as long as you shared yours with Annie, but I do appreciate the hole left behind by such a loss. A hole no one and nothing can fill. I also know the kind of thoughts that can worm their way inside your head. They burrow deep, eat away at you, and you reach a stage where you believe there is no point in carrying on."

"And is there?"

"Aren't I living proof that there is?" Bliss asked.

The living room screaming of his wife's absence, Lakeham shook his head. "You were a younger man, Inspector. You still had much to offer."

"It's not about age," Bliss argued. "It's having a sense of self-worth. You're as valuable a person individually as you were when you were one half of a couple. If you believed in yourself when your wife was here with you, believe in yourself now. Anyway, you owe it to Annie."

Lakeham frowned. "Now, that's the first time you've uttered anything trite in my presence, Inspector."

Bliss inclined his head. "Thing is, sir, I don't see it that way. I actually believe it. I am convinced that Annie would wish you a long and meaningful life. Perhaps you believe you'll be joining her again, and may therefore wish to do so as soon as possible. If so, then I don't share that belief. I think we get one chance, and when we stumble we pick ourselves back up and we go again until life decides to quit on us, not us on it."

After a few moments, the elderly man narrowed his gaze further and said, "You're quite the philosopher, Inspector."

"You learn to be when you start to talk yourself out of dark thoughts on lonely evenings. No good can come of that kind of thinking."

"You don't even know what I *have* been thinking."

"Oh, believe me I do. I saw it there on the morning I first came here. I saw it again this evening when you opened the door to me. Don't get me wrong, Mr Lakeham, I do understand why, I do see the reasoning. Like I say, I've been there. I explored all kinds of possibilities inside my head in the days, weeks and months following my wife's murder. Sometimes the loneliness is tangible enough to choke you. And I don't mean just being on your own,

I mean no longer being with that one special person who made sense of your existence. But I'm here to tell you that it passes. It never goes away, not entirely, but it does become... bearable. And then one day you realise that you're having a laugh again, having fun somewhere or doing something pleasurable, and that you're enjoying your life again when only the previous day that felt impossible to even contemplate."

Lakeham regarded him closely. "Do you provide this sort of therapy for all of your victims' loved ones, Inspector Bliss?"

Bliss laughed. "Only those who need it, sir. And there's no charge. All part of the service."

"No, I think this is above and beyond."

"With respect, I disagree," Bliss said. He edged forward and clasped Joe Lakeham's hands in his own. "My being human is the very least you deserve. The very least Annie deserves as well."

THE END

The Scent of Guilt
By
Tony J Forder
© 2017

ACKNOWLEDGEMENTS

This is my fourth book, all with Bloodhound, and the usual suspects deserve to be acknowledged. From the entire team at Bloodhound, to my fellow authors who have been nothing but supportive and welcoming into the community. From my family to my friends, including those I have met only on social media. From the supportive bloggers to the supportive reviewers. From my beta readers to my actual readers. To you all (and anyone who feels they don't fall under any of these headings) – please accept my heartfelt gratitude.

A few people deserve a special mention: My wife and daughter, of course. My step-mother, who has offered the support of two people in the absence of my father. My mother who now acts as both beta reader, reader, supporter, and head of my California readership fan club. Alexina at Bloodhound, without whom none of this might have happened at all. Jacqui at the Peterborough branch of Waterstones. Betsy and Fred from Bloodhound for creating a perfect environment for their authors. Clare, my editor who, as usual, came up with improvements and made this a better piece of work than it would otherwise have been.

And finally, to YOU. Yes, you, reading this acknowledgement. I believe most writers write first and foremost for themselves. But real pleasure also comes from having others read and enjoy our work, and you deserve a special mention because you have become a vital part of the whole equation.

Thank you. I appreciate it more than you will ever know.

Tony
February 2018